The Identity Club

OTHER BOOKS BY RICHARD BURGIN

STORIES

Man Without Memory

Private Fame

Fear of Blue Skies

The Spirit Returns

Stories and Dream Boxes (with art by Gloria Vanderbilt)

NOVEL

Ghost Quartet

NOVELLA

The Man with Missing Parts (with Juan Alonso)

NONFICTION

Conversations with Jorge Luis Borges

Conversations with Isaac Bashevis Singer

Jorge Luis Borges: Conversations (Editor)

The Identity Club

New and Selected Stories

Richard Burgin

Ontario Review Press ✦ Princeton, NJ

Ontario Review Press
9 Honey Brook Drive
Princeton, NJ 08540

Distributed by W. W. Norton & Co.
500 Fifth Avenue
New York, NY 10110

Library of Congress Cataloging-in-Publication Data

Burgin, Richard.
    The identity club : new and selected stories / Richard Burgin.—
1st ed.
        p. cm.
    ISBN 0-86538-115-1 (alk. paper)
    I. Title.

    PS3552.U717124 2005
    813'.54—dc22

                                                        2005040669
First Edition

"Vacation," "My Black Rachmaninoff," "With All My Heart,"
"Simone" and "The Liar" first appeared in *Ontario Review*; "The
Identity Club" in *TriQuarterly*; "The Spirit of New York," in an
earlier version, and "Bodysurfing" in *Witness*; "The Horror
Conference" and "The Park" in *River Styx*; "Notes on Mrs.
Slaughter" and "The Victims" in *Mississippi Review*; "Song of the
Earth," as "Private Fame," in *Prospect Review*; "Mercury" in *Santa
Barbara Review*; "Aerialist" in *Pequod*; "Ghost Parks" in *Tampa
Review*; "Carbo's" and "Miles" in *Chelsea*; "The Urn" in *Antioch
Review*; "My Sister's House" in *Confrontation*.

ACKNOWLEDGMENTS

I'd like to thank the editors of the magazines and books in which these stories first appeared, especially Ann Lowry and Terry Sears of the University of Illinois Press and John T. Irwin of the Johns Hopkins University Press. I also wish to thank Bill Henderson for reprinting "Notes on Mrs. Slaughter," "The Victims," "Bodysurfing," and "Miles" in different editions of *The Pushcart Prize: Best of the Small Presses* anthology, and Otto Penzler for reprinting "The Identity Club" in *Best American Mystery Stories 2005*. Finally, I'd like to thank Edmund de Chasca for his valuable criticism, Gloria Vanderbilt for her generous encouragement, sage advice and brilliant art, and Joyce Carol Oates and Raymond Smith for their wisdom, kindness, guidance, and for their belief in my work.

For my beloved son
Richard Daniel Burgin

CONTENTS

I

II

III

IV

The Identity Club

I

Vacation

He shouldn't have sat next to a man in a bar at night, he knew that. He'd willfully broken one of his rules, so who else could he blame but himself? Yet it had happened so suddenly, he was looking up from his drink, surreptitiously scanning the room for women, when the man settled in. He was thin and average looking, although there was something quasi-delirious about his eyes. Things were OK at first, though the man appeared to have been drinking already or (more likely) was high on something else. Then he began running his mouth about his mother. That was all right too—a little disconcerting but he could understand. Suddenly, out of nowhere, the man turned towards him, looking him right in the eye and said, "Do you think when you're old it's like being high all the time?"

He stared at him hard wanting to shout, "You're asking me? Why are you asking me, you stupid little snail?" Instead, he said, "Don't know," finished the rest of his drink quickly, then said, "I gotta roll."

That night in his apartment after reviewing the incident a number of times he decided he'd go to the salon the next day before playing ball at the playground. He watched TV and drank beer until it was past 2 a.m. but still felt preternaturally awake. When he finally did get to sleep, he once again dreamed of hurrying to a game he was late for.

* * *

He was in the salon the next morning by eleven. He figured he'd be done by lunchtime but would skip lunch so he could play with a light stomach. Then he could walk to the playground knowing he would in all likelihood be too early for a game but knowing it was much better to be early, even absurdly early, than to be late.

Besides the hairdressers, he was the only man in the salon. Sonny greeted him like he was a guest at his party, shaking hands and smiling. How was he? How were things going at the agency? He answered the questions as best he could, as he settled uneasily in the chair.

"So Gary, you want the usual today?"

"Yeah the usual, don't make it too dark."

"Would I do that to you?" Sonny said putting his hand over his heart.

"Where's your assistant?" he wanted to say. "The one with the legs and the pop-up ass." Sonny always worked with good-looking women although he was actually straight and married. Once Sonny's wife had come into the salon and she was good-looking too. Had incredible legs. But Sonny himself was not much to look at although he was in pretty good shape, still young enough and had an appealing smile, he supposed.

In the salon women were walking by in black robes with different colored dyes and transparent plastic nets over their hair as they made their way to the dryers.

When Sonny asked him if he had a date tonight he lied and said he did.

"I've got a young one this time—that's why I have to color the hair."

"Hey when it comes to the ladies you gotta do what you gotta do."

"Exactly."

He'd colored his hair to increase his chances of getting picked for a game and not get passed over for being too old, but there were other benefits too. Maybe it was irrational but he felt stronger and certainly safer walking down the street (a few years ago he'd been mugged which he'd never forgotten, and since then he usually carried a knife with him, as he did today. He'd also bought a handgun,which he sometimes took with him in his car). He figured he looked five to ten years younger now—maybe more, why put a limit on it, and would once more appear to be in the age zone where he was less vulnerable to attack. More women would be available to him too, of course. That was the whole idea of his vacation, to play basketball in the daytime in early May when it still wasn't too hot in Philadelphia and to go after women at night. He knew it was ironic to be working at a travel agency and staying home on his vacation—especially with all the vacation perks the agency offered. He also knew he'd be teased and gossiped about if anyone at work found out that he was staying home, so he'd quickly decided to say he was going to Malibu. He even had a line ready in case he ran into anybody from the agency, which wasn't that far from the salon or from his walking route to the playground. If they said, "Gary, what are you doing here? I thought you were going to Malibu," he'd say, "You believed that?" like it had been a joke all along that they'd fallen for. Shift the emphasis to them, for once.

...All along he knew he was going to Taney Park. He could have gone to Fourth and Locust where there were better players and the baskets were in better shape, or 38th and Walnut near U Penn or even to Clark Park. But he'd lived near Taney Park for most of his Philadelphia years and a number of the players there knew him, so thinking about the other parks was just a game he was playing with himself—like a hopelessly faithful man fantasizing about cheating on his wife. Yet he couldn't deny that things had deteriorated at Taney—the nets kept getting torn down and the rims getting bent. It was all a racial thing. The largely Irish Catholic neighborhood didn't like the blacks invading "their park" although it was designated a "city park" open to everyone. They figured if they destroyed the baskets so no one could run full court, the blacks would stay away. But the players fought back by fixing the baskets, even buying and putting up new nets. The last few years you never knew the state the baskets would be in till you got there—it became part of the suspense of going to Taney. He thought of the neighborhood and clenched his teeth. He hated those bigots but loved their park, just because he'd played so many games there. So he blocked out the drug dealers that walked through the park and the smashed beer bottles and broken baskets because once something entered your permanent memory, you couldn't turn your back on it, could you?

Del was there shooting. Del was always there. His shirt was off; there wasn't a pound of fat on him. He had unusually sharp blue eyes too that seemed to see everything. He liked playing with or against him because Del tried so hard but wasn't quite as good as him. Besides himself, Del was one of the few white men who regularly came to Taney and he was liked and respected by the blacks. He had a menial job at Penn, something like a janitor— but he never complained or acted embarrassed about it. The other odd thing was Del was gay, though he didn't act like it, much less flaunt it. At the same time he was open and completely unapologetic about it, which Gary found both mysterious and admirable for a basketball player. He always wondered how many of the black guys knew about Del. He knew that Del had once gotten into a fight with Barry, a tough black man with a very good physique and a big ego and that Barry had broken Del's jaw with a single punch. That was the only time Del hadn't been on the playground for a few weeks—while he was in the hospital recuperating—but as soon as his jaw healed he was back playing. It was Barry who stayed away for a while.

He was within talking distance now and knew Del had seen him but wouldn't say anything until he finished his jump shot. The ball went in, then Del turned his head a few degrees and nodded at him.

"Shot looks good," Gary said.

"Been working on the hitch in my delivery."

"Getting rid of it?"

"No, too late for that. Making it more fluid, know what I mean?"

"Sure. You been here long?"

"Half hour. Haven't seen you for a while."

"Been working. I'm on vacation now so I came here for a run. You staying?"

"No, I gotta go back to work in five minutes," Del said. "I'm on my lunch break."

Gary nodded, trying not to show his disappointment. Even just shooting with Del was soothing in a way. There was just the right amount of conversation. Half of it was about basketball—from players they knew at the park, to the N.B.A., but other times they talked about their relationships and he'd even told Del a few years back about his last serious girlfriend. Del also liked getting high and had turned him onto a pot dealer once—someone he still used.

After Del left, he took his ball out of the cloth bag he'd been carrying and shot for maybe twenty minutes—working on foul shots, his hook shot, his left hand, and his cross lane jumper. Then he'd sat on the wooden bench under a tree just behind the chain-link fence and rested, looking out every minute or so for players or for women who might be sunbathing. Every now and then a hooker might stroll through the park too. He repeated this pattern several times of shooting and resting until almost an hour and a half went by.

When the players arrived it was like a raid of soldiers. They came with basketballs and their talk and laughter from all directions. He took his ball and started shooting again so they could see his shot and couldn't ignore him. He was the only white person there and didn't know any of the players. Even a few years ago that wouldn't have happened—someone would have known him because he was playing four times a week then, but now his body couldn't take it, and he only played once a week at most.

It all happened so fast. After a few minutes of random shooting around, without any announcement, the players suddenly assembled just outside the three-point line. He was seventh in line and before he could shoot, two players made the shot and became captains. The good news was there were only 8 players to pick from so if no one else came in the next minute he'd get to play a full court five on five.

It was magical the way it worked out, especially since a half dozen new players arrived a few minutes after the game started. He realized that unless his team won, this would be his only game of the day because another team was already waiting to play.

Of course they underestimated him (this often happened the last few years) and put the slowest and shortest player on him defensively. But at least no one called him "veteran" or "old timer." The first time they passed to him he took his man into the low post and scored on a turn-around jump shot. He knew he had a step on him and could also shoot over him. It was a close game and he only got the ball a half dozen more times, making three more baskets the four times he shot. His team was ahead 13–11, in a game to sixteen, but froze him out at the end and lost 16–15.

As they were walking off the court Frankie, a tall black man who played center on his team, said to him, "We should have gone to you man, you had the match-up thing going… We should have gone to you." It was sweet music to hear and he played it over and over on his long walk home (he had left almost immediately, knowing he wouldn't get picked and not wanting to witness the injustice of it, the humiliation).

In his apartment he sat in his tub reviewing the shots he'd made; two drives, an outside shot, and the turn-around jumper that had given him his confidence. He reviewed them for a long time—it had been so vivid—until the beauty from it started to fade. Then he started to think about his hellish job and his woman situation— even worse—and the way his life was moving so fast like the game he'd just played, over almost before it began. He put some clothes on, swallowed a pill that he'd bought from the dealer Del had set him up with, and went out where it was already dark. It wasn't a difficult decision to make. He was too tired to walk so he took his car even though it was never easy to find parking spaces.

He was in a bar now in Center City. It was very dark and ornate. All the waiters and waitresses were dressed in black like vampires. There was gold on the tables and around the mirrors some form of gold that vampires probably liked. He was sitting down drinking at the gold and black bar talking to a woman in a black dress who had gold hair too. It was like the ending of *2001: A Space Odyssey* where the astronaut views himself passing through different phases of his life in a matter of seconds.

The next thing he knew he couldn't think anymore because the conversation with the woman required too much of his attention.

"'Capish,' is that a foreign word? I don't know it," she said.

"It's Italian. It means 'do you understand?'"

"Are you Italian?" she asked. She had long fingers, which were a little disturbing, but overall was strangely appealing.

"No, but I've been in Europe a lot, especially Italy."

She raised her eyebrows and tilted her head in an odd way to show she was impressed. "My name is French, I think," she said.

"What is it?"

"Renee."

"Oh, oui oui. C'est Francais vraiment."

"Jeez, you know French too. What'd you just say?"

"Yes, your name is truly French."

"So what's yours?"

"Gary," he said, "my name is Gary."

"So are you really smart or something?"

"I do my best." He was trying to think of what college he should say he was from in case that was her next question.

"Are you a lawyer or a psychiatrist or something like that?"

"Something like that," he said, touching the tip of her nose for a second as if it were a baby's and making her smile. He thought his answer was probably too vague and decided on another one. "Actually, I only work occasionally at things I enjoy now, things that are philanthropic, that help people."

"How come?" she blurted.

"Because I'm in a financial position where I don't have to work full time anymore."

"Oh," she said, quickly straightening her hair and the next second reaching into her purse and withdrawing a hand mirror and lipstick. "So how come a smart, successful, good-looking guy like you is alone?"

"I could ask you the same question," he said, resting his free hand just above her knee. She looked a little flustered, and he thought again "shift the emphasis to them." It must have worked because she started talking while also letting his hand rest on her leg.

"This is the first time I've been out by myself in a long time," she said.

"Why's that?"

"I was with a guy for a couple of years. I thought we were gonna get married but it turned out he already was. You're not married, are you?"

"No, I'm definitely not married."

"But you like women, right?"

"I find they're a necessary evil," he said, laughing a little.

"I'm not evil."

"I hope not," he said, sliding his hand to her upper thigh and realizing then that he would score.

She laughed. He liked that she laughed a lot. It kept things light and entertaining.

He wished he'd drunk more. He was being overly careful, he knew that, but now he'd just have to wait till he got home to get high.

They were outside the bar walking towards his car in silence—just her heels against the sidewalk making a weird kind of music until she said, "Do you really think it's a good idea for me to get in your car?"

"Why not?"

"I'm pretty high."

Pretty high and pretty tall, he thought, figuring that she was almost as tall as he was, and in her heels about an inch taller. "I was thinking we both should drink more."

"No, no," she said, gesturing haphazardly with one of her long, surprisingly muscular arms. "I had too much already."

"Alright, here's my car," he said leaning her against the side door and kissing her with both hands on her face. He didn't like to do that, kiss someone by surprise—especially in public—but he felt he had too. It was as if she were demanding it in order to get inside the car.

"Wow," she said. "Did you learn to kiss in France too?"

He laughed and kissed her again, this time pressing against her and feeling her a little. She was getting hot quickly, actually moaning outside where anyone could walk by and hear her. He decided they should get in the car then, had to fish and fumble inside his pants pocket for a while to find the key next to his knife but then opened the door without asking her and helped her in. They continued making out immediately as if his opening the door and getting inside the car with her was merely a tiny interval between two kisses. She was making even more noise now. It was hard to tell in the half-dark but he thought her cheeks were turning red. When you were with a hot woman like that it was like being "in the zone" in basketball—you couldn't miss.

They continued kissing. She had her hands on his legs creeping up towards his crotch. He didn't like women to touch him there until he was ready (which created a kind of catch-22 situation, at times, he realized) but to his surprise, in spite of all the alcohol, he was erect.

"Let's go in back," she said.

"Why?"

"More room," she said, breathing heavily.

"I have a better idea. Let's go to my place," he said, putting his tongue inside her mouth, as if to answer for her.

"Where's that?" she finally said.

"Just a few minutes from here."

"Can't we just pull over some place and continue what we're doing?"

"We can get a drink there, we can get high. Don't you like to smoke? We can do that there too."

"I'm already high, seriously."

"Seriously," he said, laughing a little. "I really like you Renee."

"Then pull over some place and show me." In other words show her in the car why she should go inside his home.

He felt his heart race—feeling as much anger as excitement the way he was challenged, as if he were cut by a knife, which made him feel his own knife inside his pants pocket for a second. He told himself she was probably scared to go to his place—that it was one thing to make out or even have sex in a car and another to go to someone's home you'd only known for an hour. He drove a couple of blocks looking for the right kind of parking lot, then found a street with only one other car parked—the kind of side street that still occasionally existed in the city, pulled into a space and shut off the lights.

"Come on," he said, as he opened his door. But she waited till he came around the car and opened her door. "Let's get in back." He thought they'd make out for a little while, enough time to reassure her, and then she'd go to his place.

It was more cramped than he thought in the back seat because her body was so long. Still, he managed to get most of her down and began kissing her neck, and the tops of her (smaller than hoped for) breasts.

"Hey, slow down, will you?" she said.

"What?" he said. It was like another cut, and it stunned him for a moment.

"Can you just kiss me slowly for a while?"

He went slower, thinking that was women in a nutshell: acting so passionate and impulsive but then wanting it to be as slow as Chinese water torture and making sure to criticize you as much as they could get away with in the process. But he went along with it, even closing his eyes while they kissed. It was a strange feeling, like seeing dark inside dark as in a black Chinese box.

He opened his eyes as soon as he felt his erection fading and immediately stopped kissing her. At the same moment he thought he felt something strange, as if she had a tail somehow, near her bottom.

"Hey, don't stop now," she said. "What's the matter?"

"Jesus Christ," he hissed. "Are you a man?"

"What? Are you nuts?"

"Get out of the car."

"Are you crazy, calling me a man?"

"Just get out."

"I'm not getting out in the middle of nowhere."

"You are in the middle of nowhere and you are a goddamned man. I felt it."

"You wish I had a dick 'cause yours doesn't seem to be working."

"Get out! Get out!" he screamed, throwing her against the seat, then swinging at her face with his free hand but hitting the seat instead.

It was like the first time he was stung by a bee when he was a kid, the pain shocked him and for a moment he saw orange and was silent before he began to scream. It was like life had reversed itself and was suddenly upside down. Renee was trying to get out of the car but now he wanted to stop her, make her pay for this. He put his left (and weaker) arm around her waist but she slithered away like a snake. He reached out to grab her waist again but she elbowed him in the groin and he doubled over before he could get his knife.

He was screaming again as she ran out of the car leaving the door open. Then he suddenly stopped. He could feel the cool air as the world returned to black. His pain was manageable now and he could feel his other senses intensify. He could even hear the strange kind of music she made again while running in her heels across the parking lot.

He went into the front seat, opened the glove compartment and took out his handgun thinking that she wouldn't get far in her heels. He turned his lights on too, so he could see better, see something at all, then started to run after her, not even talking any more but just running after her as if any kind of speech, any kind of sound except the one his feet were making would slow him down. It was like the world had been reduced to speed alone, yet it wasn't that simple. It wasn't pure speed, it was more like hunting. He couldn't run in a straight line—it was too dark. It was more like chasing the dark in the dark, so he couldn't shoot either, couldn't risk hitting someone else who might be there—some sleeping vampire he didn't want to awaken or some stray zombie dreaming of a meal of dead flesh.

Then there was a flash—it might have been a pocket of orange exploding again, it might have been lightning—but he saw Renee running.

"Stop. Stop running," he hissed as if he were a snake talking. He raised his gun and fired into the dark but the running continued. He fired again until he realized that he was still running. Then he stopped and listened hard. A few seconds later he thought he heard someone running in the distance like an echo of the music he'd heard earlier—heels against cement. "Thank god," he thought. It was as if the world had reversed itself again, though he couldn't be sure it was Renee still running any more than he could now be certain that Renee was a man.

* * *

He was sitting in a bar again, this time at 8th and Market. Everyone around him was black. He'd reviewed the scene with Renee repeatedly like watching a video tape hundreds of times until he drank enough to finally get beyond it. People were watching him now, smiling at him—probably because of how much he'd drunk—but he was no longer worrying. He loved black people so why should he be worried? He was in the heart of Philly's hooker district and he wanted to buy a woman to take home with him but given the shape he was in and the way the hookers looked, he was afraid to walk by his doorman (it was just his luck to have the one overly conscientious doorman in Center City!) so he'd probably have to spend the night with her in a nearby hotel.

Two or three had come in since he'd been here that he wouldn't have minded taking but he couldn't ask them in front of the black men in the bar who were watching him. How could he buy a black woman in front of a black man—though he was sure they'd seen it plenty of times. He thought he'd go out instead and get one on the street as soon as he finished his last drink. It was a much sounder plan.

He found a black hooker within a block of where he'd parked and she'd hustled inside his car as soon as he signaled to her.

"What're you doin?" she said.

He had turned on the light inside the car and was staring at her.

"Why you checkin' me out? You already looked at me on the street. You already bought me mister—don't be changing your mind now."

"You wouldn't believe what happened to me earlier," he said, wondering if he would make sense when he spoke.

"Start the car mister, then tell me 'bout it. This ain't a good spot right here."

He shut off the light and drove slowly, for a few blocks. There were three or four hookers walking near his car, nearly colliding with his windshield like low-flying bats. He turned up a lightless alley and stopped, then turned the light on and looked at her again.

"Why you still lookin' me over? You already done that. You already made up your mind and bought me."

"Earlier tonight I was with a woman, at least I thought I was, and after we started fooling around I found out she was a man."

"So? What that got to do with me? You see my titties, they half out of my dress, ain't they? These ain't no man's titties," she said, cupping a hand under each of her breasts. "These are a woman's, see?" she said, finally taking them completely out of her bra and wiggling them in the air. Gary laughed. "OK you convinced me."

"You sure now?" she said, raising her eyebrows and looking at him seriously or mock seriously, he couldn't be sure which. "I don't want you tellin' me later I'm a man. I ain't no man but it gonna cost you to know that fo sure. What you wanna do with me mister?"

He saw a chipped front tooth now when he looked at her and then shut the light off.

"I want you for the night. I want to spend what's left of the night with you."

"That gonna cost you five hundred," she said, her voice wavering a little.

"Come on, don't bullshit me. You don't charge that much."

"You heard what I said."

"Anyway, that's way more than I can pay."

"What you got to pay?"

"Two hundred. There's only three or four hours of night left so you'll still be making fifty an hour," he said, feeling strangely proud of his logic and convinced now that he wasn't drunk at all.

"What you wanna do during those four hours?"

"Sleep mostly. Just sleep next to you."

"You wanna sleep next to mama?"

"I'm tired, really tired."

"OK I hear you. But after you wake up and see how nice I been, I hope you give me a little more 'for you leave."

"I will." He said, "What's your name? Mine's Gary."

"July."

"July?"

"Yah, you like it?"

"I love it."

"OK Gary. There's a place a couple of blocks from here."

"Is it safe?"

"Sure it's safe. You worry a lot, don't you?"

"How do I know it's safe?"

"I lay my ass there every night, so it must be pretty safe."

"So, it's your place?"

"Evidently," she said.

It was on a side street, a dark walk-up without a doorman but at least you needed a key to open the doors. July lived in one room with a queen-sized bed in the center, and not much else that he could see, not even a refrigerator or a desk. It was as if the bed were the whole purpose of the room. Certainly it received most of her attention with its red satin sheets and black pillows and its coverlet with a red heart in the middle. Facing the bed on a little stand of some kind was a small T.V.

"I'm glad you've got a nice bed," he said, taking off his shoes.

"I got a toilet, but if you wanna wash yourself you got to use the bathroom out in the hall."

"That's OK."

"Hey, Gary 'for you lie down and get comfortable you wanna take care of me?"

"Sure, I was just going to," he said, reaching in his pants and withdrawing four fifties from his money clip. She took them, looking at them quickly but closely in the half-dark of the room (the only light coming from a red light bulb in a black floor lamp), then unzipped her boots and put them inside her boots in a kind of secret purse he hadn't noticed before.

"OK, you lie down now if that's what you wanna do."

"What are you doing?"

"I'm gonna smoke me a number 'for I try to sleep. Wan' some?"

She turned her back to him and stood by the window while she smoked. She had a big bottom, visible behind her semi-transparent short skirt, and heavy thighs. She was probably the fattest prostitute he'd ever been with but she had a nice smile, and there was something about her that made him feel it would be safe to fall asleep with her.

* * *

Fear sneaked up and seized him like a Zombie with its hand around his throat. Maybe he shouldn't have smoked with July. Maybe what she gave him was cut with Angel Dust. He went out on the floor—it was like the bottom of a lake with strange fish and water snakes lying in wait—trying to find the lamp. Light was the first step, he tried to concentrate on it and forget about the water snakes on the lake floor.

When he finally found it and turned it on, the lake evaporated. The lamp was like a red god, silent but powerful enough to bring back the room in an instant. He stood up (not even aware that he'd been on his hands and knees while he was looking for the lamp) and saw her big bottom sticking up in the air. She was only wearing a thong and her enormous breasts (too flabby to be artificial) fanned out on either side of her. She was snoring too, every ten seconds or so. It was a mysterious sight, a mysterious presence and for what seemed like a long time he stared at and listened to her, wondering how her life allowed her to sleep like that.

Then he lay next to her, eventually even closed his eyes. But as soon as he closed them he saw an image of Renee's face when he first kissed her—saw her purple-streaked eyes just before they closed as she started moaning when they were outdoors. Then he remembered the way she slithered out of his car like a water moccasin, and the sound of her heels running on the parking lot like rattlesnake music.

He opened his eyes and began shaking July and when that did no good punched her (though not too hard) on her shoulder.

"What, what?" she said, turning on her side away from him.

"Get up, will you? Talk to me."

"What's the matter? Shit, I was sleeping."

"What's in the pot? Is it Angel Dust or just poison?"

"The weed? Shit, I didn't make you smoke it."

"I was seeing snakes and fish."

"Ain't none of either in this place, mister."

"Give me something to drink."

"You been drinkin' too much. That's why you're seein' things."

"No, no I need to pass out. I haven't been to sleep yet."

"You wanna grind for a while, that'll calm you down. See my titties, honey. Least you know I ain't no man."

"They're enormous," he said, glad to divert himself by staring at them. "Can I touch them?"

"You bought 'em, didn't you? You can do pull-ups with 'em if you want to."

He put his hands on them—they felt warm and comforting like putting on a pair of gloves in winter. She made a few soft moaning sounds though he wasn't trying to stimulate her. It was like a juke-box responding to a quarter.

"Why don't you grind with me for a while?"

He thought about it, but he couldn't feel himself, as if his dick had flown away like a bird to a distant island.

"I can't. I drank too much."

She laughed a little. "You got all kinds of problems, don't you. Shit."

"Just get me something to drink, I got some really bad stuff in my mind, and I need to pass out, O.K? I'll pay you for it in the morning."

"Shit," she muttered as she stood up from the bed. "I got some whiskey. Ain't the best stuff in the world, but it'll knock you down. You gotta drink it warm though. I ain't going out to the hall, Gary. That's the only place where there's water, but I ain't goin out there."

"Sure, anything," he said. "I'll drink it straight."

"One more thing," she said, holding the bottle as she returned to him from across the room. "You feel like you're gonna heave go do it in the toilet over there," she said pointing in the dark. He pretended to look but even that pretend effort made him dizzy.

"Don't be puking on my bed, all right?"

Everything speeded up like the dam of his being could no longer hold back his words. It was broken, it was as if he could hear it break and the waterfall of words rushed forward no longer caring, simply needing to say themselves the way zombies simply need to move if only to feel themselves moving before they eat.

"That man/woman, I told you about, remember?"

"Sure I do."

"Something terrible happened."

"You sure you want to tell me this?"

He tried to think about what she was saying but the waterfall words kept on rushing through. "I might have killed her."

"Shit."

"She was running and I was chasing her in the dark and I shot a number of times. I don't know why I did it. I felt tricked but I shouldn't have shot at her."

"Where was you?"

"In a parking lot in the dark, as dark as this room so I couldn't be sure. I ordered her out of my car once I found out she was a man and at first he wouldn't leave and then he wanted to and I didn't want him to and that's when the chase began. But I couldn't see too well, could only see the actual body for a few seconds, maybe less. I was running and he was running, you listening?"

"Yeah, I'm listening."

"I was trying to see in the dark like a bat, but I couldn't. I'm not a bat, I'm not batman, you know what I'm saying? I could only go by the sound of his high heels on the ground. So I shot at a sound target, not even an image. And then I didn't hear the heels anymore and thought I'd hit him, that it was over but then I did hear something again. Not exactly the same sound but from a distance. It could have been Renee, it could have been someone else. I don't know. I'll never know. You understand? You listening? I've never killed anyone, I don't want to have killed him."

"You probably didn't. You heard the heels again, right?"

"Yah, but it sounded different."

"Course it did cause it was further away. Who else would it be? If someone else was there you woulda got your ass arrested."

"It was a miracle that no one else was there. A miracle." He started to shake.

"Where the gun now, Gary?"

"I got rid of it before I saw you. I got rid of it a long time ago."

"You ain't got no other do you?"

"Not with me, no."

"You ain't mad at me neither, right? I been nice to you, haven't I?"

"Yah, don't worry. I like you fine," he said with a little laugh. Then he thought of something else.

"You're not gonna tell anyone what I told you, are you?"

"Course not. I ain't dumb. I may be a whore but I ain't dumb."

"You sure?"

"Sure I'm sure. I don't blame you for what you did. You didn't want to have sex with no man. Shit—you didn't ask to be treated that way. You just relax about that. You want me to suck your dick now?"

"No, no. I'm too out of it. Just let me lie down on you, OK?"

"On my titties."

"Yes, they're warm," he said. "You don't think I killed anyone?"

"Course not. You would have heard it or seen it. You would've heard the body fall. You wouldn't have heard no heels neither."

He lay down then as if between two soft basketballs and felt he could sleep soon. That was the thing about basketball, you always knew if you made a basket or not. What kind of world was the rest of it when you couldn't even tell if you'd killed someone or not?

He closed his eyes. The videotape was finally gone. Instead he saw the playground coming into view as he was running towards it. Up ahead was Del shooting in the sunlight. Del turned and smiled at him and he looked at his eyes that were so beautiful—so wise and inviting—until he finally fell asleep.

My Black Rachmaninoff

I. THE UNENDURABLE PIANO

Sooner or later if you stay in a place long enough something odd begins to happen to it. The walls or ceilings start to contort and parts of them may begin to look like tree branches in the wind or fingers trying to caress you. Or you'll start to hear sounds from the street you hadn't heard before, a whole range of curses and groans and repetitive laughter you thought you were too high up in the building to hear. You close your window and it seems to hiss at you. You close a door and it creaks like part of a haunted house.

In my case I began to hear a piano every day in the late afternoon or early evening, as if a music box had suddenly opened in my living room. The piano was more than faint but less than loud—certainly nothing I could complain about—and audible in every room of my apartment except the bathroom. The playing was very good, too, probably professional. Bits of Beethoven sonatas, Chopin nocturnes, and Rachmaninoff's Second Piano Concerto filtered down to me or up—1 couldn't be sure. At first I remember thinking it would've driven me crazy six months ago. It was still too close to my divorce then and I couldn't bear to hear any music. At the very least I would've played some movies on my VCR (ones without painful soundtracks) that could drown out the piano, or more likely I'd have taken a walk as soon as the music started.

Now when I hear the piano, I'm just as apt to think of my father as my ex-husband, Ed. My father played oboe in the Philadelphia Symphony years ago and taught me how to play piano. I still have the upright Knabe he bought for me in my living room. But there are other times when the piano—particularly if it's playing the Rachmaninoff—makes me feel things about Ed, or even the big love of my life before him, that I'd rather not feel. When you hear the right music all the love ghosts from your past are liable to spring forth and make their claims on you no matter what you do to try to stop them. For instance, a week ago when the piano was getting to me I opened all the windows in my apartment to let the street noises in, but it didn't work. There could be an earthquake or a bomb exploding, and my ear would still go directly to a soft minor chord on the piano. It's as if I'm programmed to hear things that way.

II. MY TWO DOORMEN

The main doorman of my building is usually seated behind the counter in front of the mailboxes, at a dimly lit table, bent over a newspaper. Is he reading? Sleeping? It's impossible to tell. He wears thick, black sunglasses which perfectly disguise whatever he's thinking or doing. As a result I've never attempted to talk to him any more than I would risk disturbing anyone else who is sleeping or reading. Besides, he often isn't there; at least half the time he's missing from the lobby. I sometimes think he isn't really my doorman at all but some impostor who intermittently uses the lobby as his private lounge. There's something else bizarre about him. In addition to a uniform, complete with hat, he always wears a scarf high on his neck, regardless of how hot it is, so that almost none of his neck is visible.

"My Glenn Gould doorman," I dubbed him once when describing him to Ed. I still don't know if he's black, white, or Asian. Not that it matters, of course, but it's odd not to know.

With the main elevator man, who also functions as a doorman, it's very different. His skin is light coffee-colored and his straight hair is combed back in a pompadour and colored a dull reddish brown with golden highlights, as if part of a weird sunset had solidified on his head. But in spite of all the ambiguous colors, Howard is definitely a black man and a good-looking one too. He's also as relentlessly polite as anyone I've ever seen in that kind of a job.

"Good morning" or "Good afternoon, Paula" he'll say to me each time I get on the elevator, flashing his even white teeth in what appears to be a completely authentic smile. When someone puts out that much it almost compels you to be polite back. So I'll ask him how he is, more often than not, and say thank you at the end of the ride. Then he'll say the most enthusiastic "You're welcome" I've ever heard—always with the same intonation and at the same louder-than-average volume, as if he's tape-recorded himself and merely presses a button each time he says it.

So I began talking with Howard—obviously in brief installments—during our rides to and from the fifth floor where I live. I've learned that he loves classical music and chess and is much impressed that my father had been in the Philadelphia Symphony and still plays occasional gigs in Florida where he's retired. Howard is so knowledgeable about music that I've asked him if he plays any instrument; he said he plays piano some. I've wanted to ask him several times how he ended up at his job, but of course I never have. But I began to wonder about him, and when I'd see him working in the lobby at his doorman shift I was never quite sure if I enjoyed talking to him for a few minutes or not.

III. REVELATION IN A BATHTUB

The first day I began to think about my syndrome, which was also the first day that I really began to think, I was in my bathtub. I was following my usual routine and had allowed just the right amount of time to shave my legs, put on my makeup and clothes, and leave for work. I remember being still for a moment to listen for the piano and being relieved that I didn't hear it, then running a face cloth over the soap on my legs. Suddenly I began wondering why I was the kind of person I was, I mean why I had my particular beliefs and personality; then I wondered the same about other people. The only answer I had for this question, which I'd never really asked myself before, was a seamless programming that took place without a break from cradle to grave. A programming that my parents were only a small part of, because it was omnipresent and kept everyone focused on their syndrome (or if you want a more optimistic term for it—their lives). The programming covered all our thoughts, from our metaphysical system with its supposed heaven to our general political and racial views. It was so vast and had gone on for so long that even our authority figures, like our politicians, had programmed themselves without realizing it. In other words, no one was in charge and everyone was participating. It was an illusion, then, for me to think I thought my own thoughts or made my own decisions, about everything from the middle-management job I had in marketing to the kind of man I ended up marrying instead of, say, a cowboy from Wyoming or even Howard, the elevator man in my building.

I got out of the bathtub and began to dry myself off. I was shaking from more than the draft in my room. Society makes so much of our losing our sexual virginity, but I felt I had just had my first syndrome-free thoughts. I looked in the mirror and noticed a few gray hairs by my temples. I was thirty-four years old—it was to be expected. I thought, it's a good thing that we age or we'd have no awareness of time at all because we're programmed to block that out too. Then I thought about Ed and how he'd react if he knew what I was thinking. How he'd shake his head and probably feel sorry for me, thinking that I might be starting to lose it. I put my underclothes on, then finished dressing quietly. A few minutes later I was putting on my lipstick like a well-programmed slave. Good, I liked the irony; I could pose as a slave while secretly having my own first thoughts. I could embrace the contradiction for now and even find it oddly delicious.

IV. DISCOVERY IN A COFFEE HOUSE

The next morning I ignored the piano that started earlier than usual and reviewed my bathtub revelation, I even went into the bathroom again and closed the door to try to recreate it. Everything came back to me. My line of thought was wholly intact and still seemed clear and true. I felt so profoundly different inside that I looked at myself carefully in the mirror before leaving for work, but the face looking back at me was still mine. The same soft hazel eyes, thinnish lips, slightly limp brown hair and close-to-button nose. A passably attractive face though certainly not a thinker's face, nor a rebel's.

At the office I avoided people more than usual and ate lunch by myself. On the one hand I was dying to tell someone about my revelation but I knew there was no one at work who'd understand. Then I started thinking about telling Ellen, my hairdresser, but all we ever talked about were men. We would meet for a drink or sometimes eat dinner together, and within two minutes the men talk would begin. I knew every detail of the woman's sex life and I guess she knew most of mine, but I couldn't picture telling her about this. I couldn't picture her understanding or being interested for more than a few seconds. The same was true with the other friends I had, with the possible exception of Etta, who I went to college with and who was now a paralegal and a frustrated writer of sorts. Etta and I would go to the movies and discuss the film afterwards or sometimes we'd go to a concert. With Etta I never discussed men. It was as if sex didn't exist when I talked with her. It was odd how specialized conversation was with people. Etta might be interested in what I'd have to say about my programming or she might not let herself feel anything about it at all. At any rate, I remembered that she was still on vacation in Paris, of all places, so it became a moot point.

I remember I didn't want to go back to my apartment right after work, and wound up, very uncharacteristically, at a coffee bar near Rittenhouse Square. It's impossible to overemphasize how popular these places have become in Philadelphia, where they seem to sprout up everywhere like wildflowers. I guess it's an inexpensive way to feel hip and maybe pick someone up in the process. I wasn't interested in either of those possibilities. I simply wanted to drink something and avoid my apartment for a while, especially since the piano was probably playing now. As soon as I sat down, I saw Howard, of all people, at the table next to me,

reading a music review in the *Philadelphia Inquirer*. He lowered
his paper, looked confused for a nanosecond when he first saw
me, then flashed his smile at me with his white, impeccable teeth.

"Hello, Paula, how are you today?"

"Good, thanks," I said, with my standard perky voice. Well
this was an awkward moment, but there was nothing to do but
ask him if he'd like some company;

"Sure, yes I would Paula, thank you very much," he said, his
face unusually animated even by Howard's standards as he
began fixing up the table for me with more attention to detail than
necessary. Normally I would have asked him about the music
review he was reading, since music was what we mainly talked
about, but for some reason, even though I considered his job to be
a touchy subject, I asked him when his next shift began.

"I'm off for the rest of the day," he said, smiling, of course,
without a trace of irony;

"Good for you," I said awkwardly.

The waitress came and I ordered my cappuccino. Howard
opined that they made excellent cappuccino in the coffee house,
and although I'd never been in the place before I agreed with him.
It was as if by trying so hard to be harmonious and pleasant he
unwittingly made you his ally, even if it meant lying about
something silly, as I just had.

Then I asked him what he planned to do on his night off. He
said he was going to stay home and listen to the radio broadcast
of the Philadelphia Symphony; I felt touched for a second, felt
like giving him the money so he could walk the few blocks down
to the Academy of Music and attend the goddamned concert. He
cared so much, he deserved that at least.

"Where's home?"

"Excuse me, Paula?" he said cupping a hand over his ear.

"Where do you live?"

"Oh, I'm sorry; I didn't understand you at first. I live in the
Rittenhouse, right there in our building."

"Really? I never knew that."

"Yes, they give us special deals on the studios. It gets a little
crowded now that I have my baby grand in there but I like it. Yes,
I've been here a few months now."

Our eyes met and a strange feeling went through me. I began to ask Howard a number of more arcane musical questions and all his answers checked out. Then I felt a little ashamed. How racist of me to be so surprised that he could be a real classical pianist and live in my building. I quickly changed the subject, Howard remaining as friendly as ever, and twenty minutes later, after we'd both had our coffees, I excused myself and went back to my apartment.

There was no piano playing. I listened closely for several minutes—but there was nothing. The idea that began in the coffee shop continued inside me and was something I was sure of by night. The pianist I'd been listening to was Howard. It all fit, his recent acquisition of a used baby grand around the time I began hearing the piano (no upright could produce the sound I was hearing, especially the Rachmaninoff), and the silence I heard when I went back to my apartment because he was still in the coffee shop. In fact, it explained the long regular periods of silence I heard each day which seemed to coincide with his work schedule. When I thought more about it, I was pretty sure that a couple of times when I left my apartment while the piano was playing, Howard wasn't on his shift. Yes, it all fit and it was such a perfect irony that the best musician in the building and one of its brightest occupants was the building's black elevator operator. It made sense, too, that this would finally dawn on me only after my revelation about my syndrome, when I began to experience unprogrammed thoughts.

I had trouble sleeping that night. When I couldn't stand my TV anymore I began to think about Howard. He loved music more than anyone I knew and was a better pianist than any man I knew also. He had a pianist's hands, too, with long, tapered fingers, and a handsome face, with large, soulful, hazel eyes. He was also tall and looked fairly well built. Why didn't I admit it to myself before? I was attracted to him. As I began to touch myself, I imagined it was his dark pianist's hands touching my body whose every part was now open to his fingers' touch—all eighty-eight keys of me.

* * *

V. THE DIRTY TRUTH

Once you start to think differently you start to feel differently and you want different things in your life. Before I broke free from my syndrome, before I even realized the extent of my programming, it would never occur to me even to fantasize about Howard much less want to date him. The dirty truth is his race alone would have prevented me—not that I ever would have admitted that to anyone, including myself. As far as I was concerned I was very liberal on race issues and thought I had an impeccable position on civil rights. I got teary-eyed when I saw clips of Martin Luther King's speeches on TV: The same thing happened when I saw the movie Malcolm X, though I instinctively avoided the theaters and waited for the video on that one. I felt lots of admiration for Jesse Jackson, too, though I didn't end up voting for him when he ran for president, rationalizing that it would be a wasted vote since he wouldn't win anyway.

I was the same way on other issues. I thought interracial marriage was great and felt an inner glow every time I saw a mixed couple on the street or in a restaurant, but I, myself, had never dated a black man, much less slept with one. No one ever told me not to, by the way: My family and early circle of friends were politically correct long before there was a term for it, but in a way, silently, my whole programming had told me not to and so I never "wanted" to, or even let myself consider it.

It was that way with my husband, too, who not surprisingly held roughly the same racial views as me. For instance there was this time during a long, rainy weekend that we mostly spent in bed having sex and drinking and talking very intimately about our pasts. It was a kind of erotic game we were playing where we asked and answered lots of questions about our pasts. I'd always sensed that he feared I'd once slept with a black man and wanted to know, and I, in turn, was curious if he'd ever had sex with a black woman. He went to a very liberal college so it certainly might have happened, but I also knew he'd protect himself by not asking that question—which he didn't—then or at any other time in our relationship.

So now I was wanting Howard. Now when I heard him playing Beethoven and Rachmaninoff, I felt angry, too, for the relentlessly affable Uncle Tom mask he had to wear in public while his playing showed the inner rage I knew he felt for his job in the building and for the double life he and other black people were forced to lead. My black Rachmaninoff, I said to myself while I lay in bed again and heard him playing. My big beautiful black Rachmaninoff.

VI. THE COFFEE HOUSE ENCORE

It wasn't as easy to date Howard as I'd hoped. There were all kinds of logistical problems. For example, though I saw him every day it was always for ridiculously short periods of time in the elevator (our building has one of the very few hand-operated elevators in the city or the ride would be even shorter), or else in the lobby where he was often talking with the other doormen, including Glenn Gould doorman when he was around. How could I achieve the conversational breakthrough I wanted in a twelve-second ride to my floor?

Two things sustained me during this frustrating time. One was my conviction that I was a different person now, thinking new, unprogrammed thoughts, and so I didn't need to behave in the mousy, shrinking violet way I had in the past, always waiting for the man to be the aggressor. Given the way society had set things up, it was clear Howard could certainly never be the aggressor in this situation. It was wholly up to me.

The second thing was the anger I'd been feeling lately (admittedly a delayed hit) about my sex life with Ed, particularly the last half year of our marriage when, mainly to punish me, he'd barely touched me at all. Though I thought he'd probably been technically faithful to me while we were married, I wasn't thrilled that he had a virtual live-in girlfriend within a month of our divorce. I thought, given all that I went through—the weekends spent crying, sometimes even making my father or Ellen listen to it over the phone—that I had nothing to worry about with Howard who wasn't exactly an intimidating personality.

So one day when we got to my floor I asked him to hold the elevator for a second, and he said "Sure Paula."

I said, "You know I really enjoyed talking with you that time in the coffee house. Would you ever want to have a drink with me?"

"Yes, sure. I'd enjoy that, Paula. Thank you for suggesting that."

His smile was still intact but he looked a little away from me. Still he spoke in his typical accent-free, dialect-free, endlessly polite King's English, albeit a little faster than usual. Building Management must have flipped when they first interviewed this guy—the ultimate Uncle Tom—actually better than an Uncle Tom, since he spoke just like a college-educated white man. Not that the other door and elevator men (except for Glenn Gould) weren't Tomish—they were. Or they acted that way when anyone white was around. I sometimes felt the buildings of Center City secretly financed a kind of Uncle Tom Academy to train these guys. They were so well-trained that I often wondered if they were acting at all, except that after the O.J. verdict I saw them slapping palms and high-fiving each other in the lobby. They were so carried away with glee then that for a few seconds they didn't care that I and a couple of other white people could hear them. Suddenly it was "motherfucker" this and "motherfucker" that. I thought it was refreshing at the time. Actually I thought it was glorious, though I don't recall my black Rachmaninoff being among them that dizzying afternoon.

"What time would be good for you?" I said to Howard.

"Oh any time would be fine—whenever I'm not working," he said with a little laugh.

"Why don't you give me your phone number?" and I handed him a pen and the back of my phone bill, and he wrote it, right there against the elevator wall.

"Thanks," I said, waving the envelope in the air as I walked down the hallway. "I'll call you soon." Thank God he didn't say his usual "You're welcome"!

Two days later I called him, and the night after that we had our date—only neither of us referred to it as one. We ended up going to a Center City coffee house again—a different one that stayed open at night. That was certainly as low-key as you could get, but at the time I thought it was the right way to proceed. I didn't want to scare him more than I thought he already was, because, say what you will, we were an interracial couple and he was essentially a servant in the building I lived in. I also didn't want him to have to spend any money or possibly embarrass him by offering to pay for myself. So all things considered the coffee house didn't seem such a bad idea, what with there being so many potentially awkward moments hovering around us. The fear of embarrassing him affected my conversation too. There was certainly no talk about the O.J. verdict or the Million Man March. I also sensed that he didn't want to talk about his past, either, and of course I didn't bring up his job or the few people in the building I vaguely knew. That left the inevitable topics of music and chess, the latter of which I knew nothing about, and my job, and a few general things like movies and the weather.

He was making a big effort, a Howard-sized effort to make things go smoothly, but he was also painfully tentative as if he wasn't sure exactly why we were together and was constantly looking for a sign that would suddenly explain it all. After an hour or so of this nonsense, I began to regret the way I'd played things. What was the point of being so careful if it only produced an atmosphere of anxiety and terminal ambiguity. Besides, I knew what I wanted to have happen with Howard, though I had no idea if he liked me or was even attracted to me. There was no reason then to play these tiring social games that I'd been conditioned to play my whole life.

It was a warm night in late October and I finally suggested that we go to the park across the street in Rittenhouse Square.

"That's a great idea," Howard said. Apparently he was just as eager to get out of the coffee house as I was. "I love Rittenhouse Park. It's like a touch of Europe in our city."

"Have you ever been to Europe?"

"No, I haven't been able to get there yet, but I still hope to," he said, with a sadder than usual smile. "Have you been over there?"

"Yes, a few times," I said softly, regretting that I'd brought it up. He began asking me about Paris and Rome and did I go to the opera house in Paris and in other European cities. Somehow I answered him, but I was simultaneously getting a major hit of pain remembering what had happened two days ago. I was taking a cab back from work then, looked out the window for a second, and saw Ed with an arm around his new girlfriend, both of them smiling as they walked down the street. By the time Howard and I sat down on a bench I was crying a little and had to turn my head away.

"Is there anything the matter, Paula?"

I didn't know what else to do, so I told him the truth about Ed, told him that every time I went outside I worried about seeing him since he lived only eight blocks from me, and how two days ago I'd seen him with the new woman he was sleeping with.

"I'm sorry, Paula; I hate to see you hurt like that."

I turned to look at him. His face looked kind but older than I'd noticed before, especially around his eyes, and I realized he was at least in his early or mid-forties.

"Thanks," I said. I touched his face for a moment and then kissed him, first on the cheek I'd been touching and then for a few seconds on his lips.

He didn't say anything. He looked a little surprised but said nothing.

"I like you Howard."

"I like you, too, Paula."

"Would you like to come to my place for dinner Friday night? I make a pretty good chicken."

"I'd love to."

"I have a piano, too. I'd love to hear you play."

Howard laughed. "Oh I don't know about that. I'm not much of a pianist. I'm afraid I'd disappoint you."

I was tempted to tell him how I'd been listening to him for weeks, admiring it and feeling moved and energized by it, but thought I'd better not confess that right away. I didn't want to come on any stronger than I already had.

VII. HOWARD'S END

It turned out I needed every one of the three days I had before our dinner. I had to go to the cleaners, buy the wine and some condoms, too (to be honest about it), cook the lemon chicken and mixed vegetables, and arrange to leave work early; I also had to give my apartment a thorough and much-needed cleaning. All this was nerve-wracking but not without its occasional rewards. While I was cleaning the living room, for example, I heard Howard practicing Rachmaninoff's Second again, playing it, I felt, with a little more ardor than usual. Was this due to my influence? It was certainly fun to think so.

I couldn't really think about anything else but Howard and the dinner during the days before it, and while he was practicing I sometimes felt he was divining my thoughts and responding to them in a kind of musical dialogue. That was more than fun. I couldn't remember the last time I'd felt so excited. I thought about calling Ellen and telling her about Howard, but then I remembered a couple of quasi-racist remarks she'd made once and I decided not to. I no longer knew what I really had in common with her, anyway. If things with Howard worked out I'd have to seriously reevaluate my friendship with her. Small matter. I was completely focused on him and felt convinced that, if there was ever going to be a breakthrough with us, it would happen the night of my dinner.

So he arrived, on time of course. I was wearing a black dress, a little low in front, with a simple string of pearls around my neck. Nothing shocking, but somewhat dramatic, nevertheless. Howard was wearing a navy blue blazer, gray well-pressed slacks, and a red tie. A little too preppy for my taste, but definitely a step up from the uniform. Also his hair was less outlandishly colored and slicked down than usual. For the first time it looked like hair I could touch and I liked that idea. Other than that he looked handsome, kept his opening polite speech of thanking me relatively under control, and, oh yes, he brought flowers, the dear!

He was less self-conscious this time, which I also liked, and made sensitive little comments about the different things I showed him in my apartment. When he saw a photograph of my father he asked when he played in the Symphony. "From '62 to '93," I said.

"Then he played under Ormandy as well as Muti."

"Yes."

"Those were great years," he said wistfully. "Great years. And there's your Knabe. That's a beautiful upright."

"My father gave it to me."

"Did he teach you how to play?"

"Yes." How did you know, I almost said.

"That must have been something, to study with a great musician in your house. Would you play for me sometime?"

"I didn't keep up with it, Howard. I rarely play at all now. I play marketing games instead," I said, with a little laugh, more bitter than I intended. "Though I've been thinking lately of getting back to the piano, so who knows? Actually, I was going to ask you if you'd play for me tonight."

"Me?" Howard said, opening up his eyes wide and putting two long elegant fingers to his chest. "I don't want to ruin your dinner," he said laughing.

"That certainly wouldn't happen. Really, I'd love to hear you play anything at all."

"Are you serious?"

"Yes," I said. "You look a little worried."

"I'm no Horowitz, you know. I'm pretty much a beginner really."

"I'm sure you're being too modest."

"I don't know. Maybe later, OK?"

"Well, two shy pianists," I said, walking into the kitchen and arranging the food on the dining room table that was in the open space between the kitchen and living room.

Of course Howard offered to help, so I asked him to open the wine while I lit the tall red candle in the center of the table that I'd covered with a pink tablecloth.

Howard's table manners were impeccable and as I anticipated he was an effusive complimenter: "Lemon chicken! How did you know that was my favorite kind of chicken? Umm, the sauce is marvelous. Is that sauce homemade, Paula? Is it your own creation?"

"I plead guilty," I said, smiling from ear to ear.

"Well, you should patent it. A creation this exquisite should be shared with the world."

I started laughing, quasi-hysterically.

"I mean it, Paula. And you deserve to be recognized as a world-class chef."

I'll admit I had started the dinner still being ambivalent about whether I really wanted to have sex with Howard that night. Sex since my divorce had been quite intermittent and with generally poor results. But by the time he was through celebrating the joys of my salad and mixed vegetables, I had no more inner hesitation. I made sure I refilled his glass of wine and smiled at him again, more seductively this time, as we began my homemade peach pie. Howard praised that to the skies, too, but a moment later I had an image of Ed watching us. In my mind I was talking to him angrily about Howard, saying "He's not exactly your stereotype of the black urban savage, is he?" Ed was jealous as I exultantly delivered my cruel little speech—but then my pleasure faded and I felt guilty about how sad Ed looked and was suddenly sad myself.

I picked up my wine glass and looked away from Howard out the living room windows at the empty buildings across the street.

"Are you OK?" Howard said. My index finger went to my eye and I wiped away a couple of tears.

"You must think I'm a little nuts."

"Not at all. I think you're delightful and very talented."

"I just got a kind of flashback about my ex-husband."

"Oh."

"Maybe you think I'm a bit nutty about him, but not at all. I rarely think about him. So can we pretend this sort of sneak attack from the past never happened? 'Cause it rarely does anymore."

"OK."

I was standing up now, though there were still pieces of pie left on both our plates. "Howard, could you just come into the living room with me?"

"Sure," he said, getting up from the table quickly.

"Could you just hold me for a moment?"

He looked at me searchingly and I found myself wondering if he'd done this kind of thing before with other white women tenants. I figured either way he would have to worry about losing his job, at the very least, since there was probably at least an unwritten rule about it, and then if one of the tenants was a bit off emotionally or mentally he'd have to worry about a rape charge, too, in a situation like this.

He put his hands on my shoulders. It was almost as if we were dancing. I suddenly wished we were. I bet he was good at it. Then I put my hand on his face and caressed his brown skin, and then on his hair which felt different—like an exotic plant—but the difference excited me and I started to kiss him, on his thick, curvaceous lips, until he finally opened his mouth for me. He tasted of my food and wine and also of mouthspray he must have used recently (the thoughtful Howard touch).

When we stopped I took his hand and said, "Come with me."

"Is this what you want, Paula?" he said softly.

"Yes, Howard, I want you. Isn't it what you want, too?"

"Oh, yes."

We walked toward my bedroom holding hands. There was not much light in the room, and I suddenly wished there was even less, just the reverse of the fantasies I'd had during the week when I imagined how lovely the contrasting colors of our bodies would look in the clear, full light of my room. Moreover, I began wishing I'd taken my wine glass with me into the room so I could have some more and couldn't help seeing it in my mind shining like some kind of over-sized jewel. I thought maybe I should just make up some excuse and go back to the kitchen and gulp down a glass or two. Perhaps it was my old, programmed wife-of-Ed self trying to sabotage me one more time from beyond the grave. At any rate, I decided I'd better start paying attention to Howard.

"You're so exciting to me," I said, not knowing if I meant it or not in that moment, although I'd certainly thought it before.

Howard said something softly in my ear about feeling blessed. I wasn't sure what he said because I tried to erase it as soon as he said it. I guess I was hoping for something less religious and more lustful, so I dropped the idea of talking with him in the bedroom. Instead I began to kiss him. I felt that, if he eventually got enough confidence, his true bedroom personality might emerge, and he'd leave his amenable but passive side behind and get a little domineering, which could be exciting. Also, I was feeling a little odd, simultaneously hyperconscious and absent, as if I needed to constantly be in physical contact with him lest I lose my own physical presence in the room and become weightless and invisible—a case for *The X-Files*.

We kissed for a long time and I felt a little like I did in the eighth grade when kissing was like screwing, the maximum thing you could do and there wasn't even a thought of doing anything beyond it. Except that it wasn't as exciting as it was then, of course, being fraught with the realization that we had to move on.

Come on, Paula, I finally said to myself, you're a new person now, thinking your first thoughts; you're not going to zone out like you've done with other men since Ed. Think about what you're doing. You're making love to someone you care about and want. You're making love to a black human being for the first time after feeling so much emotion toward them from a distance, a damnable distance your whole life, and now you have a chance to share your body and spirit, so you can't just zone out.

We began undressing each other, although I initiated it and wished he had. Programmed or not, I like to have the man start taking my clothes off first. It makes me feel wanted in a way I can't usually feel otherwise. Still, things were starting to improve; our kissing had passed through the stilted and pedestrian stages to a pretty sexy rhythm and undressing each other was more fun than not. I tried not to stare at his penis, thinking that it would be kind of a racist thing to do, but wound up sneaking in a look anyway. It looked more or less average-sized to me.

Come on, Paula, said my new internal voice, getting on my case again. Resist these stupid racist fantasies you've been conditioned to have, and experience this person, this artist, who happens to be black, who's gently touching your breasts with his long pianist's fingers, whose piano playing alone, that you listened to for so many days, shows he probably has more emotional range and depth than all the other men you've been to bed with combined.

We started sinking down to the bed together. He was moaning softly and started touching me, and I closed my eyes and saw the wine glass burst softly as if the glass were no stronger than a rain drop. For a few seconds, maybe more, I thought something radically different was going to happen—the physical complement to my new consciousness—but then Howard began to very politely make love to me, as if he were painting me by the numbers, stopping methodically to ask me about how hard or fast he should do something, and I thought, alas, of how hard he tried each time to make the elevator land exactly even with my floor.

Then I felt bad for thinking that and told myself not to be so ambitious, that the first time it should be enough just to get through it. About ten minutes later he made a sweet musical kind of sound when he came, and I was glad to have given him a little pleasure.

"That felt wonderful, Paula. That was a privileged moment in my life," he said, lying next to me afterwards and stroking my hair. Ever considerate, he didn't ask if I came. I didn't—thus keeping my batting average a perfect 1,000 in not coming during intercourse for the last calendar year. Still, I didn't exactly regret that we'd done it. Things usually improve in that area in a relationship, until they get bad again. It was that way with Ed— though I didn't want to think about him now; that would be way too painful. So I snuggled next to Howard for a few minutes and it felt sweet, and my mind finally stopped racing, and I thought I might even get some sleep.

Then I felt him move. He was taking his condom off and a moment later excused himself to use the bathroom. My mind was blank at first until it occurred to me that I should put some clothes on before Howard returned. I heard the toilet flush—it makes a loud music of its own in my apartment—and merging with that sound a piano playing a poignant phrase from Rachmaninoff's Second. I felt a quick stab of pain or horror, and tears came to my eyes. So Howard wasn't the pianist; Howard wasn't my black Rachmaninoff. But, oddly, after the initial shock, I wasn't even that surprised. No, Howard wasn't an artist at all as I'd imagined; he was an elevator man. I couldn't say he hadn't warned me.

I began to feel ashamed of myself and started crying softly. Thank God he was still in the bathroom—no doubt making sure he smelled and tasted good for me. I'd better stop crying, I said to myself, quickly wiping away my tears. I certainly didn't want to talk about this with him.

Then a new anxiety went through me. What would I do if he wanted me again, because I suddenly knew I didn't. I couldn't do it again with him, and beyond that, what would I do if he wanted our relationship to continue? Obviously I'd done this for all the wrong reasons and should break it off. But if I did end it right away how could I bear to see him every day in the elevator? Would he continue to say his pseudo-cheerful "You're welcome" each time he opened the door for me, or would he not talk at all during the endless rides to my floor. Perhaps he'd tell the other doormen out of spite and they'd start hitting on me too. All these alternatives were hideous to think about. And every time I'd hear the piano, which apparently would be every day, it would be mocking me. It was all unbearable. I'd have to move out of the building as soon as possible, I could see that. Lose my deposit if necessary, but somehow leave within a week. I'd put myself in a ridiculous situation, a ridiculous trap, and there was nothing else to do.

I heard the bathroom door open and managed to get my bra and panties on just before he came back in the room. Taking his cue from me Howard turned discreetly away and put on his own underpants. When he turned around I looked at him closely. He was standing in front of my bed with a somewhat cryptic smile on his face, a slightly pot stomach, with his fleshy breasts hanging forlornly in front. A middle-aged body is usually a frightened-looking thing and his was no exception. There was a sadness in his eyes, too, and I thought that his smile was an instinctive camouflage—the way some animals and plants have protective coloration. Perhaps he sensed my disappointment, knew already this wouldn't happen again, but was damned if he knew what he should do or say next.

"Hear that music?" I suddenly blurted.

"Yes, the Rachmaninoff Second. Beautiful piece. A Korean girl on the fourth floor plays that. She's a student at Curtis who moved in a few months ago. She's very talented, isn't she? God, I'd give anything to play like that."

Yes, Howard would know all about the pianists in the building. The building was his theater and concert hall and museum. The building was his Europe. Then I got an idea. "Will you sit down and listen to it with me for a while?" I said, as I put on my dress.

"Sure Paula," he said, sitting on the bed without touching me. We began listening to the music silently and I thought that he very well might know now that the romantic part of our relationship was over, but unless he said something himself at some point, which he probably wouldn't, I'd have to make it clear in a way that wouldn't hurt him too much. It would be dreadful, but I'd have to do it.

We kept listening, longer than I thought we would. I began to picture the Korean girl who practiced these phrases over and over every day so that one day they might sound new and spontaneous. That was a kind of love, and I wondered what the source of passion was in her life that allowed her to do it. I stole another glance at Howard. For a moment I felt his loneliness, his disappointment over much more than this night, and I thought that some time in the future we might go to a concert together as friends, perhaps a piano recital at Curtis like the one the Korean girl was preparing for. Then a voice inside me said, you're still deluding yourself you foolish woman, you'll never get over your embarrassment and shame enough to do that. But later I felt maybe I would, that maybe the concert was really the first thought of my new life or at least the first one that made sense.

The Identity Club

Sometimes you meet someone who is actually achieving what you can only strive for. It's not exactly like meeting your double, it's more like seeing what you would be if you could realize your potential. Those were the feelings that Remy had about Eugene. In appearance they were similar, although Eugene was younger by a few years and taller by a few inches. But they each had fine dark hair, still untouched by any gray and they each had refined facial features, especially their delicate noses. Eugene's body, however, was significantly more muscular than Remy's.

At the agency in New York where Remy had worked for three years writing ad copy, Eugene was making a rapid and much talked about ascent. A number of Remy's other colleagues openly speculated that Eugene was advancing because he was a masterful office politician. But when Remy began working with him on an important new campaign for a client who manufactured toothpaste, he saw that wasn't true at all. Eugene had a special kind of brilliance, not just for writing slogans or generating campaign ideas, but a deep insight into human motivations and behavior that he knew how to channel into making people buy products. Rather than being a master diplomat, Remy discovered that Eugene was aloof almost to the point of rudeness, never discussed his private life and rarely showed any signs of a sense of humor. Yet Remy admired him enormously and wondered if

Eugene, who Remy thought of as one of the wisest men he knew
(certainly the wisest young man) might be a person he could
confide in about The Identity Club and the important decision he
had to make in the near future.

All of these thoughts were streaming through Remy's mind
after work one night in his apartment when the phone rang. It
was Poe calling to remind him about The Identity Club meeting
that night. Remy nearly gasped as he'd inexplicably lost track of
time and now had only a half hour to meet Poe and take a cab
with him to the meeting.

The club itself had to be, almost by definition, a secretive
organization that placed a high value on its members' trust-
worthiness, dependability and punctuality. Its members assumed
the identities—the appearance, activities and personalities—
(whenever they could) of various celebrated dead artists they
deeply admired. At the monthly meetings, which Remy enjoyed
immensely and thought of as parties, all members would be
dressed in their adopted identities drinking and eating and joking
with each other. As soon as he stepped into a meeting he could
feel himself transform as if the colors of his life went from muted
grays and browns to glowing reds and yellows and vibrant
greens and blues. To be honest with himself, since moving to New
York from New England three years ago, his life before the club
had been embarrassingly devoid of both emotion and purpose.
How lucky for him, he often thought, that he'd been befriended
by Winston Reems—now known by club members as Salvador
Dali, a junior executive at his agency who had slowly introduced
him to the club.

This month's meeting was at the new Bill Evans (who had
patterned himself after the famous jazz pianist) apartment, and
since Remy enjoyed music he was particularly looking forward to
it. He had also been told that Thomas Bernhard, named for the
late Austrian writer, would definitely be there as well. As Bernhard
was renowned for being a kind of hermit it was always special
when he did attend a meeting and it made sense that as a former
professional musician he would go to this one.

Quickly Remy dried off from his shower and began putting on
new clothes. He thought that tonight promised to be an especially

interesting mix of people, which was one of the ostensible ideas of the organization, to have great artists from the different arts meet and mingle, as they never had in real life. The decision facing Remy, which he'd given a good deal of thought to without coming any closer to a conclusion, was who he was going to "become" himself. He was considered at present an "uncommitted member" and had been debating between Nathaniel West and some other writers. Nabokov, whom he might have seriously considered, had already been taken. At least, since he still had a month before he had to commit, he didn't have to dress in costume—though he rather looked forward to that. Remy had been a member for four months and it was now time for him to submit to a club interview to help him decide whose identity he was best suited for. Sometimes these interviews were conducted by the entire membership, which reminded Remy of a kind of Intervention, other times by the host of that evening's meeting or by some other well-established member. The new member was never informed in advance, as these "probings" were taken very seriously and the club wanted a spontaneous and true response.

One of the reasons Remy was having difficulty choosing an identity—and why he felt some anxiety about the whole process—was that he'd kept secret from the club his hidden contempt, or at least ambivalence, about the advertising business and his disappointment with the emptiness of his own life as well. No wonder he found refuge in art and in imagining the lives that famous artists led. He'd heard other members confess to those exact sentiments but the public admission of these feelings would be difficult for Remy. He thought it was the inevitable price he had to pay to get his membership in the club, and along with Eugene (whose importance to him Remy also kept secret) the club was his only interest in life, the only thing worth thinking about.

Poe was waiting for him in front of his brownstone, dressed, as Remy expected, in a black overcoat with his long recently dyed dark hair parted in the middle, the approximate match of his recently dyed mustache.

"I'm sorry I'm so late," Remy said.

Poe stared at him. "Something is preoccupying you," he said.

"You're right about that," Remy said, thinking of Eugene and wishing he could somehow be at the party.

"Do you mind if we walk?" Poe said. "There's something in the air tonight I crave, although I couldn't say exactly what it is. Some dark bell-like sound, some secret perfumed scent coming from the night that draws me forward…besides," he said, with a completely straight face, as he took a swallow of some kind of alcohol concealed in a brown paper bag, "it will be just as fast or just as slow as a taxi."

"Fine," Remy said, who felt he was hardly in a position to object. In the club Remy suspected that members assumed their identities with varying degrees of intensity. Clearly Poe was unusually committed to his to the point where he had renounced his former name, become a poet, short story writer and alcoholic, and given up dating women his age. Because he worked mostly at home doing research on the Internet he was able to be in character pretty much around the clock.

"You need to focus on your choice," Poe said, "you have an important decision facing you and not much time to make it."

"I hope I'll know during the probing," Remy said, "I hope it will come to me then."

"Listen to your heart, even if it makes too much noise," Poe said, smiling ironically.

They walked in silence the rest of the way, Poe sometimes putting his hands to his ears as if Roderick Usher were reacting to too strident a sound. As they were approaching the steps to Evans' walkup, from which they could already hear a few haunting chords on the piano, Poe turned to Remy and said, "Are you aware that we're voting on the woman issue tonight?"

"Yes, I knew that."

Poe was referring to the question of whether or not The Identity Club, which was currently a de facto men's club, would begin to actively recruit women. Remy had sometimes thought of the club as practicing a form of directed reincarnation, but did that mean that in the next world the club didn't want to deal with any women?

"I'm going to vote that we should recruit them. How can we fully be who we've become without women? I need them for my poetry, and to love of course. I think the organization should try to increase our chances to meet them not isolate us from them."

"I completely agree with you," Remy said.

They rang the bell and Dali opened the door, bowing grandly and pointing towards a dark, barely furnished, yet somehow chaotic apartment.

"It's Bill Evans's home. I knew it would be a mess," Poe said quietly to Remy, drinking again from his brown paper bag.

Evans was bent over the piano, head characteristically suspended just above the keys, as he played the coda of his composition "RE: Person I Knew." He also had long dark hair but was clean-shaven. From the small sofa—the only one in the room, Erik Satie shouted "Bravo! Encore!" Remy couldn't remember seeing any photographs of the composer but he judged his French to be authentic. As a tribute to his admirer, Evans played a version of Satie's most famous piano piece "Gymnopedie" which Remy recalled the former Evans had recorded on his album Nirvana. This was the first time Remy had heard the new Bill Evans play and while he was hardly an Evans scholar he thought it sounded quite convincing. The harmony, the soft touch and plaintive melodic lines were all there (no doubt learned from a book that had printed Evans's solos and arrangements) though, of course, some mistakes were made and the new Evans's touch wasn't as elegant as the first one's. Still, Remy could see that the new Evans's immersion into his identity had been thorough. Remy had recently seen a video of the former Evans playing and could see that the new one had his body movements down pat. Could he, Remy, devote himself as thoroughly to the new identity he would soon be assuming?

"Encore, encore," said Satie again and now also Cocteau, who had joined his old friend and collaborator on the sofa. Continuing his homage to his French admirers, Evans played "You Must Believe In Spring" by the French composer Michael Legrand. When it ended Remy found himself applauding vigorously as well and becoming even more curious about the former life of the new Evans. All he knew was that he'd once been a student at Julliard and was involved now in selling computer parts. He wished he'd paid more attention when he talked with him five months ago at the meeting but now it was too late, as members were not allowed to discuss their former identities with each other once they'd committed to a new one.

After a brief rendition of "Five," Evans took a break and Remy slowly sidled up to him, wishing again that Eugene were there. Though he was often aloof, when the situation required Eugene always knew just what to say to people. What to say and not a word more, for Eugene had the gift of concision, just as Evans did on the piano.

"That was beautiful playing," Remy finally said.

"Thanks, man," Evans said, slowly raising his head and smiling at him. Like the first Bill Evans, his teeth weren't very good and he wore glasses.

"I know how hard it is to keep that kind of time, and to swing like that without your trio."

"I miss the guys but sometimes when I play alone I feel a oneness with the music that I just can't get any other way."

It occurred to Remy that Evans had had at least four different trios throughout his recording career and that he didn't know which trio Evans was "missing" because he didn't know what stage of Evans's life the new one was now living. Perhaps sensing this, Evans said, "When Scotty died last year I didn't even know if I could continue. I couldn't bring myself to even look for a new bassist for a long time or to record either. And when I did finally go in the studio again a little while ago, it was a solo gig."

Remy now knew that for Evans it was about 1962 since Scott LaFaro, his young former bassist, had died in a car accident in 1961.

"Do you play, man?" Evans asked.

"Just enough to tell how good you are," Remy said.

"So there's no chance you could become a musician?"

"No, no, I couldn't do it."

"I know the choice facing you is difficult."

"It is. It really is," Remy said, touched by the note of sympathy in Evans' voice.

"Do you do any of the other arts?"

"Not with anything like your level of skill or Dali's or any of the other members, for that matter. I write a little at my job...but you could hardly call it art. There's a man, a rising star at my ad agency named Eugene, who's working on a campaign with me now who has the most original ideas and comes up with the most brilliant material who really is an artist. If he were here, instead of me, he could become George Bernard Shaw or Oscar Wilde."

"Have you spoken to him about the club?"

"No, no. I don't really know him that well. I mean he barely knows I exist."

"Anyway, I've been speaking to some of the other members and there's definitely growing support to include men of letters in the club, you know, critics of a high level like Edmund Wilson or Marshall McLuhan."

"Oh no, I'm not nearly smart enough to be Edmund Wilson or McLuhan either. I figure if I become a member it will be as a novelist. I was thinking of Nathaniel West, or maybe James Agee."

"Either way you'd have to go young, man."

Remy looked at Evans to be sure he was joking but saw that he looked quite serious. A chilling thought flitted through his mind. Did the committed members have a secret rule that they had to die at the same age their "adopted artists" did? And if so, was it merely a symbolic death of their identity or their actual physical death duplicated as closely as possible? Was The Identity Club, which he'd thought of as devoted to a form of reincarnation, then, actually devoted in the long run to a kind of delayed suicide? Of course this was probably a preposterous fantasy, still, he couldn't completely dismiss it.

"But you'll have to die young too then," Remy said, remembering that Bill Evans had died at 51. He said this with a half smile so it could seem he was joking. Evans looked around himself nervously before he answered.

"I find that Zen really helps me deal with the death thing."

Remy took a step back and nodded silently. His head had begun to hurt and after he saw that Evans wanted to play again he excused himself to use the bathroom. Once there, however, he realized that he'd forgotten to bring his Tylenol. He opened the mirrored cabinet, was blinded by a variety of pharmaceuticals but found nothing he could take. He closed the cabinet and heard Evans playing the opening chorus of "Time Remembered," one of his best compositions. The music was startlingly lovely but then partially drowned out by a loud coughing in the hallway. Remy turned and saw Thomas Bernhard, face temporarily buried in a handkerchief.

"Are you looking for something?" Bernhard said in a German accent.

"I have a headache."

"How fragile we are yet how determined. So you are looking for...?"

"Some Tylenol."

"Ah! You have a headache and I have some Tylenol," Bernhard said, withdrawing a small bottle from the cavernous pocket of his corduroy sports jacket.

"Since my illness I am nothing but pills, my kingdom for a pill. Here..." he said, handing Remy the bottle.

Remy took two and swallowed them.

"Thanks a lot," he said. Bernhard nodded, and half bowed in a gently mocking way.

"So, have you decided to become Nathaniel West or not?"

"I understand that I'd have to die quite young then and quite violently," Remy said, laughing uncertainly.

Bernhard's eyes had a heightened, almost shocked expression. Then he started coughing loudly and persistently again. Remy waited a half minute, finally saying, "Why don't you drink some water?" He got out of the bathroom area, half directing Bernhard to the sink and returned to the living room.

"Is he alright?" Poe said, meeting him in the hallway. He was drinking from a half empty wine bottle.

"Yes, I think so," Remy said. But I'm not, he said to himself. For the first time he felt profoundly uncomfortable at a club meeting. The pressure of having to make his identity decision was oppressive and worse still were the dark fears he now had about the club's policies. The original conceit of the club had amused him in the titillating way he liked to be amused, but if he were right about his suspicions, then the club was far more literal about its directed reincarnation than he'd realized. If he were right about the death rule, to commit to an identity was to select all aspects of your fate including when you would die. And what if one changed one's mind and didn't want to cooperate after committing, what then?

The pain in Remy's head was excruciating and at the first polite opportunity he excused himself, heaping more praise on Evans for the wonderful evening before he closed the door…and shuddered.

He decided not to return the phone calls he got from three club members over the next two days. To say anything while he was uncertain what to do about The Club could be a mistake. On the one hand he'd been profoundly upset by what he thought he might have discovered about its policies, on the other hand the club was the nucleus of what social life he had and would be very difficult to give up. Besides his job, The Identity Club was his only consistent base of human contact.

Remy began to throw himself into the new campaign with more passion than he'd ever shown at the agency. Largely due to Eugene's contributions, it was succeeding and, as expected, it was Eugene who benefited the most from it with the agency higher-ups. It was not that Eugene worked harder than Remy; it was simply that he could accomplish twice as much with less effort because he was so talented in the field. Still, Remy didn't begrudge him his success. Instead his interest in Eugene grew even stronger as he continued to watch and study him. He felt if he could become Eugene's friend and confide in him, then Eugene might know just what he should do about The Identity Club.

As Remy suspected, Eugene led a highly ritualized existence in the work place. It wasn't difficult to arrange a "chance meeting" at the elevator banks and to quickly ask him to have a drink in a way he couldn't refuse. They went to a bar on Restaurant Row—Remy feeling happier than he had in days. But once outside the agency Eugene seemed tense and remote, and sitting across from him at the bar he avoided eye contact and spoke sparsely in a strangely clipped tone that forced Remy to become uncharacteristically aggressive.

"We're all so grateful for the work you did on the campaign. It was just amazing," Remy said. Eugene nodded and said a muted thank you. It was as if Remy had just said to him "nice shirt you're wearing."

"I'm really proud to have you as a colleague," Remy added for good measure.

Again Eugene nodded, but this time said nothing and Remy began to feel defeated and strangely desperate. He waited until their eyes locked for a moment then said, "Do you know what The Identity Club is?" The immediate reddening of Eugene's face told Remy that he did.

"What makes you think that I would know?"

"I know some of the key members in the club came from our agency."

Eugene raised his eyebrows but still said nothing.

"In fact, I'm a member myself or a potential member."

"Then what is it you think I would know about the club that you wouldn't know already?"

"Fair enough," Remy said, clearing his throat and finishing his beer.

"I'll be a little more candid. I'm a member in that I've been attending the meetings but I'm not a completely committed member. I've been trying to decide whether to commit to the club completely and since I respect you and admire your judgment so much I thought I would ask you about it."

"I tend to avoid organizations that have a strong ideology, especially ones that try to convert you to their world view. I think they are unappetizing and often dangerous."

"Why is it dangerous?" Remy asked.

"Any organization that asks you to alter your life, or to jeopardize it and in many cases to give it up is to be avoided like the plague. Is, in fact, the plague...I'm just making this as a general statement, OK? I'm not saying anything about your club specifically," Eugene said hurriedly, looking away from Remy when he tried to make eye contact with him again.

"Thank you for your advice."

"It wasn't advice about anything specific. Remember that. It was just a general observation on the nature of organizations."

"Thank you for your observations then. I appreciate it and will keep it completely confidential."

Eugene seemed more relaxed then but five minutes later excused himself, saying he had to leave for another appointment. Remy could barely make himself stand when Eugene left, he felt so frozen with disappointment. When he did begin to move he felt strangely weightless, like a dizzy ghost passing down a dreamlike street. It was as if for the first time the universe had revealed its essential emptiness to him and he was completely baffled by it. In his life before New York there had always been some kind of support for him. First his parents, when he was a child, of course. Perhaps he left them too soon. Then his teachers when he went to school where he also met his friends who were now dispersed around the country as he was, though none of them had landed in New York. The Identity Club had filled that void, he supposed, although not completely or else Eugene wouldn't have been so important to him. But now it was clear that Eugene wanted little to do with him and it was also becoming increasingly clear (from the meeting at Evans' house to the dark advice of Eugene) that there were real problems, some of them perhaps dangerous, with the club. But how could he bear to leave it? The truth was he could hardly bring himself to focus on these problems, much less think them through in any systematic way. He could barely bring himself to get to work on time, dressed properly and able to smile, and could hardly remember that in the past he had always prided himself on being neat, on time, and amiable—the ultimate team player. After work, the next day, he went directly home as if there were some awful menace on the streets he had to flee.

In his apartment he found it difficult to sit still, and nearly impossible to sleep. He began pacing from wall to wall of his apartment, feeling oddly like a gorilla in a cage, even to the point where he thought he felt fur on his back.

Then, finally, a change. The phone rang in his cage, he picked it up for some reason, following some ape-like impulse, and heard the voice of Bill Evans saying, "I've got to talk to you, man."

"Yes, go ahead."

"Not on the phone. Are you free now?"

Remy thought of the dark streets and wasn't sure how to answer.

"It's important."

"OK," Remy said.

"You know Coliseum Books on 59th Street?"

"Yes."

"Meet me there in half an hour. I'll be in the mystery section."

Remy hung up and continued pacing rapidly for a minute, like a gorilla doing double time. Then he stopped and began wondering if he should call a cab or not—would it really be any safer? And as he thought, the cage around him disappeared, as did his feeling of having fur and an ape persona. He was so happy about that he decided to run the twenty blocks to the bookstore, keeping his mind as thought-free as possible although he did feel a low but persistent level of anxiety the whole way.

As promised, Evans was in the mystery section in a long black overcoat looking at or pretending to look at a book by Poe with his black-rimmed glasses. Their eyes met quickly, Evans, looking around himself, half nodding, but waiting until Remy was next to him before he spoke in a low voice barely louder than a whisper.

"We can talk here, man."

"What is it?" Remy said. He wanted to say more but couldn't, as if all those silent hours in the aquarium made him forget how to talk.

"There're some things I think you don't know, that I want you to know."

"What things?"

"About the Club and its ideas. When I was talking to you at the last meeting you looked confused when I was referring to my trio, like you didn't know how old I was."

"But then I figured it out."

"Yah, cause I talked about Scotty's death and the record I made a year later. You figured it out cause you know about my career. But let me lay it out to you in simple terms cause you're going to have to make an important commitment at the next meeting and when you make it it's like a complete life commitment. When you take on a new identity there are a lot of rewards, but also a lot of demands. You have to do a tremendous amount of research too and you have to have a lot of strength to leave your old self completely behind. In that sense you have to kill your old self and its old life. The only thing you can keep is your job but you have to do your job the way Nathaniel West would, if you go ahead and decide to become him. That's why it takes so much courage and faith as well as work—time spent in a library, or whatever, doing as much research on him as you can. And finally, well let me ask you how old you are?"

"Twenty-nine," Remy said in a voice now barely above a whisper, as well.

"OK, man. You'll live the life West did at 29, you'll take on his life in chronological order, so when you turn 30 West will turn 30 until…"

"Until when?"

"Until he dies, man. I wanted you to understand that. That's where the courage and faith part come in."

"But he died so young."

"Like I said, I'm gonna pass pretty soon too, but I'm also going to play jazz piano more beautifully than any one's ever played it—that's the reward part—and besides, as long as the club exists I'll be reincarnated again somewhere down the line."

"But you'll be dead."

"No man, I'll be Bill Evans reincarnated. I might have to wait a number of years but like my song says, 'We will Meet Again,'" Evans said with an ironic smile.

Remy looked down at the floor to get his bearings.

"Do all the members understand this when they make their commitment?"

"Don't worry about the other members. Just focus on yourself."

"But what if I lack the courage and vision to do this, to…"

"Have you been studying the club literature, especially the parts about reincarnation?"

"Not as much as I should have. Look, Bill, what if I decide I can't go through with this and just want to withdraw my membership?"

"I wouldn't advise that," Evans said with unexpected sternness. "I really think it's too late for that in your case."

Instinctively Remy took a step back—his face turning a shade of white that, in turn, made Evans's eyes grow larger and more intense.

"Do you realize the invaluable work we're doing?"

"Yes, no," Remy said.

"We're saving the most important members of the human race—allowing their beauty to continue to touch humanity."

"But you're killing them again. Why not give the, give yourself, for example, a chance to live longer to see what you could do with more time?"

Evans shook his head from side to side like a pendulum.

"You can't go against Karma, man. We have to accept our limits." Remy took another step back and Evans extended his arm and let his hand rest on his shoulder.

"This world is as beautiful as it can get. You have to accept it. You know, like the poet said 'death is the mother of beauty.'"

"It sounds more like a suicide club than an identity club," Remy blurted.

"Sometimes when something is really important or beautiful you have to die for it, like freedom. Isn't that why all the wars are fought?"

"But most wars are stupid and preventable."

"Death isn't preventable, man. We know this. Every bar of every tune I play knows this. It's like we accept this unstated contract with the world when we're born, that we understand we'll have to die but we'll live out our destiny anyway."

"But all of science and medicine is trying to extend life, to defeat death."

"They'll never succeed, man. We know that, that's why we're a club of artists. Death and reincarnation is stronger than freedom. You have to give your life to forces that are bigger than you. Isn't that the unstated contract we all understand once we realize what death is? Isn't that humility the biggest part about what being a man is, man?"

Remy bowed his head, surprised that Evans was such a forceful speaker, and spoke with such complete conviction to the point where he had almost moved himself to tears. But all Remy felt was a desire to flee, to hide under his blanket and have The Identity Club, the agency and New York itself all turn out to be a hideous dream.

"As a matter of fact I took a risk seeing you like this and laying it all out for you."

"I appreciate that and I'll never tell anyone what we spoke about. I won't mention it to anyone at the agency, I promise. The agency is really a key player in all of this, isn't it?"

"I can't really get into that."

Remy nodded and felt a chill spread over him.

"Again, thank you for meeting me and for everything you told me, which, of course, I'll keep completely confidential," Remy said. He thought he should shake hands with Evans then, but couldn't bring himself to do it, instead found himself backing away from him.

"Remember how important beauty is and courage," Evans said, looking him straight in the eye.

"I'll remember everything you told me."

"See you at the next meeting then ."

"Yes," Remy said, "I'll see you then."

He walked out of the store dreading the streets, feeling someone from the club might be following him. It was entirely possible that Evans might have tipped off somebody and had them tail him or perhaps had already informed someone at the agency. Had he made Evans feel he would cooperate and go forward with his membership? He could only hope so.

It was cold, even for New York in December. The wind was unusually strong and seemed to blow through him as if he were hollow. It was odd how people often said that because New York had so many people you often felt anonymous or alone but to Remy that night, the abundance of people simple increased the odds that one of them was following him. And if he thought about it he could always feel that someone was, simply because it was numerically impossible to keep track of everyone walking near him.

In his apartment again, Remy went back to the aquarium and to his fish-like movements through it. He hated the aquarium, especially since he felt so feverish, but it kept him from thinking, which would be still worse. He must have stayed in it pacing for hours, sleeping only for an hour or two on his sofa in the early morning. Fortunately he had saved up all his sick days and could now call the secretary at the agency and tell her, quite honestly, that he was too ill to come in.

After making the call, Remy went to his room and lay down, too dizzy to keep moving around. But as soon as his head hit the pillow he was assailed by a steady procession of thoughts, images, and snatches of dialogue about the club. He saw the hard look in Evans's eyes as he said, "I really think it's too late for that." The worried look (the first time he'd ever seen that expression on Eugene's face) as he said "I'm just making this as a general statement, OK? I'm not saying anything about your club specifically." He saw the horrified expression in Bernhard's eyes in the hallway and heard his coughing fit again. He should have waited till the fit ended, he thought, and gotten some kind of definitive answer from him. Then he saw an image of Poe's face as he stood in front of his apartment the night of Evans's party, heard him say again "something is preoccupying you." Was Poe in on it too? Should he try to inform him? It seemed some members knew more than others. Perhaps there really was a secret membership within the membership that had the real knowledge of what The Identity Club truly believed and what it was prepared to do to enforce its beliefs.

Remy stayed in his apartment the entire day, eating Lean Cuisines and canned soup. Intermittently he tried watching TV or listening to the radio but everything reminded him of the club as if all the voices he heard on TV and the radio were really members of the club. He no longer was as frightened of the streets the next morning since nothing had proved to be more torturous than the last sleepless hours in his apartment. Instead, he was almost happy to return to the agency and certainly eager to immerse himself in work. Somewhat to his surprise he found himself whistling a bouncy jingle in the elevator, which, in fact, was the theme song for the new toothpaste campaign he'd worked on with Eugene.

The mood in the office was decidedly different, however. The receptionist barely acknowledged him, and when he looked at her more closely, appeared to be wiping tears from her eyes. Little groups of silent, stone-like figures were whispering in the hallway as if they were in a morgue. Remy took a few steps forward towards his office, hesitated, then walked back to the receptionist's desk and stared at her until she finally looked at him.

"What happened?" Remy said.

"It's Eugene," she said tearfully. "He died last night. Here, it's in the paper," she said, handing him a *Daily News*.

"Oh my God," Remy said, immediately tucking the newspaper inside his briefcase and walking soldier-straight down the rest of the hall until he reached his office where he could close his door and lock it. On page seven he found out everything he needed to know. Eugene had fallen to his death from the balcony of his midtown Manhattan apartment. At this point, the article said, "It was yet to be determined if foul play was involved."

Remy let the paper drop on his desk, looked out his window at the maze of buildings and streets below and shivered. Everything was suddenly starting to fall into place like the pieces of a monstrous puzzle. That so many people in the club came from the agency, that Eugene was so obviously nervous when he obliquely spoke against it, that Evans said he was "taking a risk" talking to him two days ago at Coliseum Books. Obviously, Eugene's death was no accident. He'd been punished for trying to dissuade potential members from joining, either for the warnings he gave him, Remy, or perhaps for other warnings to other people in the agency Remy didn't know about.

He nearly staggered then from the pain of losing Eugene, who'd meant so much to him and could have meant so much more not only to him but also to the world, but when he looked out the window his mood turned to terror so complete it virtually consumed his pain.

What had he done? He'd locked himself in a prison near a window on the 27th floor—but surely the higher-ups in the agency had master keys that could open it and ways to open the window and arrange his fall or some other form of execution.

There was no time to do anything but leave the building, no time even to go home, for his apartment would be the most dangerous place of all, and so no time to pack anything either. The world had suddenly shrunk to the cash in his pockets, the credit card in his wallet, and the clothes on his back. His goal now was simply to get a taxi to the airport and then as far away from New York as he could. He picked up his briefcase and overcoat, then stopped just short of the door and put them down on the floor. To leave his office with briefcase in hand, much less wearing his overcoat, might well look suspicious. He had to appear as if he were merely getting a drink of water or else going to the bathroom, then take ten extra steps and reach the elevator.

He counted to seven, his lucky number, and then opened his door thinking that he could probably buy a coat in the airport. The huddle of stone-like figures was gone. He walked directly towards the elevators, eyes focused straight ahead to reduce the chance of having to talk to someone. Then he saw an elevator open and his boss, Mr. Weir, about to get out. Before their eyes could meet, Remy turned left, opened a door and ran down a flight of stairs, then down two more flights. He thought briefly of running all the way down to the street, but if someone spotted him he'd be too easy a target. Besides, he was quite sure no one from the agency worked on the 24th floor. He stopped running, opened the new stairway door, and forced himself not to walk too fast towards the elevators. Once there he pressed the button and counted to seven again, after which an empty elevator (an almost unheard of event) suddenly appeared.

On the ride down he thought of different cities—Boston, Philadelphia, Washington D.C.—where he had relatives. But would it be a good idea to contact any of them? He had the feeling that the agency not only knew where his parents and other relatives lived, but where his friends lived too. It would be better to make a clean break from his past and reinvent himself—assume a new identity, as it were, and go with that for a while.

Outside the wind had picked up and it was beginning to snow slightly. Fortunately a cab came right away.

"To LaGuardia," he said to the driver, who was rough shaven and seemed unusually old for the job. Seeing the older man, Remy thought, the old are just the reincarnation of the young. In fact, strictly speaking, each moment of time you reincarnated yourself since you always had to attain a balance between your core, unchanging self and your constantly changing one. But when he tried to think of this further, his head started to hurt. Looking out the window to distract himself he noticed a black line of birds in the sky and thought of Eugene's falling and then thought he might cry. A man was a kind of reincarnation of a bird, a bird of a dinosaur and so on. But it really was too difficult to think about, just as infinity itself was. That was why people wanted to shape things for themselves; it was much too difficult otherwise. And, that's why the club members wanted to act like God because it was much too difficult to understand the real God.

Remy's eyes suddenly met the driver's and a fear went through him. He thought the driver looked like someone from the agency so as soon as the taxi slowed down at the airport, Remy handed him much more money than he needed to and left the cab without waiting for his change. Then he ran into the labyrinth of the airport trying to find a plane as fast as he could and like those birds he'd just seen in the sky fly away into another life.

The Spirit of New York

I scare people, usually women, I admit. I don't hurt them, or ever wish to; I simply jump out at them, or suddenly appear from a corner or doorway or from behind a parked car or tree. After they gasp or scream I apologize profusely and try to calm them down. I do it so they think it could have been an accident. Almost immediately I feel remorse and hope they forgive me, but it's also true I feel tremendous pleasure as well.

The first time was in Beachwood in the grove. My parents had chosen a Tanglewood vacation that summer, had rented a cottage in the Berkshires three miles from the concert grounds and dispatched me every morning to find my entertainment at the beach. I was ten or eleven—have never been sure which I was then. I loved the lake, blue and surrounded by hills, though I was also afraid of it. I loved the sight of the lake, the stillness of the lake, but I was terrified by the fish in it and found the occasional feeling of bluegills nibbling on my toes appalling.

There were two rafts in the water twenty yards apart. The more distant one was where the big kids often threw the smaller ones off while playing "King of the Raft." The one near the shore was like an aquatic day care center, teeming with uncontrollable young life. At my in-between age, in my in-between frame of mind I eventually abandoned both rafts in favor of the grove just behind the beach. (The beach itself was no temptation, just a few yards of undistinguished, pebbly sand.)

The games that went on in the grove were sporadic and spontaneous and much more to my liking. It was there I met Karen, who was eight and had magnificent gold hair and lake-blue eyes. Only a slightly too wide forehead kept her from physical perfection. I often focused on that forehead as if to keep myself, scrawny and practically chestless as I was, from feeling too inferior by comparison. Karen's father was in the orchestra that played in Tanglewood in the summer. Her mother and mine were vaguely friendly, the kind of friendliness my mother had with everyone. I became slightly friendly with Karen's mother myself, so she thought nothing of leaving her daughter alone with me in the afternoon. As for Karen, she was crazy about me and wanted to spend as much time with me as possible.

In the grove there were also two small wooden bathhouses about twenty feet apart. I rarely went there, being shy about my body and detesting the strong smells that filled the men's bathhouse. One late afternoon, however, I told Karen that I wanted to use it. She immediately said she wanted to go to the girls' bathhouse. As soon as we parted I began to have doubts about whether I really should go. Though it was late, someone else still could be using it; and then there was the matter of those awful smells. After climbing just one of the steps that led to the door, I turned and ran toward the girls' bathhouse, crouching low like a monkey by the side of the bathhouse, where strips of green paint were peeling in the sun. There I heard Karen's very proficient-sounding flush, a door creaking open, then her slippered feet on the steps. I didn't even have to follow her, for luckily she turned in my direction. I merely pressed myself against the wall as if I were part of the paint covering it. As soon as she came into view I jumped out with a scream that never settled into a particular word, that might have been her name or my own. For a second her eyes looked into mine. Then she bowed her head and began crying inconsolably, her little chest shaking and heaving in a kind of musical rhythm.

Instantly my thrill at scaring her turned to anguish and I began to apologize. After a few minutes she stopped crying and even let me walk her home. But I was never alone with her again, and her mother adopted a distinctly different attitude toward me those few times we saw each other at the beach.

Looking back, it's hard to remember how I felt in the aftermath of scaring Karen. For one thing, I don't remember spending even a minute trying to understand why I scared her or why I derived so much pleasure from it. Maybe I simply understood it all as a natural expression of my being, and the fact that I lost Karen as a result, as well as any happiness at the beach for the rest of the summer, made me feel I'd paid the price.

And yet, two summers later, at Cape Cod (my parents were restless vacationers), I struck again. This time it was with a little brunette I'd befriended for a few days named Margie, who was probably about ten. Unfortunately, Margie must have told her daddy, for when I bicycled past her cottage looking for her the next day he immediately came after me in his car. His lecture to me (on the soft shoulder, while some very curious drivers whizzed by) was pretty frightening itself, culminating in a promise to kill me if I ever scared his little Margie again. I nodded piously and apologized. As I pedaled away, I tried to dismiss him as a fanatic, but I did keep away from his daughter and the beach in general for the rest of the summer.

In fact, Cape Cod Daddy did such a good job of scaring me that for the next five years I put all my energy into schoolwork, instead of scaring people, and wound up at a quite prestigious college near Boston.

Then in my sophomore year, love tracked me down, just jumped out at me and set me spinning. Her name was Michelle, like the old Beatles song. She was nervous, delicate, sensuous, eager to please. Michelle was many things; that was my first surprise. My next was that our sex life was so paradoxically disappointing. I'd imagined that sex with someone you love would inevitably lead to prolonged states of rapturous closeness. I had the romantic notion that the physical climax was merely the prelude to a much longer-lasting ecstasy. Instead, more often than not, the spiritual bliss I sought died with the physical or shortly thereafter, as if our timid souls were programmed to flee each other rather than to experience too much pleasure. Our lovemaking was like a play we'd memorized, where each of us performed our roles night after night with only the slightest variation. At the time I blamed Michelle, though I now believe it's an intrinsic limitation of the sex act itself, or else of so-called human nature.

Because of this unexpected yet inescapable disappointment, I suggested a new game to Michelle. The two of us could play it in my parents' house, for they were often traveling and I'd long ago smuggled away a key. The game was a variation on hide and seek, and Michelle, of course, said she'd certainly try it.

At first I believed I would follow the rules of the game I'd, after all, devised myself. According to the rules, the hider (usually me) would jump out and embrace the seeker once the latter had discovered his whereabouts, and then begin to make love in whatever spot he was occupying. The first time we played, my parents were safely away at some convention for business lawyers. I hid in one of their bathrooms, a space so impersonal I couldn't tell which of them it belonged to. (I certainly knew it wasn't used by both of them since they lived in separate rooms and, except for their compulsive traveling, did everything separately.) I shut myself in the closet beside some cleaning fluids and a series of neutral looking, though spotlessly clean, towels.

I could hear Michelle whistling as she searched for me, and then singing some silly songs designed to make me laugh and give away my whereabouts. But I was already succumbing to something more powerful than laughter. At first I felt frightened. Then the old thrill of hiding and anticipating, of planning my scream and my jump flashed through me. Though five years had passed, I simply couldn't struggle against it and was literally quivering with excitement.

After scaring Michelle I was so elated that I found I had to think of her expression when I first scared her in order to keep up my lovemaking.

Needless to say, the game, which was supposed to be a variation, soon became a regular feature of our love life. When my parents' house wasn't available we played a scaled-down version in my studio apartment, and when the hiding spots there became too predictable, we'd take a room in a hotel; or in the warm weather we'd rent a car and drive out to the country. The Berkshires—in fact, Beachwood itself—could be reached with a very enjoyable two-and-a-half-hour drive.

I found no reason to tell Michelle why I wanted to play there in the grove at night. I was feeling too much excitement then to delve into my past, having little patience for either guilt or analysis. I rationalized it all this way: we are both consenting adults. I love the game, and by choosing to keep playing it, she indicates that she must like it, too. Although by the time of our trip to Beachwood there was a lot of contradictory evidence on that point. At first Michelle thought of the game as kinky. She thought we were pioneers creating an avant-garde mix of sex and theater, but the repetition had frayed her nerves. She had complained once, snapped at me a couple of times, and had let tears well up in her eyes the last few times I'd suggested playing.

Around ten o'clock, after checking into a hotel in nearby Lenox, we drove down the dirt road that led to the grove and the infamous bathhouses. We parked just outside the grove in a grassy area by a creek and walked toward it on a winding path, each armed with a flashlight. There were many stars out, but the trees overhead were so high and dense we felt we were walking in total darkness.

Michelle had been ominously quiet for some time. When she nearly tripped over a stray branch, she started to cry a little, then quickly said, "I don't want to do this."

"Michelle, calm down. We're safe. Our car's thirty yards away."

She stopped crying but repeated her objection.

"It will only take a few minutes," I said. "We'll play a short game. I'll give you clues."

"I'm already scared. I don't need to play the game to be scared."

"But there's nothing to be scared of."

"You're scaring me," she said firmly, and I knew then that we were headed back to the car and to a long analytical discussion. I wasn't surprised that we drove back to Boston the next morning after fighting all night long, and that the trial separation she suggested turned into a permanent one.

* * *

After I lost Michelle, for a long time there was no one. I reacted to my personal tragedy as I had before, by redoubling my efforts at school, and then at the New York advertising agency where I'd begun writing copy for accounts including an airline, a specially shaped toothbrush, and (appropriately enough) a bathroom cleanser. At the agency we were trying to make the public desire our products, but we were also trying to make them fear the consequences of not buying them. I couldn't help recognizing this strange coupling of fear and desire everywhere in New York, even in the clothes people wore. People dressed to make an impression, but they were clearly dressing to scare each other too. From the dapper young executives at the power lunches to the hookers on the street, the message was, "Look at me. Take me in carefully (though not too carefully) with your eyes. Can you really afford not to buy what I'm selling? Can you really feel safe existing without me?" The effect of it all was to make me withdraw even more.

Before I lived there, I'd often thought of New York as one of the images of infinity. (Infinity was a concept that had dazzled me throughout my adolescence.) But now I found that, while conceptually beautiful, infinity is more terrifying than anything else. You cannot defend against endlessness; it breaks down every system. I was particularly ill suited to try. The landscapes of my life were the lake and grove of Beachwood, my suburban college campus, and my parents' scrupulously neat home, where I used to daydream about the size of space and time. It's funny; I began with many romantic ideas of infinity, and now I longed for, if not a neighborhood, then at least a few streets where I could feel at home. Instead, I found chaos and coldness everywhere. The only thing that wasn't utterly chaotic was my work, but while I was succeeding in it I never considered work a real part of life. Everywhere I turned I felt blocked.

My parents' letters and phone calls were coming farther and farther apart. It was as if, now that I'd achieved economic independence, they felt they were at last independent of me, their strange and almost alien offspring, and could at last "retire" as my parents. Sometimes I didn't even feel that the woman who held the title was actually my mother. I would sit by my bedroom window (which had an extraordinary view of the sky) and try to remember as much as I could about her, such as the time she wiped ice cream off my face. Well, perhaps I had had a mother after all. And a father too, stem and forbidding though he was. Still, they weren't people I could turn to, and I continued to look to my new city for my sense of home.

It wasn't long before I made the mistake of visiting one of the darker pockets of New York—Hell's Kitchen. I thought I might play my game, the hide and seek one, with a prostitute but the results were disastrous, much too painful for me to want to even think about. The prostitutes drove me back to my apartment, as it were, where I could only pace like a caged animal and then sit on my bed staring at the intractable white walls until they fused into a single endless snowbank.

Nothing like a shiver down your spine to make you stand up and do something for yourself. I was still young, with lots of energy and ideas. Obviously I had reached an impasse and it was time to try to think my way out of it. My apartment, like the abominable snowman, had set me off running in the opposite direction. I went downtown by taxi to treat myself to a Saturday lunch at the first good restaurant I saw.

At work we had been trained to analyze products with marketing problems, to come up with scenarios to improve them. I decided it was high time to apply such a critique to myself. I was in SoHo when this happened, far out of my normal route. I was also eating lunch at an odd time, four o'clock, in quite an elegant restaurant on Spring Street. I took a window seat and noticed there was only one other couple eating, a man and a woman in their early fifties. From their snatches of dialogue I judged them to be painters; their harmless but forlorn eyes confirmed my judgment. I ate my chicken crepes and watched people parade by in their leather and furs and cowboy boots and gangster-style hats. Although it was cold, a number of women wore short skirts, their legs gleaming like swords in the street lights. When I finally turned to my left to relax my neck muscles, I noticed a wall-length mirror. At first I turned away, but then gradually I looked at myself. I was very similar to the other men in my department, I concluded, which, given my special needs, might be exactly the problem. I hurried through the rest of my meal so I could spend more time studying myself. Finally I got up from my table and walked toward the mirror to get a closer look.

My appearance had no U.S.P. (unique selling point), that was undeniable. But maybe my imagination could create an alternative. The mirror will not show you the future, that's for sure—not unless you come armed with your imagination. The painter couple now openly watched me as I practiced different walks, and even a kind of dance, in front of the mirror. I didn't care; I can be quirkily unself-conscious, like anyone else. Though I've actually been paralyzed with self-consciousness for most of my life, I also have a capacity to rise to the occasion. I was using the mirror now as a tool to re-create myself. No wonder I was dancing in slow, delicious circles near the end.

I had determined that muscles were crucial to my new appearance, and that was the natural place to develop them. But I soon found that it was not the place for me to achieve my new look. There is something about body-builders, would-be or otherwise, that is indescribably repellent. I had thought I would identify with them, but I couldn't. Besides, the awful smells there that brought back memories of the Beachwood bathhouse were much too distressing.

I left the Y after a few sessions and bought the weights and mirror I needed to work out in my living room. After a few months I'd fleshed out my six-foot frame and become quite a menacing figure. As an added touch, I bought a jet-black wig—a savage slicked-down pompadour. Then I found a T-shirt near Times Square that said "The Spirit of New York" in blood-red letters, and I began wearing it underneath my black leather jacket whenever I went out late at night. I was very unhappy when the shirt faded, for I never found another like it. Why hadn't I bought more than one when they existed?

I began walking from my apartment on lO5th Street toward Barnard College. It was a little past midnight, and I could feel my new muscles rippling like waves, could feel the new blackness of my hair and jacket. It was the first uniform I'd ever liked. I thought, If someone from work were to see me, they'd never recognize me. Not now. I was aware that my simple presence was probably frightening numerous young coeds. It was a subtle feeling, but it helped me for my first few blocks.

At lO9th Street I saw her walking alone with her head down. She was tall and thin and stooped a little. She also wore glasses and had wrapped her blue scarf around herself as tight as a mummy. Using the parked cars and trees as camouflage, kneeling down and running monkey-like at times, I managed to get a half-block ahead of her. If she turned now all would be lost, of course; but I felt that she wouldn't. I moved up one car, crouching behind a blue Buick, a hydrant, and a clump of skinny sycamores. She kept walking nearer. At the decisive moment I emerged and nearly collided with her. She seemed to reel, her eyes going up in her sockets like Little Orphan Annie's.

"Sorry," I said. "I was checking my tires and didn't see you. Are you OK?"

She nodded quickly, like a puppet. She couldn't even manage a word for me she was so frightened. I watched her disappear into her apartment two doors up, looking back over her shoulder at me once as I stood firm, like a large rock that had suddenly materialized on the street.

Then I got another idea. (I hadn't improvised like this since my days with Michelle.) I walked a few blocks further and entered the vestibule of another doormanless walk-up. If I wanted to, I could get in the building quite easily; but that could be construed as a crime, and I wanted no part of it. I found a way to curl up as thin as a carrot behind the door and then suddenly to appear when someone was fumbling with their key or waiting to be buzzed in.

I got what looked to be an eighteen-year-old undergraduate that way. Short and confused-looking, he nearly dropped the books he was holding. Later, in a different building, I had even more satisfying results. "Oh!" a blond woman with Karen-like hair gasped, "you frightened me!" I tried to hide my delight as I apologized. I like it best when someone tells me I've scared them, without my having to ask first.

Riding the wave of her testimony, and recalling her startled green eyes and her hair, which seemed to have been swept back from fright, I arrived home ecstatically happy. Was it the intoxication of my sudden pleasure or something else? I still don't know, but I felt compelled to measure myself. I made a dot on the wall where my head ended (repeating the process three times) and discovered that I was now six feet one. I had grown an inch.

Six feet one, six feet one, I repeated like a mantra whenever I went out. I had considered buying elevator shoes at one point, asking myself, Why should my body have grown horizontally but not vertically? But now it had grown vertically and I had no explanation for it, which made it all the better.

At the office no one commented on my new height. They were a perversely jealous group of midgets, and that lack of reaction was to be expected. I tried to blend in and be one of them. I was hardworking and conscientious, as I devoted myself to campaigns to scare people into buying our products. ("I've fallen and I can't get up" wasn't my line, but it could have been.) I was essentially a yes man, though I had developed a certain prickly sense of humor that I occasionally turned on my bosses, but in a playful enough way that it usually ended up pleasing them. Except for my muscles, I dressed and looked like everyone else.

But after work I was as different from them as could be. It was as if a gate had been opened, and though it was dark out, I could suddenly see the world. I felt infinitely stronger, yet my step was lighter, my senses more acute. I could feel my heart beat and when the action was good, I would sometimes grow three or four inches taller. I made the amazing discovery (which I never shared with anybody) that it's not just our genitals that can spontaneously expand or contract.

When it was over and I returned to my height of six one and was back in my apartment, I'd feel let down and I'd take a tranquilizer to ease the transition from so much excitement to the somber world of sleep and the even more somber one of work.

It was a small price to pay. My walks rarely disappointed me. The only bad times were with some of the prostitutes. They were so insensitive and uncaring. Their indifference went beyond "professionalism"; it was zombie-like. If every person is scary in their own way (and I fervently believe they are), prostitutes were scary for being like the living dead. Giving them up, and the orgasms that occasionally went with them, was a minor sacrifice. It was no more difficult, say, than leaving home had proved to be.

When it rained, the action would be slower, but one night I went to the subway and things changed again. The station lay before me like a giant Parcheesi board, but there was a difference. People were constantly angling toward the "safety spaces," though when they got there they discovered those spaces were illusory. Where was there even one safety space? It wasn't too near the track, or on the benches, or by the telephone that rarely worked. It wasn't near anyone else, for everyone else was a stranger, and in the underworld light of the station everyone looked menacing. In the subway it was always Halloween.

In such a world my opportunities multiplied, but so did my anxieties. I didn't want to frighten anyone near the tracks so badly that they might fall, and I didn't want to provoke someone into attacking me, for people have a habit of carrying and using concealed weapons in such places, a la the "subway vigilante" himself. After a ten minute tug of war about what to do that ended in a stalemate, a train roared by. I followed its sound and then its gleaming tail until it wound out of sight. Then I turned and saw some action. Usually I focused on solitary people, but a mother and daughter seated on a bench fifty yards from me seemed ideal. They were talking to each other very animatedly, and they were both wearing navy blue, which is one of my favorite colors to scare people in. I circled behind them, walking just in front of the billboards. They were having quite an argument. As their rhetoric intensified, I wondered if they were really a mother and daughter. Perhaps they were lovers instead— I couldn't be sure. I crouched as I approached them (though I could feel myself growing again). Then the younger woman turned to the older and shrieked, "You can't buy love, and if you could you wouldn't spring for it anyway!"

For a second I froze. The words were said with such cruel conviction that I thought the lover / mother might hit her. Instead she said, "You're awful," and turned her head away. I didn't see what happened next, as I was backpedaling on all fours until I could safely stand. A moment later I took an uptown train. While I was riding I thought, That's the most bitter remark I've ever heard. Then I thought it was something I had actually said myself, to one of my parents, but to which one I couldn't be sure. Maybe I had said it to both? Though as time passed, I grew less certain I'd said it at all. Sometimes, at night, my memory would grow and contract like my height.

Still, the fact that I might have said it, or could have said it, wouldn't leave me alone. I'm not going to let that remark torture me anymore, I said to myself as I got off at 110th Street. I don't deserve to be tortured by something I'm not even sure I said, something inflicted on me from the night air of New York.

I saw an older woman in a white uniform, white shoes. A nurse? A waitress? She was standing alone by a pole. I circled behind her quickly, like a pelican searching for fish, so that I could suddenly stand next to her with a dark expression on my face. She gave a little start, a spastic kind of nod. "I'm sorry, did I startle you?" She shook her head. Ah, she was a proud one, this nurse/waitress, but I'd seen what I'd seen and knew what I knew nonetheless. Not even ten minutes later I got two eleven-year-old girls by the same pole my proud nurse had just vacated. They gasped, then turned numb. I apologized in more detail than usual and raced for the next train before anything could happen. The subway had been a success.

My midnight walks got me through the rest of my twenties. Occasionally I would stray from my path and go to the zoo in the afternoon, or to a ballgame, but I felt oddly displaced and it never worked out as well. That's one reason why I stayed away from Port Authority and Penn Station. Crowds depress me in every way. A few times I went back to the flesh markets at 42nd Street; I thought I might find one or two of the girls I knew, but I didn't. What with AIDS scaring everybody two-thirds to death, I was better off staying away from them anyway. There was a whole new cast of zombies now, maybe due to AIDS, but they looked more fearful than ever. There was no point in scaring the already scared, so there was no action there.

Shortly after I turned thirty I made an important contribution to a network campaign for a fast-food restaurant. My promotion to middle management brought me my own office, which was a relief. My boss said, "You're one of us now." I must confess it made me happy. I knew he was inane, but he could make me happy. I knew he spent his life frightening his employees and plotting with them to con people into buying our clients' products; still, his praise made me happy. A paradox, but one I accepted. I won't puzzle over it anymore, I said to myself. I'll celebrate instead. They had actually wanted to take me out to dinner, but as usual I declined, saying I had to take care of my ill mother. (In reality, I hadn't heard from her in weeks.) My greatest accomplishment at the agency had been turning my dread of after-office socializing into an advantage. People said of me: "He has integrity. He doesn't scheme to get ahead by throwing parties or attending dinners." Besides, while no one liked me, no one was jealous of me either. I was regarded as a private man and a workaholic. My boss had even jokingly blessed my compulsiveness once, and that had made me happy too.

I could barely wait until midnight to put on my by now badly faded T-shirt, my wig and leather jacket. I'm treating myself well tonight, I said to myself as I left my building. I had never felt more positive or more powerful as I walked up West End Avenue. It was an extremely humid spring night. I could scarcely contain my anticipation as the blocks went by without action. Everyone was big or in groups, it seemed, but I refused to be discouraged. Instead, I turned right onto Broadway, heading for the subway at 110th.

It started happening as I walked downstairs, more and more with each step. By the time I reached the platform I was at least six foot eight. As if they'd heard the thunder of my coming and had all fled, the platform was deserted. I went to a dark space under a stairway and waited. I thought, If I keep growing my head will hit the stairway and I'll have to crouch while I wait, or else lie down like one of the homeless. I looked out again on both sides. I was hoping for a woman, of course, but there weren't any.

Finally, someone. Though it was a boy, everything else was right. He was alone with his books, about eighteen years old, with orange strawlike hair long enough to be a girl's. He sat down on a bench about fifty feet to my left and started reading. It would be difficult to circle him, but I wasn't in a circling mood anyway. If I walked right at him, my size alone would do it. At the last moment I'd veer to the right and he'd look up and find himself sitting next to a giant.

I began my walk, aiming myself directly at him. I am a mountain, I thought.

As I suspected, the boy kept his head buried in his book during my entire walk. Then, when I was two feet from him, he stood up unexpectedly and we bumped. He was startled—shocked, in fact—but he said nothing.

"Sorry," I said, but I didn't move. I wanted more acknowledgment of what had happened, so I stood in front of him.

He looked up at me, his face twisted like a corkscrew. "What's your problem?"

"I don't have any problems. Sorry about the collision."

"You walked right into me. I saw you!"

Instinctively, I put my hand over my heart to protest my innocence. At the same time he reached into his pocket and took out a switchblade. For a second we stood stunned, facing each other. Then I went into my monkey crouch, let out a scream and barreled into him, knocking him back into the bench. I punched him hard in the stomach twice, and he gasped and dropped his little knife. His face went white, like he'd been electrocuted.

"Look what you did!" I hissed, shaking my hand in his face.

"Please," he mumbled, petrified.

"Get out of here!" I hissed once more. He turned and ran to the turnstile, squirming through like a fish through a net.

For a minute I began spinning in circles like a top while I shrank down to six one. Then I looked at the platform and saw that what he'd dropped was a pen, a silver ballpoint that I had somehow mistaken for a switchblade. I stared at it, mesmerized, though I never touched it. Finally a train came. I sat in a comer thinking about his pen and the silly line about it being mightier than a sword, which in this case had been strangely true in a way, although also false. When I got to my lobby I shielded myself from my doorman, saying the quickest of hellos. Mercifully there was no one on the elevator or on my floor.

The first thing I did in my apartment was to take my tranquilizer, wash my hands, and assure myself that nothing terrible had happened. But no sooner did I feel relief than a hideous anxiety swept through me, like the clouds I could see massing outside in the night sky. Just what did I think I was doing? I had hit someone, thus breaking my own anti-violence rule not once but twice. Had I no conscience at all? Then the attorney for my defense (who these days occupies only an equal part of my brain with my prosecutor) rose up and spoke for me: It was an aberration, an incident that had never happened before; and besides, I thought I was acting in self-defense. Anyway I do nothing compared to what other people do. I don't hurt people in relationships. I don't mug, rob, rape, or pass on diseases. I don't break hearts, faith, or contracts. All I do is scare a series of strangers for a few seconds, and until tonight nothing awful has ever happened.

Then I remembered Michelle and felt a stab of pain. But that was so long ago; surely I could forgive myself for her by now.

I paced around my apartment alternately reminding myself about my promotion and trying to resolve my dilemma, going back and forth between the rebuttals of my attorney and the accusations of my prosecutor, when suddenly I saw a gigantic white fang in the sky. As soon as I realized it was lightning, I was shaken by a boom of thunder so powerful and penetrating that I instinctively knelt beside my bed for protection. I could feel myself shrinking still more as the horrifying pattern of lightning and thunder persisted, filling my window like a surging white ocean gone amok. I was too terrified to move a muscle. I thought, God is like me. He wants to scare people, so that's why he's doing this.

And still I shook with fear, though for a while I also felt a peculiar sense of mercy for myself.

The Horror Conference

A s in the past, the conference would last three days beginning
on the first Friday morning after Halloween. And for the
seventh straight year (as long as Hoover had been attending) it
would be held in the same hotel in the center of one of the city's
most fashionable districts across the street from the state's largest
park. Yet it would be wrong to infer from this that nothing about
the conference had changed over the years. In the first few years
that Hoover attended, for example, the membership consisted
entirely of people who loved horror—whether in films, books,
or music—in both the popular and high arts. But later the
membership began to include people who ostensibly hated
horror, not so much in films but in their lives, though they
continued experiencing it, couldn't, in fact, seem to escape it to
the point where it became their chief preoccupation. In Hoover's
opinion, this preoccupation had for some time been the constant
that bound not only the regional, but also the entire national
membership together. So long as the members were preoccupied
with horror (love or hatred of it finally becoming a minor
consideration) they would quite naturally gravitate to the
annual convention and enthusiastically attend the various
lectures, seminars, films and discussion groups. All this Hoover
accepted, but he couldn't help missing the sometimes elegant
discussions of *Dracula* or *Dr. Jekyll and Mr. Hyde* from years past,

discussions that might have distracted him from the terrible weight of his secret.

In protest against the method (and perhaps horror) of alphabetical selection, one's discussion group was now randomly determined by lot. Hoover had selected the group that was meeting in the Stoker room at four o'clock Friday afternoon. His after lunch nap lasting a little longer than he planned, he had to hurry through the dimly lit hallways of the hotel, nevertheless checking his fleeting appearance in the various mirrors he passed as he wondered what, if any, of his secret he would confide at the group discussion.

The thickly carpeted Stoker room featured a grand piano, ornate chandeliers and good fake Impressionist paintings. Hoover apologized as he found his seat, the only empty one in a roomful of circular tables, each with five chairs. The table leader had asked Sidney, a delicately featured man of indeterminate age whom Hoover vaguely remembered, if any important changes had occurred since last year's convention. Sidney ran his long fingers briefly across his cheeks and said that his sense of horror had become more generalized.

"Tell us," said the leader, a middle-aged woman with a full bosom and a leader's tone of voice.

"It was more focused last year," Sidney said.

"Focused?" asked a redhead, dressed in a long flowing black and purple gown as if she hadn't bothered to change her Halloween costume. She was sharp featured, even sharper-eyed, yet Hoover found her quite compelling.

"Tell us," the leader repeated.

Sidney said that last year his sense of horror was focused chiefly on sex. Hoover couldn't help but remember that years ago discussions of any kind by members about their sex lives were rare and would be uttered in hushed tones, but now such things were treated at the conference with a clinical detachment as if the group were discussing butterflies or stamps.

"Was it a feeling of revulsion or…?" the redhead asked.

"Revulsion in a way," Sidney said, "though not in the sense of being nauseated. It was more like a feeling of dread before it happened and dread after it ended and I realized what I'd done."

"Being paid back for the pleasure?" the redhead offered. She was probably a therapist, Hoover thought.

"Being paid back for participating in the horror. But..." he said, and paused with his exceedingly long index finger suspended in the air which immediately drew the group's fascinated attention as if he had suddenly exposed himself. Indeed, the fifth member who hadn't yet spoken, a portly woman in her early fifties named Tina, had become slack jawed from the sight of his finger. "It's different now. It's less exclusively attached to sex. Like I said, now my horror is more diffuse, do you understand?"

"Yes I do, I understand," said Tina, who managed to finally close her mouth after her short sympathetic speech.

Sidney said it was as if he were living in a horror movie without any particular monster chasing him. When the leader once more said "tell us," he said he'd discovered there was horror in everything and that when something was a part of everything, it naturally affected everything else around it including, in his case, his sense of beauty.

"That's really profound," Tina said.

Sidney blushed slightly then recovered his fully serious expression. "Like brushing your teeth or going to the bathroom. There's horror and beauty in everything we do that can't be separated."

I would not have picked that example, Hoover thought, yet the man had to be true to himself. He looked around the room but the only mirrors he noticed were too far away.

"My issue is trying to accept their coexistence and not frustrate myself trying to separate the beauty from the horror."

He had said the word "frustrate" with such concentrated ferocity, though he hadn't yelled, that the other members at the table fell silent again much as they had when they first saw his finger.

"Tell us more about that in the next round," the leader finally said (apparently this was still the introductory portion of the group discussion).

"Greta," the leader said to the redhead. "Can you tell us about your last year?"

She inhaled deeply just before beginning. "It was revelatory, apocalyptic, life changing, all of that."

"Can you elaborate?"

"I went to Hell last year and spent some significant time there. Hell is an objectively real physical place, by the way. I was there for a number of weeks, just last month."

"How do you know it was the Hell?" Hoover said. He didn't want to break her bubble but felt she owed the group an explanation.

"I was told by the people that were there. And then, of course, I found out myself. When you're there, believe me, you know it."

"But people call many places Hell all the time," Hoover said. He could feel his heart beating fast.

"Trust me, it's real."

"Where is it?" Sidney blurted.

"OK, it's not like other places, like any other place. It's portable, OK? It chose, a month ago, to be in my particular building and in the block around it in Philadelphia."

"I find this extraordinary," Sidney said.

"I don't know why it came or why it left...I don't know if or when it will come back."

"Outside of its moving around so much," said Hoover, "what's it like?"

"It's definitely an alternative world. It's like you're scared all the time, in that sense it's not that different than here. But everything is a little off and everything is addictive," she said looking at Sidney.

"I believe you," Sidney said, meeting her eyes. "I believe her," Sidney said, looking at each person at the table.

"I think we all do," Tina said.

"I didn't see you there," Hoover said.

Greta turned around to face him. They were standing in line next to each other at the hotel bar during happy hour.

"Where?" she said, her face registering more perplexity than disappointment.

"You know, in Hell."

"Maybe that was your punishment," she said.

Hoover smiled. "I'm serious. I was there and I didn't see you."

"I'm serious too," she said, as the bartender handed her drink to her. "Completely serious."

"You suppose I could sit and talk with you for a minute?" Hoover said, his face reddening slightly.

She smiled ironically and shrugged. "Why not?"

Hoover ordered a whiskey sour to match hers and later at their table, when he was halfway through it, said "I didn't mean to put you on the spot, when I said I hadn't seen you."

"You didn't. I don't get defensive anymore. I learned that once and for all in Hell, didn't you?"

"I didn't have any teachers there."

"Listen, let's get one thing straight," she said, placing her drink down on the table. "I don't care if you believe me or not. It's not like you're a talk show host and I'm trying to sell a book about it on your show, you understand?"

"I understand."

"I was asked a question in group and I told the truth, that's all. Don't you try to tell the truth when someone asks you a question, all things being equal."

"Yes, I do. I see your point."

"So why is it you want to interview me about it?"

"Just because I was there, and didn't see you."

"That's not my fault. And if you were there how come you didn't bring it up in group?"

"I was going to but you beat me to it. You'd already introduced the topic, so I spoke about something else."

"You might have supported me."

"If I'd seen you there I would have."

"OK. So who did you see there? What did you see there?"

"That's just it," said Hoover.

"What's just it?"

"I didn't see anyone there. It was just slivers of myself sometimes in the mirror. There was no one else there."

"You think you're important enough to have Hell exist just for you?"

Hoover bent down and swallowed his drink, feeling a pain in his chest and at the same time an unmistakable hunger. "That feels more like an insult than a question."

"No one ever gave me an award for tact. On the other hand, I owe it to both of us to say what I think and you have been strongly implying that I'm a liar."

"I don't say that you lie. I'm just trying to make sense of it all. How could there be two separate Hells? That's what I'm trying to figure out."

"I don't have a problem with it. I already told you that Hell is portable. There are mountains in more than one place and forests and oceans in more than one place and there's space everywhere. Hell can travel. Why does this surprise you?"

Hoover took another swallow and finished his drink realizing more deeply how attractive Greta was. Perhaps he should soften his tone. "So were there mountains and oceans in your Hell?"

"I said in group that it was in my apartment and the block around it. I don't think there were any mountain ranges there the last time I checked."

Again he felt the stab of pain, no longer sure now what it meant.

"I need to know who was in Hell with you. Can you tell me?"

"I don't know you well enough to tell you that. You're the one in the group who doubts me the most, yet you're the one who wants to know about it the most. Why is that? Can you tell me that?"

"I need to know why you were there. I don't disbelieve you anymore but I need to know if it was a situation where you thought you deserved it or if instead some power…"

"Listen, if it's based on sin, there's not a person in this convention who doesn't deserve it, but there's also not many people who do deserve it either. I mean does a woman ever deserve to be raped? Does a man deserve to go to war?"

"I'm trying to figure out why you were there. I'm trying to figure out if you deserved it."

"You talk as if I should know everything about it. What about you? Did you deserve it?"

"That's just it," Hoover said, looking down at a pattern on the tablecloth. "I don't know. It was something I fell into. Like falling into a hole. There seemed to be no warning, no memory of a warning. It's like the moment between two moments—it was too small to exist. I was out of Hell one moment and I was in it the next. There was me and this understanding that I'd lost all my moments and then it was like I died and yet in the next moment I didn't die, only the moment before me did. I was dead but I was needing," he said, suddenly fearful about what he was saying. "There were no devils or fire in my Hell, by the way. Were there in yours?"

She looked hard at him with little tears in her eyes. "There was a fire that nearly burned me down but it was inside of me. I couldn't stop it."

"I'm sorry," Hoover said. As if his words released them, two tears slid down her cheek.

"Listen, can we continue talking somewhere else?"

Hoover nodded, then said yes.

"Were you going to go to any of the events tonight?" she asked.

"What are they?"

"There's a seminar on drug addiction and later they're showing 'Night of the Living Dead.'"

"I don't need it. I don't need a movie."

She reached across the table and put her hand in his. "Let's take a walk then."

She wanted to go to the park and he felt he had no choice but to comply although it was already too dark to appreciate the trees and ponds. It was cold out too, yet she wore no coat, making him think about the fire she'd said had burned inside her. "Aren't you cold?" he'd said after they entered the park and she had just looked at him. If you're not cold now because of your fire, what will happen to you in the summer, Hoover wanted to say. He remembered that he'd enjoyed it when she held his hand in the hotel bar (though he hadn't felt any great transfer of warmth) but now wished she hadn't done it. It was probably also good that she didn't want to talk but he missed that now, in a way, as well.

"Are we going any place in particular?" he finally said.

"Yes," she said. "Right here."

Hoover looked around thinking if I were a bat perhaps I would know why. "Is there anything special I should know about this place?"

"The ground is soft here. The grass is thick and pretty much stone free."

"How do you know that?" Hoover said as he sat down with her and discovered she was right.

"I don't have any trouble seeing in the dark… Listen, are you gonna keep asking me questions all night?"

"Don't you want to ask me any," Hoover said, "like about my job?"

"I've got a good reading so far about you. As far as your job goes, I figure anyone who can afford this convention must have a profession. I know I do."

She sat down next to him and touched his face then immediately began caressing his legs and kissing him.

"Did you bring anything, 'cause I didn't," Hoover said, in between kisses.

"Just myself."

"No, I meant…"

"I know what you meant. Don't worry, the only disease that I have is I need to do this a lot."

"'Cause we could go back to the hotel."

"It's too hot in the hotel," she said, suddenly getting on top of him. She is almost as tall as me Hoover thought. A moment later, when she seemed to expand like a snake, he thought no, she is taller.

She was kissing him ravenously, which reminded him of his own hunger. That, combined with the strange sounds of the park and the near total darkness made him feel he was dreaming—just the reverse of what he wanted to feel.

"Stop it, stop it," he blurted.

"What?" she yelled. She had been riding him hard and dug her nails into his wrists for a moment in anger.

"I can't do it."

"You've been doing it. Why did you have to pick this second to stop? Jesus! You conference guys are all a bunch of weirdos."

"I need to stop. If you want to go back to the hotel and continue there that would be fine. That would be something I could look forward to."

"Jesus!" she said, as she finally got off him. She didn't talk to him for the first few minutes of their walk back. Then she suddenly said, "You've got a secret, don't you?"

Hoover felt his heart beat again. "What makes you say that?"

"I notice you're not denying it. Maybe you have an aversion to female orgasm."

"No," he said, "it's nothing to do with that."

"It has something to do with sex. Why else would you stop when I was so hungry?"

"I'm hungry too."

"Oh, so that's it."

The highway that separated them from the hotel came into view, the cars and the lights from the buildings.

"You're a zombie, aren't you, or you think you are."

"What?"

"You think you're a zombie and you had an attack of conscience and didn't want to kill me."

"No way, that's not it. And I don't appreciate the suggestion. It's...insulting."

"I'm not insulting you. Just trying to crack your code, guess your secret. My time in Hell has made me utterly sincere."

"Look, about what happened in the park, it was what I said it was."

"You didn't say. You just told me to stop."

"My head was spinning. It felt like a dream, and I needed it to be real."

"I'm not real enough for you?"

"You're fine. I'm talking about me and what I'm hungry for."

"OK, we're on our street now. You can go your way in the hotel and this whole convention and I can go mine. And that's what I plan do to if you don't tell me what you're hungry for. You already know what I'm hungry for, don't you?"

"I could be hungry for that too."

"I know—if you were only in a hotel room."

"Now you're being sarcastic."

"Why is setting so goddamn important?"

"I told you. In the park I felt I was dreaming. I couldn't see anything."

"I like that feeling."

"But I need to not feel like that."

"Why?"

"Because I always do. Almost always."

"What are you talking about?"

"I either feel like I'm dreaming or just like I'm a little puff of air. Nothing but the single moment I'm in or sometimes, like a sluggish pair of eyes just watching things."

"So you're hungry for...moments?"

"Moments, memories. Can I at least talk with you in the hotel?"

She looked at him. "Yuh, we can do that."

She didn't talk to him in the main lobby, but in the elevator she took his hand and he felt his hunger again. She continued to hold it until she opened the door to her room. He was glad to see that it was just like his.

"OK," she said, as she put one hand firmly on his bottom, "let's be sure you have everything the way you want it before we begin. You want the lamp on or off?"

Hoover looked at the mirror facing the bed, relieved to see that he was in it. The lamp was on a table in front of the mirror. He had already told her that he felt like a cavity instead of a man and that parts of him were sometimes missing in mirrors. Even now, though he saw his dark hair and the general shape of his body, his face looked vague, like a smudge. None of this seemed to make any impact on her. It was because she was so locked into what she imagined to be her own Hell, Hoover thought, though it was he who lived in the real one.

"On," he finally answered. He figured if she wanted to be on top again he could still lift his head from time to time and check on himself in the mirror.

"Does it always take you this long to make decisions?" She had already taken her dress and panties off and Hoover realized he should begin to undress too.

"Come on cowboy, off with your chaps," she said laughing. "Don't worry, mamma's gonna make decisions for you now."

She fell on top of him again. There was red in her face and chest. "You are sure you want me, aren't you?" she added, looking hard at him.

"Yes," he said. "I want you to be inside me."

"Sorry, but you got the dick, honey."

"That's not what I meant," Hoover said into her ear, feeling a sudden impulse to bite her and make it hurt.

"Oh. So you are like a zombie, or a woman," she said, laughing again.

"Don't talk that way to me," ever again, Hoover added to himself, as he gritted his teeth in anger.

"Mamma's just teasing. You want a 'moment,' right? I'll try to give you one."

She took off his underpants and started sucking him. Hoover liked the feeling and closed his eyes, calming down for a moment but he soon started to feel weightless and dizzy and quickly opened them. It might be better this way with his eyes open he figured, so he could, in effect, photograph her.

Then she started rubbing up against him and soon was riding him again, getting ever redder until, it appeared, she finally came. Hoover tried to also, out of politeness and also to make it more potentially memorable but couldn't get there and eventually gave up. Later she asked him if he got his moment. "Yes," he lied, to be polite.

"It's funny you wanting to remember moments, when I want to erase them," she said.

He didn't say anything to that. He felt he was missing again and couldn't feel his penis, his face or his mind.

"You didn't come, did you?" she said, looking at him.

Hoover didn't answer. He had sat up in bed to check himself in the mirror.

"What are you doing? What are you looking at?...Jesus! Stop looking at yourself," she yelled, as she got up from bed and shut off the lamp.

"Turn that back on," Hoover said.

"You're yelling. What in the hell are you yelling about?"

"Turn the lamp back on."

"OK buddy, that's it. The party's over. It's time for you to go."

"What?" Hoover said.

"Go. Leave," she said, looking angrily at him.

"Who are you telling to leave?"

"You. You see anyone else here?"

"You ordering me to leave?"

"Yes. Out, out damned spot."

"I told you not to talk to me that way." Didn't I, Hoover asked himself, suddenly as uncertain now about the words he'd said as he was about his fleeting appearance. "What makes you think you can bludgeon people like you do with the words you use? You think your stinking time in Hell gives you the right? You've never been there!"

"Go to Hell," she hissed.

"Stay in Hell," he said, as he stood up and turned on the lamp. She was up in a second now too, red and furious and just a foot away from him as she shut off the lamp and took control of it in her hand. "You don't need a light since you have fire, you hissing Devil," he said, suddenly pulling the lamp from her grasp and swinging it down on top of her head. She fell to the floor with a strangely dull thud as if she'd hit her head on a rock in the park, and for a moment he wondered if they were still out there in the dark where she'd first gotten so angry. But she appeared to still be in her room, lying motionless on the dull brown carpet as still as a rock herself.

Hoover let out a little gasp and backed away from her. The oddest thing was happening to him as he stared at her body. The usual cold, silent feeling of being a cavity was missing, replaced instead by the overwhelming pressure of memories of other women in other rooms, including one horrible one at the convention three years ago from this same hotel. He looked at the mirror and saw the memories; he looked at the ceiling and the floor and they were there too, howling like wolves. Hoover screamed once, then ran out of the room, barley remembering to close the door, as he fled down the corridor. By the time he reached the elevator, he realized that he had to stop running and had to calm down in general. Three fourths of everything people judged about you depended on the appearance you presented, he'd remembered hearing at a training session for salesmen years ago. Probably true, Hoover thought as the elevators stopped, annoyingly enough, on the second floor. A woman walked in smiling in a menacing green dress.

"Hi there," she said.

Hoover stared at her and then realized it was Tina from the discussion group.

"Are you going to the movie or the drug seminar?" she asked perkily. He shivered at the memory of discussing this less than an hour ago with Greta.

"I don't know. Which do you think I should go to?"

"The movie seems like it would be a lot more fun."

"I guess I'll go to that then."

"I was going to go with Sidney but at the last minute his stomach started bothering him."

The elevator doors opened, which was a good thing because Hoover didn't know what to say. He felt calmer but talking any more seemed too difficult. He walked behind her for a few feet until he suddenly realized it might be necessary to be seen with her.

"I could go with you if you'd like," Hoover said. Tina turned and smiled at him.

"I would like. Good deal," she said, as they began walking towards the screening room already filling up.

"I liked what you said about zombies in Group today," Tina said.

"I don't remember. What did I say?"

"You made an analogy, how people who have trouble remembering or experiencing things are like zombies. It was very powerful," she added in her breathy voice. "And now we're going to see a movie about zombies, so that's pretty appropriate."

"It's the classic zombie movie. The classic of them all," Hoover said, trying to sound enthusiastic.

They sat down just before the lights dimmed and then, in the next moment, it seemed they were watching. In the half dark, Hoover reached in his pants pocket and took one of his tranquilizers and within minutes the memories began to subside, to howl less and press on his head less, though they still bothered him intermittently throughout the movie (which he scarcely paid attention to). He was trying to remember if he'd wiped his finger prints from the lamp, trying, so far in vain, to see a picture of his doing it in his mind. Of course he should have done it but that alone hardly guaranteed that he had.

"Is anything the matter?" Tina asked after the movie ended and they were walking towards the lobby—the people around them still buzzing about the movie they had stood for and applauded a minute before.

"I'm feeling like it's time to go out and leave the hotel before it eats me up."

Tina looked concerned, almost wounded. Hoover saw that and then looked to the left just past her head at the huge lobby mirror but couldn't see himself. "Would you like to go with me now?"

"Oh, you surprised me," Tina said, putting her hand to her heart. "But yes, I would like to. But where would we go?"

"I don't know. Get some air, take a drive, or maybe just a walk in the park. The park sound okay to you?"

"Yes," she said. "The park sounds fine."

He took her hand, as they walked out the door, feeling nothing but ice.

Notes on Mrs. Slaughter

I'm living with Mrs. Slaughter in her apartment in Cambridge. She's not a bad housekeeper and now that the Mafia is beginning to leave her alone, she's regained her skill in cooking. Really I can't fault her at all. She doesn't even demand that I work, for example. Money is the farthest thing from her mind. For weeks I lived here without doing a thing, but then I began to feel guilty—I went out and got a job in the library stacking and sorting books. In the early stages of this situation I occasionally took walks (although Mrs. Slaughter hated to be left alone) even on the worst days of winter.

I don't want to rhapsodize unnecessarily about them but these were walks like no others I had ever taken. When you have no direction in mind your walk is bound to be different. The colors, for instance, you take more note of them. You see that the snow isn't just white, or even predominantly white. You see all the black and gray there is in it, and you also see the blue. And the trees, even the birch trees have orange in them, as if part of them is always on fire. But nothing is so modified for me now as the sky. I would no longer say that the sky is blue, or the sky is gray. I see too many colors in it that there aren't even words for (for example, what color is the cross between salmon orange, tongue pink, and pebble pink), and so I have stopped talking about the sky.

Of course, if one sense is modified the others change also. For example, the sidewalk began to feel different. Sometimes I had the sensation that I was walking on a river, other times that it was rising over my feet like quicksand. And the buses, the buses seemed to roar past me like tigers.

Once when I went to Harvard Square I began to read a newspaper in front of one of the outdoor magazine stands. Suddenly, I was overwhelmed by the work that went into producing it, the work that was in it. Afraid of bursting into tears, I quickly put it back on the stand.

Maybe there were too many newspapers in Harvard Square. That may be why I started to take the bus out to the suburbs, to Watertown and Newton and Waltham, and do my walking there.

I'll tell you what I saw there once. It was the warmest day of the winter and the snow was melting. A group of very old people, all of them over eighty, were out on their front lawn lining up for a picture. From across the street it was hard to tell how many of them were men, and how many were women. At a certain age the importance of that distinction begins to disappear. One of them, who held the camera, was arguing about how they should pose and soon a yelling match started. Insults were traded back and forth, and even when I inadvertently stopped and stared at them, it seemed to make no difference. No witness could deter them from their fight. Finally, they made a kind of compromise. They lined up in front of an oak tree, and smiling and holding hands, they held their pose so that the picture could be taken. Then all of them began to smile from ear to ear like choir boys. The sun was shining on their white heads, lighting them up like crystals. They began fussing over each other and soon they started taking pictures again, as if nothing could stop them, one after another—varying the pose just a little each time, the way models do on assignment.

...When I would go to the suburbs I'd naturally come back to the apartment later than when I'd walk around Cambridge. It was during those times that Mrs. Slaughter really suffered. She'd pace her floor, she'd fill up the bathtub with water only to empty it again, sounds would become amplified, even the air itself seemed to be full of Mafia fingers reaching for her throat.

She couldn't help cross-examining me. She wanted to know where I went on my walks, she wanted to know what I did. When my back was finally to the wall, when she fired one too many questions at me, I'd go to the mantel and take out my pen and only then, as if I were brandishing a whip, would she back away like a scared cat.

It was a necessary defense, as well as being convenient. Of course, I couldn't have explained. Silence was the best course, I was sure of it.

So I continued my walks, I continued my rides, soon I began to go all over Massachusetts. Now how can I explain the things that happened? In Marblehead, for instance, as I was walking up and down those sloping roads that lead one away from the water, I stopped to look at a house that was white with dark green shutters and a little petunia garden in front. I looked at the wind blowing the petunias—what can I call those feelings?—I've had them before at zoos. I know that real astonishment is our deepest taboo—that even Spinoza would not consider wonder to be one of our emotions.

It was never difficult, after that day in Marblehead, to call up those feelings again. Sometimes it caught me unaware, in the most "incongruous" places. Once it happened in the urinal at the Boston Garden, another time waiting for the train to Park Street, when a man gave me a certain look as he was lighting a cigarette.

Little things, little acts could do it, you see, but still I kept up with my walking, even though it did take a lot out of me.

Now if I ever encountered a woman during my walks it was by pure chance. It would be something that happened to me, rather than something I caused, or even participated in. One of them I met during one of my rare walks through Boston. It was in the Boston Common, as a matter of fact. We met on the bridge, where the boats pass under in the spring and summer. I walked around the park with her for a few hours. She wanted to be something— a singer, a writer—I can't remember exactly what it was.

Probably because I said so little, she assumed that she liked her. She invited me to her apartment, and I followed along dutifully like her dog. I don't remember where she lived. I can't remember the exact location, but I do have a good picture of what her bedroom looked like. In fact, that turned out to be a problem. She was taking her clothes off, she'd gotten down to her bra and panties, and I was still fully dressed and staring at her bureau drawer at the little chips in the thin pink paint. Mistakenly thinking that I wanted her to undress me, she started undoing my belt, but I was already fascinated by the wood on her floor, by its delicate varnish and its slender cracks.

You see how it was. Finally she lay down on her bed with her legs apart. I watched her vagina for a few seconds, it looked like a miniature violin with a dull finish; to me the bed post proved much more fascinating, there was so much labor in it, so much time in it.

Things were made out of matter but things were also made out of time. Does that sound like a principle? I don't want to convey the impression that I have any. I wasn't trying to prove a thing with my walks, I'm almost positive of that. Supposedly philosophers have stopped asking what things are made of anyway. They want to know how things behave. Behavior is interesting—that's their slogan, apparently directing their lives.

...After a week or two of my walks I began to go to some restaurants, simply because as my walks got longer it became necessary to eat. Of course, I can't claim to be a connoisseur of good restaurants. I can't even say that I had a favorite place, but there was one cafeteria near Harvard where I went quite often, because no one noticed anyone else in there, and if I wanted to sit in solitude it was fine, and if I wanted to look at other people I could do that just as easily.

I never saw anything that made an indelible impression—oh, I saw lepers, queens, spastics, impassioned lesbians—but nothing that really left an imprint until I saw this fellow I'll call Mr. Egg. He was very tall, his neck was especially long, and he was thin. He looked as if he'd had a trauma, say in World War II. The remarkable thing about Mr. Egg, who sat in a corner near the water fountain and never dreamed he was attracting anyone's attention, was simply the way he ate his eggs. Or maybe I should say the way he didn't eat them, the way he guarded them. He stared at them reverently as if he were watching twin suns surrounded by a white cloud, then he would bend over them to almost eat them, but at the last moment he would refrain from touching them, the way a person may stop just short of touching a painting in a museum. How he loved those eggs! And what concentration. He was like a scientist laboring over chemicals, or a surgeon studying a heart. Nothing else existed but the eggs on his plate. No other reality was whole for him and he simply couldn't bear to disturb it, he would instead let the eggs grow cold as plastic while he never so much as touched them with his fork.

...I don't know why I wrote so much about Mr. Egg. Really, I only saw him there twice. Maybe I want to cling to my picture of him because it was, in a way, the last picture I had before I began to be chased.

I shouldn't say chased, because I was at first simply being followed. As I recall, I left the cafeteria one afternoon after watching Mr. Egg and I walked a few blocks toward the river, and then I realized that I was being followed—the same steps, the same shadow and sound.

I was surprised that I kept my equilibrium. I didn't even deviate from my course. I didn't, for example, bolt for a bus or else try to hail a taxi. Instead I kept my course straight for the river and my pursuer kept behind me, maybe a half a block behind, stopping to hide behind trees or else a parked car whenever it was necessary.

Quickly I searched myself. I was without any weapons. There was nothing in my pockets but a few small coins. Immediately I wondered why I was going toward the river. Wasn't this just what my pursuer would want? In fact I was sure it was the worst possible thing I could do.

I took a right at the stoplight instead of crossing the street. Nobody was walking on the bridge, but when I looked a second time I saw a little girl leaning over.

Would my change in direction be detected? Would it be discovered that I was walking in a circle? I reminded myself that it was important not to increase my speed. It was necessary to act as if I didn't know I was being followed.

It was very cold out. I hadn't dressed warmly enough—Mrs. Slaughter had offered me one of her sweaters but I walked out without taking it. The wind picked up. When it blew hard it seemed to go through my neck.

We were like soldiers in a procession, there was always the same distance between us. He is being polite, I thought to myself cynically. Quickly I envisioned a scenario for the pursuer's future actions. Probably it would be weeks, months, before I'd be taken. There would be phone calls first and no matter what ring I answered on the party at the other end would hang up. There would be perhaps some threats by mail, maybe even a rock through the window, though that seems too barbaric. Maybe this operation would go on only outdoors while I was walking. It would probably consist exclusively of trees and cars and steps and shadows, and nothing so abrasive as a phone would ever be employed.

So the chase by the river never came to pass. Instead I took the bus to Porter Square, as soon as I reached Harvard, and left my Pursuer behind. But all the way back to the apartment I wondered if he knew where I lived, if that information were already his property.

...Once in the apartment again, it wasn't long before I confessed everything that had happened to Mrs. Slaughter. This surprised me because I didn't think I would ever confide in her. Of course she had her own theory about it all. She was sure the Mafia had spotted me and had assigned a man to tail me. I didn't say anything to that. I never paid much attention to her anxieties about them, but in this case, while not accepting her explanation, I was willing to follow some basic rules to protect myself.

For one thing, we agreed to stay inside as long as our food held out. In light of this it was also necessary to keep the door and all windows locked, and to keep all the blinds down. Finally we decided to stay close to each other while we figured out what to do. The argument, such as it was, came down to this: either my Pursuer didn't know where we lived and had no way of finding out (in which case we were safe for now), or else he knew, in which case it would do little good to leave town. It was hard, of course, to determine just what he did know. Since we had to stay in the house there was little chance for any real scouting of our own. The only thing we could do was to peek periodically through a few inches of curtain at the street or at the alley in back, and these watches never produced a result.

The other thing Mrs. Slaughter asked of me was to stay in the same room with her all night, since I had developed the habit of pacing the floor at night and sometimes ended up sleeping on the living room couch. But as to what we did then, could one actually call it sleeping? We lay rigid and cold under the sheets with our eyes open like mummies.

Maybe one of us would get twenty minutes or so of sleep on occasion, but then the other one of us felt a special obligation to keep guard. Worst of all, perhaps, we hardly talked at all. Whether from fear of embarrassment I don't know, but we confined ourselves to abortive speculations about what we could do.

The apartment was like a dark aquarium now. In the daytime we moved by each other with our mouths closed like fish. If we opened our mouths it was to suck air rather than to talk. Even the feel of the skin on my body began to drop away from me, as I began to feel more like a fish.

Of course a fish still has a clock in its blood, it knows when to swim south, for example, but I had lost the clock too. Consequently, I did everything on impulse. I circulated around and around the house like a fish in an aquarium. Sometimes there would be an obstacle to go around but then I began to master the obstacles. In time I became familiar with every inch of my environment as I kept moving through it, varying only slightly the pattern of my passage each time, and also passing through with a perfect equilibrium, with exactly the same amount of tension, that remained as constant as the fixed temperature in a pool.

...At night, the darkness in the house doubled. We would take our food from the cabinets in the pantry because everything in the refrigerator, all the fruits and fresh vegetables, were rotten by then, and we had already run out of meats. We were eating out of cans exclusively. Unfortunately there was no milk or fruit juices. We had to eat dry cereal straight from the box, Cheerios and Sugar Pops without milk, and corn flakes. For our main meals we had tomato soup or ravioli, or canned pineapple, or tuna fish. We had no bread, only a half box of Triscuits.

After dinner we would light two candles and place them on the floor in the middle of the living room. Then we would lay down the game board of Chinese checkers or Parcheesi on a table and try to get through a game. Not only was it hard to finish our games because we had other things on our mind, but by evening we'd already played each of the games for about an hour in the daytime. There was nothing else to do. Mrs. Slaughter didn't want to play any music. To us the record player was like a coral reef that cut into our space. It was a kind of intruder.

Once, after we finished our game, we began in a serious way, in quiet measured voices, to account for the time that had passed between my discovery of the Pursuer and our present discussion. How much calendar time, for example, had gone by? What had we done in those moments or what were we in those moments we were in? It was like investigating the history of a fish, like compiling the biographies of two fish in two different aquariums. In the aquarium there are no traces. A dog may leave tracks but fish never do. The water is always still, there is never a sign of motion.

No, we had to give it up, it was too much for us. We began instead to discuss our Pursuer. When we talked about him he became more astonishing, more real. One could not even say we had any emotions one way or the other toward him, though it would be wrong to say we regarded him as merely a force. But as soon as we got some insights into the Pursuer, we ceased talking about him, simply because we could not talk about him without referring to our safety, and the topic of safety was essentially beyond discussion. It was a double-headed monster—for to talk about safety was to talk about danger and we hardly needed to talk about that. It's true, we could make a run for it but we had no place to run to, no money to go anywhere with, and then we didn't want, really, to stick our heads out of the house. We were like termites now—we belonged in the house. If we could have we would have started living between the walls.

Besides, what assurance was there that the Pursuer wasn't waiting outside in the alley watching the house, wondering if we were in it or not, looking for a sign, a light, wondering what was going on behind the drapes, wondering if anything could be alive in such constant darkness? No, there was no assurance that that wasn't exactly what he wanted, that he wanted nothing more than for us to make a break for it. And he must have realized that we hadn't called in the police. Even if we had wanted to, there was nothing to show them—for the policeman was a man you had to show something to just like the fireman. He wasn't interested in your stories, he wanted evidence he could see with his eyes, he wanted proof. We had received no letters, no threats on paper or on the phone. To us the policeman was becoming even less substantial than a rainbow—he had the thickness of dew.

...I don't know how long the discussion lasted. At the end of it I suggested that we buy a gun. Mrs. Slaughter moved back a few steps from me when I said that so that I could hardly see her face.

...We didn't make any decision on the gun then. But don't think the gun left us. It floated over our heads while we circulated through the house. There were signs of it all over the aquarium. And when we ate, while we picked at our corn flakes or ravioli, the gun was beside it on our plates.

Then one afternoon while I was circulating, Mrs. Slaughter signaled to me with her index finger to come into her bedroom. Somewhat mystified and anxious, I obeyed her. When I was in front of her she suddenly opened her bureau drawer and showed me a pistol lying against a green felt cushion, like a strangely shaped jewel.

Perhaps to keep my confidence in her strong, she felt compelled to explain why she'd concealed it from me. It hardly mattered that I told her I wasn't interested in her explanations. Nothing could stop her then. She took it as a trial. She said she'd had it for a long time, a good many months before I'd moved in. But it frightened her. She hated to show it to anyone, to admit to anyone that it was there in her room. Now that she'd exposed it, it would be different, she said, and as if to assure me, she cradled it in her arms.

The gun soon began to preoccupy her. She would keep it beside her plate as she ate breakfast in her underclothes. That, and the food on her plate, were the only realities for her now. She scarcely noticed that I existed. Of course, I could understand. For example, Mrs. Slaughter had gotten quite fond of ravioli, but that's how it is when you don't have much food and you stick to the same diet, you start to have love affairs with your food. They are strange affairs too, they are apt to be cruel, but in the end it is real love and there is no mistaking it or pretending otherwise. That's essentially what happened with Mrs. Slaughter and the ravioli. It began with aversion and from there to ambivalence, and there was even a long period where it seemed they were fighting. But underneath the constant bickering a passion was developing that was bound to surface sooner or later—that simply couldn't be denied.

The ravioli soon became like a theater to her. The actual eating was only part of it. She seemed fascinated by its form and color and would stare at it intensely for long intervals before placing even her fork on one of the pieces. Then she'd smell it, positioning her nose just a few inches above her plate, as if she were inhaling the most exquisite perfume. Also, she loved to touch it, and would feel several of the pieces from time to time. In a way I felt bad to merely eat my ravioli, and would have gladly given her some of my share, but I realized it would only detract from her theater. Part of her enjoyment, I realized, lay in watching me consume my portion. In fact, that was the only time, in those days, when she seemed aware of my existence.

But, you see, there wasn't enough food of any kind left to eat more than twice a day, and since we were still determined not to go out to get any more, the gun was, in a manner of speaking, far more important than food. The gun she could take with her while she took her hour-long bubble baths, and when she wanted to use the toilet she could hold it like a life saver in her hand.

And then at night while we were under the sheets listening for sounds of the Pursuer because she had said she'd heard him singing under our window one night, singing softly like a bird or a lunatic, at night the gun lay between us on the bed and she would periodically slip her hands over it and caress it until it seemed to lull her to sleep.

…While Mrs. Slaughter was so fascinated with the gun and the ravioli, I was becoming interested in the drapes. The drapes, I realized, in a very intimate way were protecting me and so I felt a sense of indebtedness to them. Also, at the same time, they were allowing me to investigate the situation, to peek through a few inches of the window and look at the snow on the streets, where I thought I might catch a glimpse of the Pursuer.

I don't remember how many times I stared at the drapes, as if to discover the secret of their fiber. I do not know either how many times I parted them as if I were parting a woman's lips, just an inch or two to get a view of the outdoors. It is also difficult to know if the repetition of my actions increased my anxiety or diminished it.

The one thing I feel certain of concerning my relationship to the drapes is that there came a different stage when I realized rather deeply that while the drapes were in one sense protecting me (since they obstructed the Pursuer's line of vision into the apartment) at the same time they were calling attention to me, and maybe they were even tipping off the Pursuer.

Just as I began to mistrust the drapes, Mrs. Slaughter in time grew skeptical about the gun. First this showed simply in her reluctance to touch it anymore at night, when there was no light on. She was afraid it would go off; she was afraid it was loaded. It wasn't long before she refused to touch it at all, and so left it on the table without moving it, as if it were somehow sacred. When I suggested that she check to see if it were loaded, she grew petrified and then furious with me. Didn't I know that it might explode in her face while she was checking? Did I want her to go blind, or get scars like some of the other Mafia women? I didn't say anything to that. I was content to let it stay on the table where she'd look at it with an expression of both fear and longing.

...But soon she stopped watching it so much. We were beginning to play games again on the living room floor. At first we played backgammon but soon tired of it, and switched to Chinese checkers. Chinese checkers, you see, is not a game like backgammon where you can outwit your opponent and suddenly move ahead at the end of the game with a kind of O. Henry finish. There is no luck in Chinese checkers because you do not play with dice or cards. Each marble is an image of your mentality. It advances according to your design. The way we played, with each of us playing for three men, it took as long as a good game of chess.

But here there were also some drawbacks. After fifteen or twenty minutes there would be a big tie-up in the middle of the board. A series of blockades had caused it, and now it was difficult to move any of our pieces more than one space at a time.

And sometimes we would have to move sideways or backwards, sometimes at angles that didn't advance a piece but would merely permit a different piece in the near future the chance to advance two places. These are called preparatory moves.

...Several minutes later the blockades would multiply. We would be quiet and intense. We were laboring over our moves. Then I'd say, "Do you want to continue this tedium?"

She'd shake her head and we'd drink some vodka. Then we'd set the marbles spinning, set them free from their places, disrupting the board, and have a good laugh over it. We'd begin instead to play Parcheesi.

Parcheesi is a game played with dice and four pieces. A piece is always vulnerable and can be sent back to its starting point on any place on the board except the safety places. The object is to get all four men home. You can also form blockades in Parcheesi but they can never last for long because the pieces forming the blockade have to get home too. Parcheesi is a game of running and hiding and searching for safety. Above all it is a game of chance and chance lands on you like a thunderbolt. When you play while drinking vodka it is apt to make you laugh until you are hysterical. But when the hysteria wears off, you may have an empty feeling, you may even feel upset or frightened.

...And so we abandoned the games. For a while everything was quiet. Then we discovered, or rather we admitted what we had discovered for a long time, that there was no food left.

"This is the end of reality," I said to myself as I went outside in my overcoat. The walk consisted of two blocks to the nearest grocery store and then back. Except for one turn the walk would be a straight line.

...The light outside was brilliant yellow and white. The cold stung me and the light made me dizzy. My mission was to buy milk, cheese, eggs, bread, and, of course, ravioli. I walked briskly, like a man who wants to catch a train but is too dignified to run. I hardly allowed myself to think about what I was doing. It was only later, maybe two hours after we ate, that I dared to think about what had happened. Mrs. Slaughter was taking another bath and I was alone on the couch. But it wasn't fear I felt then. Suddenly I had a picture of myself walking through the snow with the bag of groceries. It was so beautiful, why hadn't I looked around and seen more of the outdoors?

True, I did get some reward for my daring venture. Mrs. Slaughter lavished a lot of attention on me. She became suddenly very affectionate and kept kissing me on the neck.

Is it any wonder, then, that the next morning I went out on another walk?

This time I saw green and white houses on the snow. I saw a car sputtering out of its driveway like an angry little whale. I saw sand spread out on the sidewalks like caviar and little girls walking to school with their green school bags over their shoulder, and the gray oatmeal-colored sky where two dark clouds hung like ships about to converge, over them and over all.

I saw a butcher's shop, a dry-cleaning store, a liquor store with its orange neon sign. I saw a shopping center with stores as wide as mountains. I saw the procession of people that passed in and out of the stores like fish in the sea. I examined them closely, as if I expected them to be an hallucination. The woman in the black kerchief who had just bought some lamb chops and was heading toward her car as if it might be on fire, I strained to see the color of the mole above her chin, as if it might lend her some more dignity.

It was stunning, humbling, beautiful, and humiliating to walk around. I looked at the Star Market—suddenly so sturdy, so much time in it, a somber and compact paradise. I looked at the sky and back at the ground in front of my feet and then back at the sky again. I felt hopeless, dizzy, in the moment I was in the Pursuer was gone! ...I continued to look, first at the telephone wires as thin as necklaces and I tried to imagine how the signals traveled through them. Then I watched the people on the far corner, so unafraid of each other, so trusting as they waited for their bus.

...I began to walk up the sidewalk looking into all the store windows as I passed the liquor store, the drugstore, and the camera shop. I turned the corner. In the last window a man was throwing a pizza in the air. I looked at my feet, my black shoes as they walked over the snow.

...In the next moment I began to succumb to a strange feeling of helplessness. It was hard to know who I was. Nothing can threaten identity like a flight into ecstasy—no matter how brief. It was almost with relief, then, though I was still afraid, that I saw him trailing after me again driving a long black car. I turned a corner heading back to Mrs. Slaughter's and the Pursuer followed me. I couldn't resist turning around to try and catch a glimpse of him, but the driver was wearing dark glasses, and besides he was too far away.

II

Bodysurfing

There was a rustling, then Lee saw it, fat and gray and big-eyed with an orange crown, as it slid across the path. They were going to have the last laugh—the iguanas—that was for sure. There were so many of them, Costa Rica was going to be their world some day. The path ended and the boogie board banged against his knee. He swore out loud as he began walking down the road. It was madness, sheer madness, to have rented the board. He knew that within two minutes; he knew that when he reached the first wave. There was the wave and his body and nothing ever should come between them, that alone should be pure. Sheer lunacy to think otherwise. He looked at it—baby blue with a dangling wrist strap like an umbilical cord, this boogie board with its silly name— it was idiocy in its purest form to let it ruin his rides, to let it bang about in the wind and hit his knee. Why had he done it, why? It was because he'd remembered his wife saying they were so much fun. Years ago she'd said that; he had a distant memory of it. It was that and the surfboard morons who were taking over the ocean, crowding him out of his space. He'd let them intimidate him, let them infantilize him into thinking he should maybe get some kind of board of his own, so when he left the beach and saw it in the store he'd rented it on an impulse.

It was the same store that was in front of him now. The Palm Store, a combination travel agency and gift shop run by a good-looking man and his wife with a yellow-haired kid who didn't look like either of them, certainly not the man. So he would return it now, eleven minutes after he took it. Of course he wouldn't ask for his money back. He would take responsibility. They would wonder why, perhaps ask him why, but he wouldn't let himself worry about it. He was about to lose his job in two weeks, about to be transferred to a lower job in the bank in a different city, to be screwed over like that at his age, and with his mother at death's door, too. No, he wasn't going to worry about returning a boogie board to a store that looked like it was made out of cards (as every other store in Tamarindo did), with its pathetically corny painting of a sun sinking below the waves, a store that rented surfboards and goggles and boogie boards and tickets for turtle tours!

He went inside the Palm Store. A tall attractive blond man, a surfboardoron, perhaps two inches taller than he was, perhaps a dozen years younger, perhaps with fourteen better-defined muscles than he had, had finished talking to the owner and was fingering a surfboard as Lee placed the boogie board beside it. He is going to ask me how I liked the boogie board, Lee thought. He is going to try to have a conversation with me. The blond man turned toward Lee. He is from California, Lee thought.

"How did it ride?" the blond man said.

"How did it ride? It didn't ride at all. I didn't have any use for it."

"Surf too strong today?"

"Board too superfluous today, or any day."

"OK, I hear you."

Lee was struck by how straight the surfer's teeth were, which perhaps accounted for the extraordinary hang time of his smile.

"I don't like anything to come between me and the wave, me and the water. I think that relationship ought to stay pure. Today I violated that relationship, I'm sorry to say. Today I let myself be conquered by a product and I corrupted that relationship."

The blond man's smile vanished and Lee felt vindicated.

"I don't think I get what you mean."

"These boards," Lee said, indicating the blond man's surfboard with his gesture, "they're just another way people've found to make money off the water. They're about buying and selling, that's all."

The blond man showed a second smile, a quizzical but still friendly one. "I guess I don't see it that way," he said.

"Really? How do you see it, then?"

"They're just a piece of equipment for a sport. They're just a means to an end. Like you can't play baseball without a bat or football without a ball, can you?"

Lee felt an adrenalin rush. Apparently the man really wanted to discuss this. "There was a time when you could play sports without buying things," Lee said. "To me the more a sport costs the less its value. The more it's about buying these accessories, the more of a fetish it becomes instead of a sport. By the way, I hope I didn't desecrate the flag, so to speak, with my remarks about surfboards. I know you guys get sensitive about that."

"No, man. I don't mind. I just never met anyone who thinks like you. It's kind of interesting, really."

Lee felt flattered in spite of himself. Ridiculous to feel that in this situation, though he did for a moment, and thought he should soften himself. Besides he was beginning to get an idea and he needed time to figure it all out. Just before he spoke he made a point of looking at the surfer's eyes.

"And by the way, I know whereof I speak," Lee said. "I'm a banker. You can't be much more of a whore than that. My whole life is buying and selling. I'm in middle management at Citibank. Need I say more? Or I soon will be. I was actually at a somewhat higher level of management but that's like bragging about being in a higher circle of hell, isn't it? But at least on my vacation I want to stay pure when I'm in the water. I said to my secretary, 'I don't care what kind of hotel you get me (and she got me Le Jardin del Eden, the most expensive one in Tamarindo) but I insist on big, world-class waves. I want you to research that for me.' Well, the waves here are certainly world class and they deserve the best from me."

Lee looked closely at the man, who in turn appeared to be concentrating intensely on what Lee said. "So, I'm on my way now, I'm going to have my twilight drink, and again, I hope I haven't offended you at all."

"No way; I enjoyed talking with you. You're the first American I've spoken to in three days. I don't speak Spanish so I've practically been talking to myself since I've been here."

Lee looked at him closely once more, wondering if he were gay or just needy, or perhaps one of those friendly, new age types. He had decided something important, something definitive in the waves yesterday but this young man might make it even better. Besides he was a surfer and that would make him the cherry on the sundae and his possible gayness would never enter into it.

"I've enjoyed it too," Lee said. "Hey, you know the restaurant, Zullymar?"

"Sure."

"That's where I'm going for my drink. Why don't you join me and have one on the bank."

The blond man laughed. "Sure. My name's Andy," he said, extending his hand.

"I'm Lee Bank or should I say Le Bank, and we all know what shape banks are in."

Lee turned and walked out of the store and Andy followed after him, still laughing.

"Is Bank really your last name?"

"I'm sometimes known as Lee Bastard, or when I'm in Paris as Le Bastard. But we are far from Paris now, aren't we?"

Lee looked straight ahead as they walked down the dirt road and seemed unaware that Andy was walking beside him. It was not much of a road, Lee thought, full of holes and rocks and puddles, so they could have, should have left it alone and not put up so many toy-like stores. Laughable really how small they were—the little shack that probably doubled as someone's home—with the giant sign saying "Nachos and Ice Cream," a sign that was half as big as the shack. Pathetic really, the hut beside it—called Jungle Bus—that advertised "Killer Burguer and munchies." If the puddle on the road in front of it rose a couple of inches, it could swallow the Jungle Bus.

Zullymar was on the other side of the road, facing the Jungle Bus on one side and the beach on the other. It was a big (by Tamarindo standards) open-air restaurant and bar filled with surfers, the same crowd that forced him off his path two days in a row in the water and actually made him yearn for a lifeguard to patrol things. A wall mural that clashed with the red floor depicted a pink pelican, circling over some anchored boats and a small island beyond that—

the approximate scene outside. Across the street at another bar, a man was playing the marimba with two little boys.

Lee and Andy sat down at a table facing the water and looked briefly at the half-filled room. As soon as they focused on each other Lee said, "You'll want a beer, won't you? Isn't that the drink you guys favor?" He had a tight, semisarcastic smile and Andy smiled back.

"What do you mean?"

"You surfers, you surf wizards. You don't want to drink anything too hard, anything that might put you at risk when you go out on your boards again."

"I'm done surfing for the day and I drink lots of things. No routine."

"Fine. Dos mai tais," Lee said to the waiter.

The incredulous smile reappeared on Andy's face. Lee was going to say something to try to get rid of it but Andy spoke first.

"You've got some negative feelings toward surfers, don't you?"

Lee shrugged.

"What did they do to you, man?" Andy said, half-laughing, his hand absently caressing his board for a moment, Lee noticed, as if he really thought the goddamn thing was alive. "Did they run into you once or something?"

"No, that would never happen, though they have crowded me out more than once here in Tamarindo, kept me from where I wanted to go, but believe me I stick to my own path. I don't mingle. I am not only on a different path from them, I'm in a different world."

"But what's so different about your world?"

"Night and day, Andy, night and day."

"Why, what do you do? You bodysurf, right? I respect that. So I get up on a board and you bodysurf. Have you ever surfed?"

"I do surf."

"I mean with a board."

"Years ago when I was actually young."

"So what do you have against it?"

The drinks came. Andy took a big swallow while Lee let his sit.

"It's about buying and selling again. Kids see it on TV in ads and think 'that's it.' Then they make movies about it and create a surfing tour and sell all this equipment, all these fetishes, and the young guys think if I do this I'll be a man, if I do this I'll get some first-class pussy. It will all happen if I can just buy the right board."

Andy was laughing now. He was not an easy man to offend, Lee concluded, as he sipped his drink.

"I'm not agreeing with you, by the way," Andy said. "I just think what you're saying is funny and interesting in a way."

"Of course you think that surfboarding is the greater sport, the greater challenge, don't you? After all, you stand up, you are Homo Erectus, whereas I am still on all fours. You go out further to sea whereas I am nearer the shore. You walk on water like Jesus Christ whereas I only ride with it like a fish. And then when gravity must eventually bring you down you take the deeper, more heroic fall. You think all those things, don't you?"

"I just enjoy surfing. I haven't thought it out like that really. And like I say, I respect what you do."

"I wonder if you know what I do. Because there are a number of bodysurfers out there—it isn't just me—and very few of them know when or how to jump, and once they do jump how to go with the wave. They almost always start too late."

"I probably wouldn't know man—isn't that the way it is with everything? We don't really understand the other person's thing or point of view."

"Dos mai tais," Lee said, catching the waiter's attention, although he had not yet made significant progress on his first drink.

"So, now tell me your story, Andy. What brings you to glorious Tamarindo?"

Andy looked flustered, ran his fingers twice through his longish blond hair. He could be Kato Kaelin's younger brother, Lee thought.

"I just came here to surf."

"From whence did you come, then?"

"Santa Cruz, in California."

Lee smiled tightly again. "This is your vacation then. You came to Tamarindo directly on your vacation?"

"Not exactly. I was in Monteverde first. I went to Costa Rica directly but I went to Monteverde first, you know, in the mountains."

"Then you are a mountain man, too."

Andy lowered his head a little. Lee couldn't tell if he were burying his smile or giving birth to a new one. In Tamarindo smiles were the iguanas on every surfer's face. Lee distrusted smiles in general because he had discovered that if you believed in them a time would come when that belief would hurt you. He remembered he had once been very moved by his wife's smile.

"So how were the mountains?" he finally said.

"Some bad stuff happened there so I came here earlier than I expected."

"I'm sorry to learn that. What exactly was the bad stuff?"

The waiter came with the new drinks and Andy took a big swallow as the waiter took his first glass, while Lee carefully placed his second glass next to his first (which was still three-quarters full) as if he were positioning two bowling pins.

"The woman I was with went bad on me. She met a dude on the tour we took in the cloud forest. He was older than me, around your age I guess, and he had a lot more money than me, you know. I was never very good at making money; I just help run a little Xerox store. But this rich guy was a businessman, a big businessman, though he was in the same hotel as us, only he was in some luxury suite. Anyway, she told me she was sorry; she said she didn't plan it that way, that it was a one-in-a-million thing but she thought he was the man for her and she was going to go with him for the rest of her vacation and beyond. So…"

"So what could you do?"

"Just got drunk. Woke up alone the next morning and got in my Suzuki and came down here 'cause they said this was where the surf was, and they didn't lie about that. The last couple of days I took it out on the waves, six, seven hours a day, and just flushed that bitch right out. It hurt though, I'll tell you. So when you talk about money corrupting things, I really hear you."

"And when you talk about women being bitches, I hear you. I lost my sense of smell from a woman once."

"How'd that happen?" Andy's incredulous smile had snuck back, Lee noted, as if it were taking a curtain call.

"I discovered my female friend had cheated on me and I got extremely ill in an odd way. I developed a sinus condition that's never really gone away. I think it was my ex-wife who did me wrong, though it might have been someone else before her. Over the years people tend to blur together, don't they? Anyway, I have very little to do with women now. The only woman in my life besides Mother Sea is my secretary and she's far too valuable to bother having sex with. I am completely dependent on her. It was she who arranged this trip for me. Of course I'll lose her when I'm transferred to my next job but that's the way it is with women— we always lose them. They were put here on earth so we would know what losing is. Even when we have them we lose them— did you ever think about that?"

"What do you mean?"

"We watch them lose their looks, their charm, their ability to have children, their sex. We lose our mothers, too, and then our wives become our mothers and we lose them again. We lose our mothers a second time."

"But men age too," Andy said.

"But we don't notice it as much since we don't desire men, do we? Anyway, you don't have to worry about all this now. It'll be years before you'll have to realize this."

"I realize it; I realize some of it now."

"Then you might consider giving them up as I have. You can get a greater high than the orgasm from bodysurfing, at least you can the way I bodysurf."

Andy looked away morosely. Lee waited a minute. There was a rustling sound in the restaurant as if the waiters were really iguanas. Lee couldn't stand hearing it so he spoke.

"Thinking about her?" he said.

"Yeah."

"How long were you two an item?"

"Just a couple of months but..."

"Impact can be made in a couple of months. Impact can be made in a minute if we allow it to happen. I understand."

"Yeah, I thought this one would work out. I had hopes..."

"Ah hopes," Lee said, gesturing vaguely toward the sea. "Listen, I have an idea for you, a proposal to make to you. It does not involve hope, but something better. It involves a challenge."

"Go on."

"Something very special happened to me yesterday. Do you know that inlet that separates our beach from the other one, the one that goes straight to the mountains?"

"Yes."

"Have you ever been on that other beach?"

"No. No one surfs over there so I just assumed there wasn't much there."

"That's precisely the point. The beach goes on for miles but because there's no access from the road, because there is a thick jungle of trees to walk through and no other way to reach it unless you swim across the inlet, there is almost no one there. Well, yesterday I swam across that inlet. It was sunset, a little earlier than now, and the swim wasn't easy but I found the beach deserted and astonishingly beautiful. There were no footprints on the sand, just the swerving lines of hermit crabs and twisted branches from trees. I don't think there were even any butterflies; it wasn't civilized enough for them. It was like being on the moon or on a new planet. The waves were enormous and there was no one around to get in my way. My path was totally clear. Why don't you go there with me now and bodysurf with me? Leave your board at your hotel room and just go there with me now. I know you've only known me thirty minutes or whatever it's been. I know it's getting dark and it's a little dangerous."

"It's not that dangerous. I could do that."

"Fine, marvelous. Here, why don't you have my other drink, I haven't touched it, and I'll finish my first one and then we'll go out together and meet the waves with our bodies alone. I promise you it will be extraordinary."

"Yeah, OK," Andy said, looking Lee straight in the eye. "I'll go with you. I'm open to it."

They finished their drinks quickly and Lee paid the bill. The moment he put the money in the waiter's hand he saw the sun slip below the water. Some people were watching it in the restaurant and beyond them others watched from the beach. It was an understandable ritual, Lee thought. It had been advertised, like a Citibank card, and people needed to see the promise delivered. In her condominium in Florida, his mother was probably watching it, too, from her wheelchair, perhaps with one of her nurses. She more than anyone believed in advertised beauty. All her life she believed in Jackie Kennedy and Marilyn Monroe and Marlon Brando and Holiday Inns and sunsets. It would not do any good to tell her the deeper beauty came after the sunset, came with the night when the whole world slid below water. She had never listened to him. They should have switched positions. She should have worked for Citibank and he should have been the cripple. He might have done well in a chair...

There were only occasional street lamps outside but he could see the night was thick with butterflies. They were not talking now, so he could hear another iguana slide past in front of him. Then he decided it wouldn't have mattered if they were talking— he would have heard it anyway. In Tamarindo every sound on earth was an iguana; you could only escape them in the water.

"There's your hotel," Lee said, pointing to the Diria, barely bigger than the travel agency it seemed. "Why don't you drop your board off here, you won't be needing it. It'll only get in the way."

"OK," Andy said softly. He walked off in the dark and Lee waited in the road, thinking he should have told him 'go put your dick away there too. That's what your board really is. You won't be needing it where we're going. There aren't any dicks in the ocean, not in the night ocean.'"

Andy came back. Lee had never really considered that he wouldn't.

"Let's go," Lee said. There were about fifty yards of road before they reached the path that led to the beach. The deep orange of the sky had passed. It was now a dark purple and silver, tinged with spots of fading pink. There were not many people on the beach and most of them were leaving. Except for the white of the waves, the ocean was dark.

"It gets dark quickly," Andy said.

"Drops like a plank," Lee said. He is very young, Lee thought, and his fear is showing. Lee thought of himself as a thousand years old. This will be good for him. He needs to put on a hundred years. Then he didn't think about him anymore.

They walked the length of the beach toward the inlet. Andy was talking about the girl who had dumped him, whose name was Dawn.

"Forget the girl," Lee said. "Drown her in the ocean."

When they reached the inlet the sky was nearly black. There were lots of stars out and three quarters of a moon.

"I was hoping it would be low tide so we could walk across," Andy said.

"We can swim it," Lee said. He threw the towel he'd been carrying into the sky and the black swallowed it.

"What did you just do?"

"I threw my towel away; I won't be needing it. It's a hotel towel."

"Yeah, you told me about your hotel. Very impressive. It's supposed to be the best hotel in Tamarindo." There was sarcasm, even a trace of contempt, in Andy's voice that stung Lee for a second.

"The hotel can drop dead," Lee said as he walked into the water. He was surprised again by how wide the inlet was but he didn't feel tired this time while he was swimming. He could hear Andy breathing heavily, almost gasping, as he swam beside him and thought for a moment that he shouldn't have let him drink three mai tais.

"Stop racing," he said, nearly yelling. "Stop trying to beat me. It's not a race. You have to pace yourself."

Andy slowed down the rest of the way. When they reached the shore of the deserted beach there were only a few slivers of sky that weren't black.

"I wish it were lighter, man," Andy said.

"Why?"

"I can't see things you said would be here. I can't see the things you promised."

"Yes, you can. Look harder."

"I can barely see in front of myself."

"I can look at anything and see the beauty in it. Especially the dark."

"Tell me what I was supposed to see here again, and walk slower, will you? I can barely keep up with you."

"Twisted tree branches and hermit crab lines," Lee said.

Lee walked briskly, saying nothing for the next few minutes. Andy ran after him, stumbling occasionally, trying to keep up with him or at least keep him in sight, feeling like he did when he was a child trying to keep up with his father's longer, relentless stride.

"Come on, we're going in the water. It's time to face the black water now."

Lee walked toward the ocean in fast, imperious strides like a fixated scoutmaster, Andy thought.

"Slow down, will you, why are you racing?" Andy said, and then repeated himself, yelling this time because the ocean was so loud he felt he wasn't being heard.

Lee kept walking into the water without changing speed, the big blustery businessman from the fancy hotel who had to know it all, who had to take what he wanted when he wanted it. Why had he listened to him, why had he come with him to this crazy beach. He was chasing after him in the water now while his legs felt like rubber. The water was up to his knees and he knew something was wrong, had known it for some time.

"Lee," he yelled. "Lee. Lee Bastard."

A few seconds before he'd seen him fifteen yards ahead propelling himself forward, not even ducking for the waves but somehow willing himself forward like a man walking into a wall, into the earth, until the water covered him. Andy heard himself scream. It might have been "Lee," it might have been "Help." His legs wouldn't move at first and when they could he knew he wouldn't move them because he'd already known Lee wanted to be witnessed while he disappeared by a sucker like Andy; just as Dawn had, and one of those humiliations was enough. Lee Legend gets back at a surfer. Lee Lemming. "Lee," he screamed. "Lee Bastard," knowing he would see and hear nothing now except the constant roar in the black and his own sickly voice boomeranging back at him like spit in the wind, because the bastard had wanted it this way.

Song of the Earth

After his phone call to Perry, Ray let out a little scream and jumped with raised fists, slightly bruising his knuckles against the wooden beams. Then he ran around turning on every light he could find, for the trees were thick and so near the windows that the cottage was already dark and chilly. He thought of trying to start a fire to surprise Joy when she got back from her run but doubted there was enough time, so he fixed himself a drink instead.

When Joy returned, Ray was finishing his second whiskey sour. While she toweled off by the fireplace she told him a long joke about a couple she'd seen at the beach; he pretended to laugh but took advantage of the moment to study her. She looked amazingly good. She was thirty-five, his age, but he thought she looked younger than he did. She'd always had what he considered a classic female figure except for her unusually broad shoulders, which, coupled with her height (she was only an inch or two shorter than he was), at times gave her appearance a forbidding quality. Yet when her long blonde hair hung down straight, as it did now, her shoulders were tremendously exciting; the more he thought about it, they were exciting regardless of her hairstyle, perhaps just because they were so dramatically incongruous in her otherwise gracefully proportioned body.

"Did you speak to Perry?" she said, stretching her legs out as she spoke. She was wearing her navy blue running suit.

"He invited me to his home tomorrow for lunch."

"Wow!" she said, springing forward as her face exploded into a smile. "Congratulations! You're going to have lunch with Perry Green! What a coup!"

"Take it easy. It's not as if I've just won the Pulitzer."

"I'd say you just took a big step toward winning it. Perry Green is probably the only legitimate triple threat in music now that Bernstein is dead, except for maybe Lukas Foss. He's one of the most prominent conductors of modern music in the country. He's definitely one of the most influential critics, and he must be on eight zillion juries or boards of directors."

"He's also a famous composer. You forgot that."

"That too."

"No, not that too. As far as he's concerned that's his real identity."

Joy nodded uncertainly, as if barely able to repress another joke.

"Yes siree buster, I'd say it's a coup. It's working out just as you'd hoped."

"Do you think you can drop me off there tomorrow?"

"I'll do better than that. I'll make you dinner tonight if you'll promise to tell me all about the fast society you're running with these days."

Ray smiled and said it was a good deal. She made chicken crepes, broccoli and carrots, and tapioca pudding—all his favorites—and he told her an edited version of how he had met Perry Green. There was a party of musicians in the Village, what he had thought would be basically a bunch of composers kvetching and flattering one another. He'd heard a rumor that Perry would be coming but hadn't fully believed it until he saw him, looking slightly frail in a pale blue suit and yellow Windsor tie, in a corner of the living room. Then it was simply a matter of screwing up his courage (a whiskey sour helped him there) and striking up a conversation.

"What did you talk about? Did you tell him you had an old girl-friend who once sang in one of his song cycles at Tanglewood?"

Ray laughed and said he would tell Perry all about her tomorrow. At the time, though, he had thought it best to steer clear of shoptalk. Instead they'd talked about books and movies and New York politics—although they did talk about Perry's book in progress on Stravinsky's ballets. Ray barely mentioned that he was a musician, much less a composer. But it worked, or something worked, and Perry suggested they have lunch, which they did a week later in the Village. Then they talked more freely about themselves, and when they discussed summer plans Perry said he'd be at his house in Tanglewood and invited Ray to visit. Ray hadn't thought Perry meant to invite him to stay at his house, so he had thought of calling Joy. And now here he was, tremendously in her debt.

He stopped talking to finish his drink and saw something unsettling in Joy's face. Had she assumed that there was more to the story? For Perry Green was rumored to be a homosexual and was often seen with men thirty or forty years younger. Was it that, or something else from her own agenda? Quickly he offered to introduce her to Perry and she said that would be great.

"Of course, I should have made that clear to you earlier. Actually, I meant to tell you when I first called that you could benefit from this too."

"Not to worry," she said, but that anxious expression was back in her face. Ray watched her closely. Maybe it had nothing to do with Perry and she was instead concerned that he might make a pass at her now. Over the years they'd both worked at becoming friends who could joke about their past relationship and still do occasional favors for each other. Yet here they were, in her cottage in the country. Neither was involved with anyone else, and it seemed they'd never gotten along so well.

"I'm getting really tired," Joy suddenly announced, before yawning with exaggerated emphasis. "Will you need any help fixing up the sofa?" He said no; she wished him good night, and as quickly as he had envisioned the possibility it was removed from him.

"Who are you staying with?" Perry asked. They were sitting at a white patio table shaded by a white and blue umbrella sprouting from its center.

"A woman named Joy Davis. We're just friends," Ray said with a wave of his hand. "She's a teacher and singer who sang in the chorus of your 'American Song Cycle' actually, at Tanglewood a couple of summers ago."

"Really? Did she drive you here?"

Ray nodded. "I wanted to introduce her to you but she turned shy at the last minute."

Perry chuckled and adjusted his sunglasses. "I have a friend staying with me too—the young man who brought us our drinks. His name is Bobby. You'll have to talk to him later. He's delightful."

"What would we do without friends?"

"Indeed!" Perry said, still laughing. Then he fell silent until, just as Ray was about to compliment his yard, Perry asked the magic question.

"Tell me what kind of music you write. I'm sorry I'm not familiar with it."

"There haven't been many performances of it in New York. And, of course, no records yet. But I keep plugging away. It's tonal, mostly. Some might call it neo-Romantic, though I don't like the label."

"Labels are for librarians. They call me a Romantic too, and a conservative. But I think I'm kind of a wild man, wouldn't you say?"

"Sure," Ray said. Then, after Perry began laughing, he laughed too.

"I hope you brought a score for me to read."

"I have some back at Joy's house. A short symphony I've just finished and a string trio I'm working on."

"Splendid! You'll have to bring them to me tomorrow, or tonight if you can come over."

"Really?"

"Of course. Bobby will fix us all dinner. He's an excellent cook."

"Thanks so much."

"And bring Joy too. I'd like to meet her."

"She'll certainly be thrilled to meet you," he said, immediately wishing he hadn't been so florid. He reminded himself that he was succeeding by staying in the background and letting Perry orchestrate everything.

Between four and five, Perry went in the house to take a nap. He'd invited Ray to use his guest room but Ray told him he'd like to stay by the pool and maybe swim again.

"It's so exciting to be young," Perry said. "All that wild energy." He laughed a little, then walked down the steps in a careful, almost stately manner (not unlike the way he approached the podium when he conducted) before disappearing into his house. Ray had gotten up from the chaise longue and was watching the house from the diving board. Perry was definitely playing some kind of game with him, but what was it? First he was the relaxed but dignified host. Then he seemed to show a possibly jealous interest in Joy; yet a moment later he invited her to dinner. Of course, he had asked him about his music and offered to look at it, but was that said out of mere politeness?

Perry was certainly a master of mixed messages and as a result, he'd kept Ray off balance all day. The nadir of the afternoon had to be when Bobby, after serving them lunch, sat down to join them. It turned out Bobby was not merely a waiter but a sometime actor. Perry's bright blue eyes sparkled as he talked about Bobby's auditions. Was this his way of demonstrating that he had no vulnerabilities in his love life? Yet Bobby was also naive, bordering on goofy, and not particularly attractive. He even had a fairly substantial case of acne. It was true that Perry was somewhere in his sixties with thinning hair, but he was still Perry Green, and on stage (albeit with his hairpiece and elevator shoes) he was an imposing figure. At Tanglewood, Joy said his poster sold better than ever.

For several minutes Ray had been walking from the diving board to the patio table and then back, turning every few steps to look back at the house below. On one such trip he stubbed his toe near the table, swore out loud, and then sat down in a chair, telling himself to calm down. He inhaled deeply a few times and watched a pine needle drift over his head in the light breeze. Above him the cloudless sky was a deep azure. When he was young and came to Tanglewood with his parents he used to call them Mahler skies. How inexpressibly beautiful it was to hear Mahler's Resurrection Symphony or "The Song of the Earth" under such a sky across from the tree-lined lake. Of course

Tanglewood was much more built up now, and more businesslike. He could never feel about Tanglewood (or even about Mahler) the way he did twenty years ago.

Looking down at the pool he remembered the most stunning event of his afternoon with Perry. They had gotten up from their seats to go swimming. "It's a little obscene to have a pool here, I suppose," Perry said, "but I often feel too tired to bother with the lake." Then they went into the water together, laughing while they waded.

"Look at our feet," Perry said, pointing below the water. "They look identical. That must mean we're twins."

That moment in the pool was the closest Perry had come to flirting with him. But was it serious flirting? And if it was, and if Perry persisted, what would he do? He knew one thing: He would call Joy before she left for Perry's and ask her to bring his scores with her. He was going to put them into Perry's hands tonight.

That Joy chose to wear probably her best white cocktail dress might have worked, but with her long turquoise earrings, her pearl necklace, and gold and turquoise rings, she looked top-heavy and garish. She'd even worn twice as much eyeliner as usual, and a fat smear of red lipstick. It was immediately obvious to Ray that she'd tried too hard—a big mistake in dealing with Perry. Moreover, she talked too much and too loudly about all the wrong things.

Perry, of course, remained unflappable. He allowed himself to be interviewed about a bevy of subjects Ray thought indiscreet, and he complimented Joy a number of times on her appearance, as if hoping his praise would have a tranquilizing effect on her. Meanwhile, Bobby, acting preoccupied with his dinner, said nothing but was unfailingly able to laugh whenever Perry made a joke or laughed at one of Joy's.

For the first half-hour Ray tried to contribute some comments of his own in the hopes of slowing Joy down. When this failed, he concentrated on drinking wine and staying silent. It was only shortly before they left (while Joy was in the bathroom) that Perry turned to him and said, "Did she bring your scores?"

"Yes. I have them in my briefcase, actually." He went on to say that he would greatly value any comments Perry might make. Perry removed his glasses and smiled at him as he took the scores, while Ray tried not to stare at his wrinkles.

"Are you free to come for a swim tomorrow before you leave?"

"Sure," Ray said.

"Say twelvish?"

Driving back, Joy sang bits of various arias, mixing in dirty jokes and laughing continuously. He could never tell at such times if she was truly happy or just projecting an elaborate cover.

"Isn't Perry amazing?" she said once they were back in the house, as she again made up the couch for him.

"He's very nice."

"Now I can die and go to heaven, I've dined with a great man. Aren't you happy too? He said he'd look at your scores, didn't he? God, what an opportunity."

"I'm pleased," he said with a tentative smile.

"I should think so," she said, putting a hand on the hip of her white dress. "Haven't you gotten everything you wanted?" Their eyes met and he felt she was looking at him meaningfully, as if he could sleep with her. He was excited too, but something froze him. Instead of trying anything he yawned and let the moment pass.

But he couldn't fall asleep. He felt vaguely as he had years ago, the night before his master's exam. It was the knowledge that something momentous would happen tomorrow, for he was certain that Perry would look at his work before they met for their swim. Regardless of what he thought, Perry would have to say something positive; but what he said would hardly matter. It was really a question of what Perry would or wouldn't offer to do to help him, and then, of course, what Perry might expect in return.

He thought of Perry's own music, buoyant, crisp, and civilized. It was also romantic but always controlled. Might Ray not expect reasonably controlled conduct from him too? He reminded himself that Perry was over sixty and had complained about his heart. Perhaps he merely enjoyed flirting and wouldn't want anything too drastic to happen right away. Of course, Perry could just as easily make a pass at him tomorrow and end by asking him to do something unthinkable. He didn't really know Perry and could hardly predict his behavior. But what would he do if something did happen? He had never had sex with a man and there were certain things he knew he couldn't do, especially with AIDS around, when sex with men had become like Russian roulette.

He tried focusing on the question of just what he would do with Perry but found it too difficult to think about. Instead he started thinking about the look in Joy's eyes that night, her long blonde hair and big shoulders. It was odd, but he'd wanted her more than he ever had during their relationship. Why had he turned away from her? Was he already punishing himself for his thoughts about Perry?

But maybe it wasn't too late. If Perry Green could champion his music, anything was possible. He turned on a dim lamp by the couch, put on his slippers, and walked to her room, the floor creaking with his every step.

"Joy," he said softly as he tapped twice on her door in the near total darkness.

"What's up?" she said matter-of-factly. "Come in."

"Me, obviously. I'm having trouble sleeping."

"Sounds like the Ray I know."

"Were you having trouble too?"

"Me? No, I'm too uncomplicated to be an insomniac."

"Sorry. I guess I'm disturbing you then."

"No problem," she said, her voice still even and toneless.

"Can we talk for a few minutes?"

"What's on your mind?" she said, turning on a bedlamp before he could ask her not to. Her face looked strained in the light, as if it were fighting against something, and he thought she was keeping her eyes on a point just behind him while she talked.

"I guess I'm nervous waiting to hear what Perry will say tomorrow."

"Don't worry, it'll work out. Why wouldn't it? Your music's good, he seems to want to help people he cares about, and he certainly cares about you, don't you think?"

Something in her tone stung him. It was one thing to be sexually rejected by Joy (which she'd all but made clear by now) but quite another to be put on the defensive like this.

"I think he cares equally about you. And you certainly showed the whole night long how much you cared about him. I've never seen you so enthusiastic."

"I don't get your point, Ray."

"There's no point. It's just that I never knew you could flirt so relentlessly."

"That's a strange thing to say. God, Ray, I don't know that I appreciate that. It seems a little hypocritical too, under the circumstances."

He felt his heart pound and took a step back toward the doorway.

"How's it hypocritical?"

"I didn't leave my scores with him."

"You're not a composer."

"1 didn't leave my business card either."

"So what are you saying? That it's a sin for me to try to help myself? That I shouldn't show him anything and should just be a meek little music teacher the rest of my life and never get anywhere?"

"I'm saying I think you're maybe accusing me of something you're doing yourself."

"And I'm saying you're maybe a little jealous." He shut the door—he didn't think he slammed it, but it made an inordinately loud noise. By the time he reached the sofa he already regretted it and realized he should apologize. But how? It suddenly seemed an incredibly difficult thing to do. What was happening to him that it was so hard to say he was sorry? He had always considered himself direct and spontaneous, but now he was becoming so ineffectual, so Hamlet-like. Was it this Perry business? Or maybe it had really started years ago, when he moved from Somerville to New York. But that was too painful and ridiculous to think about. In Somerville he had been a child with no conception at all about how careers were made. Somerville was about long afternoons at the piano, summer trips to Tanglewood, and dreaming about being the next Mahler. A movie a few years ago had shown how Mahler converted to Catholicism to help his career. Was it true? Even Mahler probably wasn't what he seemed, and had had to put in his New York years as well.

Ray walked across the living room and again knocked on her door. "I want to apologize. You've been exceedingly generous to let me stay here, and I was a pig to say what I said."

"I'm sorry for some of the things I said too," she said, once more in a matter-of-fact voice that gave away nothing. "Why don't we get some sleep and I'll see you in the morning?"

But in the morning her face had only softened a little and that maddeningly neutral voice was still intact. Moreover, she continued to avoid his eyes, something she used to do years ago whenever he had disappointed her.

In the car on the way to Perry's he thanked her profusely and she smiled. But when he asked her to the concert and proposed a farewell dinner afterward, she quickly found a reason why she couldn't do either. He felt so discouraged that he lied and told her that Perry had offered to give him a ride back so she needn't call for him. Then there were some awkward words, a tepid kiss on the cheek, an inscrutable and probably forced smile on Joy's face before she drove off, leaving him at the iron gate to Perry's house.

"This is ridiculous," he said out loud when he discovered that the gate was locked. It took him a confused minute or so to ring the buzzer, and another few minutes before Bobby emerged in a pair of madras shorts and white T-shirt to let him in. He had his characteristic smile that Ray alternately saw as either innocent or empty. After he opened the gate, he shook hands with Ray effusively. "I'm going into town to do some shopping for Perry."

"To Stockbridge on foot?"

Bobby giggled. "I need the exercise. At least Perry thinks so." He began his high-pitched quasi-hysterical laugh, which Ray determined to cut off with a question. "Which store are you going to?"

"A lot of them, practically all of them. He has very particular tastes. I'll be gone for hours, but I guess exercise is a good cause."

"Well, if I'm gone before you come back, good luck to you."

His smile faded. "I'm sure I'll see you soon. Oh, by the way, Perry's in his room. He asked if he could meet you there."

"Sure," Ray mumbled.

"You can get in the house from the back." Bobby waved and smiled again, then began whistling some innocuous tune as he headed down the road.

Ray walked up the stone steps cut into the front lawn, then circled around the left side of the house, where there were alternating gardens of petunias and tiger lilies. In the backyard he stood on tiptoe to view the pool, but he could see just a sliver of water before he was in the house. For a moment he wondered which way to turn until he heard Perry's voice.

"Ray, is that you? Keep turning left and then left again." Perry was sitting at his desk arranging papers. It was a bright, airy room filled with photographs on the walls and dominated by a large unmade bed against the far wall. Perry rose from his chair and shook Ray's hand warmly, asking him to sit down on a green velvet chair just behind him.

"You can see I didn't quite make it to the pool yet."

"Did I come too early?"

"Not at all. You're as punctual as ever. I just went a little overtime on my book. I'm writing about the opening of Orpheus. It's kind of silly to try to put it in words, don't you think? The whole book may really be kind of silly, but I'm supposed to be a champion of Stravinsky. The Stravinsky Society even gave me their medal," he said, pointing to his wall where it hung between autographed pictures of Koussevitzky and Copland.

"Say, you look even more glamorous today than you did yesterday. I love your pink shirt, especially with those sleek black bathing trunks. And your sunglasses make you look so mysterious—like Marcello Mastroianni."

Ray laughed a little, then took them off. "It is silly wearing them inside, however," he said.

Perry studied his face. "Well, maybe you're right. You do have such expressive eyes that you should never hide them for long, though right now you look a little anxious. Would you like it better out by the pool?"

Ray shrugged, too boyishly he thought.

"I think so," Perry said, still pointedly studying him. "I'll change into my suit then if you don't mind."

"Of course not," Ray said. He kept his eyes fixed on the photograph of Hindemith, resolving not to look at Perry for a second as he fumbled out of his pants.

"I looked at your stuff last night. Seems pretty interesting to me. I like the flute against the drums in the waltz section."

Ray felt his heart beat again as he waited to hear more, but all he heard was the sound of Perry changing clothes. Finally he said, "Thank you."

"You look a little sad, but now that I know you're a composer it makes sense, I suppose. That's a good enough reason to be sad."

Ray turned and looked at him. Perry was wearing a baggy navy blue bathing suit and a white polo shirt. He looked short and a little shriveled. At least he doesn't try to look young, Ray thought.

"May I keep your pieces a little longer so I can try to understand them better?"

"Of course."

"I get the feeling that I've disappointed you somehow. I hope not, of course. I liked a good bit of what I saw."

"Oh no. I'm very grateful. Anything you say means a lot to me."

"Tell me the truth, Ray. Do you really want to be a famous composer?"

"Only if my work deserves it."

"That's a good answer. The problem is so many people think their work does. It's curious why people chase so hard after public fame when they can make each other feel famous so easily."

"How do they do that?" Ray said. He could still feel his heart, but everything else in the world seemed to have receded from him except this conversation.

"Why, through love, of course. But people hold back so stupidly. It's a tragedy, really."

"But you're famous. You're famous all over the world. Are you the exception to the rule?"

"I never expected it. I did hope for it at a certain time in my life, and I did do things to help my cause, but I never compromised myself, I don't think. At least not too badly," he said laughing. "I haven't, at any rate, been as lucky in my pursuit of private fame. I think you have a much better chance of getting public fame than I do of getting my private one."

"Why's that?"

"I think it's very obvious why. You're young and crushingly handsome and you have drive and talent, and I'm getting older, my energy's petering out, and I just feel my chances dwindling all the time," he said, looking deeply, almost incriminatingly into Ray's eyes, as if begrudging him his relative youth. "Let me ask you another question, Ray," Perry said as he took another step toward him. Ray had gotten up from his chair as well; they were now standing a few feet from each other in the middle of the room. "Do you think of your life as a challenge or a disappointment?"

He thought of Joy and of his tiny apartment on the Upper West Side. "Both, probably."

"Touché. Well then, do you consider yourself disappointed with your life so far? That's a better way to put it."

He felt then that he had never loved anyone happily, never accomplished even one of his career goals.

"It's fair to say I'm somewhat disappointed so far. So where does that leave us?"

"How rare are absolutes attained, how valuable are compromises," Perry said smiling. "You see, I've always believed the way to avoid disappointment is not to expect absolute victories in either work or love. Take solace in small victories whenever you can. You can believe they're real, at least. That's why they call the other fantasies or dreams."

Ray stopped himself from making a joke about Perry philosophizing so much. Instead he said, "But you've gotten so much success, you've realized your dreams."

"Ah, you can't be too sure about what I've gotten. You'd have to know what I wanted first. For instance, I'm not going to get you the way I want, am I?"

Perry's lips trembled as he asked his question. Ray stared with fascination at them, and at the moisture that had gathered above his upper lip.

"No, I guess not."

"And maybe you had hopes that I could make you famous, but I can't. It's really beyond my power. So much for absolutes. On the other hand, I could lend a hand here and there, help you out a bit every now and then. I think you're very bright and just tremendously attractive."

"And what could I do for you in light of what I just said?"

"The pleasure of your occasional company is the main thing. Small things. No absolutes. Can I, for example, give your back a massage now?"

"Here?"

"Don't look so mistrustful. I mean literally what I said. A backrub, that's all. Just lie down on my bed. You don't even have to take off your shirt if you don't want to."

Ray looked up for a moment at the rows of autographed pictures before he walked toward Perry's bed. Every time he thought he'd seen them all there'd be a Shostakovich, a Casals, or a Heifetz he hadn't noticed before. It was as if these were magic walls perpetually revealing the images of new musicians.

When he lay down he tried to understand what he was feeling. He decided he was anxious and slightly angry—nothing he couldn't control. He closed his eyes and tried to imagine they were a woman's hands, perhaps Joy's. Then he tried to think of analogous situations, how baseball trainers routinely rubbed the arms, shoulders, and backs of their players. But this didn't work either, and his eyes stayed open the rest of the time.

Perry's touch was surprisingly strong and skillful, and so far he was sticking to the rules. "These hands have played duets with Heifetz and Hindemith," he said softly. "You shouldn't find them so repulsive. On the contrary, you should find them at least somewhat interesting. After all, they can make a hundred men sit down and play beautiful music. How does it feel to have them rub your back?"

Ray said nothing. He was certainly not going to say anything that might excite Perry, but if he stayed silent much longer he worried that he might seem too passive. "You're very good at it."

"Ah, and I'll get better yet. You'll see. You merely have to tell me what you like and I'll adjust."

For the next minute the only noise Ray heard was his skin being rubbed. It sounded like the lake lapping up against the sand. Then, without warning, except for his slightly heightened breathing, Perry broke the agreement. His hands began moving down Ray's body without the slightest hesitation. Ray wanted to say something, but the longer he waited the more impossible it became to speak. Finally he said, "Just be careful, I have to insist on that. Just promise you'll be very careful, OK?"

With All My Heart

The woman was crying.

"What's the matter? Why are you crying again?" he said.

"Because you're hurting me. I don't understand what you want from me. Maybe if I knew…"

"What I want from you. Sweetheart it was you who seduced me. Remember back in the bar. It was all of two hours ago when we met. Are you listening?"

"Yes, I'm listening."

"But how are you listening? Are you listening with all your heart?"

"I'm listening with all my heart…"

"And?"

"And soul," she said, biting her lip as she repeated the routine.

"Because what you say is ridiculous. It was you who started talking to me, laughing at my jokes, staring at my chest and touching me. Right?"

She nodded, then mumbled "yes."

"And then back here you practically attacked me before I could take off my coat. So what are you talking about?"

"I don't mean that. That part was fine."

"Fine? It was fine?"

"It was magnificent."

"How magnificent?" he said, putting as much pressure as he could on her arms.

"It was everything I could have hoped for."

"So don't you think I deserve to have a conversation with you afterwards given what I've contributed to your life?"

She started to cry again.

"Come on, answer me. Stop crying and answer me."

"Yes, you do deserve it."

"And that, therefore, I deserve to talk about what I want to talk about."

She nodded. "I agree," she said softly. "I want to hear it. Please."

"Earlier you told me that I was vain."

"I'm sorry."

"You also said I was crazy."

"I'm sorry, I..."

"I'll admit I'm vain. That I'll admit, but I'm not crazy. Now say you're sorry for that."

"I am sorry but please stop hurting me. Please take your knees off my arms."

He eased the pressure a bit.

"Why are you doing this?" she said. "I don't understand what I did."

He ignored her question and continued talking.

"Do you want to hear how vain I was? Do you think it would do you some good? When I was a kid I lived in fear of my older sister seeing my toes and on my way to and from the bathroom to take my shower I always wore a long white robe and white rubber slippers that covered my toes completely."

"Why aren't you living in fear about what you're doing now?" she said, staring at him hard.

"Because I'm in control now, I'm much more in control, obviously. But then I was afraid of her seeing my toes and underpants, can you imagine? And my deepest fear was that she'd see my chest. That's why I didn't learn how to swim till I was eleven."

The woman sighed and rolled her eyes. She noticed the half-empty bottle of vodka on the floor and wanted to scream, but when she'd screamed before he'd slapped her face. Besides, she had the feeling, as she looked at the walls, that the room was soundproof anyway.

"Why are you doing that? Why are you rolling your eyes?" he said, moving his knees up higher on her arms again.

"You think you get stuff by me but you don't. Nothing gets by me."

She closed her eyes for a second and a new tear rolled down her cheek.

"What? I'm sorry. It's just that you're hurting me and scaring me a lot."

"Do you or do you not want to listen?"

"Yes, I'm listening. I'm listening. I want to listen."

He looked at her closely, as if finally deciding to give her one more chance, and then continued. "Once in the car on the way to the beach with just me and my parents and our dog, my father made a joke about me. Do you know what it was?"

She shook her head no.

"His joke was that I was afraid to have our dog see my chest. I went along with it and let my parents laugh too, but I wanted to scream that I didn't care if anyone saw my chest except my sister, Julie, that they'd got it wrong because it was only her I couldn't stand to have see it. I was churning inside, churning, but I kept it to myself."

He paused and looked away from her and she snuck a look at her wristwatch. He'd been sitting on her for about twenty minutes though she'd thought it was almost an hour. She wanted to give up then and just pass out.

"What do you think of my chest now?" he said, sitting up a little.

She nodded appreciatively.

"Look at it. Look at the muscle definition. Look at my abs too. What do you think?"

She forced herself to look.

"It's a good chest."

"Good?" he said, contemptuously.

"It's beautiful. It's probably the most beautiful chest I've ever seen."

"That's why you were attracted to me in the bar. Because of my chest, right?"

"Yes."

"Because you could see it through my net shirt, couldn't you?"

"Yes."

He took a breath and continued talking. "With my younger brother, on the other hand, I didn't mind if he saw my chest but I couldn't bear to be defeated in any game by him, not even once. As he got better at some of them I had to eliminate the number of things we competed in. You get it? By the time we were teenagers it was down to badminton, Chinese checkers and candlepin bowling. Can you imagine?"

She nodded.

"Now with my parents it was a different kettle of fish. Are you paying attention? Do you know about different kettles of fish?"

"Yes."

"With them I couldn't bear to lose an argument. I could say I was sorry, let's say, for accidentally breaking a window with a baseball I'd hit in our yard, but couldn't admit I was ever wrong on any issue I argued about with them even if I didn't know a thing about it. The thought of losing to them was too humiliating and I wouldn't acknowledge it."

She nodded. "That's awful. I mean that's really sad."

There were a few seconds of silence and she found herself reviewing (pointlessly she realized) her meeting with him at the bar to see if there were some clue she missed. But she couldn't find it. It had all been, unfortunately, typical one-night-stand behavior from both of them. He was a normal looking guy in his early thirties, kind of attractive if a little pudgy—but still attractive enough. The sex had been nothing unusual either. Despite her drinking she'd even remembered to fake her orgasm. It was odd. She'd begun the night feeling sorry for herself, thinking about her stupid job and that when she went to the bar she would find nothing again or a man that would end up being nothing and that she certainly wasn't getting younger, but now she worried that it would be her last night because the man (who said his name was Greg) appeared to have no conscience or empathy at all.

"Stop thinking."

"What?"

"I can hear your thoughts so stop thinking them."

She wondered, could he? Perhaps he had special powers which accounted for the way he thought and acted.

"Listen, I would get off your arms if I felt I could trust you to be still and quiet."

"I will."

"No, I don't think you would. So far you've taken every opportunity I've given you to make as much noise as possible."

"What can I do to make you trust me?"

"You should have thought of that earlier."

"What do you mean?"

But he didn't answer her question, increasing the pressure on her arms instead.

"Jesus Christ do you realize what you're doing to me?" she blurted, and then immediately regretted saying it. On the one hand she wanted him to realize, hoping he might have an attack of conscience and let her go, but on the other, stronger hand, if he really realized what he was doing he would worry about her calling the police later and could feel the need, very possibly, to kill her like a bug.

"I ask you the same question," he suddenly said, as he stared at her intensely.

"Did you realize what you were doing to me? Did you? Do you? Did you even have a clue who I was when you decided to sleep with me? Think about it."

"I knew you as well as you knew me," she said, thinking it was sometimes better to challenge him, sometimes better to appease him and say exactly what he wanted to hear, though she'd been trying out different responses and nothing had really worked so far.

"But you were the aggressor. You have to acknowledge that."

"Yes. OK I was."

"So what was your plan for me? To use me like a piece of gum. Just take the flavor out of me and then spit me out?"

"No."

"But you have no interest in me at all. That's obvious by all the sighing and crying and eye rolling you've done once I started to talk."

"I'm crying because you're hurting me, and are still hurting me. I would have enjoyed talking, I still would enjoy talking with you and listening to you if you'd just stop hurting and scaring me."

"I don't think so. I think that's a lie like all the rest of this evening."

"You see? You won't give me a chance," she said, her cheeks turning red with frustration as she started to cry.

"Shut up. Stop crying. I find it personally offensive when you cry."

She tried to stop but the effort made her choke and cough.

"Whenever I would corner my mother and confront her with something she'd done to hurt me, she'd start crying or coughing or choking or monologing about some unrelated issue, anything to avoid saying she was sorry and wrong."

"I am sorry. I was wrong."

"Tell me what you were wrong about?"

She hesitated. She knew she had to be extra careful about what she said now.

"Stop hesitating," he said. "Whenever you're hesitating I know that you're lying and faking and I hate lies."

"I was wrong to go to bed with you so soon when I barely knew you."

"Less that an hour by my count."

"Yes. I was wrong to do that."

"Why did you?" he asked, with a little smile. He was strangely complicated, insisting on the truth on one hand and extreme flattery on the other.

"I couldn't help myself."

"Why? What about me made you lose control?"

"Just how handsome you are, how sexy your voice is."

"Was it just my voice?"

"No, of course not. How well you spoke, the way you touched me and kissed me in the bar. It was everything about you. I knew you'd be a great lover."

"And were your suspicions correct? Was I a great lover?"

"You were the best lover I've ever had in my life by far."

He eased the pressure on her arms, though he still held her hands firmly as he slid down a little on the bed.

"You see, now that you've told the truth I've decided to stop hurting you. That was the truth wasn't it?"

"Every word of it."

"Because earlier in the night I thought you were faking. I thought you were trying to make a fool of me."

"I don't know why you thought that."

"Because I've made it my business to study the female anatomy and yours didn't seem to be responding in bed the way you claimed."

"I know what I felt."

"I wonder…so what you told me about what kind of lover I am is the truth?"

"Yes."

"Can you swear to it?"

"Yes."

"No, say 'I meant it with all my heart.'"

"I meant it and mean it with all my heart."

"And soul."

"And soul."

"It doesn't matter anyway. It's too late," he said, still sitting on top of her. She guessed he weighed fifty more pounds than her, maybe seventy.

"What's too late? I don't understand."

"Everything's too late. Too late for you, too late for me. Too late for us."

"What do you mean? What are you saying?"

"We have the same disease, you know what that disease is, don't you? It's the vanity disease. We have it, and turn to it just like people turn to sex and drugs and whatever…God, religion all of it, wouldn't you say?"

"Yes," she said. She was panicking again and his words made no sense to her. She thought she could feel her face turn paper white. "That's very wise," she said. "So when you speak about it being too late for me it's like a way of saying that it's too late for me to love someone, that's what you mean, right?"

He smiled. "Oh I see. You're wondering what I'm going to do about your life. You're really wondering about whether I'm going to end your life or not."

"No, what are you talking about? I…"

"Don't lie to me," he said, raising his voice. "Given what you are and the way you think, it's understandable that you would want your little life to continue. It's all part of the vanity disease. Just think, God may or may not know or care about what's happening to you, God may or may not exist, but I exist and I can decide what happens to you. Maybe you should start praying to me."

"Pray to you. Is that what you want?"

"Yes, I'd like to hear it."

"Now?"

"Yes, now."

"But how can I pray without my hands?"

"What do you mean?"

"I need to clasp my hands together to pray, don't you?"

"I don't pray. I wouldn't know."

"That's how I pray, that's how I have to do it. So if…"

"Listen, if I want you to pray you'll pray the way I tell you to. OK?"

"OK."

Then he suddenly moved down her body some more, setting her arms and hands free.

"See I've already granted one of your prayers, haven't I?"

"Yes, you did. Thank you."

"Now get on your knees and keep your hands together and pray to me."

"Now?" she said weakly. She was feeling strangely passive and yet self-conscious about her nudity, especially her skinny breasts that she felt drooped too much for a woman in her twenties. That and the unfortunate tattoos on her bottom.

"Now, come on let's hear you do it on your knees, right now on the floor. And no funny business, either."

"Out loud?"

"Yes, out loud to me. You're the one who says you pray. I want to hear it."

"Dear God…" She looked at her knees on the carpet, her hands clenched tightly together and thought she was dreaming.

"Dear God, what? Come on, pray for what you really want. And pray to me, Greg, not to God, OK? We agreed on that."

"Greg, I pray that..."

"It's dear Greg."

"Dear Greg, I pray that you...I pray that you will let me live."

She couldn't say anymore, her teeth were chattering and she found it impossible to talk. Meanwhile he was staring at her with a curious expression on his face.

"OK. Get up. We're going now."

"What?"

"Was there something unclear about what I said? We're going now. Right now."

"Are you going to shoot me?" she blurted. She was still shaking.

"No more questions. Come on."

She reached for her panties but he grabbed her wrist and held it hard.

"Just your overcoat. That's all you'll wear. Got it?"

"Where are we going? What are you going to do with me?"

"No more questions. I mean it. Come on. I'll lead, you follow. I'll talk and you listen and do what I say. Got it? Just, trust in Greg, OK?"

She noticed that he was picking up her clothes, her skirt, silk shirt, panties and high heels—while watching her at the same time the way some men fish, and carry on a conversation with their eyes turned away from the water. Then he started putting on his clothes, still watching her every second.

"What are you doing with my clothes?"

"Didn't you hear me?"

"Why can't I have my clothes?"

"Because we're doing things my way. Trust in Greg, remember?"

"No, I won't go without them," she said.

"Yes, you will," he said, reaching into his sport jacket pocket, some kind of hidden inner pocket she hadn't noticed, and removing a gun. She felt herself reel as if he'd just hit her again. It was the first time she'd seen it. Then she remembered that a few minutes ago she'd asked him if he were going to shoot her so maybe she had seen it before or somehow sensed that he had it. Perhaps he'd even showed it to her when they were drunk, before it all started.

"You will do things my way, if you want to keep doing things at all. Got it?"

She nodded, then got up from the floor she wasn't even aware she'd been sitting on.

"Now listen to me. You're going to go out the door, then down the steps and straight to my car. I'll have the gun aimed at your back the whole time and I'll also be holding your hand, hard, like this. Got it? So, no funny business. One yell for help, one foolish scream and you will be shot and permanently silenced."

"Yes, yes. I'll do whatever you say."

"Now open the door." She could feel the gun on her back, hear his breath in her ear as she had in bed less than an hour ago. They'd been in a plain one-bedroom walk-up on the first floor. It was all so convenient for him, she thought, wondering now if this place so far out of town were actually some kind of motel.

"Can I put on my shoes?" she asked softly.

"I told you to shut up about your shoes. You won't die from hurt feet," he said, moving one of his arms around her waist as if to be sure her raincoat wouldn't open.

It had rained while they were inside as it had threatened to all day. She could feel the wet sidewalk on her feet. She walked straight ahead as she was told. She felt she could hear him move his head to check both sides of the street and couldn't resist looking quickly herself but there was only one person within shouting distance and he soon disappeared around a corner.

"OK," he said, opening the door. "Get in the car now."

She got in on the driver's side, the steering wheel digging briefly into her ribs.

"Now put your seat belt on," he said, after he closed the door. "We wouldn't want anything to happen to you, would we?"

What did he mean? Did he mean he wouldn't want a car accident to happen with her not wearing a seat belt, or did he mean something else? She thought he was deliberately talking in riddles to torture her.

He drove with the gun in his left hand and his right hand on the steering wheel. She'd wondered if images from her past would start to parade in front of her, then thought they wouldn't because her past was even skinnier than she was. Nothing but routines and disappointments. But then without seeing any particular image, she started feeling that her life had been rich, after all, especially before she started sleeping with men and that even that part with all the bars had a strange beauty to it.

She could tell that he was driving well out of the city. It was getting more and more quiet with fewer and fewer lights. He took so many turns and took them with such authority that she felt sure he'd done this drive before.

"You never cared about me or took an interest in me," he said, "just like all the rest."

It was her cue to flatter him, she knew, but she couldn't speak. All her life she'd flattered men and this is where it landed her. She wouldn't do it anymore, nor would she beg. She closed her eyes and felt that richness comfort her again.

"It doesn't matter. We were just two strangers in the night, you and me. Two fires that will burn apart forever. You'll never see me again. This isn't even my car and I don't really live anywhere near you."

She didn't answer, just stared straight ahead thinking suddenly of her mother's face.

He turned the car and they seemed to enter a world of huge trees and darkness. For a few miles they rode in silence until he finally spoke.

"Ever see *Blair Witch Project*?"

"No. Yes," she said.

"This woods is like that woods. But you'll find your way out, eventually. High heels won't do you much good though, neither will walking. I recommend you wait till morning when you can see where you're going. By then I'll be far away in another world so don't even think of calling the police. Besides, what could you tell them anyway?"

He stopped the car suddenly.

"OK. Open the door and start walking."

"You're not gong to shoot me, are you? You're not going to shoot me in the back?"

"No, I want you to live because you'll never forget me, will you? I'm burned into you forever, aren't I?"

"No, I'll never forget you," she said. Then, trembling, she opened the door and ran out into the blackness of the woods.

He backed out and drove away, she could hear the car leave, but she kept running anyway. Then after a minute or two, when she started bruising her toes, she stopped, panting so loud it was like a kind of singing. When that stopped it was completely black and she was wet and alone, waiting for the light of morning when the world would begin. "I'm not dead," she thought. "I'm not dead at all. Something completely different is about to happen."

Mercury

There was a party in TriBeCa, what Larry thought would be the same group of writers his age or older complaining and consoling each other. The party's host, Aaron Reisman, once had a brief flurry of success with his metafictionist stories, but that had all ended years ago. In fact, Aaron had already, in his own words, "surrendered" to his "bad karma" and now wrote only for an hour or two every other weekend. His one enduring piece of good fortune was the loft he'd bought cheap in the late '70s, which, of course, had now sky-rocketed in value. Every year, shortly before Christmas, he'd have a party in his loft for the writers and sympathizers in his circle who all brought wine or whiskey (Aaron somehow constructed the dip), and each year the humor got a little more desperate and bitter.

Until the last minute, Larry thought that this year he'd skip the party. He was in a writing slump, badly stalled on a novel he'd been working on since his book of stories had been published three years ago. Moreover, he was out of fulltime work now, wholly reliant on substitute teaching to make money. Under the circumstances, with all that was on his mind, how could he stand to go to Aaron's party? Still, there was one reason to consider going. He'd heard a rumor that Kenneth Alters would be there. Initially he'd dismissed it as an attempt of Aaron's to ensure a good crowd or maybe a fantasy of one of the guests. Why would a young, glamorous writer/celebrity like Kenneth Alters attend such a scruffy affair? Yet, such things did happen in New York and he couldn't discount it. The more he thought about meeting Alters, perhaps even being able to befriend him and all that might mean, the harder it got to stay home. Finally, he drank a glass of vodka and soda water, then selected a pair of jeans and a purple wool sweater, trying not to look overly concerned about his clothes but not wholly unattractive either. Then, before he'd gotten halfway to the elevator, he went back to his apartment to get a copy of his book of stories, and his knife. He'd been mugged by three teenagers a few months ago and, without telling anyone, had bought a large pocket knife which he generally took with him now whenever he went out at night.

There were dark clouds outside and he nearly ran from the corner liquor store (where he bought a bottle of gin for the party) to the train stop. On the train to TriBeCa he spent the whole trip thinking about Kenneth Alters' sudden and stunning success.

An elevator led directly to Aaron's loft on the fourth floor where Larry was greeted by the familiar scene of men mostly on the edge of middle age in their de rigueur minimalist dress of jeans and tee shirts, men who still looked puzzled as to why their stomachs were sticking out and their hair lines receding, holding their drinks while they talked to each other or to the mostly younger women they were with. But the loud laughter and quasi-hysterical talk that usually filled the air was strangely muted. Larry thought that it was like a theater shortly before the lights dimmed. The glances were mostly directed toward the punch bowl in the right side center of the loft where Kenneth Alters, looking infuriatingly as good as his photographs, was standing alone, cool and self-contained in a gray suit and baby-blue tie.

Immediately Larry went to the bar, about twenty feet behind Alters, and fixed himself a vodka tonic, leaving his bottle of gin on an adjacent table. When he looked up again, Alters was still standing alone. In a bizarre (yet somehow predictable) gesture of collective insecurity or perverse pride, the other guests were pretending not to pay any attention to Alters, although, period-ically, everyone in the room was actually looking at him. What provincial idiots they are, Larry thought. Someone a little famous comes to their party, and immediately he paralyzes the room. He drank his vodka quickly, deciding that the less he thought about what to say to Alters, the better. He would simply tell him that he admired his work (he had only allowed himself to read a single story of Alters', which he'd considered more precious than precocious) and then at some point tell him about his own book, hopefully giving him the paperback copy he'd brought. It was imagining all the consequences (that never happened anyway) and giving time for anxieties to multiply that intimidated people.

When Larry finished his drink he began walking directly toward Alters, then seeing that he was talking with Aaron, he went to get another vodka from the bar. With his new drink in hand he looked out at the rest of the loft and soon noticed an attractive brunette, a poet he'd spoken to for a few minutes at a couple of downtown parties. For some reason, probably because of his fixation with his former lover Debby, he'd never called her and couldn't even remember her name. Was it Jama, Janette, Janine? Anyway, it was "J" something, so he thought of her as Lady J. She was talking to Morty, a forty-something writer who dressed like a hippie and wrote simple-minded parable-like stories—a third-rate Brautigan. Lady J, wearing a very nicely cut black dress, looked like she was humoring Morty. Larry began to move toward her but before he could make any meaningful progress he was stopped by a less attractive woman, a redhead with darting, almost comically intense green eyes.

Gesturing slightly with her head, she said, "Is that who I think it is?"

"That's Kenneth Alters, himself."

She looked perplexed and astonished. She was overly dressed, Larry thought, and was wearing too much makeup and jewelry.

"Wasn't he on the cover of *People* last week?"

"He wasn't on the cover, but they did a story on him," Larry said.

"Yeah, that's right. It was about this three-picture movie deal he signed. God, can you imagine being that successful at his age and that rich, if you can believe the story."

"Normally, I don't read those kinds of magazines but since I'm a writer myself, I was curious to see what they'd say. It's so rare that they do an article about a writer."

"You write novels, too?"

"Yes, and short stories."

"Do I know your name?"

"Larry James."

Larry watched her studying him skeptically for a few seconds as if he might be lying about being a writer. The thought made him bristle and he finished his second drink. She looked like a poor man's Lucille Ball anyway, he thought.

"So have you met Alters yet?"

"No, I haven't."

"Oh," she said with what Larry thought was obvious disappointment. "I was going to ask you to introduce me, but what the hell, he's just a person. I can introduce myself. After I've had a couple of drinks," she said, laughing loudly. Larry tried to suppress his anger while he waited for her laughter to subside, then excused himself, still keeping his eyes on Alters who was giving Aaron a lot of time.

He went to the bar and fixed himself a new vodka tonic. It was strange to think that just three years ago Alters was completely unknown. That's when his first book of stories had gotten both extraordinary reviews and sales. A host of articles with pictures of the young, golden-haired writer began appearing everywhere as if he were a movie star. Of course, Alters' youth (he was only twenty-five, ten years younger than Larry) was used to help promote him as a phenomenon. That and the brilliant way Alters himself marketed his California friendliness. Surprisingly, his antisnobbism was seen, even by cynical New Yorkers, not as disingenuous but as refreshing. At the time Larry reassured himself that his own first collection, published the same year, had also gotten some very good, thoughtful reviews, though his small press publisher could hardly compete with Alters' major New York house in getting anything like the amount of attention Alters got. Still he could at least consider himself a part of the same general literary universe. But when Alters' novel, published just last year, eclipsed the success of his first book and became a bestseller, everything changed. Now at twenty-eight, Alters really did inhabit a different literary and social world. He'd been on late-night talk shows, there were articles speculating that he might act in one of the movies that he was writing, and in an interview with the *Times* he expressed an interest in directing. Could one doubt it would happen? When he moved to New York and bought a loft in SoHo, *New York Magazine* wrote about it. Columbia University immediately signed him to teach one hour a week for who knows how much money, and seemingly every university or writers' series in the city wanted him to read or lecture—offers that Alters kept accepting. To top it off, despite his bestseller, Alters had actually increased his involvement in *Mercury*, the young literary magazine of which he'd been West Coast editor and which had also enjoyed a quick rise in status. It was as if he couldn't bear to let go of anything in his impeccable resume, and now that he'd moved to New York, where the magazine was published, he'd become associate editor, and the main fiction editor as well.

Larry finished his drink and noticed that Alters was finally alone, but Aaron had spotted Larry and was smiling broadly as if he wanted a witness to congratulate him on his social coup.

"Glad you came, Larry," Aaron said as they shook hands.

"How could I miss this?" he said, gesturing toward Alters, who was still alone.

"How's it going these days? Nobody ever sees you anymore."

"I need a job for one thing. Substitute teaching is all I've got now."

"I'll definitely let you know if I hear of anything. How's Debby? Are you two together by any chance?"

Larry looked away for a moment. "No, we're not. So how's Kenneth Alters?"

"Very nice."

"I guess I'll pay him my humble respects now."

"By all means, you'll enjoy him."

"Then I'll talk to you later," he said, patting Aaron on the shoulder.

"Good luck," Aaron said, smiling even more broadly than before.

Alters, whose wavy blonde hair reached to the tops of his shoulders, looked to be consulting his watch. Was he planning an early exit, already regretting that he'd attended this nebulous event?

"Excuse me, I'm Larry James," he said, shaking Alters' hand. "Like everyone else, I admire your work a great deal and I'm glad you've come to New York."

"Thank you, Larry," he said with his by now famous smile, long lashes shading twinkling eyes.

"It must be a very exciting time for you."

"It's been busy more than anything. I've certainly spent more time with agents, lawyers, and interior decorators than I've ever wanted to."

"You've become an event."

Alters laughed and took a sip from a drink that Larry hadn't noticed.

"I understand that you're also becoming more involved with *Mercury*."

"That's true, too."

"The magazine is really hot these days. It keeps getting terrific publicity."

"I hope I don't jinx it."

"I don't think that there's much chance of that. You're the main reason it's so successful."

Alters looked at him more seriously for a moment. "I don't think so, but thanks again. Are you a writer by any chance?"

"Yes, I am. I published a first collection of stories with a small press the same year you published your first book. And I'm working on a novel."

"What's the name of your book?"

Larry looked down at the floor for a second. "Rights of the Moon...and Other Stories," he said spelling out the word "Rights." "It was done by a small press and..."

Alters knit his eyebrows for a moment.

"I'm sorry I don't know it, but I'll try to get a copy."

"It's a pretty weird title but..."

"Don't apologize. I like it. It sounds different from so many other collections that come out these days." Alters turned to the vodka punch bowl. "Want a drink?" he said. "It's not bad stuff."

Larry thanked him and took a new drink, thinking that Alters was being pretty decent—though he didn't like the words "Don't apologize." Christ, Alters was almost young enough to be his student, yet there he was being subtly patronizing. He took a big sip of punch and asked Alters what he would be doing now at *Mercury*.

"Reading lots of fiction."

"I wonder why you feel the need…" And then, seeing Alters' face tighten, Larry quickly added, "Or have the time when your own writing is so successful."

"It's something I've always cared about and enjoyed doing. I've always been involved in literary magazines. At least since high school. Maybe it's my kind of security blanket."

"And you still need it, successful as you are?" Larry said, trying to control the edge in his voice.

"You can never have too much security, can you?"

"So you're going to be the main fiction editor, then?"

"That's what they tell me."

"Any changes you plan to make? Anything in particular you're looking for?"

"Umm…I guess, as the cliche says, every editor likes to make discoveries."

"So you plan to publish fewer famous people then?"

The tightness reappeared in Alters' eyes.

"I mean, in the past *Mercury* has published a lot of famous people, and now you'll be looking for unknowns?"

"The famous people will not entirely disappear, but we will be looking to showcase more unknown talent."

"Does unknown mean young?"

"I'm not sure I follow you."

"Take me for instance. I was young once and unknown and now, as you can see, I've gotten older, I'm sure I've got at least ten years on you, but I did publish this one book in a small edition and it did get some good reviews, some of them as good as the reviews you got, even, and some of the stories in this book had been published in pretty good literary magazines, too. So do I qualify as an unknown or am I just a little too old to qualify and so fall somewhere between the cracks?"

He was aware that he was rambling, that something unpleasantly aggressive was happening when he spoke, but he couldn't seem to stop it.

"I'd be interested in seeing anything that's good published in *Mercury*."

This seemed unsatisfactorily evasive and Larry felt stung. Perhaps he should force the issue and give him the copy of his book now.

"Well, assuming you mean it, maybe I'll take you at your word and send something your way."

"You seem skeptical."

"Skeptical?"

"And a little cynical."

"Like I say, I've been around awhile and I've seen this kind of thing."

"What thing is this?"

"Some new young person comes along who gets sensational press, signs a big book deal and then figures it's smart to do something 'altruistic,' fears there might be some kind of backlash of resentment otherwise and so gets nominally involved in a project that's supposed to help young writers. Like Norman Mailer starting the *Village Voice*. It happens all the time."

"Well, I'm not 'some young person.' I'm a real person just like you are and I do care about writing by young people and older people, but I don't think I like the way this conversation's going."

"What's wrong with the conversation?"

"It seems tense and a little angry and also aimed at making me acknowledge some dark crime of hideous self-interest. Outside of that, nothing."

"Look, I'm just a hard-working writer trying to get somewhere and not succeeding very well," Larry said, looking slightly to the left of Alters while he spoke. "I don't even have a job or a girlfriend and I meet someone like you, which doesn't happen very often, and I hear you talk about helping unknowns and I wonder how you could know at your age what it means to be unknown, to struggle year after year in bad living conditions. I mean a bug-infested, heat-saturated apartment like I live in where you can hear your neighbor's answering machine, hear his toilet flush 'cause the walls are so thin, and meanwhile people are selling crack in my neighborhood and on any given night I can get mugged like I was two months ago so that now when I go out I have to carry a knife."

"Do I need to know all of this to be the fiction editor of a literary magazine?"

"I just wonder, if you want to help young writers so much why don't you finance a magazine instead and let some talented lesser-known writers edit it."

"Like you?"

"No, not at all. Though I would know certain things about how to deal with unknown writers, especially the older ones who've been doing good work for a long time. What they've been through...and how to treat them. But, what I'm really wondering about is, if the world's given somebody everything right away, how can they judge others?"

"You do a fair amount of judging yourself, as far as I can see. Excuse me," Alters said, turning away.

"Don't blow me off like I'm a fly, like I don't exist. Why don't you stay and talk?"

But Alters had already left him and was surrounded by a semi-circle of people, some of whom were giving Larry funny looks. How loud had he been talking? How many people had heard him practically begging Alters to talk to him? The loft had snapped back into view, and he saw again the grotesque ballet of the guests as they assumed their strategic positions around Alters like so many little birds along the shoreline waiting, small and stupid and squawking, for something they hoped the next wave would deliver.

Larry turned back to the punch bowl and poured himself another drink, keeping his back to them. He finished the drink in four bitter swallows, then fixed himself another and drank it only a little more slowly.

Walking a few steps away from the people around Alters he closed his eyes. What had happened to him, why was he shaking in anger? It was as if he'd always felt this way, but that couldn't be true. He knew he was happy the day his book was accepted, but that was followed by so many days of anxiety trying to help market it and get it reviewed that he'd nearly sunk under the weight of it. No, the kind of happiness he was trying to remember was all bound up with women, especially Debby, but that was too painful to think about now. Suddenly he turned around, his eyes focusing immediately on Alters who was talking to Lady J, the brunette poet he'd fantasized about going out with. She was smiling almost as wide as Alters was, eating up his words as if listening to him were a kind of sex act that gave her ultimate gratification.

When he first started talking to Alters he'd figured he had an inch on him and simply by being older was probably more muscular, though with the loose clothes Alters wore, it was hard to tell what kind of body he had. Now as he walked toward him, he knew he was taller and bigger than Alters.

"Why did you walk away from me? Why did you insult me?" he said loudly, forcing Alters' conversation with Lady J to stop. He kept his eyes on Alters, who looked startled, profoundly disrupted, in fact. Lady J's mouth was open, and she, too, looked deeply confused.

"It's you who insulted me. Why don't you just leave me alone?"

"I want to know why you won't finish what we were talking about, man to man." Some more people had stopped talking and had begun gathering around them, including the overdressed redhead with the glaring green eyes.

"There isn't anything more I want to say to you."

"But you insulted me, and then..."

"Look, I don't want to spend any more time with you, that's all."

A worried-looking Aaron appeared in front of him.

"Come on Larry, stop it. You've had too much to drink. You're drunk."

He'd put an arm around his shoulder, but Larry threw it off. He remembered his knife then, felt it folded in his jacket pocket, thought he could feel it pressing, cold and heavy, against his flesh. Then he stepped forward and pushed Alters' shoulders. "You condescending little bitch."

Alters went back a couple of steps and the guests gasped. When Alters came back he threw a punch which grazed Aaron, who'd stepped between them again, in the neck. Aaron let out a yowl of pain but managed to grab Larry in a bear hug.

"You jealous jerk, are you out of your mind?" Alters said, teeth flashing.

"Come outside and fight me," Larry said in a voice he hadn't used since his playground fights twenty-five years ago.

"Please, Larry, stop it," Aaron said. Larry saw fear in Aaron's eyes and let himself be led away, a few feet at a time, while Aaron kept saying softly, pleadingly, "Just go home and rest Larry; you're drunk, go home and rest."

At the elevator door Larry turned and pointed at Alters but Alters had turned his back to him. Before he could yell again Aaron said "Please," his sad middle-aged brown eyes looking desperate. "Get in the elevator. Go home and you'll feel better."

Larry took a deep breath.

"I'm sorry for this," he said. "Really sorry."

"Just go home. Call me tomorrow if you want," Aaron added before the elevator doors closed.

"Are you all right?" she said, an unintentional parody of concern on her face.

Alters looked around in an exaggerated manner at himself to try to make her laugh, then said, "As far as I know."

"Why did that maniac attack you?" she said, brushing a few recalcitrant strands of dark hair from her forehead, then rearranging her dress to make her breasts more prominent. Alters simply shook his head while she introduced herself as Janice.

"I'm Kenneth Alters," he said, shaking her hand.

"Of course, everyone knows who you are."

"As for my assailant, I have no idea. I was going to ask you. Is he a maniac or maybe he just drank too much and is angry at some image he's projected onto me."

"I've seen him at parties before. He tried to hit on me once but he didn't get anywhere," she said, trying to align her eyes with his.

"Well, nobody's punches landed though I'm afraid one of mine hit…" He paused, unsure if the host's name was Arthur, Arnold, or Aaron. "…the man who organized the party."

"Yes, wasn't that awful, I mean, awfully bad luck? But I'm sure he's all right."

"Oh, of course, I'm hardly Mike Tyson."

"In fact, here he is now."

Rather than guess from the trinity of names, Alters stepped forward and shook Aaron's hand. "Sorry that you caught my right hook. Obviously it wasn't meant for you."

Aaron, uncertain if Alters meant to be funny, was temporarily paralyzed between a laugh and an apology.

"I'm sorry that all this happened to you—when we all feel so lucky that you came here."

Alters winced and tuned out the remains of Aaron's tribute. He waited for an appropriate moment to lighten things up, but before he could a number of people began introducing themselves to him and shaking his hand. It was going to take a lot longer than he thought to get out of here.

The people who talked to him all exaggerated his virtues and strengths as much as that freak, Larry, diminished them. But in his forced courtesies to them he realized that his behavior was distorted as well. That's how fame distorts everyone in its orbit, he thought, chastising himself mildly for his habit of thinking in aphorisms. Christ, can't any of these people see I'm real?

"Why was that man, Larry, I think his name is…"

"Yes, Larry," Aaron said, glad to be of use.

"Why was he so angry at me?" Alters asked.

"He's just in a funk right now," Aaron said. "And he was drinking and for some stupid reason took it out on you. I'm sure he feels terrible about it already and will probably write you an elaborate apology in the morning."

"Is his life really as pathetic as it sounds?"

"When he's drinking, he thinks it is. But really, he's published a good amount of work, more than most of us, and he's got some good reviews, too. He does have some money problems right now, and he's a little insecure, but nothing he hasn't dealt with before."

"He mentioned something about not having a girlfriend."

"Maybe not now," Morty said, joining the conversation. "But he'll have one again soon."

"Well, the paradox of human motivation. Why did the not-so-young man attack me? In creative writing class, we're told to provide our characters with motivation, but it's always more mysterious in life, isn't it?"

"Amen," Morty said. Alters then asked if there was a phone he might use and Aaron directed him to one in the bedroom portion of the loft. On the way, Alters grabbed an abandoned drink by the punch bowl. Maybe he should have reassured Larry, or expressed an interest in his work, and all the ugliness could have been avoided. God, the guests had actually succeeded in making him feel guilty. Larry had started the fight and now they had him doubting himself. That's the thing about sycophants, he thought, as he closed the door to the room. They meant to make you feel totally supported but because you couldn't believe anything they said, you believed the opposite of what they said or you at least read between the lines and they ended up making you feel worse. Of course, there was no way for him to talk honestly with them, either, and that was the only thing that could make him feel better. It would shock them to know the kind of pain he was in, how on the edge he really was living, he thought with a bitter laugh as he sat down on the bed.

He decided he'd better call Tommy before he began to pity himself too much. With Tommy—an unemployed actor he'd met a few weeks ago and who'd become his first boyfriend—he could at least be quasi-honest. It was funny, when his interest in women began to fade he used to get relief from drinking but now, when he was trying to make a big decision, was on the verge of making it, instead of bringing relief, it just made everything worse. Things weren't simple, either, the way Tommy tried to make them seem. There was a lot to lose, and people who said it was fashionable now, at least in New York, were lying or deluding themselves. His fiction, his audience, his image were all straight and there was even serious talk of his getting one of the romantic leads in the next movie in his deal. How would everyone react to him as a gay writing star? Was there really such a creature today in supposedly enlightened America? Yet he felt he had to do it and sooner rather than later. Tommy was probably right about that.

It wasn't until the sixth ring that Tommy answered: another childish trick to make him jealous? Alters cursed himself for giving him the key to his loft so soon, especially now that sex with him was only intermittently successful.

"Hi. I was just about to give up on you."

"Sorry, I was outside. It's snowing out! It's amazingly pretty, delicate snow, and I was just coming in when the phone rang. How are you?"

"Not tremendously good. I'm also more than a little high or low."

"Oh, I thought you said you didn't do that at parties."

"It's not a normal party."

"I told you you should have brought me with you."

"No, it's a normal party, almost all of the people are normal and all of them are straight, but this one frustrated macho writer in his late 30s started in on me about *Mercury*. Very sarcastic and nasty."

"He probably has the hots for you and doesn't even know it."

"I doubt it."

"The strain of your secret life is probably making you touchy, then."

"Anyway, he started a fight with me."

"Verbal?"

"No, physical."

"Are you all right?"

"Everyone's all right. It was broken up very quickly. I threw one punch and hit the host...by accident."

Tommy laughed for a second. "I told you I should go with you. Why are you so afraid of going to a party with me? Don't go without me again, OK?"

"OK," he said softly.

"When are you coming back? I miss you. I have the hots for you too."

"Tonight would be a very poor night for that."

"I didn't necessarily mean sex. I just want to see you and have fun with you."

Alters sighed. What a child Tommy was, albeit an adorable one.

"Did I say something wrong again, am I exasperating you?"

"No, no. I'm under a lot of pressure, that's all. I have to do an impossible amount of work."

"And keep up an impossible image."

"That's true too."

"No wonder."

"What? No wonder I can't 'do it' so well these days?"

"No, never mind. Just 'no wonder.' Just come home."

"So what is it you want to do so much if you don't expect to have sex?"

"There're lots of things to do. We could go outside and play in the snow. If it starts snowing harder, like it's supposed to, we could build a snowman together. How about that? Wouldn't you like to help me build a snowman?"

Janice wasn't going to give up that easily. You didn't meet a Kenneth Alters every day, you didn't meet a Kenneth Alters in ten years, even in New York—not in her circle. And it was all going so promisingly. He was definitely looking at her breasts when that Larry moron made his psychotic bid for 15 minutes of party fame. Pathetic.

She thought of all the dreary readings, receptions, and parties she'd gone to faithfully over the years since she'd moved to New York from Florida. They said it was a golden time for women but men still held almost all the power positions in literary publishing. You still needed a male protector or male allies, but since she hadn't done an MFA, she'd missed the male teachers available at a writing program, and at the parties all she'd met were a couple of poetry editors from really little magazines, one of whom she stupidly talked herself into sleeping with. But nothing like *Mercury*, nothing like Alters, who knew everyone in New York and who could get more or less anyone published if he endorsed them. She moved closer to the room where Alters was still on the phone and clenched her teeth. She saw the redhead who'd been trying to angle into her conversation with Alters before. She had her hair done up like Lucille Ball, and Janice gave her a dirty look. It's not a costume party, Lucy, she wanted to say, so why don't you drop the wig and clown makeup and try another approach. Pathetic. Janice kept her post directly in front of the door and turned her head away from Lucy. There was no reason now, nor any space, for Lucy to either cut in front of her or wait—no hope of conversation, either, as Janice had made plain, and eventually Lucy slunk away. Meanwhile, Janice had another drink and waited.

When Alters emerged from the bedroom, he had a look of purpose in his eyes that was temporarily disrupted when Janice stepped towards him.

"Hello again," she said, feeling immediately after he said hello back that he wanted to leave this foolish party as soon as possible.

"You were such a good sport to put up with that twit..."

For a moment Alters looked puzzled.

"You know, the jerk who attacked you."

"Oh, yes," Alters said smiling. "I'd forgotten about him and wasn't sure who you were talking about for a moment."

She laughed to show her empathy. "I meant to say it was generous of you to stay on at the party the way you did. I'm sure it meant a lot to the people here."

"Thank you."

"I know it was a thrill for me to meet you."

He thanked her again. Somewhat to his surprise, he felt the first stirring of an erection. Life was so complicated, he thought with a smile, as his eyes drifted down towards her breasts. Which, now that he thought about it, he'd enjoyed looking at before.

He managed to simultaneously keep talking to her, validate his erection, and do some quick thinking. From many parties before this one, he'd developed the technique of doing some of his most serious thinking while talking about completely unrelated things. He was wondering if she was the one who could end his sexual drought with women. More to the point, could he really afford to pass up the chance to find out with all it would mean to him professionally and personally? She certainly knew how to talk sweetly to him, and, at least with women, he found their flattery was the most effective aphrodisiac, far more effective than pot, although delightful in combination with it. With Tommy, he was very rarely flattered; in fact, Tommy seemed to delight in thwarting him that way. He also didn't like the way his conversation with Tommy had ended and was still angry that Tommy had let the phone ring so many times before answering. Why didn't the answering machine pick up as it was programmed to do after four rings? Another trick of Tommy's to make him jealous? Or perhaps Tommy wasn't really out in the snow but was spreading his legs for some new stud he'd found in a bar, Alters thought, and getting back at me for not being invited to the party while risking my health, my life, in the process—the stupid, sex-addicted little prick.

She was telling him about her poetry now, then about her home state of Florida. She was awkward and naive, but trainable and definitely appealing. He made a few comments, asked a question, and before he knew it, she was telling him how magnificent the ending of his novel was, which made his erection stiffen another degree, until it reached its maximum potential.

She was definitely opportunity incarnate, and he decided he should certainly explore it—or try to. He could do that and still get back to Tommy tonight if he handled the situation right.

"You look like you're thinking about something real serious," she said.

"No, only that I was wondering if I'd stayed here long enough to be polite, so I could leave now."

"Oh."

"And also, if you'd like to leave, too, and go someplace else with me?"

Her crestfallen look of a moment ago was replaced by a wide smile.

"Yes, I'd like that. Where would you like to go?"

"Oh, anywhere with you would be fun, I think," he said, and then drawing her close to him, kissed her a little more than briefly on the lips.

"What's your apartment like? Is it far away?" he said, after they separated. She already looked flushed, and he was encouraged. Perhaps she was one of those women who came very quickly.

"No, it's in the village. We could go there, though it's a mess right now," she said. "I just need to get my coat."

"Fine, marvelous," he said, smiling, before he realized that he needed to get his own coat as well.

Was it in the elevator that he got his idea? He couldn't be sure as he stood behind the dumpster, on the street just to the left of the entrance to Aaron's loft. On the elevator, he seemed to have no memories, he was just a shape falling then, and now he felt his whole body again as he crouched behind the dumpster watching the door. It was dark and cold but he felt no change of temperature or light while he waited, was even unaware of the snowflakes falling lightly but steadily on him as he crouched.

He thought he wouldn't have to wait long. After their fight how could Alters bear to stay there for any length of time? On the other hand, he couldn't really leave right away. Impeccable diplomat that he was, Alters would wait ten or fifteen minutes to show that he was not only unafraid but unruffled. But by then, after he joked and thanked a few people, the party would have exhausted what little use it had for him, and he would have to walk a block to get a cab. No taxis would be cruising down this little side street.

The door opened. For a split second he was stunned by the light and his hand went to his knife as he stared at the man just now walking under the street lamp. It was Morty—short, fat, balding Morty—walking home alone and still unpublished, still bookless after all these years, his snow-covered beret sitting absurdly on his head. He quickly ducked behind the dumpster until Morty slowly passed out of sight. It was then he first realized that the snow was falling on him too. The door opened two more times but it was people he didn't know or couldn't recognize except that they weren't Alters. Then he began to doubt that Alters would walk out alone. Why would he walk down the street like a plebeian when he could order a taxi to come to the door? With his money, taking a cab wasn't anything he'd fret about for a second. And what made him think that Alters would leave alone anyway? He remembered the rapt expression of Lady J's face while she listened to Alters. Why settle for her phone number when he could leave with her and salvage something pleasant from the evening? He imagined Alters making love with Lady J, then imagined him doing it with Debby. He'd intended to focus on these images for a moment to help keep up his resolve but found that, once in his mind, they stayed longer than he wanted. The snow was falling harder now. He imagined himself slowly being crowned with snow, head first, then over his dark clothes until he was white and immobile, a snow man with a knife, with the white, unwritten pages of a novel sitting at home as he realized that he must confront Alters again, that he couldn't endure the humiliation he'd suffered and must fight him in the snow, must make Alters acknowledge him and apologize, that he must use whatever he needed to use and do whatever he needed to do to make Alters taste this dirty, relentless New York snow.

The door opened again and he saw them. It was like black magic. The image in his mind was prophetic, was happening now. Alters was walking with a brunette, and for a moment Larry couldn't tell if it was Lady J or Debby. He heard the steps get closer, like a bizarre dance routine reverberating on the frozen sidewalk—not enough snow on it yet to soften it. He saw Alters with his arm around the brunette, his hand sliding down to where her bottom was underneath her coat. He waited another set of steps and then stood up and away from the dumpster and made a running jump like a praying mantis. He had intended to say a sentence to him, something like, "Fight like a man, bitch!" but he was so astonished at the size of his jump and his feeling that he had done it like a praying mantis (that he was somehow insect-like now) that he didn't think he said anything—only emitted a strange sound, between a yell and a hiss.

Then the hitting began as they half-boxed, half-wrestled each other on the snow while the woman screamed. Alters hit him in the stomach, but Larry countered with an uppercut, followed by a left hook, and then he tackled and sat on him. He could see blood on Alters' face, while the woman yelled, "You'll go to jail for this. You're gonna do time."

That's all I've ever done, he said to himself. Then she ran down the street. Larry took out his knife and held it over Alters' dazed eyes. "This is for humiliating me, asshole. Now say you're sorry."

Half-conscious, Alters whispered something that sounded like "Sorry, Tommy." Larry wanted something better than that— Alters didn't even remember his name—but he realized Lady J was probably already calling the cops, maybe had already called them, so he got off Alters' chest, still holding the knife in front of him.

"Don't follow me," he said, before he began running as fast as he could down the dark narrow street.

III

Simone

He saw her for the first time near Broad and Tasker on his way to the store. It was like everyone else was dead and she was shining. There were fifty or sixty feet of gray city between them. He kept walking towards her. She was wearing a pink plaid skirt and matching shirt—cheap clothes but they looked good on her. When he got nearer she raised her blouse halfway up trying to tempt the drivers passing by. She had a small chest and looked very young and pretty. When he passed by they smiled at each other and said hello and he asked her how she was doing. He could feel himself being pulled towards her and had to use all his strength to keep going to the store because he'd promised himself years ago—once AIDS started getting big—no more hookers.

He walked into the Rite Aid to get his evening candy, instinctively looking away from his reflection in the mirror. Sometimes he'd look at it to see if maybe the color under his eyes was somehow less severe, or the hair on his head a little fuller, but most times he didn't look anymore. It was as if his body now bore a sign saying "Good for no more than thirty years," and as far as anything that mattered, for no more than ten. No point nurturing his little flirtation with a young girl like that, hooker or not, he thought, as he paid the cashier. But he thought about her nonetheless. She reminded him of his 16-year-old girlfriend many years ago when he himself had barely been 20. Similar soft brown hair and glow to the eyes, though his girlfriend's skin was lighter. Terrible to think nothing like that would ever happen to him again but it seemed it wouldn't. Since his divorce five years ago, he'd had only a couple of uneventful relationships (if he was to use the last word generously). It was true he had a wonderful son, Kenny, but he only saw him on weekends, and as far as his job at the magazine, designing ads and occasionally articles, it was simultaneously dull and full of pressure—a real spirit killer.

On the way back to his place he looked for the hooker again. There was no sign of her, but her image stayed in his mind intermittently for the rest of the day and for the day after that, too.

He thought it was maybe because he was on vacation and had lots of time to think. It was odd how once people had a vacation they thought they had to go somewhere. He'd always been so grateful not to have to go to work that he enjoyed simply staying at home and just doing whatever he wanted. This summer, since Kenny had wanted to go to baseball camp, he was staying home for the whole vacation. As a result, he became more aware of his neighborhood. For instance, he hadn't noticed before that there were prostitutes a few blocks from his apartment. There could be two explanations for that. He could simply have been so tired from his job that he was oblivious to them or they could have moved there recently from a different part of the city. Prostitutes were always migrating like schools of fish to wherever the climate was better (i.e., fewer cops).

Two nights later he saw her again. First it was from a distance—their eyes seemed to lock and he immediately took off his glasses so he'd seem younger and more attractive. She was wearing a white undershirt without a bra. When he got closer he thought she might be part black—that she could possibly pass for either race.

"Hello again," he said, staring at her chest for a few seconds. "You're really beautiful."

"Thank you."

"I've been thinking about you. Are you gonna be here tomorrow?"

"I can be."

"What time will you be here?"

"What time do you want me to be?"

She was smiling still. Her eyes were lovely. "It's just that tonight isn't good for me."

She pouted and he felt his resolve melting.

"You sure?"

"Can you tell me how old you are?"

"I'm twenty-two," she said softly.

"What's your name?"

"Simone."

"Hi, I'm Jerry. You really excited me the other day, Simone. Can I date you?"

"Uh huh," she said.

"Come on let's go," he said, "but act straight, OK? I live on the top floor of a house and my landlady's home, not to mention there are all sorts of cops around."

"Don't worry," she said confidently, as they started walking.

"Where are you from?" he asked, detecting a slight accent.

"New Orleans."

"Really? I love New Orleans. How did you happen to come to Philadelphia?"

"I went to college for a little while," she said, with an ironic laugh. "To Temple."

"Temple? No kidding. How long were you there?"

"Three months," she said, with another ironic laugh. He liked that she was being honest and ironic. He asked why she left and if she'd like to go back to school and she said it was because of money, and that she'd definitely like to go back.

"Of course. Education is the paramount thing," were the words he remembered her saying. He was impressed by the word "paramount" and asked her more questions. It seemed he couldn't stop asking her questions. "Let me ask you the obvious question, why a beautiful, clearly intelligent woman like you is doing this?...I mean, would you like to get out of it if you could?"

"In a heartbeat."

"Maybe I can help you," he said. He wanted to screw her and help her. Or not screw her exactly, but have some form of sex where he wouldn't feel too much anxiety afterwards because of AIDS. She seemed to be a bright and interesting hooker. He hadn't remembered many of those when he used to deal with them a lot. He was happy. It seemed like such a long time since anything had excited him in his life—since well before his divorce. It was like having a wonderful glass of champagne.

He saw his building come into view and wondered what the neighbors would think if they saw him, as one or two of them almost certainly would. Since his last relationship, the only person the neighbors ever saw him with was his son, and he was much younger than Simone—though Simone was certainly young enough to be his daughter, too. He decided to look straight ahead and screw the neighbors.

While they were climbing the stairs, he lightly patted Simone's behind. He was so happy he was giddy. He said he knew a lot of people in the city who could maybe help her get a job. She said she had no home and he said she could always stay with him, or at least use him as a reference and use his address as hers.

When they passed through his living room she asked if she could take a shower.

"Sure, can I go with you?"

"I'm kind of funny about needing my shower space but you can watch."

"Thanks, great, I will," he said, leading the way to his bathroom. She was out of her clothes in three seconds.

His first reaction was she was really lovely. Then he was struck by how skinny she was and by the profusion of red sores and cuts—like a rash, but not exactly, all over her lower back and rear end. But she was enjoying herself so much and also looked so beautiful while she washed herself that he couldn't bear to ask her any disturbing questions about her health. Still, while he was admiring her and feeling his champagne kind of happiness he wondered if her sores were one of the symptoms of AIDS. He knew weight loss was, but he wasn't sure about the sores.

When she was done, he picked up her undershirt, which looked filthy, and followed behind her, tapping her bottom lightly a couple of times, as they walked through his living room into his bedroom. She was completely naked, standing in front of his bed in a relaxed way.

"OK. What do you want to do?" she said, a little too matter of factly for his taste, with one hand on her slender hip.

"What's that stuff all over your back and bottom?"

"That? Most of it's from stress. Some of them are pimples I scratched."

"They look a lot worse than pimples to me. How do I know you don't have HIV?"

"I don't have any diseases. I go to the clinic across the street every three weeks."

Jerry wanted to believe her but her skin looked pretty awful. "Why are you so skinny? You look like you've lost a lot of weight."

"'Cause I'm hungry," she said angrily.

He looked at her. At first her tone startled him, then he felt a sudden wave of pity. "Look, I don't want to do anything with you. I can't...I feel sorry for you."

"You're not going to give me any money?"

"I'm going to help you. I want to figure out what you need and help you."

"My need is money. I have a five-year-old kid and I'm hungry."

"I have a kid too. Let me show you his picture." He realized he was being self-centered but couldn't stop himself and soon had opened up a desk drawer and was showing pictures of Kenny to her (including some of Kenny's baby pictures). She looked at them briefly in silence, and he felt guilty.

"I don't understand why you're in this mess. You were at Temple a few years ago."

"I told you it cost too much money."

"OK. But why not take a regular job? What did you do before you were on the street?"

"Worked for an escort service."

"But that's the same thing, isn't it?"

She considered his observation for a few seconds, then shrugged.

"Why can't you get a job at the Rite Aid as a cashier or something?"

"They wouldn't hire me. If I could get some kind of home and get cleaned up maybe I could get a job."

"OK. OK. Calm down. I'm getting the picture. How long have you been on the street?"

"Six months. Why are you asking me all these questions if you're not even gonna date me?"

"I need to know as much about your situation as possible if I'm going to help you. I need to know about your life. Do you have a pimp?"

"No!" she said contemptuously. "I work for myself."

He looked at her doubtfully. Prostitutes never acknowledged their pimps.

"So how did you really get those sores? I don't understand. I need to know all this to be able to figure out how to help you."

"But it's totally irrelevant," she said, louding up again. "I have a babysitter to pay to take care of my kid, I have no clothes, I sleep on the street and I'm hungry."

"OK. Calm down. I understand that you're angry, I don't blame you. But try to realize that I'm on your side. I'm going to help you. I'm not gonna just give you money."

"But money's what I need."

"You need a job. You need to change your direction in life."

"Jesus Christ! Can't you just date me?"

"I'm sorry. I'm just frankly nervous seeing all those things on your body. If it clears up in the future I'll date you, but now... Please don't look so discouraged. Look, do you know anybody who sells pot?"

"Sure."

"Could you get me some?"

"Yeah I could do that."

"It's just that at my age, at my job, there's no one I could ask, but I wouldn't mind having some."

"Yeah, OK."

"OK, maybe we can work something out, but meanwhile have some faith. Trust me. I'm going to help you. You can eat here, you can shower here...if you need to, you can stay here."

"Can you give me a tee shirt?" she said. "Mine's dirty and I'm getting sick of standing here naked."

Jerry looked more closely at her undershirt and saw there was dirt smudged all over the front of it. He opened his closet door and started looking for a shirt to give her but for some reason it was difficult to decide which one to part with. There were different memories associated with each shirt. Finally, he picked a purple tee shirt and handed it to her. She put it on. He was glad he gave it to her. Then he opened his desk drawer where he kept his petty cash.

"I'm going to give you twenty dollars," he said. She took the money out of his hand quickly. And I'm also going to give you some Valium to help you sleep at night or just to calm down. Would you like that?"

"I'll take a couple."

"And I also want to give you a box of Triscuits in my kitchen and any fruit you want."

"Can I have some of your jellybeans?" she said pointing to his bed table.

"Yes, of course. And one other thing. You could help your own cause if you were just a little nicer to me. I know you're angry but be nice to people like me who are trying to help you. Believe me, I'm one in a thousand, in a million."

She looked at him with her big eyes and said nothing. "Now give me a hug," he said, extending his arms. She hesitated for a moment and he thought if she didn't hug him he'd feel utterly lost. Finally, she moved forward and he held her a few seconds. When it ended, he started to worry about seeing her again. He began writing down his phone number to give her, while keeping one eye on her to be sure she didn't take some of the money that was lying around his desk.

Meanwhile she'd gotten her skirt and shoes on. She looked adorable in an offbeat way wearing his purple tee shirt. It would probably help her earn more money.

"Simone I want you to take my phone number, OK?"

She looked a little surprised but took it.

"If you're ever in a jam, ever in any real trouble and need me or just a place to stay I want you to call me," he said, handing her his name and number on a piece of paper.

"Thanks," she said.

He looked at her. He could see the intelligence and feeling in her eyes. "Give me another hug," he said softly.

She gave him one that was less emotional than the first, and to blunt his disappointment, perhaps, he lightly tapped her rear end a couple of times and then she disappeared, though not before he called out, "Act straight when you go down the stairs and be polite if my landlady talks to you, OK?"

Two days passed without seeing her. He went out looking for her on the streets both nights but no luck. He felt lonely and tried to think who he could call. His ex-girlfriend? His ex-wife? Either would be awkward and unfulfilling. What was happening to him wasn't anything they'd understand. The only person he really wanted to see besides Simone was Kenny, who was going to be away for two more weeks at the baseball camp. He sat down and wrote Kenny a letter and immediately felt better. How many times when he was dodging mirrors or thinking how few years he really had left to live or just how much he hated his job, had the image of his son's shy blue-eyed smile saved him? Here was another time, he thought, as he wrote an extra "I love you" at the end of the letter. Then he left the apartment to mail it, looking up and down the block for Simone. It seemed that every time he went outside he was really looking for her.

That night while he was watching TV, Simone called him collect.

"How are you, where are you?"

"A few blocks away. The phone kept eating my quarters so I decided to call you collect. You know that thing we talked about?"

"What thing?"

"The thing you asked me to get. Well I got it."

"That was fast."

"I told you I could do it. So you wanna pay me now, I've gotta move it fast."

He realized, of course, that he didn't want the pot but he also felt that he was being hustled, that she should have called him first to ask him how much stuff he wanted and let him know what it would cost. But he agreed to meet her, insisting, however, that she come to his place alone. She agreed to meet him in front of his house in ten minutes.

He felt that she wouldn't come on time, that something would go wrong. Hookers aren't exactly the world's most responsible people, he thought. They're habitually late, if they show up at all. They forget and lose things. They are the least dependable people on earth except, perhaps, for junkies, and since most hookers are also junkies it's a moot point which of the two is less dependable. He waited exactly ten minutes then went out to his stoop (noting that his landlady was in her bedroom with the door shut and the TV on) and waited another ten minutes, alternately looking both to his left and right for Simone. Then he began to walk towards the street corner where she said she slept. He was wearing slippers and shorts—rather pitifully dressed, he knew, to go walking through such an unsavory neighborhood as 15th and Tasker where so many questionable people were walking around.

He saw a room with the door open on the ground floor of a vacated building and stuck his head in. There were four women in the room who all looked vaguely Hispanic. Dark-haired women with sad faces.

"Does Simone live here? Do you know Simone?"

One of the women tilted her head a few degrees and looked at the others, who in turn shook their heads and/or shrugged in a way that conveyed the least possible interest in his question. He left the room and kept walking, feeling more anxious by the moment.

Then he heard someone calling his name. He looked up and saw her about a block and a half away, seeming to skip towards him in his purple tee shirt, and he smiled. As he walked towards her he noticed a black man trailing a little behind her on a bicycle. Jerry gestured with his hand for Simone to follow him, then turned his back and started walking slowly towards his place. When she caught up with him he said, "Where were you? I was starting to worry about you."

"I had business to finish."

"A date?"

"No. It took more time than I thought to get the stuff."

"I thought you said you already had it on the phone. Never mind. Who's the guy trailing us on the bike? Is he your pimp?"

She gave him a look. "No way. That's Ron, the guy who gave me the stuff. He's my friend. He listens to me and lets me cry on his shoulder when no one else will."

Jerry felt a pang of jealousy and tried not to give into it. "I thought we agreed you'd come to my place alone. I don't want to deal with anyone else on this."

Then Ron rode up beside him, which forced Jerry to look in his direction and acknowledge him. Ron was a big man with a toothy smile.

"I'll be selling you the weed," he said.

"I don't know you," Jerry said. "I'm dealing with her alone on this or just forget it," he said, walking more quickly towards his place. He couldn't tell if he was more jealous or scared, or simply angry at feeling double-crossed. Simone caught up with him a block later.

"Why is that guy still following us? Can't you explain to him that I'll only deal with you alone?"

"Ron isn't going to do anything."

"Then tell him to go away. I'm not going to talk to him again."

Simone turned and gestured to Ron, and though he continued to follow slowly, the distance between them increased.

Then Jerry closed the door behind him, looked at Simone and forgot about Ron. He felt happy again and patted Simone's rear end a couple of times as they walked upstairs to his apartment. In his bedroom she put the plastic bag of pot in his hand and said, "OK, I got you a quarter."

He looked at it and said, "How much is it?" He felt stung again by her completely businesslike attitude.

"Eighty," she said.

"Eighty dollars? Jesus Christ."

"That's a good price. This is really good stuff."

"I can't pay eighty dollars."

She turned away with a look of anguish in her eyes and paced a couple of steps. "You can't fuck me like this. I already put up the money."

"I don't understand."

"This will cost me. I had to pay up front. You said it's what you wanted."

"We never agreed on or discussed a price. Come on, don't fuck with me, don't manipulate me."

"I'm not manipulating you."

"I've given you food and clothes and money and medicine. You should have called and asked me what I wanted to pay, or if I wanted to pay what he asked."

"I couldn't."

"Why? Why couldn't you call me?"

"I lost your number."

"But you called me collect."

"I thought it was lost when I could've called you, then I found it later. I misplaced it."

"You've always got an answer for everything, don't you?"

"I thought I was doing you a favor."

"Eighty bucks, some favor."

"Look, I'm gonna get screwed for this if you don't give me the money."

"OK, calm down. No one's gonna let anything happen to you. I'll cover you this time," he said, going to his desk drawer again, withdrawing four twenties and handing them to her.

"Thank you," she said.

"Just don't pull that shit with me again, OK?" She said nothing and he worried that she might leave. He quickly started asking about her day, and she answered him in what he thought were rushed, half-hearted sentences. He couldn't tell if she was still hurt (or ever hurt) by his initial anger about the deal, or if she was just in a hurry to get back on the street. Hookers were always aware that their meter was running, he knew that, but he also remembered how awful he'd felt when he couldn't find her the last few days. He felt panicky again and shifted the conversation to ways she could make money, ways he might be able to hire her. She said she could type but of what use could that be to him? Plus he knew how to type himself. His son was still young enough to need a sitter sometimes, but Simone was no baby sitter (although he enjoyed picturing the three of them together) and he never used a sitter when he had Kenny with him. He'd fixed his schedule so he wouldn't have to.

He could sense her growing exasperation and felt frustrated himself. "If only you didn't have those sores I'd date you."

"It'll take months before they go away."

"If only you'd tell me the truth about how you got them."

"If only you'd stop asking me questions. You ought to pay me to answer all your questions."

"But how can I trust you if you can't level with me?"

"I told you it's hard to talk about," she said. He was facing her but she looked down at the floor.

"Please," he said.

"OK," she said angrily. "You wanna know? I was shackled to a board."

"What?"

"I was shackled to a floorboard for a week and I had to pee in my pants and have my period and what you see, some of it is stress like I said, but it's mostly floor burns, OK? It's not AIDS."

There was a knocking at his door. His landlady was calling him and he ran to the door before she could walk in.

"There's a gentleman here to see the young lady who's visiting you," she said, the blue eyes in her big round face looking at him without a trace of irony. She was either terminally naive or very discreet, he could never be sure which.

"Thanks, she'll be right down," he said. He felt angry. He walked back to his room wondering if Simone had had enough time to take any of his money.

"Lord Ron, your protector, is here. I told you I wanted to be alone. Now my landlady knows what I'm doing."

Simone's face turned white as she got up to leave, and he followed her to the stairs. "Go ahead, go. This whole thing is a fucking mess. Don't ever come here again…unless you call first," he added, as she ran down the stairs.

He went back to his room, and slammed the door. He didn't like that pimp, Ron, knowing where he lived, and couldn't believe he was brazen enough to knock on the door, to stand there like a father collecting his daughter. But a minute later he started worrying about Simone. He ran to his opened window, couldn't see much on the street, but thought he heard some yelling. He kept looking, was frustrated by a tree that blocked his view, then thought he heard a scream coming from across the street. He ran downstairs, opened the door and looked out. Across the street in front of the empty health clinic he heard Simone yelling "You bastard" and worse at Ron, then saw her punching him a couple of times, before running down a side street, still swearing. What had Ron done to her? Had he hit her first, or was it possible that she was angry at him for coming to the house and interrupting their conversation? Could he, Jerry, be more important to her than he realized?

He went up and down Broad Street the next night, walking a mile north and south, but saw no sign of her. Then he walked back to Tasker a couple of times but didn't see her there either. He remembered thinking that his vacation was like a noose around his neck, that he needed to get back to work so he wouldn't have to deal with so much time.

The next day, he tried reasoning with himself. This was all so inappropriate on so many levels: her age, the fact that she was a prostitute, for God's sake. But that night he went out looking for her, without success, anyway, and began asking other hookers if they'd seen her, or knew where she was. Nobody knew. One black woman in absurdly tight jeans with five earrings on her face said she thought Simone had gone to New York on a date.

Jerry took two Valiums, then stayed in the next day when it rained. What did Simone do when it rained, he wondered. Was it true that she'd really gone to New York and, if so, for how long? It was disconcerting to simultaneously worry about her as if she were his daughter and to also be so excited by her.

Around 3:30 in the afternoon he went outside, though it was still drizzling. He told himself he was going to Rite Aid to get a snack, but he also knew he missed Simone horribly and was still hoping to see her. He stood on his stoop for a moment scanning the street when, incredibly, he saw her. Or thought he did. He had wanted to see her so much for so long that he couldn't fully believe it was her. Also, she was so chameleonlike—could be lovely in so many different ways that didn't resemble one another that even after staring for a long time he couldn't be sure it was her walking a block and a half past his house.

"Simone," he called out, almost yelling. The woman stopped walking, turned, and looked at him. He gestured for her to approach him, she hesitated, looking confused, and he left his stoop to meet her on the sidewalk.

"I've been looking for you. I was very worried about you."

"You said you didn't want me in your house again."

"I didn't mean that. I meant without calling first and without that guy tagging along. I was just worried about my landlady."

"Did you see what Ron did to me?"

"I saw what you did to him. You have a pretty nice left hook."

She smiled for a second.

"You saw the tail end of it then."

"Why? What did he do to you?"

"He hit me upside the head. He had me down on the ground, practically strangling me."

"Jesus Christ! Why? What did you do?"

"I don't know."

"I gave you the money."

"Yeah and I gave it to him like I was supposed to. I don't cross anyone on deals."

"So what was it? Was he jealous?"

She shrugged.

"Had he ever hit you before?"

"No."

"So what was it? It doesn't make sense."

"Maybe he thought I was taking too long, but I told him 'I gotta spend some time talking with the guy': I mean you had to see the dope."

"Come upstairs with me," he said putting his arm around her waist.

"You wanna date me?"

"I want to give you some money. I've thought of a way I can pay you for your time. I mean it, I'm very serious about this, so just listen, OK?"

They went inside his apartment and he explained his idea while she sat across from him in his room. It was something he'd thought of the night before while he was looking for her on the streets, something inspired actually by her remark "You ought to pay me to answer your questions." Well, he would do just that. He wanted to write a story about her, he said, a fictional story, but he needed to do research. He proposed paying her a dollar a minute, if she'd answer his questions about her life, in a series of half-hour sessions over the next few weeks.

"I thought you were a designer," she said skeptically.

"I am, but I want to write this story." That was only partially untrue. He did want to learn about her as much as he could and perhaps really would write it down at some point, though he had no interest in turning it into fiction.

"I don't know. It's hard for me to talk about my life. You said thirty bucks for thirty minutes, right?"

"Yeah, and you don't have to talk about anything you don't want to, anything that's too painful. Just tell me the truth whenever you do talk, alright."

It was an even more tangled and painful story than he'd imagined, featuring a heroin-addict father whom she rarely saw and who eventually died of AIDS, a brother who sexually abused her, and a mother who was a prostitute and who once locked her in a closet for two hours. It sounded like stuff he'd heard on the Jerry Springer Show and he wondered how much of it was true. Hearing about the nuclear family took up the whole thirty minutes. When the time was up (she'd checked it on the desk clock), she stopped talking abruptly.

"You're more ruthless than a psychiatrist," he said.

"We made a deal," she said, "and every minute counts. You know," she added, "this isn't easy for me."

It was more of the same the next day, when she was late again. She was businesslike, a little distant and curt, and left after exactly thirty minutes, with his last question unanswered. She seemed both depressed and angry and he wondered how well his idea was working. But the day after that she arrived close to their agreed-upon time in an unusually good mood. He hugged her, then asked if she was on anything special. (A couple of times he'd felt she was hopped up on some powerful drugs.) "Nothing special," she said, and he let himself feel some hope. Maybe his listening would make her get closer to him, or at least appreciate him.

This time he'd written out a group of questions starting with her early years away from home which had led her to the business, and then some additional questions about her present life. Those were the questions he cared the most about, though he was almost afraid to hear the answers. Do you ever get excited having sex with clients? Do you ever get a crush on a client or even fall in love with one, etc.? What do you feel for me? Do you think you could ever love me? What would it take to make you happy living with me? He had fantasized about her answers to the last three questions all morning long. He felt he'd made some decisions yesterday, and here was the time to act on them. He knew he couldn't make her love him, at least not right away, but he did think he could make himself indispensable enough that she might get out of the business and stay with him, perhaps in a completely different neighborhood. For his part, all he wanted was to see the printed results of a recent HIV test, and God knows he was ready to make love with her, to live with her, and support her, if necessary, though he would also try to help her get a job.

Was he thinking foolishly, was he out of control? He considered the possibility, but only briefly. For years now everybody everywhere had been telling him to trust his feelings. Talk show therapists, the occasional real-life therapist, newspaper columnists, people in general. It was the mantra of the day. He looked at Simone in her clinging black skirt with no panties underneath, her legs spread apart, and his purple tee shirt matched with a dab of purple lipstick. He looked at her eyes, pregnant, it seemed to him, with all the pain and yearning and contradictions of the world— like a heroine in a Russian novel—and he knew what he was feeling. She was shining like she had the first day on the street.

He heard another tangled story about six months in an abusive mental institution, about dancing on drugs in New York strip clubs with the room in back that customers could have her in, of her life in a New York escort service where she was ripped off and humiliated, outraged, to her life on the streets of Philly, which she admitted was run by somebody other than herself, though not Ron, she was quick to add.

He no longer dared to ask about her attraction to clients. He'd already been hurt when she had alluded to "the love of her life," a window-washer in New York who had fathered her child. She blamed heroin for ruining him, too. There was little mention of evil or weakness in Simone's conversation, simply heroin or crack, which explained all bad behavior—just as success in her eyes was, regrettably, only measured by money. He watched her wipe away a tear and could barely stop himself from saying how he'd never take drugs if he were taking care of her. He felt he was turning red with jealousy and as a compromise decided to ask her then if she thought she could ever love him so at least he could tell her how much he already loved her.

"Time's up," she said, with a mischievous smile, pointing to his desk clock. He smiled too, in spite of himself.

"Just one more question, Simone."

"But the time's up."

"It's important."

"No, it wouldn't be fair," she said, getting up from her chair and walking by him without giving him the kiss or hug he'd hoped for.

"Simone," he said, racing after her. "Give me a hug good-bye."

She stopped at the beginning of the stairs and hugged him saying, "You can ask me your question next time."

After two days had passed without seeing her, Jerry tried to reassure himself that this had happened before, that it was the rule rather than the exception. But this time he felt something was different, and he suffered more acutely than ever when he couldn't find her. Perhaps it was because he was returning to work, which meant there would be less time to look for her— though, as he unfortunately discovered, just as much time to think about her. There was an unreal quality to his job now and to much of his life in general.

It was the strangest thing to think about, for those few moments when he could think about himself. There he was, a blur in space, moving about—an image in a coloring book suddenly given life or animation. He hardly had a conception of himself, as if he were merely an impersonal product of time. And other people, too, were blurs, time-products as well. Some simply knew it and others were protected and didn't. His son mercifully was in the latter category, perhaps also his ex-wife. He wasn't sure if Simone sensed it or not and that made him worry and long to be with her even more.

It was only while he looked for Simone that he felt himself to be more than a time-product, felt his heart was real and beating in his chest.

But if the act of seeking Simone seemed real, the information he received from the street often wasn't. A black hooker named Daisy, who had a front tooth missing and worked in front of the health clinic at night, told him she'd heard Simone was in jail.

"She be out soon. Don't worry honey. Why don't you date me in the meantime?"

He walked away disbelieving it. Simone was too shrewd and too paranoid to get arrested, wasn't she? Daisy was simply lying to him to make a buck. A fat white prostitute with dyed yellow hair, named Blondie, told him she'd heard Simone skipped town. That her pimp was mad at her and beat her and she'd gotten scared and gone to D.C. This sounded just plausible enough to scare him, but under more intense scrutiny—scrutiny he paid ten dollars for—she admitted she wasn't sure. "You hear things all the time—it's not always true, you know, it's street talk."

A week passed. He was spending four to five hours a night repetitively walking over Simone's territory near Snyder and Passyunk and then around Tasker and Morris. He began to notice the same men on his route—other Johns—solemnly, silently searching for hookers (or the right hooker), like junkies. One of them near Rite Aid nodded to him once and Jerry approached him.

"Hey can I ask you something? You got a minute?"

The man looked a few years older than him—early 50s—with restless eyes and stubble on his face, as if he'd been too preoccupied hunting women to shave. The man looked up and down the block for a moment, probably to be sure he didn't miss a girl, then said, "Yeah, I gotta minute."

"You know a girl named Simone?"

"Maybe."

"Come on, it's all right. I date her, you know, it's OK. We both know who she is."

"Yeah, I know Simone."

"When was the last time you saw her?"

"Not for a while."

"I ask because I've been looking for her for a week and I'm worried about her."

The man looked away again, dragged on his cigarette before speaking. "You never know with these girls."

"What do you mean?"

"A lot of 'em get sick and just disappear."

"You mean AIDS?"

"Yeah, whatever. They're not built to last. That's why I'm careful not to do too much with 'em when I do see 'em. I don't want to catch what they have, you know?" .

"Yeah, me too, I hear you," Jerry said.

"All I do is spank them sometimes because I figure that's OK," the man said, "but I'm scared 'cause I don't want to get what they have, right?"

"Right," Jerry mumbled. He couldn't bear the image of this faint-hearted pervert spanking Simone, so he kept walking.

In the weeks after Simone disappeared he felt that he'd done nothing but walk the streets searching for her, or else stay in his apartment thinking about her, and that the former was often done to find relief from the latter. Not that there weren't some rewards from thinking about her—remembering phrases she'd said and expressions on her face as she'd said them. And then her body in his shower, her legs strategically spread so he could see her crotch while she'd sat across from him in his room, and then the feel of her when he'd hugged her or felt her breasts or bottom and, of course, all the emotions he felt. There was great beauty in remembering that, but also pain as well.

Then the act of memory inevitably was followed by regret and self-recriminations. Why hadn't he tried harder to have her stay with him during all the times she did visit? Why hadn't he asked her to live with him and gotten a new place, if necessary? He knew that was what he really wanted. Why hadn't he even made love with her once? It was his fear of AIDS, of course, that had stopped him more than anything, but now he was faced with his empty, overcivilized life. And there were things he could have done to mitigate the health risks—tests at the clinic across the street, condoms....He knew if he had the chance again that he would press her to his flesh and not let her go, that there was nothing he wanted more than to be inside her body and to cover with kisses the very sores he'd let scare him.

The fear that it was too late now and would never happen, that what he'd felt with Simone was something he'd never feel again and that he'd let it slip through his frightened fingers, was more than he could stand and got him out of bed— sometimes at two or three in the morning—to hit the streets again, moving without any concept of time, it seemed to him, or even memory so that later he barely remembered that on one of these walks he'd been mugged and had to give his assailant almost a hundred dollars.

Meanwhile, Kenny had come back from camp and Jerry thought he could finally spend a night not looking for Simone and perhaps stop looking for her forever, because a part of him now knew it was hopeless. At first he'd postponed seeing Kenny (something he'd never done) saying he was sick, but he'd felt ashamed of himself. He'd promised to make it up to him and took Kenny shopping Friday evening at a new sports store in Center City, buying him lots of baseball equipment, though the summer was almost over. They'd talked easily and laughed a lot and for a while Jerry felt a serene and exquisite pleasure.

"OK, my man," he said as they left the store, "I'll take you to any restaurant in Philadelphia. You name it and we're there."

Kenny considered the matter for a moment, then said, "Can we go to TGIF?"

"Of course, we're there, dude," Jerry said, smiling. Kenny was always a cheap date.

The restaurant was crowded and noisy. On the way to a table Jerry thought he saw Simone, stopped a moment, looked again, and saw that it wasn't her. But a few minutes later, while they were eating cheeseburgers, her image was vividly in his mind again. She was wearing the same clothes she wore that first time he saw her sparkle in the street and he felt the feeling he'd felt then—like a gravitational pull. Kenny asked him what was wrong and he said nothing and began asking Kenny lots of questions about the baseball camp. But for the rest of the meal, and then in the car, as they drove back to his apartment where they were going to watch a football game, Jerry struggled with her image.

He found a space near his building (looked up and down Broad Street, just in case) and said, "Hey, did you know we're near a Rite Aid where they've got an enormous selection of candy? How about it?"

"Sure."

"Come on, it's only a few blocks away."

"Aren't we gonna drive?"

"No. We need to walk off those cheeseburgers we ate to make room for the candy."

"But we'll miss the beginning of the game."

"We won't miss anything."

"Yes we will."

"Besides, you need to keep developing your leg muscles. Didn't your coach tell you cars are the death of legs?"

Kenny continued to ask questions but Jerry kept walking and reassuring him, while intermittently looking for Simone. At times he worried what Kenny would think if Simone did come running up to them, but all things considered it would be a small price to pay.

In the Rite Aid, Kenny's eyes got big and he stopped complaining. He bought a Mike and Ike, a Snickers, cheese popcorn, a bag of jellybeans, Twizzlers, and a big bottle of Coke. Jerry barely had enough money left to pay for it.

As he was coming out of the store, the spanking man gave him the high sign. "Excuse me a minute. I see someone I know. Wait here," he said to a puzzled-looking Kenny. Jerry walked about twenty feet away from his son. The spanking man was characteristically looking away from him, dressed in his usual uniform of lightly frayed sports jacket and navy-blue baggy pants.

"What's up?" Jerry said.

"Heard something."

"What's that?"

"Something about Simone. Yuh....Heard that she died...heard they found her in the river. The Hudson River in New York. She killed herself probably, or maybe someone killed her. They can't be sure. Can never be sure with that kind."

"What are you saying? Are you sure?"

"That's the word. That's what I heard. They found her body a few days ago."

"You know this to be true."

The spanking man looked him in the eye.

"I don't lie about it. Her real name was Ravetta Stone."

Jerry walked away from him and started heading home. "Who was that man, Dad?"

"Nobody," he said softly.

He could barely think of anything to say to his son on the way home. He knew it was wrong and focused on saying what few words he could (with eyes averted) till they got home and Kenny turned on the set and started eating his candy.

Jerry went to the bathroom, took a double dose of his new sleeping pill, Restoril, and finally allowed himself to cry softly. Then it occurred to him that he was mourning someone he couldn't be totally sure was dead. How could he 100 percent trust a character as nebulous as the spanking man? A fetishist and borderline idiot! That stopped his crying, though he still felt desperate, still felt he'd lost Simone forever. When he came out of the bathroom he forced himself to watch the game for an hour with Kenny and say some things before pleading fatigue, when the pills clicked in, and agreeing to let Kenny watch TV as long as he'd like.

That night Jerry dreamed he was alone on a long street, perhaps a boulevard. It was his neighborhood but it was also someplace remote and exotic like Egypt. He thought he was looking for Simone but then it was for the girlfriend of his youth, and then he no longer was sure what he was looking for, though he continued to ask the few people he saw on his walk. The sun was hot; a blazing blue light filled the street. Finally a man standing in darkness by a large black fountain said, "You're looking for God, yes?"

"Yes," Jerry said.

"There's no chance. Your lives are too different."

He woke up with tears somehow in his eyes. Then he sat up, hearing a faint sound from the living room. Looking down he saw the empty cot in his room where Kenny was supposed to be sleeping, felt a moment of horrible panic, and opened his door. Kenny was asleep on the couch in the living room facing the TV which was shining like a weird little sun, showing some science fiction show. Kenny's eyes were closed. He looked incredibly young, like he did as a baby. How had someone like him managed to produce such a beautiful child? Jerry tiptoed up to him and kissed his forehead lightly, half hoping he might wake him up so Kenny could sleep on the cot and so he could talk to him for a few seconds. But Kenny didn't wake up. That was all right, though. Better to let him sleep, now that he could. When Jerry was a child he'd slept that way, too. Such a private act, going to sleep, that each person did it his own way. Who knew what sleep rituals or pills Kenny would have to adopt (as he had) in the years to come? Undoubtedly, women would drive his son crazy too, but he hoped less crazy than they'd driven him. Jerry smiled, in spite of himself, but an image of Simone went through him then like a tremor. He felt he might be close to tears again and so breathed deeply and stopped it, didn't cry. Then the image went away. He looked at Kenny once more, thought about kissing him again but decided not to. The next thing he knew he bent down and shut off the TV and everything was dark but still.

Aerialist

First I want to write what my impressions were of the apartment and what my life was like before the change. I'd intended to take an apartment on the second floor (due to my fear of heights), but after I paid my deposit the manager told me the only place still available was a large studio on the top floor, the thirty-third. I was told I'd be living at the highest point in the city.

When I saw it for the first time the sun came through the windows lighting up the just-shampooed carpet. It was so extraordinary I forgot about my fear right away and spent four hours feverishly unpacking. I thought, My whole life is here, all my possessions, but there are so many closets they'll all be tucked out of view. Besides wall-to-wall carpeting the apartment came with a brand-new stove and refrigerator, a laundry room two doors away, an exercise room in the basement, a dry cleaners on the main floor where there was also a mail drop, and newspapers on sale in the lobby. It's all a very good marketing strategy, I remember thinking. They want to get you dependent on the building so they put everything in it.

But the most remarkable thing about the apartment was the view. Eight large plate-glass windows covered the length of the studio. There was so much space and so many things to see it was a completely new puzzle every day. Looking left to right I could see the museum, the railroad tracks, center city itself—with high-rises, banks, office buildings, and an elementary school playground where children were always playing basketball. Farther to the right were Veterans' Stadium, the Walt Whitman Bridge, some trees, and a slice of the river. In the mornings everything was bright and at night there were lights everywhere—searchlights, streetlights, office lights, lights reflected in glass.

In many ways the apartment was the opposite of where I'd lived before on Pine Street. I'd spent a year in an area filled with prostitutes, in a third-floor walk-up with low ceilings and uncarpeted floors. My windows looked directly into the apartment of a woman in the adjoining building who had never bothered to buy a window shade for her room. Every time I'd get back from the bank I'd sense she was looking at me, whether she actually was or not. It was pull down the shades and live like a bat or feel her eyes on me, and when you're a teller peoples' eyes are on you all day long. As it turned out, however, I began to watch her. Her name was Lisa and her occupations, I quickly learned, were modeling and studying art.

I soon found myself following a routine. I'd come back from work, turn on the TV, and watch Lisa during the commercials. When it was time to eat I'd bring my TV dinner into the room. Shortly after the eleven o'clock news she'd shut off her lights and I'd usually go out for a walk, down Spruce or Locust and then circle back to my place. One night I saw a banner draped across Locust Street:

An Evening of Cha Cha
A Benefit for AIDS

It occurred to me that there was a lot of dying in my neighborhood, which happened in all neighborhoods, of course, but this was contagious dying. Halfway down the block a group of prostitutes were running and laughing whenever they saw a police car, as if they were trying to outrun a wave at the beach. Meanwhile, on the corner, a boy was pretending to use a pay phone so he'd look like he had a reason to be on the street. He was, of course, hoping to be picked up. A bottle crashed behind me and a drunk started screaming at the sky. I figured that's enough for tonight and I went back to Pine Street.

When I walked into my room I saw Lisa lying in her bed reading *Jokes and Their Relation to the Unconscious.* Just before I pulled the shade she looked up at me from Freud and our eyes met. I turned off the lights and tried to get to sleep but I kept seeing images of her face, which was pretty and round and lit by bright, light eyes. Once I watched her talking and laughing with a man who had just finished working on her portrait, and I noticed a slight and very appealing space between her teeth. The man was probably a fellow student, or maybe a young teacher or a young-looking teacher. He was one of her most frequent visitors and once accompanied her to a modeling agency while I followed less than a block behind. I began to suspect that he might be in her room now and debated whether I should pull up my shade. Eventually I compromised by walking to the side of the window and moving the shade a few inches.

My suspicions were correct. They were in her room, lit only by a dull gold lamp on the floor. She was wearing the nightshirt she normally slept in and he had on a shiny pair of pink satin pants. At first I thought they might be rehearsing some kind of play, their gestures were so sweeping and theatrical, until I realized they were actually making love. That surprised me. I knew Lisa to be earnest, idealistic, accommodating, even a little passive, but in the scene I watched she was both the aggressive star and the director.

I felt hurt and disappointed. I'd always found something depressing about combining theater with sex, something I may even have considered evil, yet I watched, as I'd watched every other aspect of her life in her room. In a little while I wondered if she might not be performing for me. After all, I was her devoted audience, our eyes had met many times and many times I'd thought of signaling to her and saying out my window, "Look, we've watched each other for a year, why don't we say hello?" I'd also considered calling her and asking her out, of course, but didn't. There were the usual inhibiting factors, not the least of which was my dark and disgusting apartment.

That night I forced myself to confront certain truths about Lisa. I'd watched her so much, and occasionally followed her, because

I was attracted to her. From my eyes alone I'd, in a way, fallen in love with her. I'd pursued no other women because I wanted Lisa, but what, really, could I offer her? As long as I lived in this cave I'd never be able to call her, and as long as I stayed where I was I'd continue to watch her and that obviously wasn't a healthy situation for me.

At the bank the next day I applied for a special loan available to five-year employees. One of the tellers named Frank told me about the high-rise and how my social life would improve if I moved there. He said I owed it to myself to live better. A month later (exactly six weeks ago), I moved in.

I know now that the change began then, though I didn't realize it at the time. That it happened to me validates my idea of God as being unconcerned with human notions of status. For who could have been more ordinary than I was? I'd worked at three or four jobs since I graduated from college. I'd never been married, though I had one "wife equivalent" back in the '70s in a different city. Always I'd lived in a marginally middle-class way. If there was anything unusual about me, besides being an underachiever, it was my lack of a social life. Before the change I had no real friends at the bank, no girlfriend, no one I was even fantasizing about except Lisa. My father was an accountant, my mother a substitute English teacher. I saw them three times a year in Poughkeepsie. And then the change.

The first time I felt some inkling of it was when I started to look out my new windows for long periods of time. Apparently my apartment was in the middle of so many competing signals that none of the TV channels came in well and with most of them I saw double. So I started to stare at my view. One morning I got up earlier than usual. When I raised my shades I was shocked. Great patches of color were in the sky forming a huge belly of purple with a salmon orange underbelly. Submerged beneath that was a stream of light green. As the orange intensified it suffused the purple, making it look like an enormous crater. Meanwhile, when I looked again at the green part, I saw that it wasn't really "green" at all but that there was no other word for it. A flock of birds appeared, forming a kind of figure eight in front of the crater. Then the sun split the crater like a bomb slowly exploding upward and my apartment was filled with warm orange light. I couldn't take my eyes off all of this and was ten minutes late for work.

I went to bed early that night to be sure I'd wake up in time for tomorrow's sunrise. (Needless to say I'd stopped pulling my shades down at night.) In a few days I discovered that there was always drama in the sky equal to that first sunrise, always more colors and shapes than there were words for, and always more order than I could conceive.

Why did it take me so long to understand, I wondered? Why hadn't I seen this before? I tried to recall other times I might have looked at the sky and could only remember watching a fly ball in a baseball park or some construction workers on top of an office building or once, as a little kid in New York, ducking from a waterbomb someone threw at me from a high-rise. I hadn't noticed simply because I'd never watched.

After I began sky-watching I quickly established a pattern of three hours of watching in the morning, then home during my lunch break for forty-five minutes, then two more hours in the late afternoon. Of course it was an inexhaustible subject, yet I felt I was learning things in a cumulative way. For instance, just from altering my position by a step in the living room I could make the moon appear, or when I lay down in bed with one pillow under my head instead of two I could make the skyline vanish and just see sky.

Once during my lunch break, while I was watching some clouds, I got so involved I forgot to go back to the bank. When this happened a second time Frank called to tell me that I'd better watch it, that the supervisor was getting angry and I was skating on thin ice. "You already can't afford your fancy apartment, what are you gonna do when you lose your job?" he said in a clipped, prissy tone.

I was tempted to tell Frank what was happening, but wisely I didn't. His whole world was Equi-bank. How could Frank at the bank understand? The sky was completely enveloping—everything was in it. It was also communicating to me, telling me things I needed to know and changing me in ways I couldn't express.

After my mother called to bawl me out for not calling on her birthday, I also didn't explain. The truth was that except for some images of Lisa, whom I sometimes saw after I finally closed my eyes and tried to sleep, the sky was all I thought about. I knew that the change was happening but I still struggled to keep a strong foothold in my everyday world. So I apologized to my mother and sent her flowers, and I began setting my alarm clock to ring forty-five minutes after I'd come back to my apartment during lunch break, which helped my attendance at the bank.

By then I'd bought two six-by-four mirrors and put one on the living room table in front of the through-space to the kitchen and the other against the wall where the television used to be. (I'd long ago put my TV away in the storage closet.) Now, in those rare moments when I accidentally wasn't facing the windows, I had a way of monitoring the sky. I was living in a state of constant expectation, but I was constantly having my expectations fulfilled. Really, I was simply experiencing the natural rhythms of the change, so of course there was no way my watches could ever disappoint me.

But how did I manage to go to the bank every day and concentrate on my job? It's true I'd sometimes see little suns where George Washington was supposed to be on the dollar bills, but somehow I got through that time with no major errors. Also, as my mental and spiritual strength increased I trusted my instincts more and they told me to keep going out into the world and to keep my job but to separate it completely from the time in my apartment. Toward that end I unplugged my phone a few weeks ago.

One morning right after I got up I was stopped by an image in the mirror. I turned around and found myself feeling each stage of the sun's rise into the heavens. I understood how we were related—how we were equals, really—both shot through with rays of divinity. I knew then that all entities are a part of God and that my purpose was to put this knowledge to active use. Immediately I decided to call Lisa.

This was the kind of decision that might have paralyzed me before, but now I merely had to think of a single sunray for a second to feel sure of myself and begin dialing. I told her I'd been her neighbor and had often wanted to speak with her; that I'd definitely planned to call her when a stroke of good fortune happened and I'd moved. I gave her my new address and she seemed impressed. Then I asked if I could see her, but she hesitated. There was actually an embarrassing silence during which I asked if she remembered me. "Maybe," she said and hung up.

I refused to be discouraged. Instead I went straight to my windows and had a meditation with a pale white cloud. When it was over I knew my next move. I remembered that I'd followed her on three separate Wednesdays to the Star Watch Modeling Agency and that the agency closed at five. The next day I was waiting in front of the agency with a bouquet of roses.

Lisa was so heavily made up I almost didn't recognize her. She was wearing skin-tight pants, and for a moment I wondered what kind of modeling she did, before realizing that it no longer mattered.

"Hi, I'm your old neighbor who phoned you the other day. I brought these for you," I said, holding the roses out to her. She looked uncertain whether to accept them but her hands finally took them as if they'd made the decision independently from her.

"So what's this all about?" she asked, looking at me skeptically but half smiling.

"I just want to talk to you for a few minutes. Can I walk with you for a while?"

"I'm catching a bus on Chestnut," she mumbled, increasing her speed.

"May I walk you to your stop?"

"I guess. So what are you, the last chivalrous man in the city or something?"

"I hope you like roses."

"Who doesn't like roses? They're really pretty."

"Actually they're a bribe because I need to speak to you and I need to show you something very important."

"Oh, yeah?"

"Yes. Right now as a matter of fact."

"Is this the part where you rip open your raincoat?"

"No, it's nothing like that," I said, feeling wounded but laughing along with her. I was glad she had a sense of humor. It wasn't an entirely appropriate thing to say but I had to remember that I'd changed and she hadn't. I decided to go slowly and stick to small talk for the rest of our walk.

"Well, what can I say?" she said, indicating the flowers. "You've made my day. Look, here's my bus, thanks again for the roses."

I smiled and waved goodbye, perhaps once too often, but I did manage to keep her smiling.

For the next three days I wired her different kinds of flowers, which gave me the excuse to call her each day to ask how she liked them. On the first day she said, "You're really something. I love orchids, they look nice with the roses." On the second day I sent daisies and her enthusiasm diminished a little.

"My apartment's starting to look like a hothouse. By the way, I hope you're rich, otherwise I'm gonna start to feel bad about this."

"Forget about the money. I just want to see you soon. I have to tell you something extremely important."

"Tell me now. You obviously know how to get my attention."

"It would be better in person."

She paused. "We'll see," was all she said.

On the fourth day I sent lilies and called her a little later than I normally did.

"Look, it's been a lot of fun and I'm very flattered but please stop."

"Why? I thought you liked them."

"I loved them all but it's starting to get creepy, getting them every day from someone I don't really know."

"But I would love to get to know you."

"Well let's start by stopping the flowers, okay? It's making me nervous."

"I'm sorry."

"It's just that with gifts come expectations. You know what I mean?"

"I only mean to give you an infinitely greater gift."

"I'll bet," she said, laughing.

"No, you don't understand....Look, I promise I'll stop if you'll just meet me for coffee someplace, okay?"

She hesitated but finally agreed to meet me two days later. Of course I kept my part of the bargain and stopped sending her flowers. I unplugged my phone again and spent my time at home watching the sun rise and feeling the change and at night feeling my closeness with the stars. I also began reading, really for the first time since college, because I was curious to find out about other people's experience of change. I read parts of Dante's *Divine Comedy* and St. Augustine's *Confessions* and all of Franz Kafka's "Metamorphosis." The Kafka story was very interesting. Of course his character's metamorphosis was backward and mine was completely forward, but I could still relate to it.

When I wasn't sky-watching or reading I'd think about Lisa. What a busy, contradictory soul she had! She was so sweet and funny, but I also had to remember (as if I could ever forget) that she was the same person who wore those skin-tight clothes on the street, who didn't even bother to buy a shade for her room, and who stood over her painter friend that way. Clearly, she was a soul in peril who needed to channel her energy into a higher form. Did she ever look at the sky and see what was there? It was up to me to show her and the rest what would happen naturally, as it had for me, I was sure of it. After all, isn't the world proof that good people can sometimes do evil things?

…In the coffee shop I was both polite and restrained and only flattered her selectively. Toward the end I finally told her that I had a secret that had changed my life.

"So am I supposed to guess it?" she said, smiling just wide enough for me to see the little space between her teeth.

"You're supposed to *see* it."

"Are you a mystic or one of those 'New Age' people or something?"

I shook my head. "It can change your life too. You just have to come to my apartment for ten minutes and I'll show you."

"I'll bet. Wow, what an original approach you have."

"It's not an approach. Why are you so skeptical?"

"You think so? I was just wondering why I keep listening to you."

"Because you sense that I'm honest, you can feel me telling you the truth."

She still wouldn't agree to anything definite, but I sensed she was weakening.

The next day when I called she said she'd come over at five o'clock for fifteen minutes. I hung up and began dancing all over my carpet. But after I finished dancing I realized there were many things to do. I had to vacuum the carpet, clean my living room table which also functioned as a desk and dining table, clean the kitchen and bathroom, and buy a bottle of gin, some cheese, and some fancy crackers. Later, while I was ironing my suit pants I remembered that toward the end of our meeting in the coffee shop she'd talked a lot about her career, to the point where I agreed that my secret would help that too. But would it? I only had to think about my miserable attendance record at the bank, the thin ice Frank said I was skating on, to feel anxiety about my own career. What was it that Lisa hoped for? I knew a lot about her in one sense, but she had many secrets that the darkness of her apartment made it impossible to know. Maybe this is a terrible mistake, I thought, turning away from the windows. But when I turned back I saw an image of myself smiling in the sun and I regained my confidence in an instant. Good thing, too, because my doorbell was ringing.

"Come right in," I said, cheerfully, extending my hand, which she shook. She was wearing a white dress with little pink flowers and pink lipstick that highlighted her full lips and made the little space between her teeth that much more exciting.

"You surprised I came?"

"You said you would, so of course I hoped you would."

"I decided to trust you," she said, still smiling a bit skeptically, I thought.

"Good decision," I said. The sun was pouring through me and I was speaking confidently and spontaneously, although this was my first date in half a year.

"Come in and sit down at the living room table."

"I can only stay a little while."

I decided not to respond to that. Instead I fixed two drinks in the kitchen. "Like one?" I said, after I returned from the kitchen. She nodded, skeptically of course.

"I'll sip it."

I sat down, half facing her, half facing the holy late afternoon light.

"I like your mirrors, they're really big."

"I don't want to miss a thing."

She looked down at her drink, blushing, and I said, "I mean with the sky. Incredible things happen every moment out there."

"It's a real impressive view."

I got up from my seat, drink in hand, and walked to the windows. "Everything is out there," I said, looking at the first signs of sunset reflected off an office building, then looking at her. "Why don't you come over here and look up? You can see better."

"I can see fine from here," she said, reaching for a cigarette and lighting it. "Why don't you tell me your news now. You said you had this important thing to tell me, remember."

"This is my news, this is my important thing," I said, indicating the sweep of the sky with my arms and spilling a couple of drops of gin on the carpet.

"I don't follow," she said, inhaling more rapidly on her cigarette.

"This is the power that's changed me. It's been in front of us all the time."

"You're talking about the sky or what?"

"Yes."

"How did it change you?"

"It tells me everything. It told me that my body may die but that I'm part of the world forever. It told me that I'm as much a part of God as anything or anyone. And it told me to call you."

She snuffed out her cigarette and looked down at the table. I saw her cheeks turn dark red.

"You're serious, aren't you?"

"Very much so."

"That's why you sent me the flowers and everything, so I'd see this?"

"I knew you couldn't see it where you lived, and I wanted you to be changed too. It's changing you even now...."

"The sun is?"

"Yes, the sun, the sky, all of it. It's changing you even though you don't realize it. But if you spent a month or so watching it, you'd feel it in a totally overwhelming way."

"Well, it's certainly a beautiful view and thanks for sharing, but I think I'll be leaving now."

She got up from the table and walked toward the closet where her coat was.

"Wait. Please give me a minute more of your time. Two months ago, if someone said to me what I just did, I would've reacted the same way. Let me just explain why I asked you here instead of meeting you in some restaurant."

"You already explained."

"Just give me another minute."

She looked surprised, or maybe frightened, but I went on.

"Have you ever noticed how our ideas of spirituality are connected with heights? How we say 'Our Father who art in Heaven'."

"So this is supposed to be Heaven?"

"It's become Heaven."

"And that would make you God?"

I smiled. "No more than you are."

"Yeah, well the difference is I don't think I'm God so I don't try to play God with people's lives. See, I'm just a working girl plugging away at my humble career. I'm not really the religious type."

"It can help more than your career. It can help you in every way."

"What, looking out the window? Well, start a church then, charge admission. Call it the First Church of the High-Rise. Anyway, I'm going now." She opened the closet and pulled her coat off the hanger, which fell to the floor like a cymbal crashing. I rushed to the door and touched her arm.

"Hey, don't touch me, okay?"

"I'm sorry. Listen, everything I told you is true. I used to see you a lot when I lived next door to you and I thought you needed this."

"Yeah, I remember you," she said just before she opened the door. "You used to try to watch me every time I got undressed. You didn't seem like God then and you don't now. Maybe you made some money, but it's just you in a high-rise."

"You're trying to make me doubt everything."

"No, really, I'm busy. I gotta go. Good luck with the sky," she said, closing the door. I pressed myself to the door and stared out the peephole and saw her running down the hallway toward the stairs. Ah, she wasn't even going to take the elevator, she was so eager to escape from me.

...After I watched Lisa leave I felt dizzy and sat down at the living room table. I closed my eyes and concentrated until all I saw in my mind's eye was a blank, clear area like a lineless piece of paper. When I was still in school and had to write in class I'd sometimes close my eyes and actually see the question I had to answer better. That was how I saw what I was thinking about now, like a question written on an empty piece of paper: "Is Lisa evil?" If she was simply confused and panicked in her confusion, if I maybe revealed too much too quickly, I could still call or write to her explaining things in a less-threatening way and everything could be saved. But if she planned to make me doubt myself the way I did when we were neighbors, that would call for a very different response.

...My head hurts. I find this excruciating to think about. I close my eyes again and feel like I'm on a roller coaster tilting downward, then like I'm a mere waterbomb dropping from a high-rise that space itself has cast down. Totally excruciating. I open my eyes and feel an urgent need for...perspective.

I walk to the windows trying to keep my eyes above the building tops. The sun is setting on the other side of the high-rise, but I can see part of it reflected in the bank windows on 19th Street. I try to peer around my building to see the sunset better, but I can't. Meanwhile a cluster of birds fly by in different directions, although there are only supposed to be four major directions. Then I see an image of Lisa's face smiling in her dark apartment. I breathe deeply. I shudder. I hold onto the air conditioner and try to focus on my next move.

Ghost Parks

His wife, Ellen, had yelled at him, then left to go to work at the museum, somehow implying that he, too, should work on Saturdays to better himself. She thought nothing of his current job, that was obvious. Selling disgusted her. It disgusted him, too, but he couldn't see any real difference between her job and his (wasn't she selling herself every day to her bosses?), so why criticize? And why yell? She made him feel seven years old again, trembling with rage as if before his mother. Why did he put up with this? He felt he was getting so old now; he was already past thirty and he was still being yelled at by his wife. It was ridiculous, but there it was.

Andy paced in front of the picture window. Outside the sky was almost insanely bright. He looked down repeatedly at the elementary school playground where the basketball court was, but no one was on it. It was cold and he could hear the wind, but the court looked good in the strong sunlight.

There was a line, Andy thought, as clear as the foul line on a basketball court, and she had crossed it. Certainly, there were a number of ways you could cross the line—he'd thought for some time that she would cross it with a single outrageous act like sleeping with her boss. He still thought she'd probably done that, but he couldn't prove it. Instead she'd crossed it with her yelling and the abusive things she said. It was not any single thing she said, but rather the number of times she said them, the number of times she yelled at him until she yelled herself right across that line. He stopped pacing, looked out the window again, and realized that it was over—that much was certain. There was something pure about knowing this, something as pure as the sky. Still he felt nervous, as if uncomfortable in his own skin, and decided that despite the weather, he'd go outside and shoot some baskets, by himself if necessary.

It was more windy than he expected, and unusually cold that morning even for December, but he was still glad to be outdoors. His first thought was to go to Taney Park five blocks away on Pine Street, but then he remembered that the new Park Commissioner had taken the rims off the backboards to keep blacks away. Just like that, one hundred people disappeared. Some of the white players in the neighborhood even complained, but it came to nothing. Now the single basket on the elementary school playground three blocks from his apartment was the only place left to shoot in Center City. Philadelphia was getting more stupid every day, he thought, destroying its own playgrounds for no reason. This basket, which he was now forced to use, was old with a large gray wooden backboard and a slightly oversized rim so that you could never even be sure you deserved the shot you made. Most of the time Andy didn't let that bother him, but this morning it bothered him a lot. Moreover, after his first basket he missed his next six shots. It was the wind, it was the sun in his eyes, but most of all he was still stunned by his latest fight with Ellen and the realization that she had begun to hate him, and perhaps had hated him for some time.

That he hated her was completely different. He was sure she didn't know, so as long as he kept it a secret it didn't hurt anyone. Besides, his was not a cold or pure hatred—it had been balanced by memories of happier times with her and by the desire he still felt. He often thought of it as a close and vastly complicated basket-ball game—a game of streaks. When she got angry or wouldn't sleep with him the Hate Team surged ahead, but if she were nice even for ten or fifteen minutes, the other team would rally. But always it was a game he was officiating, and if it got too lopsided one way or the other he could end it and make it disappear.

This morning while she yelled at him he had seen something in her face that was undeniable. She wasn't playing any secret game; she wasn't ambivalent. She simply hated him and it shocked him, though he knew things had been going badly for some time. She was bitterly disappointed in their marriage and was probably sleeping with someone or soon would. She would never want him again as she once had—his sex life with her was lost. His own complicated game was now over as well. The look in her eyes had ended it in an instant. That look made her cross the line even more than her yelling, he realized. He hated her totally now and only hoped she would leave him soon or else let him go. If she wouldn't, if she were afraid of having to pay alimony or else was insane enough to expect some from him (for he had some money from his parents), he'd do something if he had to, anything to be rid of her.

Finally, he made a hook shot. Andy turned instinctively to see if anyone was watching, and saw a black man coming toward him, wrapped in a cheap green cloth coat that reminded him of the army coat he used to wear in college. The man had a thin beard which circled his face and gave him a look of sternness and conviction. Andy thought they were about the same age, that he was maybe an inch or two taller, though it was hard to tell because the man was walking hunched over a little with both arms folded against the cold.

Andy turned to him and said, "Wanna shoot?"

The man unfolded his arms and opened his hands to catch the ball. For a few minutes they shot in silence. Andy immediately considered himself a better player and hoped there'd be no challenge for a one-on-one. He hated such situations where he had to determine how hard he should try so that the game could be close, and no one would be too hurt or angry. He'd been the starting off-guard on his high school team and generally was one of the best players on any given day at a playground, though of course he'd slowed up a little in the last few years.

"Damn! Can't get one to go down," the man said.

"The wind's brutal. You gotta play the wind today."

They shot another two minutes without speaking. Andy thought about Ellen and began missing his shots again. When the man hit a couple of jumpers, Andy said, "All right!" with sportscaster enthusiasm.

The man walked over to him carrying the ball and extending his free hand. "My name's Graham."

"I'm Andy." They shook hands and Andy asked if he lived nearby.

Graham said no and Andy immediately regretted his question because Graham looked like he was probably homeless. His chinos were badly torn and his shoes looked like strips of bacon. Ellen had upset him so much he couldn't think right any more.

"Hey, man, I want to show you something."

Graham reached inside the pocket of his coat, which came down to his knees, and pulled out a wallet. "See this? I used to be in a group, man. You know music?"

"Sure, some."

"Here's a picture of my group. We was called 'The Thunderballs.'" Andy nodded. He had never heard of them. He saw a picture of four black men in tuxedos smiling in front of some palm trees and asked what Graham did in the group.

"Sang, played keyboards, sometimes sang lead. We travelled all over when things was good. Then we hit a down time in L.A. See this dude? Recognize him? That's Quincy Jones."

"Sure." It was a colored Polaroid—all the pictures were—of Graham standing next to Jones in a club. Andy found himself checking for inauthentic details, in spite of himself. Graham showed him similar pictures of himself and Whitney Houston, his group hovering around Danny DeVito (of all people), his group sitting at a table with Luther Vandross, and then one of himself and a smiling Cher.

"Amazing," Andy said, in part to make Graham feel good, in part because he was kind of amazed to see a picture of this street person in such friendly proximity to Cher, who had long been one of his fantasy women.

"Yeah, things were cool for a while."

"What happened?"

"Give me the rock, man; I've got to stay warm."

Graham hit a jump shot and Andy applauded. He thought that he had to do this to keep Graham talking.

"Income tax problems is what happened. I didn't do it. Just trusted the wrong people. Shoulda stayed with the brothers, I guess. Done three years for it, I know that."

"Prison?"

"Three-and-a-half years' time. Just out a few weeks ago."

"How come you're in Philly?"

"Long story, man. I'm trying to get down to Florida. Got a wife and kid in Jacksonville," Graham sighed. "Yeah, I really miss 'em."

Andy stopped himself from asking Graham why he didn't go to Jacksonville. It was obvious he had no money.

"You gotta old lady?" Graham said with a little smile that showed a chipped front tooth.

"Yeah, but I'm trying to get away from her. Can't stand her anymore. She yells at me all the time."

"That's cold."

"Yeah, it shouldn't happen, should it?"

Graham shook his head. "Come on, check me, man," Graham said. He began dribbling with rapid, low bounces toward the imaginary key.

"Remember Earl the Pearl? Watch this." Graham tried a spin move, but his shot only nicked a side of the rim. Then he insisted on going through the routine three more times until he finally made a basket, Andy all the while playing only token defense. After his basket Graham said, "See that, the Pearl is back. Now I'll turn into Clyde Frazier and check you. You old enough to remember those dudes, ain't you? How old are you?"

"Too old to keep guarding you. You're wearing me out." He still wanted to avoid a game, and besides he'd gotten an idea that was still so vague he didn't know if it was an idea or a dream, but to find out he knew he needed to talk some more to Graham. Andy took a jump shot, missed, got his own rebound and passed the ball to Graham.

"Let's just shoot, OK?"

Graham rubbed the ball and smiled. "Long as I get to shoot the rock, I'm happy. Long as you have a rock, you're never alone, right man?"

"Right," Andy said, but he hardly heard him. He was thinking about his idea again and for the next five minutes, while they shot, he tried furiously to remember bank statements and deeds and insurance policies. When he was unable to visualize each document he felt that it might no longer exist, and he'd start to panic. Then he'd turn his back and dribble the ball hard on the concrete with his eyes closed until he found he could see the lease or the last bank statement, could make them exist again through concentration. He turned to Graham. "Where are you staying now?"

Graham smiled ironically and shrugged. "No place particular, man. I'm trying to get enough together for a room but they want all this security shit, first two months, then the last month...Maybe they're insecure or something," he laughed. "Course you can't get a job if you don't have an address." He swore and spat with disgust, the wind barely letting the spit leave him.

"Sounds rough. I'm sorry."

"I don't know what they expect when they let you out. They don't give you nothing...you can't get a job, that's almost impossible. I'm trying to be good. I'm trying not to slip up and do something wrong, but they're not making it easy. Every day I'm tempted 'cause I got to eat, you know? Yeah, I'm tempted every day."

Andy looked at Graham closely. His big dark eyes looked angry, and for a moment Andy was frightened.

"You could stay with me for a while, if it wasn't for my wife. She wouldn't go for it. She doesn't care about helping people. She's one of these unconscious racists, if you know what I mean. She doesn't know herself well enough to even understand it, but she is."

"I hear you."

"But look, I can give you a few bucks so you can eat something today."

"Thank you, man."

"I'll have to get it in my apartment, if you don't mind walking me there."

"That's no problem."

They took their last shots, each waiting till the other made a basket, then left the playground, walking up Chestnut Street. Andy lived in a high-rise filled with what he considered yuppie creeps and future yuppie creeps (University of Pennsylvania business students). It was his wife's idea to move there. He'd wanted to stay in West Philly where they'd lived near Clark Park, a playground where there were always lots of games and where he'd earned something of a reputation. But after Ellen's promotion, she'd insisted on moving. She became impossible on the subject so quickly he couldn't muster a defense. She was hot to live at a semi-status address, and also, Andy thought, hot to get away from black people. Their new building fulfilled both her wishes. Except for the doorman and maintenance men, who were all black, and a prostitute accompanying a blushing business student, he'd never seen a black person inside the building. Just another example of apartheid Philadelphia-style, he thought. That Ellen loved the building convinced him she was a racist and made him hate her all the more. As they climbed the steps to his building, he wondered if he should introduce Graham to James, the somewhat supercilious doorman now on duty, but decided to say nothing. So a poor black man in shabby clothes was in the building; let the building make an issue of it. He knew the building wouldn't, that the building would back down.

When they walked into the lobby, James looked at Graham with slightly raised eyebrows, but as soon as Andy looked at him, James buzzed them both in. On the elevator the presence of Margaret, the legal secretary who lived on the same floor, temporarily inhibited them, but as soon as they began walking down the hallway, they started talking again.

"You got a nice building, man."

"The accommodations are nice, but the people are a different story."

Andy turned the key, and they walked into his apartment. "Make yourself at home, sit down if you can find someplace where there isn't a plant or tree growing. My wife likes to pretend she lives in the jungle—a high rise in the jungle, I guess. But no natives, just her and the trees."

Graham sat in a brown leather chair and laughed. "Reminds me of my time in California."

"Wanna beer?" Andy asked as he opened the refrigerator.

"Sure.

Andy took out two cans of Heineken. "I can't find a clean glass. Is the can OK?"

"Sure, man. Can's great."

He handed Graham the Heineken and sat down in a green La-Z-Boy opposite him. To their left a large picture window overlooked Center City. Periodically they looked out the window while they drank and talked.

"That the playground where we was?" Graham said, pointing at the window and then momentarily turning toward Andy. Andy nodded.

"Do you check it out to see who's there before you go down? Is that what you do?"

"Sometimes," Andy said, while Graham laughed.

"You got a real setup man. Yes sir, a real setup."

Andy didn't say anything. He didn't want to begin talking until they'd both had a second beer or something stronger. He was trying to remember where he had hidden his pot (his smoking was another thing Ellen and he fought about), thinking the pot might be what he needed to implement his idea. Meanwhile, Graham was talking about his salad days in California.

"When I was in Santa Monica I was three minutes from the beach. That's three minutes if I ran, and I used to run there at first, just to see how fast I could get there. That was beautiful, man. The waves and the sun."

"What was your place like?"

"Two-room apartment we were renting. Got a little crowded 'cause one of the guys in the group was staying there too."

He felt a flash of jealousy which he tried to stop by focusing on Graham's present condition. Graham was looking at him quizzically.

"Course, even though I could get to the beach in three minutes, I couldn't see it from my window, man. You're three minutes from the park and you can see it too. That's a setup. Yes sir, you're in a real classy building."

"I didn't want to come here. I liked where I was before better, but my wife made me move. She wanted a big deal address."

"Where were you before?"

"In West Philly; in a regular apartment. I was near a park too. I couldn't see it from my window, but there were games there all the time with all kinds of people. I don't have anyone to talk to here. Everyone here is the same, if you know what I mean."

"I hear you."

Andy felt odd, as if he were starting to vibrate inside, and took a breath to steady himself.

"I'm getting another brew," he announced.

"Sure, man. We gonna drink the blues away." Graham laughed and Andy laughed too, before stopping himself in the kitchen. He would get nowhere acting like this; he would lose track of his idea. He decided he should change the mood, so when he returned with the beers he asked Graham about his wife and child.

They were in L.A. with him when he was arrested and had gone back to Jacksonville to stay with her relatives, Graham explained. His son, Tommy, was four-and-a-half years old, and for three of those years Graham hadn't seen him. Andy looked at the pain on Graham's face and felt nervous.

"You and your wife have any children?" Graham said.

"Well, there's the two of us," he said, and Graham laughed.

"See my wife doesn't want to have any children. There's not much happening in our bed these days. She thinks she's so successful now that she doesn't have to deal with the likes of me. Want some of this?" he said, holding out a joint and lighter he'd found next to the steak knives in the kitchen.

Graham gave him a funny look. "With my empty stomach, this gonna go right to my head." But he took the joint, inhaled deeply a couple of times, and passed it back to Andy.

"Like I said before, I can give you about ten bucks or so. Wish I could give you more, but that's all I got on me. My wife makes most of the money; and she doesn't share. She hides all her cash, too." He took a hit, passed it back to Graham, then waited until Graham smoked some more.

"Your woman ever cold to you? I mean one or two times they all say no."

"Yeah, one or two times a week, you mean," Graham said laughing.

"Yeah, really," Andy said, forcing himself to laugh. He waited until Graham stopped laughing, which seemed to take a long time, then said, "No, I mean has she ever shut you down for a long period of time?"

"A long time?" Graham asked.

"Yeah."

"Course that's one of those relative terms. 'Cause sometimes a week's a long time and sometimes a day is. Every damn day I spent in jail was long to me."

"I was thinking more like a month than a week."

"No man, that never happened to me 'cept in jail."

"I hate it when they use their pussies as a weapon to shut you down."

"Hey, better they should shut you down than chop you down, right? Like that Lorena Bobbitt did to her husband while he was sleeping. John Bobbitt was his name, wasn't it? Then she drove off and threw it away like an old useless bone. Cold, man."

"Yeah, she got off with nothing, man, nothing but a little counseling, as I recall. Hell, she probably enjoyed whining about herself and having someone there who had to listen. That was probably pleasure for her. I know my wife would rather complain than anything."

Andy inhaled on the last of the joint then said, "What did you say you were arrested for?"

"I told you, man, income tax problems. My manager did it. I trusted the wrong dude, that's all."

"That's a lot of time for income taxes."

"Hey, you ever notice life ain't always fair?"

"Right," Andy said, nodding. "Must have been tough in jail. Was there a lot of violent stuff in there?"

"What you think? Wasn't no tea party: you got to be alert, you got to take care of yourself. That's why I can do it now on the streets. I learned how to survive in there."

"But you said you aren't getting into any fights now."

"No. I'm not fighting anyone 'less they fight me first. I told you that. What you think? I tell you one thing on the playground and another up here?"

Andy made a conciliatory gesture with his hands. "Not at all. I'm just trying to understand. 'Cause you said you were tempted."

"Sure, I'm tempted."

"That's interesting 'cause there are probably other people who are tempted too, who might pay you a lot of money to do something for them."

"You mean, pay me to pull some job for them?"

Andy finished the joint and tried to make eye contact with Graham. "It could be that or something that might be worth a lot more money to you."

"Like what?"

"Say there was a man who really hated someone he was living with. Say this man had been stepped on and humiliated by this person and felt he'd come to the end of the line." He felt his hand shake but kept on. "Now he might not be a man who looks like he has money, but he might really have some money plus be absolutely sure of getting some more so he could put, say, ten thousand bucks in your pocket. Let's also say that he already has an excellent plan worked out, and he's only looking for someone like you to put the plan in motion so he can put a stop to the cruelty of this terrible person he happens to live with."

Graham leaned forward in his chair. "Am I reading you right? You serious?"

"Could be, Graham. You might be."

"Well, that person wouldn't be looking for me 'cause I wouldn't be doing nothing like that. I draw the line, see. And on one side of the line is money and property, and on the other side is people, even racist pigs—unconscious or otherwise. They're still on that side of the line."

Graham looked directly at him, and a terrible fear swept though Andy. "That's a very good answer," Andy said. "That's a really impressive answer."

"There's lots of temptation out there, but that ain't one of them. Never be one either. I'm a father, you know. You can't bring one person into the world and take another out. I'll be going now."

Both men got up from their chairs, and Andy mumbled something about how strong Graham's character was. Then he took fifteen dollars from his pocket and thrust it into Graham's hands, worrying that Graham might realize that he'd had money in his pants all along, but not wanting to lie about it either.

Graham said, "Thanks," and put the money in his coat. He had pulled his coat tightly around himself and was heading toward the door.

Andy rushed up behind him and began asking if maybe they could meet to play ball again. He picked up the basketball from in front of the door and followed Graham out into the hallway, but Graham was already standing by the elevator. "Hey," he said, passing the ball to him, "take it. It's yours."

Graham looked down at the ball he had caught, running his fingers over it for a few seconds as if he were combing an animal's fur before he passed it back to Andy. "You need it more than I do," he said. Then the elevator came and Graham left.

In his apartment Andy paced in front of his picture window thinking that Graham saw right through him, which was why he wouldn't take the ball or even say good-bye. But what would Graham do? Would he go to the police, or try to warn Ellen some way, maybe leave a message for her with the doorman?

He ran into the bedroom and, after searching the room quickly, found Ellen's Ativan in the bathroom cabinet. He took a pill and returned to the living room, letting his head fill with a different voice that the mere taking of the Ativan seemed to have set in motion.

He thought, I've been smoking, which is making everything seem worse. The bottom line is it's his word against mine (and I never even, technically, said anything), plus he's a homeless ex-con who's high. Besides, he took the money so he can eat—he just wants to eat. He doesn't want any new trouble; that'd be the last thing he wants.

He sat down in the brown leather chair and his anxiety began to give way to an immense sadness. He started running his fingers over the leaves of a jade plant. How had he come to this point? He could still vividly remember the time when they loved each other. What had happened to those people? It was like time just took them away and replaced them with two angry ghosts. At any rate, he now knew he wouldn't have gone through with it. It was only a temporary rage he was in and now it was over.

When Graham spoke of drawing the line, he'd felt strangely moved. He stopped stroking the plant and stood up to see if Graham might be back on the playground or else walking on the street, but all he could see were buildings and the blinding blue sky. It was too cold to be out walking, much too cold.

A few hours later, he fell asleep in the bedroom. When he heard the door open he woke up instantly, but instinctively stayed still.

"Christ, what a day," Ellen was muttering, either to herself or to him, he couldn't tell which. He could hear her undressing, making more noises of exasperation in the room. Be nice, he warned himself. Things can be made better just by being nice. But he was afraid that if he talked she'd find out he'd been high and pick another fight. Tomorrow he'd be nice first thing, but for now it was best to say nothing and just vanish. So he closed his eyes, pretending to be asleep, but the uncomfortable feeling in his skin returned, and for a moment, he thought again of hiring someone else for the job Graham wouldn't do. His head ached, too, but he'd get no sympathy talking about that to Ellen, so he just kept his eyes closed and soon rolled over to make room for her in their bed.

Carbo's

She walked across Lindell Avenue, high heels clicking on the street, her necklace of bells ringing slightly. She liked the music she seemed to be making. It was a warm night in a typically un-predictable St. Louis winter and she was glad she'd worn her short skirt. It had played well at Mardi Gras, so why not at Carbo's on her date? Besides, on the phone she'd told him she had good legs so she might as well showcase them. His voice had turned husky when she'd described them and he'd made a joke she couldn't quite remember, though she'd laughed at the time. He was good on the phone. Smooth, deep, appealing voice, intelligent sounding. He said he was a businessman, an officer at Ralston Purina no less, so obviously he had bucks. And he was funny too—the best of both worlds—but of course she shouldn't start building up too much of a fantasy about him too quickly. Nick had been funny in the beginning too. He used to make her laugh, and he laughed himself before he started yelling. Men were like that. They lost their humor faster than they lost their erections. So it wasn't the biggest deal in the world that Davis had made her laugh on the phone, although certainly it was a good sign.

She was five minutes late as she walked into Carbo's. She wanted to be ten minutes late because she knew guys liked to feel the anticipation up to a point, valued what they had to wait a little longer for. But she also knew some pretty hot women hung out at Carbo's on Friday nights and she was afraid to let him be among them for too long. (That had happened to her before, and once the bastard had pretended he didn't know her when she walked up to him.) The really cool women, the confident ones, were ten minutes late but she supposed five minutes was better than nothing.

She saw him almost immediately. Dark blue pin-striped suit, red power tie, pretty tall, not too heavy, blue piercing eyes. He looked like a corporate officer as he walked towards her with big power strides.

"Are you Nancy?"

"Yeah, hi, are you Davis?"

They shook hands and smiled.

"I brought you something," she said, opening her purse and withdrawing another necklace. "Just pretend you're at Mardi Gras," she said as she helped him put it on.

He smiled. "Come on, I've got a table for us," he said, taking her hand and holding it until they reached the table. He was a bold one all right, already getting physical, but so far she kind of liked it.

He helped seat her (which she thought was classy) and ordered the drinks from the waitress who instantly materialized by the table. Ten minutes, two drinks, and a few jokes later he put his hand on her thigh.

She looked at his hand as if it were a blemish on her clothes. He didn't remove it and then she felt she couldn't ask him to. She knew how men were. She finished her drink and when the waitress came to their table ordered another.

She noticed his jokes had stopped somewhere around his third drink. Just flew off and disappeared like a flock of birds. Meanwhile his hand kept moving up and over. It felt like a mouse on her leg but she couldn't scream, couldn't even say a word about it. She had another drink, thinking that if she drank enough she could maybe like that mouse.

Then it seemed they were arguing. Again she didn't know how it had started. He'd been talking about his ex-wife darkly, bitterly—started saying some negative things about women in general—and she'd reacted and said some things back about men. It was that simple, that childish. It was short, intense, like an angry screw, and then it ended. He looked worried, went back to his jokes, and the hand that had practically been pounding the table went back to her thigh. She had to get up, to breathe, to compose herself (plus she was suddenly worried about what she looked like) and said she'd be right back, that she had to use the bathroom.

Davis wasn't exactly sure how long Nancy had been gone, but it seemed too long and he was getting nervous. He began looking around the bar incredulously. He felt he'd never been in a place as ridiculous at this. There was a woman—late 30s, maybe early 40s—ten feet in front of him in the middle of the bar wearing a skintight red, white, and blue skirt that said Budweiser all over it and barely came down to her crotch. She was surrounded by five men her age, all dressed up and laughing loudly as they eyed the woman in the center of their circle.

He'd been told about this Carbo's place—he should have known. He looked out towards the light behind the bar where a platform was set up. The blonde singer was wearing a clinging black vinyl skirt. She seemed to come in three parts. Body looked young, not fat, lots of work—maybe some surgery to make her breasts firm—the hair dyed, of course, in some way, the face of ambiguous age because the bar lights were dimmed. But her neck showed she was definitely past 40. No one knows how to operate on a neck, Davis thought. No one knows how to make a neck look younger than it is, and so his eyes always went to a woman's neck. Her neck told him she was in the 43 to 45 zone. He could read it like the rings on a tree.

He turned away from the lights and remembered earlier that night, sitting in his chair that faced the television, wondering if he could bear to turn off the living room lamp, if he could risk that plunge into half-darkness. Had the Ativan kicked in enough to face a darkened room with only the hallway lights on, muted and partly hidden by a wall? They were more like pale slivers of moon than sunlight. His whole apartment seemed vacant, cold, and light resistant, like the moon, which made him use 250-watt bulbs in all the lamps that could hold them.

Nancy was still in the ladies' room, probably doing make-up inspection. She'd come from Mardi Gras in Soulard and was dressed in purple and bright green on top and a black miniskirt. She wore three rows of beads almost the size of small Christmas bulbs around her neck. He'd finished his second vodka tonic and was wearing the necklace that she'd given him. She was a strange one but so far not too strange. (The last three women he'd met through the ads were all on antidepressants.) Nancy's ad was longer than most of the other ads he'd answered, and though it was filled with much the same information (she liked "movies, dining out, travel, the outdoors," etc.), its very length and detail gave him a certain confidence. Also, to be honest, he'd answered her ad because she'd said she was 41 (younger than him), attractive, and a natural blonde with blue eyes "and long, shapely legs."

The waitress came to his table to ask if he wanted another drink. Davis shook his head no. Couldn't she see his glass was half full? The waitresses here were clearly trained to never leave you alone for more than ten minutes. It wouldn't surprise him if they wore some kind of timing device that rang whenever the time for a particular table was up. You could be making out with your girlfriend, you could have your tongue halfway down her throat, and if the waitress's timing device went off she'd trot up to your table and earnestly ask, "Can I get you some dinner now? Or another drink?"

Where was Nancy? What was she doing? She seemed to be capable of anything. She also seemed divided into separate parts, like the singer who was now belting out her version of "Strangers in the Night." There was Nancy's head, which spoke most of the words between them, which picked an argument with him before she went to the bathroom about men being manipulative and only caring about sex, and then there was the Nancy from the waist down, who was letting him press his leg against hers and keep his hand on her thigh, even move it around a little, as if all this were going on in a separate world—the below-the-waist world that was of little concern to the Nancy-head world.

Davis got up from the table and started walking towards the ladies' room. She said she'd come to Carbo's before and had already said hello to a couple of men. Who really knew what was going on in the bathroom?

Davis walked into a lighted area. He found he was at the edge of the singer's pool of light and, looking over his shoulder, stopped for a moment and tried to make eye contact. But the singer avoided him. One hand on her hip, the other clutching the mike, she was working a man in the front row who'd been ogling her all night.

Davis turned away and started thinking again about what Nancy was doing in the bathroom. He didn't like the images in his head but couldn't get rid of them. Was he high enough to walk in there and find out for himself? (He could always claim he'd misread the black stick drawing of a woman on the door.)

He'd moved closer to the bathroom now, thinking that perhaps he'd try to listen first for a few seconds at the door, when Nancy suddenly walked out.

When she saw him she smiled semivacantly. "Hey there," she said. Davis realized she was still high and felt better for a moment.

"Hey there yourself. I was just stretching my legs. Our table's still there if you want it," he said, pointing to it.

"Sure," she said, walking ahead of him.

At the table she sat a little apart from him and Davis felt miffed. The waitress came by again and he glared at her until she left. He was remembering his last girlfriend, Lori, who had left him two months ago. He hadn't touched a woman since then and felt he was going crazy. (Every one of the personal ad dates so far had ended in disappointment or humiliation.) It seemed there was always one of three feelings he'd had in the Lori aftermath: a sickening kind of deja vu anger at her and how she'd hurt him; a panicked feeling that he would never make love again, at least not that way; or finally, missing aspects of her such as her smile or voice, missing her and feeling guilty for his part in things. The feelings were separate and at the moment all-encompassing. It was like each feeling was a television channel of its own, playing the same show over and over again, though at any moment a new channel could be pressed and he'd have no choice but to surrender to it. On those occasional times that more than one of the channels played inside him simultaneously, Davis would start drinking and then call one personal ad after another.

Nancy said something to him that he didn't hear. He waited a few seconds then said, "What were you doing so long in the ladies' room?"

She smiled. "Girl things."

"That hardly answers the question."

"What do you mean?"

"Girls have been known to do all kinds of things, both in and out of bathrooms."

She looked at him quizzically. "You saying something?"

"I thought so. I thought I was saying something. It might have been a mutual illusion but I don't think so."

"I was fixing my hair and my make-up. What else did you think I was doing?"

"I didn't know. That's why I asked."

"Christ, Davis, I hope you're not gonna be one of those jealous, adolescent-type men."

"Adolescent? That's a curious choice of words to use with me. Why adolescent?"

"Because grown-up people wouldn't say what you just did, would they?"

"Grown-up people wouldn't come here."

"Excuse me. I thought you'd get a kick out of this place. On the phone you said you liked to have fun."

"Yeah, fun, for the middle-aged challenged."

"You've certainly enjoyed the musical talent."

"What talent?"

"The singer. I've noticed you can't seem to keep your eyes off her."

Davis felt himself bristle. He decided not to point out the obvious irony in light of her calling him jealous. There was something more important that he needed to get straight. "Do you realize how ludicrous the word adolescent is applied to me? I have approximately 110 people directly affected by my decisions. Did you know that? But that's just my branch, and my influence extends far beyond my branch. Do you think Ralston would entrust that kind of responsibility to an 'adolescent'?"

She looked at him closely and didn't say anything for a moment. "No," she said. "I don't think they would."

"Would an 'adolescent' earn over $150,000 a year? Because that's what I earn."

"No."

"So it was stupid, really, to call me that, wasn't it?"

"I'm sorry."

"It's just a trick you women do to belittle a man, using a word like that. You cut off a man's dick before he's even had a chance to use it."

"Hey, watch it. I'm not a slut that you can talk that way to me. I know you think I'm stupid but I don't think I am, and I'm definitely not a slut."

"On the contrary. I've never said or thought you were stupid. I did wonder a bit about your standards when you started flirting with so many men on the way to the bathroom and then stayed in there so long."

"I talked to the men that I met here before for about half a minute. Big deal."

"And how long were you in the bathroom after speaking to them?"

"I don't know, I didn't time myself. What's the matter with you? Did you just get divorced or something?"

"I told you about that on the phone."

"Well stop taking your anger at your wife out on me. I didn't do anything to you."

Davis said nothing. In his mind he saw the word PROOF in big black letters. It was true he had no proof that she'd done something. With women it was always a question of proof, and you had nothing to go on but the words they said to you. So you began developing your memory, you realized at an early age or perhaps just by instinct to remember all their key words and store them without even knowing it. Store them up for the times when they'd contradict themselves even as you also remembered all the compliments and reassurances—the castle of words you clung to so you could go on and believe in them.

Both were functioning simultaneously—the memory of the reassurances in all their forms and the memory of all the contradictions and doubts. Meanwhile the women knew what you wanted to know. They knew if they came or not, they knew who really was the father of their children. They knew everything you wanted to know and so focused on other questions. They wanted to know if you loved them or not. They were always getting abstract on you. But without the concrete, who could get to the abstract?

Their superior knowledge gave them complete control of the word game. They decided whether to release compliments or contradictions, reassurances or doubt. It had been that way with Lori and with his wife and the women before her. It had always been that way with women and now, within an hour, it was already that way with Nancy.

"Hey, Davis, what's the deal? You going silent on me?"

"Sorry," he said, instinctively.

"Have another drink," she said, pointing to the new vodka tonic beside him, as she took a swallow of gin.

"I didn't order a new drink."

"The waitress left you one anyway."

"That's disgusting."

"What?"

"To be that sneaky. They'll do anything to hike up your tab. She probably thought I was too high to notice."

"Yeah. Little did she know you were too angry."

"What? You want to pick a new fight with me now, is that it? We have a certain number of nice minutes and then your timer goes off and it's time to fight."

"No. Sorry. Look, I just want to have a few laughs with you like we did before I was a bad girl and stayed in the bathroom too long."

Davis laughed, then took a big swallow of his new drink.

"Really, what is it with you guys? You're always so primed to get mad. A woman can bat her eyelash the wrong way and you start yelling. You see that movie *Raging Bull* about the jealous boxer who abused his wife?"

"Yes, I saw it."

"Yeah. He lost everything 'cause of his temper and jealous mind. Far as I'm concerned I think you guys are all raging bulls. You can't wait to start yelling and pointing fingers and worse. It was the same way with Nicky, my ex. Always getting angry. We could be at the beach lying on our chaise lounges. Nice sunny day. He could be totally relaxed but if for one second I looked at him the wrong way, bam, he's pissed off. You're all like that. You're all angry little bulls. But what's the point of going through life like that?"

"Beats me," Davis said. He wasn't angry anymore but couldn't help feeling sad. He regretted his temper and the things he'd said to Nancy. It was the type of thing he'd done too often with Lori and with his ex-wife, too. Was he a drugged rat in a maze that he kept behaving the same way? Yet he wasn't really a rat because he alone knew why he'd lose his temper and sometimes say and do mean things. There were reasons; he was a rat with a reason and so not really a rat at all. The irony was people never saw the reason, only what you did in the moment in front of them. Only when you were in a court of law did anyone consider your past, and even then most of it was thrown out as inadmissible. So many times he'd wanted to say to Lori, "If you could see a videotape of my life, you'd understand." He wanted to say it now to Nancy too but couldn't. Yet if she could see even just one scene with him and his father, for instance when he'd used the belt on him, not that that was even the worst of it, wouldn't it soften her heart at least a bit?

"So we went to the goddamn Jersey shore, not that it's the worst place in the world for a vacation, but I'd hoped for something quieter and I knew it meant he'd spend a lot of time at the casinos, which I had no use for."

"Who's this again?"

"Nick. My ex-husband. Haven't you been listening?"

"Yes."

"This is on the vacation that's supposed to make up for his roughing me up when I got on his case about gambling and then about his female assistant I was sure he was screwing, or wanted to. Anyway I hoped this vacation might be different. And I don't want you to think I was some kind of jealous freak always checking on him or some kind of puritan angel who had to live by the word of the Church. I wasn't. I wasn't either thing. I just liked peace and quiet and I tried to always trust him, though, of course,

I had my limits. But on this trip (which I thought might be the last of our marriage if it didn't work out) I really hoped it would be different. And for a few hours it was. He made love with me in the morning, spent a little more time with me than usual. Then he went out to the beach with me and sat in a chair we rented, though I knew he didn't like the sun. He even took off his shirt for a while. Honestly, his skin was as white as a piece of paper—it was almost funny—but he was being a good sport. I remember he even walked down to the water with me for a few minutes.

"When we got back to the chairs, he put his sunglasses on and got quiet. It was like he'd used up his speech quota on me for the day and I knew he was getting restless—he kept tapping his knee—so I said, 'Why don't you go to the casino? You know you want to.'

"'Just for an hour,' he said. 'You come get me if I'm not back by then.'

"'Sure,' I said and I think he even kissed me good-bye on the lips and called me a good girl.

"I remember I felt a strange sense of peace, so strange that after ten or fifteen minutes I became afraid of it leaving and to sort of protect against that I fell asleep. When I woke up at first I saw these colors floating..."

"What colors?" Davis said.

"Red and yellow and pink and baby blue, the colors of the kites and people's bathing suits and the sky. Just the colors of the beach, but when I first saw them after waking up I swear to God I thought I was in heaven or something.

"Then I looked at my watch. He was already fifteen minutes late but I said to myself 'I'm not going to be a shrew': I decided I wasn't even going to go over there. Another fifteen minutes went by and I got up and started to pace a little near my chair. I was beginning to worry about how much money Nick might be losing, then when another fifteen minutes passed I started wondering if he'd picked up some girl at the casino, or maybe a hooker on the street.

"I began walking then, thinking I'd walk along the shoreline holding my shoes and at least let the water go over my toes every now and then. But when I reached the shoreline a weird thing happened. I began walking in the opposite direction, away from the casino. The colors began to blur together and I just started crying to beat the band, thinking, 'It's over this time, I just know it's over this time.'"

She continued talking. It was a painful story all right, like a long slow aria in a tragic opera. Davis couldn't focus on her anymore and began to wonder where the waitress was now that he needed her. But he couldn't turn and call for her while Nancy was still talking, nor could he get up and go to the bar to order a drink, and he wanted a drink badly. He'd been thinking about his father and then his ex-wife and then his father again. Repetitive, torturous images. He feared the onset of sobriety, thinking his thoughts would become still worse then.

How had this happened tonight? How had he been ambushed like this? It started when Nancy had criticized him, called him adolescent and jealous and then started in on her own pain like his father would do and his ex-wife, too. They were like hit-and-run drivers. They would hurt you when you least expected it and then desert you once you confronted them, or worse, start in with their own pain and turn you into their audience, still without dealing with how they'd hurt you in the first place.

He began feeling in his pants pocket for an Ativan, then in the pockets of his suit coat and shirt. Could he have forgotten to bring it somehow? Could it somehow have fallen out?

The image in his mind turned from a glass of vodka to the small white pill on his kitchen counter by the sink. If he didn't picture the pill he would see his father's face, or his wife's, or some hideous fusion of the two.

"I need to get out of here...soon. This place is making me sick," Davis said. He noticed that he was half out of his seat already.

Nancy stared at him in a stunned way, her eyes wet with tears.

"I'm making you sick?"

"No, it's not you. It's this place. I said it was this place, didn't I?"

She looked at him. It was like being on the beach again when it got dark.

"You go ahead," she said. "You do what you have to do."

"You're not coming with me then?"

"I'm comfortable here. I'm OK. I'm fine. But you go ahead, I understand."

He took two twenties out of his wallet and put them on the table to pay for the drinks.

"I'm sorry," he said.

He'd said more too, two or three sentences more by way of apology or explanation, before finally saying good-bye. He tried to remember exactly what he said as he drove back in his Lexus. Tried over and over to recreate the circumstances, to visualize the scene in the dark, irregularly lit bar, the better to recall the last words he'd said, but couldn't ever be sure. Then he wondered why he was wondering.

It was the hit-and-run syndrome again—he was sure of it. She had hit him—hurt him—and then disappeared into the black hole of her own pain. It had happened to him before. There was a photograph of his father on his bureau and in it he had that expression on his face too—the look of a hit-and-run driver.

He slammed his car door shut, then could barely bring himself to acknowledge the doorman on his way to the elevator. There was a rumbling in his head in the elevator, a rumbling and a roaring. Just before he opened his apartment door he thought the noise was coming from inside, that somehow a group of horses were running around in his apartment.

He opened the door and saw nothing but a few specks of lamplight from the park through his living room window. The roaring subsided. He turned on the kitchen light, reached for his pill, held it, looked at it, swallowed it, then sat down in his chair and held himself because for some reason he was shivering.

She was still in her seat with a new drink beside her, trying to figure something out. Why was it like the beach again, like that afternoon at the shore? How could it be? Was it just because they were both dark? But was there music playing on the beach like there was here? She supposed there was from the transistor radios. Yet then she had been walking on the beach and could still feel the water over her toes, the soft, wet sand under her feet, and here she was sitting like she was paralyzed, her face painted, her skirt hiked up like a whore, unable to move. So how could they feel so alike it was like deja vu?

She took two swallows of her drink and then it hit her. It was the same because in each case she'd been left by a man. At a certain point it didn't matter if it was by a stranger on a first date or her husband who had become a stranger. They each took what they wanted, or tried to take what they thought they wanted, and then left.

She took another swallow. A man stood over her. "You want some company?" he said. He wore a sports jacket and a red tie. She didn't have anything to say so she smiled as he sat down. When he got settled she looked at him and the oddest thing happened. She couldn't see his face. She knew he was a man, but where his face was supposed to be there was a blankness like a white sheaf of sky.

IV

Miles

"You're the rookie, I'm the veteran—you should listen to me," the veteran said, turning towards her in the front seat. She didn't acknowledge him, just kept driving her route, staring ahead poker-faced, maddeningly placid from the veteran's point of view, Miles thought. "See, it's not about what's comfortable and convenient for you, it's about time-is-money; you hear me rookie?" She still said nothing. Kept her poker face, although Miles thought it was a pretty poker face and he'd been trying, so far without luck, to make eye contact with it from the backseat via the mirror in the front seat where the rookie and veteran sat. In that regard he sympathized with the veteran. Miles's hope was that if she would look back at him he'd show some sympathy for her, try to talk to her and maybe find a way to get her phone number later. But, realistically, he thought this could never happen. She was simply driving the shuttle to his home—there was no basis for contact. Besides, there were several other factors going against him. She was probably black, she hadn't said more than three words to him and she was under a great deal of pressure from her mentoring fellow driver, who might or might not be involved with her and who was certainly more than a little mean.

It was starting to get dark out. Five minutes ago, the last people besides Miles had left the shuttle and the veteran began to get even angrier. He pointed out with more than a little contempt that the elderly couple they'd just dropped off lived in one of the wealthiest communities in Delaware County, then said how he hadn't appreciated their oversized guard dog that'd charged him. The veteran described the dog's charge and its relentless barking in some detail, although nothing had happened to him bite-wise.

"I wish that dog did bite me so I could sue their ass," he said, and Miles made a little supportive sound—something like a part laugh, part uh-huh.

Speaking of money made the veteran think again about the longer, cost-ineffective route the rookie was taking and he lit into her once more. Now Miles started to worry. It was like becoming aware there was a bee flying near him, not exactly on his nose but perhaps two or three feet away.

He thought it was hard to know if it was worse being a rookie or a veteran, then checked again and saw that the rookie being criticized was definitely black. He tried one last time for eye contact with an expression that he hoped combined both lust and sympathy, but she still didn't respond. Once more he wouldn't get his way.

He remembered sitting in the backyard of his building complex a week ago, shortly before he started packing for his company's latest trip. He'd moved his white plastic chair off the five feet of concrete in front of his sliding doors onto the backyard itself, then started picking some blades of grass and rubbing them against his face. A fat bumblebee was flying around in an irregular pattern as if it were drunk. Miles had been thinking: there are as many people in the world as blades of grass in this yard but it's only the few blades you can pick and rub against your face that you feel. It was the same with people. The ones you picked weren't any more different from each other than the blades of grass were. They wanted light and water and growth and maybe to be picked by the right hands. They wanted their way—it was built into them, just as it was built into the grass. But how long could you accept your will being denied?

It was a tricky question, especially with women. He remembered when he started with them, in his late teens and early 20s, thinking the pleasure lay in getting as much of your way as you could. He would look for and eventually find ones who would let him mostly do what he wanted, but they always thwarted him one way or another. Either they said too many words or not the right ones afterwards or none at all, or else they would simply lie to him or ultimately leave him, or if one ever did do what he wanted he found out that wasn't what he really wanted either.

The veteran was talking warmly to the rookie now, even laughing, and Miles wondered what was behind this good cop/bad cop behavior. Was the veteran becoming worried about the way he'd acted in front of a customer, or was he merely trying another approach to get some response from her? Then the rookie asked Miles in a toneless voice if his home was off Route 113. Miles answered and the veteran started speaking sarcastically to the rookie again, but by then Miles had turned back to his own thoughts.

He was thinking about his sister now—sibling rivalry would be too weak a word to describe the intense, complicated power struggles between them that took place over the years on the playground, in their yard and, of course, inside their home in the form of endless games and competitions. Much more often than not, however, when he would win in monopoly or basketball (and especially when she'd cry afterwards), instead of feeling happy he'd feel a sadness verging on despair. It was almost the same thing, years later, when he got divorced. The fact that his ex-wife didn't find anyone for years, and he did, didn't make him feel happy or vindicated—though she'd left him and falsely accused him of so much. Instead her loneliness caused him more pain than if she'd married again right away and he'd been left like a dog chasing its tail or like that drunken, useless bee.

"OK, you gonna stop this bullshit right now," the rookie said. She still wasn't looking at the veteran when she spoke, but then she'd just left a red light and couldn't afford to.

"You saying something to me?"

"You heard me."

"You talk that way to me, you're looking for trouble."

"You're the one doing all the talking. You're the one in trouble talking like that to me in front of a customer."

"I'll talk any goddamn way I want to, I'm the supervisor in this car."

"I'll talk to the supervisor, all right. You can be sure of that."

There was another red light; then catlike, she got out of her seat belt and slammed the door.

The veteran swore out the window at her but she was running and soon turned a corner (perhaps into the woods) and disappeared. Meanwhile, cars were honking behind him and the veteran had to switch to the driver's seat and start driving.

"Jesus Christ, do you believe that?" he said.

Miles couldn't think of anything to say in response and made one of his semisupportive sounds again.

"That woman's crazy. I'm trying to help her do her job, I'm *supposed* to ride with her and help her do her job and she refuses to take the route I tell her to take. It's like she wanted trouble right from the start."

"Do you think she'll be all right?" Miles blurted.

"Oh, she'll be all right. That bitch is tough as nails. I'm the one's gonna come out getting screwed by all this. She's got a cell phone that she's probably using right now to file a complaint on me."

"I thought I saw her run into the woods. How will she get home?"

"She'll get home OK. She'll get them to pick her up and when they come she'll say I abused her, maybe even tried to rape her. I wouldn't put it past her. Matter of fact, you're my only chance here 'cause you're the only goddamn witness knows what really happened."

"I really wasn't paying attention."

"That right? Funny, I thought I saw you looking at her a couple times, like you were interested…anyway, you know I didn't lay a goddamn finger on her. If I lose this job, it's all over for me. Your telling the truth—that's my only chance. What's your name…sir?" he said, adding the sir as a kind of afterthought.

"Miles."

The veteran pulled the car onto the soft shoulder and stopped. "Miles, I'm gonna have to get your name and address, OK?"

The veteran produced a notebook and pen and turned on the light in the shuttle. Miles thought briefly of lying, but what would be the point since the veteran would see where he lived when he dropped him off? Besides, he'd already given the company his last name and phone number when he called the shuttle service from the Philadelphia airport.

The veteran wrote rapidly (though his hand was shaking), asking Miles to repeat everything twice. He had a mustache and dark, intense eyes. Then he started the car up and drove in silence for a while. When they were ten to fifteen minutes from Miles's housing complex, the veteran finally spoke.

"Hey Miles, I hope I didn't offend you with what I said earlier about you looking at the driver."

"No, forget it. Besides, I guess I was looking a little."

"Hey, I don't blame you. We all look, right?"

"Sure."

"Be worse than hell if we couldn't even look."

"That's for sure...these days."

"Hey Miles, you mind if I ask if you're married?"

"No, I'm not married. I was once, but I'm not now."

"Anyone special in your life?"

"No, not now. I couldn't say there was."

"So it must have ruined the ride for you when she left the car, huh?"

"The whole thing was just upsetting."

"But if me and her didn't argue, she might not have left and then you could have kept looking and maybe talked with her and who knows what might have happened? So I guess I ruined that and I owe you one, right?"

It was a strange, though not inaccurate line of argument—like a panicked kind of logic—and Miles didn't know what to say.

"Yeah, I can see what I ruined for you—especially since I'm gonna need you to be on my side and say that I never touched or threatened her, never did nothing like that to make her leave the car and desert her job."

"You don't owe me," Miles said, although he was thinking the veteran did owe him for this nightmare of a ride and should give him the ride for free.

"No, no, I think I do, and I think I know a way I can pay you back and square things between us, but first I need to know if you'd like a little action tonight; I mean a woman, Miles. Could you use one?"

He thought of his empty apartment. The traveling life of his new job in a new place made it almost impossible to meet anyone, and the only women who'd been in his place in the year that he'd been there were the building manager once—for two minutes— and an equally brief visit from a middle-aged tenant with a petition. It was as if his will to find anybody at this point had been worn away. At 29, he knew he shouldn't be feeling that way.

"Yeah, I could use one, I guess."

"It just so happens I know one who lives pretty near you. I can make a little detour and get her for you right now. If you want me to."

What's this gonna cost me?"

"No, no, you don't get it. She's for you, on me, to show my appreciation for your testimony for me in the future, OK?"

"Yuh, OK," Miles said, feeling uneasy.

"Good, so long as we understand each other. 'Cause I didn't hear you volunteering to speak for me, and I have to be completely clear about what you're gonna say, you hear me? I can't take no chances with you."

"Yes, yes, I hear you."

"'Cause if I lose this job it's all over for me. I'd rather be a corpse in the ground than be out of a job, and I'll never get work in this business again if that bitch starts flapping her lips. See I've got no defense, you get the picture, Miles. You sure you get it?"

"Yes, I understand…"

"So that's why I'm rewarding you like this."

"OK. So how's it going to work with this girl you're gonna get me?"

"I'll pick her up, we'll drive to your place or you can do it at hers. You do it at hers, I'll wait in the shuttle and drive you home after. You do it at yours, I'll wait in the shuttle and drive *her* home. Would an hour be enough time? Maybe you could have a little more."

"Yeah, sure."

He was trying to figure where it would be better. He didn't like the idea of a stranger in his house with the veteran right outside.

On the other hand it would be easier to do it in his own apartment and safer, too, since he knew where everything was.

"You just say the word, buddy, and I'll call her on my cell phone right now so she'll be ready."

"Yes, OK. I guess my house would be better."

"You got it, chief."

The veteran began to dial and Miles leaned forward slightly, like a jockey. He was trying to figure out if he was getting his way or if the veteran was. Or was this one of those rare times when both could benefit? The veteran was talking in a low voice and it was difficult to hear much of what he was saying. Miles thought he said, "You *have* to do it," then, "Be ready…ten minutes, no more."

The veteran cursed softly, but with great bitterness, after he hung up. Neither of them said anything for a while.

"What's her name?" Miles suddenly said, surprised by his question.

"Who? The one I'm getting for you?"

"Yes."

"Her name's Silver."

"Sylvia?"

"No, Silver, like the horse, and you can be the Lone Ranger. Me, I'll be Tonto waiting off-screen. There a place I can get a drink near you?"

"Yuh, there's a couple."

"Good. You tell me where they are when we get there so I'll have something to do. I could use one."

"OK," Miles said. He was wondering just how big a pimp the veteran was, how many girls he had in his stable. It couldn't be too many, otherwise he wouldn't be so worried about losing his driving job.

They reached Paoli (15 minutes or so from his home), the veteran still muttering about the rookie. Then he took a couple of side streets and a moment later pulled the car over and said, "Wait here, I'm gonna get her."

Was it his home? Hers? A few seconds after the veteran left the car, Miles looked out the window to get a sense of the neighborhood. It looked dim and gray, even under the stars, more

shabby than sinister. The few people he saw walking were not
well dressed but appeared to be ordinary citizens.

He heard them walking, or thought he did, a split second
before he saw them, and saw them too late to tell which building
they came from. He felt oddly frightened and exhilarated at the
same time—like a child at a horror movie. Then they were at the
car door—Silver making a move to get in front.

"You get in the back seat," the veteran said authoritatively.
"Come on, don't start getting shy on me now, I'm in no mood."

Miles moved over to give her room, then tried to figure out
how old she was. It was hard to tell because she didn't look at
him directly and, at any rate, seemed to have an unnatural
expression on her face. As for her body, again Miles couldn't be
sure. She was wearing jeans and a long black blouse. No skin was
showing, but he thought she was maybe a little overweight.

As if he were reading Miles's mind, the veteran said, "I told her
to get in a dress but she wouldn't. I guess this is the night no one
listens to me."

Miles looked at Silver reflexively, wondering if she'd start
fighting with the veteran like the rookie did, but she said nothing.
This time he noticed that her eyebrows were dark and quite pronounced (which made him think she was hairy in other parts of
her body too—something he had mixed feelings about). Her eyes
were also dark, though smaller than he would have hoped, as if
they were on the verge of closing to protect her from something.

They rode in silence, no one talking except the veteran
occasionally cursing the rookie or else life in general.

"I like your name, Silver," Miles finally said, to say something.

"Oh yeah? Thanks. What did you say yours was?"

"Miles."

"Right....'And Miles to go before I sleep.' That was the name
of a poem I learned in school. You know it?"

He did know what she was talking about but didn't want to
correct her and so said, "No, I don't know."

"Where'd you say that bar was?" the veteran said.

"On 113th about a half-mile from where you'll drop me."

"Gonna get wasted tonight. 'Cause it's a cruel bitch world,
right Silver?" the veteran said.

She said something under her breath, then settled back in her seat, rigid like a mummy. "Hey Miles-to-go, you got anything to drink at your place?" Silver said.

"Yeah, I got something," Miles said.

"Good."

Miles made his little supportive laugh, trying to make eye contact with her. Instead he saw the veteran glaring at him in the mirror. Silver still hadn't looked him straight in the eye, and Miles began feeling that this all wasn't going to go well. It had been exciting at first, the thought of a girl in his apartment, and it all happening so unexpectedly. It was as if, to return to his earlier thoughts, he was not just getting his way but getting it in a guilt-free manner and with the full cooperation (enthusiastic in the case of the veteran) of the other people involved. Of course it was unclear how much he would have to say later about the rookie. That was troubling, since the veteran had scared her and Miles didn't blame the rookie for leaving the car. As a result, he had to remind himself that the rookie had never really spoken to him. There'd been one plaintive look that had encouraged him, falsely, he now saw, so really what was she to him? Still, it was troubling. Was it really, then, his conscience bothering him about her that could account for his mood or simply how sullen Silver was acting?

Once again, the veteran seemed to read his mind. "Hey Silver. I don't hear you talking to Miles. You supposed to be friendly, I told you that. Miles is going to do something very important for me, and he's supposed to be happy, you got that?"

She said a single "yeah" in reply. He didn't like the way the veteran was bullying her.

At his home, Silver got out of the car and walked ahead of him through the parking lot, still not looking at him, stopping only so he could open the door. He turned the light on immediately and walked to the refrigerator, where there was a bottle of gin.

"You want a gin and tonic, or maybe a beer?"

"Gin's good. I'll fix them."

He stood a few feet away now, thinking that there was something oddly sweet in the way she looked, that she was really pretty and that perhaps this would work out after all.

"Hey Miles, what're you thinkin' about?" Silver said, handing him his drink. He saw that she'd finished half of hers. "You look a million miles away."

He quickly took a large swallow of his drink. He liked that she was speaking lightly to him. She asked him about his job and he told her, without telling her how much he hated it. They joked for a few minutes more until he said, "I'm thinking you have a pretty face," and touched it with his free hand. Then he drank some more. He was pleased that she let him touch her there, since he thought prostitutes usually didn't like to be kissed or even touched on their faces. She looked at him closely and he saw a softness in what he'd thought were her hard little eyes.

"I like looking at it" he said, continuing to touch it and then her hair. She seemed to be under his spell for a minute, but then broke away.

"It's not my face you want to spend time with."

"What do you mean?"

"That's not the part of me you're interested in, right?"

Miles made a semi-shrug, uncertain what to say. The alcohol seemed to have made her much bolder. She was walking ahead of him towards his room, holding the little bottle of gin and her glass, which she set down on his bureau. He was embarrassed that his room was so small and uninteresting. It lacked distinction or even any secrets. He thought it would be fun to share secrets with a woman under his spell, but they were all in his mind and there seemed no way to get them out. He thought he would drink some more then, like Silver.

"What are you looking at? You keep looking outside," she said.

"My blinds are open and I can see him in the car."

"Yeah, that don't surprise me."

"Feels kind of weird, like he's spying on us."

She finished her drink and started another. She was standing a few feet away from him by the far side of the bed.

"Why don't you shut them then?"

"Think it would make him mad? I notice he's got quite a temper."

"It's your house. Besides, he told me he was doing you a favor. He's worried about making you feel good, not about me."

Miles shut the blinds, then walked towards her. He thought of kissing her but began trying to unbutton her blouse.

"I'll handle the clothes," she said, turning away from him. "Why don't you shut off the light? You'll like me better in the dark."

"I like you now," he said, but shut off the lamp anyway. He was starting to trust her more now, or at least trust her judgment, since he did feel both more excited and confident in the dark. The only thing that bothered him was that she was still drinking in bed, apparently straight from the bottle.

"Put the bottle away, will you?"

"One second," she said.

The only thing that bothered her once they started having sex were his attempts to satisfy her. "Quit doing that, will you? What are you trying to do?" Then later, "Go faster, OK? No point in anything else." She said the last remark so ardently that he finally obeyed, uncertain again if he'd gotten his way or she'd gotten hers but reasonably content for a few seconds with the outcome. Then she started talking in a rush. It was like a fast and complicated passage in a piece of music that took him by surprise and seemed to be already well underway by the time he tuned in.

"I was always like that," she was saying, "wanting to know the reasons for things, even as a kid. But after a while you got to wonder what's the point of learning about dresses and make-up or even brushing your teeth if you end up like this," she said, starting to cry softly.

"What's the matter?"

"Nothing. Don't worry about it."

"Come on, tell me. What is it?" he said, embracing her and letting her cry against his chest. It was a refined kind of crying, too, that almost made him want to cry himself.

"I shouldn't have drunk so much. It makes me weepy afterwards."

"Haven't you done this a lot? I mean…"

"No, not a lot. A few times when he made me."

"What do you mean? What are you saying?"

"What do I mean? What am I saying?" she repeated.

"You mean you never get paid?"

"I'm no whore. It's him, he gets paid from it one way or another."

"So why do you do it? I don't understand."

"You're asking a lot of questions, aren't you? Especially since you wouldn't like none of the answers."

"I like you, I…"

"Oh really."

"Yeah, that's why I want to know."

"It's an evil story, Miles."

"He's your boyfriend, right?"

She laughed ironically, but said nothing.

"That's it, right? And he gets off making you do this for him whenever he wants to use you."

"No, that's not it."

"What else could it be? He's not your pimp, you don't get paid. Why don't you just tell me?"

"It's not that way."

"Come on, why bother to lie about it?"

"I'm not lying. He's my brother, OK? You satisfied now?"

"Your brother?"

"You couldn't understand. We've been together a long time. You couldn't understand. My father crossed the line on both of us. My brother helped us get away. We've been together a long time. He seems mean, but he's kind too."

"So, you're lovers, right?"

"What? Why are you asking me that?"

"'Cause I'm thinking that you are unless you want to lie and tell me otherwise. Look, I have a sister. I've had dreams about her. It's not like I don't understand."

"It was only once or twice; we did it years ago when we were first away from my father, but then he stopped, 'cause he said he wanted to live right."

"Then why does he make you sleep with other people?"

"You wouldn't get it. He has to do that 'cause he's like me. He has to ruin things. See, you were a nice man, you touched my hair and face and said nice things and I had to ruin it by telling you this. All my secrets."

He picked up the bottle from the floor and took a drink. Silver was perceptive enough, he decided, she *had* ruined things. He thought he wanted her to talk but, as had been the case before, he regretted it when she did. If only people would occasionally say things you wanted to hear. The way it was, it was nothing but a recipe for confusion. You pleaded for communication and you got overcommunication that ended in pain. No wonder you couldn't win.

He sat down on the bed, feeling angry and sorry for himself but not wanting her to leave either.

"My problem is I'm never able to get my way in anything," Miles said, "no matter how hard I try. It's like you can ruin things just by wanting them. Sometimes it looks like I'll get my way but then something always ruins it in the end."

"Well, I'm sure I kept your streak going."

"No, I didn't mean you," he said, thinking that of course he did mean her. "I'd like to get to know you."

"You'd be disappointed." She had stopped crying now and said the last line coldly. It made him miss her crying. He felt he had to do something lest he lose her completely, but first he got up from the bed and peered through a slat of his blinds.

"He's still out there."

"I'm not surprised. I hate it when he waits outside like that."

"Why's he doing it?"

She shrugged. "Like I said, he's a ruiner."

"You think he's getting madder by the minute?"

"Probably."

"Why?"

"Just the way he is."

"What if you wanted to stay longer? Could you?"

"How would I get back? I have a regular job, you know. I work behind a counter."

"I could call a cab. I just want to know if that's something we could do, or would he blow his stack?"

"Probably."

"What?"

"Probably blow his stack."

"What would he do?"

"Try to make you pay one way or another."

"But it was *his* idea."

"The sex part was his idea, not anything else. He'd probably feel you were cheating him—he's a great one for feeling cheated. Not that he cares much about me. I don't flatter myself that way."

"I don't get why he'd feel cheated."

"He'd feel you were trying to get more out of the deal than you agreed on. He'd end up turning you against him too. That's one of the ways he ruins things for himself."

"Maybe we could see each other another time. You could give me your phone number."

"My phone number is his phone number."

"You could call me. I could give you my number. I really want to see you," he said, squeezing her hand before getting out of bed to check on the veteran's whereabouts.

"This night would torture you once you started to remember it. I ruined it by telling you too much."

There was a sudden knocking at the door.

"Jesus!" Miles said, trying frantically to at least step into his underpants before walking to the door.

Should he open it? It was the veteran, of course, and the knock sounded angry. But if he didn't answer it, the veteran would only get angrier. Besides, hadn't the veteran made good on his deal? He had no grounds not to answer the door. He certainly couldn't bring up what Silver told him without getting her in trouble, so after hesitating and listening to it again, he opened the door, then immediately stepped back as if he'd just let in a cold blast of air.

The veteran stared hard at him. He was actually an inch or two shorter than Miles, not heavy at all, and probably at least five years older. Yet there was something menacing not only in his face but in his whole lean, tight body.

"Hey Miles."

"Hey." Miles said, feeling childlike by merely echoing him.

"You enjoy being the Lone Ranger? It looks by the way you're dressed that you did."

Miles looked at him silently.

"Now I need to have you write a statement about the incident tonight with my co-driver. You know, like we agreed."

Had he agreed? He wasn't sure but he said he'd write the statement (thinking what will it mean, if it isn't notarized? He's really not so smart after all).

"Just write a few lines on your company stationery saying I didn't abuse her in any way and that she left the car completely on her own…impulse. Then sign your name."

Miles nodded. "Will do," he said. "Did you ever go to that bar?" Miles asked as he wrote out the requisite lines on his TV table a few feet away.

"No, but I see that you been doin' some drinkin'. Where's Silver anyway? Silver!" he called, raising his voice a little.

She walked out into the room, blouse hanging out, head averted from both of them.

"You been drinking, Silver?"

"What?"

"You been drinking this man's liquor?"

"Just a little. Why's that so bad?"

"'Cause we all know how easy it is for you to keep your mouth shut when you drink."

She looked away and Miles looked at the floor.

"You been flapping your lips again? You flap your fucking lips worse than Donald Duck, don't you?" The veteran turned towards Miles. "She been telling you her life story?"

"No." Miles said.

"You been telling him all about us, haven't you?" he said to Silver. She shook her head unconvincingly. It was almost as if she couldn't lie to him, Miles thought jealously.

"Christ, what difference does it make, anyway? My life's over. I ain't gonna keep my job no matter what he writes, they're gonna believe that bitch over me, we all know that. My life's over. You could flush it down the toilet in less than a second—that's how little of it's left, so why the fuck should I care what you two talked about? You always were a stupid snitch, anyway. So how 'bout letting me have a drink too?"

"You sure?" said Miles.

"What do you mean 'am I sure'? You ask a man with a dagger hanging out of his heart if he's feeling any pain? Jesus Christ, what do I have to do to get a drink in this world?"

Silver left the room then.

"Where you going?" the veteran said, taking a step forward, but Silver returned with the gin before he walked any further, handing the bottle to her brother.

She didn't even ask me if it was all right, Miles thought, as the veteran hoisted the bottle and drank it straight.

"Jesus Christ, this stuff stinks!" he said after the first long swallow. Then, "Damn it to hell," and, simply, "Christ," after the second and third. He seemed to get high immediately—perhaps he'd been drinking from a bottle of something in his car all along.

Silver's eyes never left the veteran's face, Miles noted, like an actress waiting for her cue. Miles was also watching the veteran, anxious and dumbfounded.

"Jesus Christ, I'm a real spectacle, drinking and crying in front of you two."

"You aren't crying," Silver said.

"Whoring out my goddamn sister to…"

"Don't," Silver said.

"…a stranger. A stranger, for Christ's sake."

"Don't say anymore."

"Depending on a goddamn stranger to save my life. You can't get any lower than that, for Christ's sake, can you?…So, you enjoy her?" he said, turning towards Miles, with a strange smile on his lips.

"Why don't you sit down?" Miles said.

"If I sit down I will sit in hell, that's why. I will fall into hell and never get up. You learn to stand, after a while. I sit all day and night in my job…. So you sorry you did her now?…Now we're like family and you got to listen to me."

"I said I was on your side."

"I don't even care about the fucking job. What kind of job is it anyway? You think it's so wonderful driving strangers back and forth from the airport all hours of the day and night for peanuts? For peanuts! You drop them off and get attacked by their dogs in the dark. You get lost, your fellow driver deserts you, you have to pimp for a stranger so he'll testify *if* they even give you a hearing. What am I fighting for? For twelve hours a day of that? It's over, it was over a long time ago."

"Why don't you sit down?"

"I told you why already. Are you completely unaware of hell?" he said, raising his voice and glaring at Miles. "Nothing can save you when you're in hell. You can't rest in hell. You got to stand at attention, that's all. You're trying to get me to sit in hell so you can squash me like you squashed my sister."

"Stop it," Silver said.

"I've been squashed by better than you my whole life," the veteran said, his face wrinkled with grief and rage. He pointed directly at Miles and Miles felt a rage of his own surge up in him.

"Give me that," he said, snatching the piece of paper that Miles had been holding for several minutes now.

"This is what I think of your fucking statement," he said, tearing it into several pieces and throwing them on the floor.

We are going to fight now, Miles thought. It will be my first fight.

"Come on," the veteran said to Silver, "let's go. Let's leave this squashing factory."

"He didn't do nothing," Silver said.

"He took ADVANTAGE!" the veteran said, screaming the last word before he stormed out the door. Silver followed but walked slower, turning towards Miles at the open door.

"Good-bye Miles-to-go," she said, somewhat sadly. He wanted to say something to keep her but she followed the veteran into the car. A moment later the tires screeched and they were gone, Miles staring after them from behind his blinds.

At first he felt as if he were spinning like a top as he walked around and around his apartment, checking for something they might have stolen. Except for his TV and stereo, there was nothing worth taking, from an objective point of view—he had no jewelry (they'd left his car) nor any hidden money, yet he kept checking anyway.

Finally he stopped. It was totally silent in his apartment except for the crickets outside. The next thing he knew, he was opening the sliding door onto his five-foot patio and walking through the grass in his bare feet. It was dark out despite the stars. He could feel himself tempted to go back to his apartment, as if to recapture some traces of Silver, who he was already missing, but he resisted and kept walking, concentrating on the countless blades of grass.

He wondered if he could avoid a bee in the dark that could well be outside about to sting him, but he decided to sit down on the grass anyway. He thought about the grass, then looked up at the stars, trying to keep from thinking about Silver. If the world goes on forever, it doesn't matter what anyone does anyway, he thought. That was the world—nothing but endless miles....Then he started worrying about the bee, as if it were hovering a few feet from him poised to attack, and he headed back quickly, locking himself into his silent home.

The Park

Don't think I leave for the outer dark,
Like Adam and Eve put out of the park.
—Robert Frost

A t first it was like an invitation from the sky which there was no possibility of refusing. He began going to the park every day knowing something important would happen. He found a favorite pond, later a favorite bench facing the pond, and waited surrounded by a group of delicate, oriental-looking trees with their red and green, gold and orange leaves. Then her image appeared before him one day like a delicate little tree itself. It was as if she were born in the park, as if that were her true home and her life at the travel agency a mere illusion. Vince wasn't even surprised or disappointed when the image left him a few moments later—he already knew what to do.

The next afternoon he returned to the agency where he'd met her just the week before. He'd gone there twice, once to buy a ticket to Chicago, then to buy one to New York. At the time he figured he needed to travel since it had gotten so quiet in his apartment building where he hadn't yet met anyone.

This time he didn't go inside but watched her through the street-level window, seeing mostly the crown of her yellowish hair. When she was ready to leave work, he followed from a safe distance until she got to the Metrolink stop, pressing himself against the side of a lamppost and waiting until she got on her train heading west.

He began going to the agency on the pretext of planning a winter vacation in Bermuda or Jamaica and soon started finding out some things about her. Her name was Janice and she was twenty-five, quite young, but not necessarily too young for him. She lived alone near the airport outside the city and seemingly had traveled everywhere, taking advantage of her reduced travel rates, she'd said, laughing. Her teeth protruded a little, yet this didn't inhibit her from having a full smile, which Vince found extremely appealing.

On his third or fourth visit Janice started asking Vince some questions, too. What exactly did he do? He told her that after his mother died he'd inherited some money and eventually had come to St. Louis a month ago to start a small business. "Why here?" she asked. There were so many better places to start a business back East, she would think. Because he'd had some happy years here before his parents moved, he said. Also, he knew it was a buyer's real estate market in St. Louis and he was interested in buying a house and settling down. His parents had bought a wonderful house here, but then they sold it to make money and moved East. He wanted to buy a house and *stay* in it, he said. She seemed impressed by that and by the time he left her office he wished he'd asked her to lunch.

He went directly home and watched the sunset over the park, seeing an image of Janice's toothy smile above the multi-colored trees, then later the interplay of moon and clouds like a mother holding a child. When he looked more closely, he saw Janice's profile in the moon and knew he would have to talk to her tomorrow and certainly, this time, invite her to lunch.

While he was shaving the next morning, he wondered what he would say when she'd inevitably ask him some more questions about his life. Since he wasn't working now and hadn't had a history of remarkable jobs, there wasn't much to talk about there. He'd been one of those students whose ambition was genuinely intellectual, and even spiritual, but definitely not material. He was like his parents that way: they had had only minimal experience with the working world. Their money, like his, had been inherited. They were fearful and suspicious of society in general and the business world in particular. That much Vince knew. But he couldn't tell if they created his own similar fears, or simply had the ability to understand them. They'd had him late in life, after a miscarriage and years of trying for a child, and seemed to guard him like a jewel. Yet he loved them deeply and often thought they were the only truly kindred spirits he'd ever met. Should he talk to Janice about them or focus more on his own life (since his parents were both dead now) and his plans for the future?

Perhaps there was one thing he definitely should tell Janice about his past—"the genius hour." The few people he had told seemed to find it quite intriguing. Every day, beginning with his freshman year in high school, his parents insisted he have at least one hour of contact a day with a great mind. It was one of the few things, besides basic honesty and not driving while drunk, they ever demanded of him. The hour could be served, as it were, in a variety of ways. He could listen to an hour of Beethoven or Bach, or go to a first-rate museum and look at Rembrandts or Picassos, or he could read an hour of Kant, Shakespeare, Spinoza, etc. The important thing was developing the discipline to do it every day until it became a habit. Though his parents checked on him, and two or three times a week listened to music or read and discussed philosophy with him, much of the genius hour was done on the honor system. But there were few times he didn't do it on his own, even during his college years while he was away from home. It was only after his father's heart attack that he stopped doing it regularly; yes, he would definitely tell Janice about that, if she agreed to have lunch with him.

Inviting her wasn't as easy as Vince had hoped. He hesitated on the phone until he could sense Janice beginning to get exasperated, then blurted it out. She surprised him by suggesting they meet in an hour and a half during her lunch break. But this was said in such a casual way, as if he were her college roommate, that he felt deflated and wondered if she wanted him to know that in her mind this meeting had absolutely no romantic potential.

He remembered thinking there was no time to indulge such worries, no time for anything other than to shower, shampoo, and get dressed. He decided to wear a blue shirt, because his mother had always said it set off his blue eyes to great advantage, and having decided that much, he continued to pick blue as the color of his jeans and sports jacket.

He felt that he was racing too much, getting too nervous, so he stopped and gazed at the park for a moment from his bedroom window. It looked wise under the full sun. "That's where it all began," Vince said to himself. Then he left for the Greek-style diner that she'd suggested. She couldn't have picked a more pedestrian place but he tried not to interpret that as a bad sign. He had to stay strong and positive and reassure himself. At least I'm tall, he thought, as he approached the door of the restaurant, and that's almost always something. And wasn't it also true that he was intelligent and relatively well-read and, for now, financially independent, and that he had slept with a number of attractive women? The problem there had been his always wanting it to lead to something emotionally important and his pressing for that goal too quickly. His parents had told him that even geniuses don't matter much unless their gift helps or sustains people in a lasting way, and Vince felt the same about relationships. He made a mental note not to demand too much of Janice too fast, were he lucky enough to get involved with her.

She arrived a few minutes later, in a shortish black dress with gold hoop earrings and a matching necklace. She looked smart—she always looked smart and acted calm. She didn't seem to be the slightest bit nervous as she slid into the booth the way she slid into her swivel chair at work. He noticed, too, that she spoke to him in the same voice she used on the agency phone. Was she still thinking of him as a client, and of this as some kind of business lunch? He closed his eyes for a moment and concentrated on the image of her he had seen in the park when she appeared as an Eve-like figure of destiny in his life.

When he opened his eyes she had a puzzled look on her face and he wondered how long his eyes had been closed. "Is something the matter?" she asked.

Vince felt nonplused. He had to explain but how could he without lying? He said he'd been visualizing part of Forest Park because it made him feel good to do that.

"Are you a nature lover?" she said, still in her pleasant professional voice. Her Greek salad had arrived and she was already eating it in a perfectly relaxed way, whereas he felt befuddled by his Gyro plate and wished he had ordered something easier to eat. "Do you know the names of the different trees and flowers and what not?"

"Some of them, not many: that's not really why I go to the park."

She raised her eyebrows as if still puzzled, and he explained that he went to the park to get ideas.

"What kind of ideas?" she said.

"Ideas and…feelings about myself and life in general, and how I fit into it. That's what the park gives me."

She momentarily looked away, and he began thinking it might all be over with her, all be vanishing as her image did that day in the park.

Suddenly she turned toward him and looked him straight in the eyes. "I know what you mean about wanting to know how to fit into life. When I first started working in the agency, I couldn't stop flying."

For a moment he thought she knew how to fly like a bird or an angel, but she meant traveling in planes, of course. It began with her trying to take advantage of her reduced employee rates by flying a lot to the Caribbean but continued because she was lonely then and traveling was something to do that could give her life structure. "That's what I thought you were doing, too, when you kept buying plane tickets."

"I did that before I really discovered the park…but I used to do something else to give myself structure," he said, and then began telling her about the genius hour.

She followed him closely with her eyes while he spoke, which made him feel oddly important, then looked unusually animated when she answered him. "That's really neat the way they wanted you to develop your mind and all, and the way you stuck with it. Maybe you should keep doing it. I mean, why stop?"

Vince looked at her closely, himself, and felt transfixed.

"Would you consider the park? Would you consider going there with me sometime and just seeing what happens?"

"Thanks, that sounds nice, but I'm just so busy lately."

"I know it sounds a little odd. I know there's always a resistance to trying new things that we have to overcome, but believe me the rewards are immeasurable. There's a wonderful world in the park, a magical world where you can transcend the normal fog we walk around in, and pierce through to a different level of perception. There's a…"

"There's something else," she said cutting him off. "There's a special guy in my life and he might have trouble understanding why I'd go to the park with you, you know? See, I spend almost all my free time with him."

"I see."

He felt a pressure shoot up near his eyes, stopping perhaps a quarter inch from his eyeballs. It was all he could do not to scream. Somehow, five minutes later, after she'd finished her pecan pie, he walked her back to the agency. He could scarcely feel his feet, while a pins-and-needles sensation was resonating everywhere in his body, as if it had replaced his blood and flesh and he was all discordant nerve now.

She didn't comment on the way he walked or looked, but he turned his head away slightly so she wouldn't get a direct view of his eyes. He said good-bye and turned into an almost blinding sun streaming directly at him as he started to walk home.

So she had someone else. He'd never had a chance then. He stopped walking around his living room and sat down on the sofa, so lost in thought he barely noticed the park, though it was shimmering under the full sun. Then he got up from the sofa. What if she merely said she had a boyfriend just to get rid of him. Was that possible? Foolish to wonder about that now, though. Either way, she'd made it clear she wanted little to do with him. And was there such a great wonder there? He was tall (sometimes in the park he felt like a tree himself) which would be good for a tall woman, but she wasn't tall. Besides his height there was probably nothing outstanding about his appearance. His mother had loved his blue eyes and told him he was handsome, but that hardly meant other people thought so. The women he'd slept with had not said as much as he wanted (though he always yearned for a lot, he knew), and when they did he couldn't tell if they were merely flattering him. He could believe only in his parents' praise, but paradoxically, that was why you could also grow to distrust your parents. For what did their love do but paint a false or distorted picture of the world, since no one else would ever love you half, or a quarter, as much. And what was the purpose of this great early love in your life if they were going to die while you were still young, as his parents had before he was thirty? How was he to fill up all the years that were left him?

He was glad when the dark came. He was glad when he could lie in his bed and close his eyes at last and let sleep come. He fell asleep easily enough, but woke up with a jolt at 2:30 in the morning. It was as if he had been dreaming a long, puzzle-like dream and had woken up with the knowledge of the final piece. His lunch with Janice had not been in vain. The purpose of meeting her was not simply his own humiliation and defeat—far from it! Instead, it was that she might tell him, as she had during lunch, to resume the genius hour. That she should be so emphatic about its value and the importance of his returning to it instead of the park, which she scarcely mentioned, that she should say to him, "Why stop?" Why indeed? Stopping the genius hour was the worst thing he had ever done to himself, and now this message was sent through Janice, as if by some higher force, to set him back on the right path.

Tears came to his eyes as he thought about why he *had* stopped. In essence, he hadn't thought he could do the genius hour without his father being alive. It seemed to be something that was so connected to his parents that, when one of them died, the spell was broken and he lacked the will to continue. Then after his mother died, his will to do it left him completely. It was a step he was incapable of taking, but now a step he suddenly needed to take again.

How much time had he lost? It hadn't been part of his daily life for at least five years. Well, now that he wasn't working, now that he had the time and money for at least a year before he would have to work, he'd spend six genius hours a day, every day, to make up for the lost years.

He began turning on all the lights in his apartment. He hardly knew where to start. Finally he decided to continue where he thought he'd left off, by finishing *The World as Will and Representation* by Schopenhauer, which he'd abandoned around page 100 five years ago, just after his father's heart attack. Certainly it wasn't easy reading (he had forgotten, for example, what the "Principle of Sufficient Reason" was), yet his concentration was so unusually intense that he was able to understand most of what he was reading and to read for two straight hours before he felt the need to stop.

After Schopenhauer, he listened to three of Bach's unaccompanied cello suites, then to Mahler's "Das Liede Von der Erde," whose haunting finale seemed to recreate in musical terms the experience of dying. He grieved for his parents, then, seemed to see them smiling at him in the sunrise's silver-white points of light. After that he fell asleep, but resumed reading Schopenhauer after lunch in his kitchen until he reached his six hours. He repeated the routine of reading, music, and reading for the next two weeks, always pushing himself until he finished his hours.

Meanwhile, the leaves were still mostly out and full of color, but he'd stopped going to the park. He seldom even looked at it through his windows. It was as if one night it had gotten up and moved away from him, so that when he did look now the park seemed to be quite far away. Only occasionally would he wonder why he didn't go there anymore, and when he did, the reason came to him quickly: if the park had a purpose, it was to lead him to Janice, whose purpose, in turn, had been to lead him back to the genius hour. That purpose had been served. Moreover, it hurt him to remember the look on her face when he told her about the park and finally her rejection when he asked her to go there with him. Perhaps in addition to telling him to resume the genius hour, she was also trying to tell him to stop putting his faith in the park. To move on. What had the park really ever done for him? The park didn't love or educate him, the way his parents had, the way the genius hour was doing now.

It seemed easy not to think of the park, but at night he couldn't help dreaming about it. He might read all day, but at night he dreamed about the park. He would be on the bench by the pond, or walking deeper into the forest with the bright leaves blowing around him. Sometimes one of his parents would be with him. In one dream both of them were sitting on the bench laughing at a dog that was doing tricks in the pond. Whenever he had such dreams they would make him think much more about the park than he wanted to the next day. One afternoon while he was reading he found he couldn't stop looking at the park through the living room windows, until finally he got up from his chair and pulled down the venetian blinds. Then he pulled the blinds shut in each of his other two rooms. There had been way too much light in his apartment, anyway. Now with a few flicks of his wrist he could keep the park out almost completely.

But that night, he had his most powerful dream yet of the park. He was walking in the woods when he heard his mother's voice calling from a field up ahead. "We're here," she said, referring to herself and his father. "We're here." It was so strong a dream that when it was over it seemed to pull him out of bed, until the next thing he knew he had put his clothes on and was walking past the quizzical-looking doorman, across the street toward the park.

It was almost completely dark, except for the half moon, and there were hardly any cars on the highway. He knew he should walk slowly to avoid falling but he could hardly keep from hurrying, moving as much by memory as by sight, while trying to keep alive the sound of his mother's voice in his mind.

There was a field near the pond, above and to the left of it, which he had sometimes walked through. Of course there were several—perhaps many—fields in the park, but it would make sense for his parents to choose the one nearest his favorite spot in the park if there were going to be any sort of meeting or communion. Besides, it would be impossible for him to find, much less explore, the other fields tonight.

He was walking through a clearing toward the bridge that led to the pond, when he heard a rustling sound. The shock of it made him stumble and almost fall. He stood still and, looking toward his right, heard, then half-saw, someone walking his dog and talking to it. It was a man with a flashlight (which Vince wished he, himself, had taken), very possibly someone from his building. It surprised Vince that he was not alone, that other people, even at 4:00 in the morning, were also in the park. He stared in the direction of the man (who had been keeping a steady stream of chatter going at the dog) until his voice faded away; then slowly, vigilantly, Vince crossed the bridge that hung over the highway; stepping off it, he slipped and fell to one knee near a rock, his hands pressing against the leaf-covered ground. He got up slowly, checked to hear his mother's voice, then kept walking. Somewhere up ahead was his bench, where he yearned to rest for a while. He took a few more steps, then saw the moonlight reflected on the water. With the pond in sight, he knew his bench was near; in fact, he appeared to be walking directly toward it. It was only when it seemed no more than a few yards away that he realized there were people on it who were having some form of sex. One appeared to be seated on the bench, the other standing. It was probably two men, but he couldn't be sure, their genders being erased in the dark. Vince began backpedaling, then turned around. "It's a good thing I saw that dog walker earlier or I would have been really startled," he thought, and it was a good thing in a way that the bench was occupied, since his purpose was to go to the field and he really had no time for rest or diversion.

He walked more quickly then. The voice was beginning to fade and he wanted to still be hearing it when he reached the field. The clearing grew wider, the moon more visible. He could feel the ground become smoother under his feet and knew he was finally in the field. At first he circled and walked across it several times. It was very quiet. There was no sign. He sat down in what he imagined was the center of the field and waited. The ground was cold and slightly wet and Vince closed his eyes tightly to re-capture the sense of his dream and his mother's voice.

Once, while he sat, he almost felt the ground give way and open up, could almost feel himself tunneling down to where his parents were waiting to embrace him in a world of light below the earth. But it didn't happen. There were always signs like the feel and smell of the wet, bumpy ground that reminded him he had gone nowhere.

Sometime later, he gave up and began to walk toward his apartment. "So that's the park," Vince thought, "a place where dogs shit, people screw, and the dead make false promises to rejoin the living."

Still, when he was back in his room, in the half light of early morning, he missed the park and wished he had been there when he could have seen it in the daylight. After all, he had gone there on a mission filled with desperate hope. He shouldn't judge the park too harshly in light of those conditions. The park, itself, was not to blame, nor was there any point in trying not to see the park if he still saw it in his dreams. No point in keeping his blinds shut either and walking with his head down if he thought about the park while he was walking. It would be better to acknowledge it, to even walk through it every now and then, as he had an hour ago, as long as he divested it of its former significance. Yes, the key was not to believe that it had any special powers. The key was to simply let it be a park.

Twenty minutes later he got out of bed and opened the blinds in his bedroom, then in the living room and study: the park looked as it did in his dreams—immense, serene, and, under the pebble-pink patches in the early morning sky, slightly mysterious. He thought he would go to it after eating breakfast, perhaps before all the dogs and dog walkers got there. Later, thinking about the park so much, he had trouble reading Schopenhauer. He kept rereading the same paragraph, which no longer made any sense to him. In his mind he heard again, though faintly, his mother's voice from his last dream—"We're here. We're here." Then he grabbed his jacket and left his apartment, not even remembering to lock his door.

The elevator stopped three times before it reached the lobby. Four people got on. They seemed to ignore him but small-talked with each other. Small matter; he yearned to get to the park and hoped for no more delays. The doorman was not at his desk in the lobby as Vince walked as briskly as he could toward the door, nearly bumping into an elderly lady with a large bag of groceries who was standing outside the building by the doorway; she looked at him with slightly stunned, saucer eyes. He apologized, then realized she was waiting for the doorman to help her with her overly full grocery bag.

"Would you like some help with that bag?" he said. It wouldn't kill him to help this poor woman for a minute. She looked at him doubtfully. It had been a long time, if ever, since Vince had seen a

person with such a vulnerable expression. Perhaps he had had
such an expression in his eyes'when he first met Janice for lunch
and it had scared her away.

"Oh thank you, so much. That's very kind of you. I'm afraid
my shopping cart broke down...I wonder where Walter is," she
said, referring to the doorman.

Vince opened the door, picked up the bag, and carried it to the
elevator. It occurred to him that it would still be difficult for her
to carry it into her apartment. The woman was so small and frail,
and at least seventy years old. Now that she had opened her navy
blue coat she was even skinnier than he realized. He asked her if
he could bring the bundle to her apartment and she thanked him
profusely and told him she lived on the eleventh floor—one floor
above him.

"I wonder why I haven't seen you before," he said to her in the
elevator. Her eyes were friendly looking now, he decided. They
were warm and blue.

"I don't get out much, but I've seen you. You always looked
like you were thinking about something."

"I guess I was."

The elevator door opened and he walked her to the door.

"Could I bring it in for you?"

"Why, thank you. You're being very nice," she said, fidgeting
with her key. "Would you like a cup of tea?"

"Yes, thanks, I'd like that." He set the bundle down on the
counter by her sink and began unpacking it and putting the
perishables in her refrigerator. When he was finished, she
thanked him again and invited him to sit at the table in her living
room. Her apartment was filled with rose and green furniture and
paintings. They were ordinary enough colors on the one hand, yet
heavenly in a way because they were so appropriate to her life.
He thought he could feel a part of her life in each piece of
furniture. Her table was in the same place as his was, just in front
of her long counter top. He noticed that her living room window
also faced the park and turning his head he looked at it briefly. It
was just a park. A pretty, though muted-looking, group of trees
now that most of their leaves had fallen and their color gone. He
sat down with his back to it. He was vaguely aware that he was

smiling. The woman was wearing a blue dress that matched her coat and was smiling at him, too, as she brought in the tea and cookies.

"Well, we're here," she said. "I hope you like oatmeal cookies; I made them yesterday."

"Thanks, I do. I haven't had any homemade food in a long time."

She looked concerned for a moment. "Really? Well that's a shame. You're such a kind young man to help me the way you did. My name's Gertrude," she said, extending her skinny arm to shake hands with him.

He felt he was feeling the touch of destiny at last.

"I'm Vince," he said, smiling widely now and grasping her small hand in his.

The Urn

It was preposterous to be in such a beautiful city as Madrid without your mother (like a fairy tale with a wrong ending). She, who always believed in you, who loved you with her whole being and was sure you would one day be a famous writer—but there you were walking in its biggest park without her but with her money in your pockets. She not dead even two months and you walking around at 33 with enough money to last the rest of your life without even a sibling to share it with or a father (because he'd left you and your mother when you were eight— the better to try and con the world—though he'd be sorry not to have a cut of what you had now, you knew that). There was no wife of course either, Barry thought, nor cause to give it to—not with what you knew of the world. So far you were giving it to women. You were traveling to places, ostensibly to see the sights but wound up chasing after women and getting into trouble.

You thought that in a new place things would be different. You were in New York now pacing in your living room in your shrinking circles, remembering everything, but you were in Madrid then. Your mother was dead but you were still stepping on leaves in Retiro Park, looking at the boats in the lake, the children playing by the water and towards the end of the park the drug dealers from whom you wanted to buy pot or something stronger.

While you walked towards the dealers you began to pace (as you did now in New York) as you always did, at least since your mother died. It began with her kidneys—you thought of a kid's knees, a child's knees because you had always loved her knees and had often kissed them when you were a child. You took her to the hospital with her failing kidneys and it was as if she'd gone inside a cave or some kind of awful fun house that swallowed her.

You visited her every day and sometimes stayed all night. Other times you walked the streets of New York at two in the morning all the way back to your apartment. Each day she got weaker like a softening cloud blending in with the eventually indistinguishable air. Still she held your hand, she said things to you you'll never forget. At the time you told yourself she'd died a beautiful death.

Afterwards it was like having a heart attack in your brain. You thought the only way to escape it was to leave New York, then to leave America itself, which in many ways had mistreated your mother and therefore mistreated you. But you had to hang around for the will, the funeral, and settle various other financial matters. You wondered now that you were coming into a lot of money (the same way your mother had inherited hers), if you'd suddenly hear from your father, but you didn't. When it was over, or mostly over, you went to London for a week and after that to Madrid. In London you had a couple of bad encounters with women you met in bars. One ended with you screaming at her before she ran out of your room. The other one you still couldn't bear to think about.

You hoped you would begin living differently in Madrid and began carrying your mother's urn with you in part to share what was beautiful in the city, in part just for the company. Madrid was beautiful, heartbreaking really with its fountains and cafés and its endless avenues of flowers and statues. The city itself was a work of art—you knew that—but it was also menacing as if while you walked through it, it was also walking after you. Part of it may have been political—they hated your government, the way it was pushing around Iraq and preparing for war—you couldn't blame them for that—that was part of it but not all of it. You were an interloper with filthy American money. Behind the warm smiles and friendly words you felt targeted like the city was preparing to mug you. Some of this was irrational you knew, but still you walked quickly with your urn in hand and you looked over your shoulder too.

You remember that you started talking to yourself in your mind, then, the way you are now in New York, never calling yourself "Barry" but addressing yourself in the second person instead. Between talking to yourself and talking to your mother it got pretty complicated sometimes. You also remember that you began to go to bars but your Spanish wasn't very good and you couldn't bear to talk to an American. You were afraid to be away from the urn too and carried it everywhere with you, once even to a bar. Then you worried that you'd drink too much and leave it in the bar or else on the metro.

You gave up on the bars and you left the urn in your hotel room and took the metro to Sol. It was like the Times Square of Madrid, and you started to walk the streets looking for hookers. The buildings were yellow and white and faded pink with black iron grills on the balconies. The streets were thick with people and very hot and humid. You started to see the girls then, half undressed in tight fitting shorts or jeans, many of them tattooed; a surprising number of them fat. You bought one who seemed to have a simple face. Again it was difficult to speak to her in either English or Spanish. You wanted to take her to your hotel but she insisted, so far as you could understand, on hers. You were afraid to go to her place—who knew who else would be there or might appear later. You wound up paying twice as much to get her to go to your hotel.

She took off her clothes right away. She was dark-skinned although not exactly a negress. She had a tough, vacant expression; protruding teeth which perhaps explained why she kept her mouth closed and didn't smile. There were some indecipherable tattoos on her shoulders, stomach and left buttock.

You looked at her and didn't think you could do her. You began thinking about the urn again but when you thought of it, it was like a bar of gold, floating in space—untouched by anything else on earth. You felt profoundly separated from your mother and wanted to crawl inside the urn and be with her. Meanwhile the girl was looking at you and spoke to you sternly in Spanish.

You spoke back sternly too, and she suddenly bent over completely naked in the middle of your room thinking that you wanted to spank her. You did want to hurt her in some way, although her life or even just her mouth seemed punishment enough. You looked at her bottom, sad and vaguely muscular at the same time, and then you did want to spank her, which you did several times in succession.

She straightened up and turned around to face you with the same look in her eyes as before and told you how much money you owed her, in Spanish, then, eventually, half in English.

"Fine," you said (you could actually watch and hear yourself say things as if you were a character in a movie). "I'll pay you."

Then you pushed her shoulders and forced her down on the bed underneath you. She looked too frightened to scream and a moment later you were sitting on her, right on top of her skinny tattooed arms, then up to her face.

…You gave yourself a lecture about never doing that again. It was wrong and it was dangerous. You'd made the hooker cry and run out into the night barely remembering to take her money. She'd tell her pimp and he might come back and break your legs or even kill you.

You began pacing in ever-narrower circles. Then you realized there was not even time to pace. You threw your things together—you were moving as fast as a cockroach or a frenzied wasp. When you checked out of the hotel only twenty-six minutes had passed since the whore left, yet it still felt as if her pimp could appear any minute.

Madrid suddenly seemed like a small city. You told yourself there were many other hotels, of course, in other parts of the city but you didn't listen to yourself, you weren't really listening. You imagined the pimp had seen you get into the taxi and that he'd follow you to any hotel and wait for you or even pay off the concierge and come to your room with a couple of goons and do the job there. You told the driver to take you to the airport. You looked at the urn you were cradling in your lap, which you would now have to put back somewhere in the maze of your suitcase.

"Why didn't you stop me?" you said to your mother. "Why didn't you stop me?"

...It could have been any city. It was simply a question of which plane was leaving first that you could still catch. You told yourself to take the first available plane and for once you listened to yourself. It was a flight to L.A. It could be a lot worse. Get on it, you told yourself. Get on it no matter what.

On the plane you remembered that Santa Barbara was only an hour and a half north of Los Angeles. You'd gone there with your mother once after she got her inheritance for a short vacation. You remember columns of sunlight shimmering on the water, the backdrop of the mountains and the elegant courthouse illuminated in lemon-colored light and all the palm trees and flowers on State Street. She was happy there and would appreciate going back. You remembered in your hotel room in Santa Barbara she'd noticed some food that had stuck to your lips. She wet a face cloth and wiped it off. She had washed your face in Santa Barbara. It was a memory you would never lose.

Santa Barbara would be a good place to cool out; you would sit on the beach and feel the wind. Maybe you'd climb a mountain. You would swim, of course, let the waves crash over you. "The sea whispered me," you said to yourself over and over on the plane.

...When you arrived in L.A. you were more tired than you thought, too tired to rent a car and drive to Santa Barbara. You were exhausted and just wanted to sleep—you could drive to Santa Barbara in the morning.

...It was the middle of the night. You took a cab to Hollywood and checked into a Motel 6 using your fake I.D. because you were still nervous, and paying in cash. You took the urn out of your suitcase and placed it under your bed and then you made an effort to sleep, you remember that. You took your clothes off and got under the covers. You felt bad about the whore in Madrid and kept replaying the whole scene with her. Your mother was shocked and angry—angry that you had bought the whore and then shocked at what you did to her. Then you remembered that you couldn't be sure what she felt since she was dead. So you really couldn't be sure and yet you knew.

You took a tranquilizer—one of the pills they gave you after your mother died, but you couldn't sleep. You had an erection that you couldn't get rid of, so you got out of bed, put some clothes on and hit the streets.

Perhaps you'd outsmarted yourself going to Hollywood where all the hookers were when you could have simply stayed at a hotel near the airport, especially considering how tired you were. It was surprising that you didn't realize what you were doing at the time, that you were able to sneak it by your own police.

You were on Sunset Boulevard, then you were walking past Hollywood High School. Soon you saw hookers everywhere. It was prime time for them. Without a car, though, you had a handicap. They'd think you were a cop or else figure you had no money since you were searching for them on foot but you kept pursuing them anyway.

You took a side street off Sunset and followed a young black girl. She was not dressed as outrageously as the others but you could still tell she was selling. When you got closer you saw her face looked like a wounded animal's. You decided to call her Bambi, in your mind at least. She had big, liquid, still innocent eyes that you remember even now as well as you remember your mother's face. That shouldn't be possible but it was true. Life was cruel that way. It was like your mind was a maze filled with hundreds of conflicting tunnels and passageways and at the end of one of them was a secret switch that determined which faces you remembered and which ones you forgot and Bambi had found her way through the labyrinth and pressed that switch and while she was there pressed your videotape switch as well so you'd always have to watch and hear what happened with you two. You might not have to watch it for a day or two or even for a week but eventually you would have to watch and hear it simply because she, or something else—some ghost or spirit— had pressed the right switch in the dark.

You finally approached her and looked at her face trying to determine how old she was.

"Hello officer. How are you tonight?" she said.

You laughed a little. "Pretty horny thank you, only I'm not a cop."

"Really?"

"Yes, really. Why do so many girls think I'm a cop?"

"I don't know. You just look like one."

And you look just like Bambi, you said to yourself. Now that you were closer you could see she was no great beauty but she was pretty in a way hookers usually aren't. There was a softness to her face.

"What you want, then?"

"Excuse me?" you said, though you had heard her.

"How can I help you, mister?"

"In so many ways," you said. "So many ways, so little time."

"You want to date me, is that it?"

"Yes I do, but please call me Gordon," you said, using the name on your fake I.D.

"OK Gordon, what did you have in mind?"

"I have to know in advance everything I want to do with you? Where's the spontaneity? Where's the romance?"

She laughed. "That's not the way it works. Haven't you done this before?"

"Oh yes. I'm just in a funny mood, capish? And I'm glad I am because it made you laugh and you look even prettier when you laugh."

"Thank you, that's very nice. We need to talk money up front though, capish?" she said with a little smile.

"Touché. Have you been in Italy?" you said, thinking more likely Italy's been in her.

"Something like that. So what do you have in mind, Gordon?"

"You want me to make you an offer you can't refuse, or at least one you can't refuse at 2 o'clock in the morning."

"Something like that," she said, smiling again.

"OK. How about two hundred dollars for two hours? Will that cover most things?"

"Yah, most things. Where do you want to spend time with me? You got a car?"

You told her that you didn't have a car at the moment but that you did have money, some of which you took out of your pocket to show here. To her credit, she barely looked. You went on to tell her that yesterday you'd been in Madrid and had to get out of there in a big hurry—all this to explain the no-car situation and also why you were staying at a Motel 6.

"That's fine," she said. "We can go to your hotel."

Already you knew you wanted her for more than an hour and you tried to calculate how much you could actually spend on her: five hundred, six hundred tops.

"Can you tell me your name?" you said, as you started walking.

"Jordan," she said, in a matter-of-fact voice that made you think it really was her name, and so you stopped calling her Bambi to yourself.

"Jordan? After Michael Jordan?"

"Not even close."

"After the country?" you said, trying to remember where Jordan was and whose side they were on politically.

"After the river. Rivers last longer than countries."

"Longer than athletes too. Is that your goal…to last a long time?"

"Why not? If I last long enough I figure things'll get better and I'll come out on top in the end."

You felt unaccountably nervous then. You wished you didn't but you did. You felt other things too but you mostly felt nervous.

"So, Jordan, let me ask you if you happen to have something I can get high with… I'll pay you for it of course."

"How high you wanna get?"

"Pretty fucking high."

"All I have's some weed and some sleeping pills."

"Whatever. I'll pay you for the weed."

"That's cool. I just have two joints so you can have one but I want you to pay me for my time before you smoke, all right?"

"Here," you said, taking a hundred dollar bill out of your pocket. "Here's a hundred dollars for walking down the street with me. Can that be a deposit?"

She laughed a little and waved her hand dismissively. "Put your money back in your pocket, man. I just want you to pay me when we get to your room before you get all messed up with my weed, OK?"

"Fair enough."

"Speaking of your room, when we gonna get there?"

"Sorry about that. It's not too much longer—just a couple of blocks."

At the next corner another hooker nodded at Jordan and said, "Hey girlfriend."

Jordan smiled and said "Hey" back. You decided that you couldn't really imagine her life.

...When you got to the Motel 6 it didn't seem like your room, it was more like a place you were visiting in a dream only this time you were visiting it with someone else. This feeling was heightened because you entered from the street without anyone from the motel seeing you. It was exciting, but it was making you nervous and you began to pace.

Jordan asked for her money then. You knew she was going to and you knew you were going to pay her but it hurt you anyway. Also, you couldn't help feeling a little angry which made you still more nervous.

"Where's that joint, can I have it now?" you heard yourself say.

She produced it like a magician from some hidden opening in her skirt. Hookers always had more exits and entrances to their clothes than you could imagine.

"I don't have any matches," you said, and a moment later she produced a match from another secret exit. You admired how calmly she lit it, you found the confidant expression on her face exciting. It was sharing space with her vulnerable expression as if they were uneasy roommates in a double bed.

You touched her finger as you took the joint and inhaled. Immediately your erection came back to you. It was as if it were impossible to be in this room in Motel 6 without an erection. You inhaled some more and thought vaguely about starting a hotel called Hotel Erection based on the same idea. A lot of men would check into that hotel.

"Let me have some," Jordan said, taking the joint from you. She was a little too confident. She would have to find out who was really boss. You saw an image of your mother's face then, free of the urn, simply stationary in space, and you took the joint back from Jordan and inhaled some more. It was very strong, maybe mixed with something else.

"I want us to forget about time," you said.

"OK," she said. She sounded like an angel—it seemed possible—so you smoked some more.

...You began looking at her smile then, at the structure of her lips and mouth. It looked like a kind of pristine tunnel—like the first thing you'd ever seen. You felt drawn to it and wanted to kiss her but were afraid she wouldn't want to.

You were done smoking now. You were very stoned and when you closed your eyes you didn't know where you were. You refocused on her tunnel/mouth and soon felt drawn to it again. You moved closer and kissed her and she didn't stop you. She looked strange, almost shocked, when you saw her again but she didn't say anything.

"I really want us to forget about time," you said.

"All right," she said. You put your arms around her and realized that you were both naked but it seemed almost too trivial to bother having sex. You looked down at yourself and realized that your erection was gone and that your underpants were off, but for once you didn't care that a woman saw you without it. You felt accepted by her and by yourself—it was hard to remember why you ever worried about it.

You felt dizzy then and lay down. You closed your eyes but felt even dizzier so you opened them again, not really knowing where you were. "What's in this stuff we smoked?" you managed to say. She shook her head, said she didn't know.

"Can you lie next to me?" you said. "I think we should stay close to each other while we're both so high."

She didn't say anything or at least nothing you heard or remembered but she did lie next to you. When you touched her arm she seemed to be vibrating or else just trembling a little. There was a difference. If she were vibrating it meant one thing, but if she were trembling it meant another. You decided that this time it was going to end tenderly—that you were going to stop the pattern of which the whore in Madrid was only the latest, if most extreme example. If you were really free, as you believed you were, you could do it.

She looked at you and nodded. You remembered that you never had intercourse with hookers, that it was too dangerous, but you could only half remember why. Then you remembered that hookers never kissed you or let you kiss them but she'd already kissed you—something you found to be very touching.

You kissed her then and when you closed your eyes you couldn't really remember what a prostitute was.

The light around you grew lemony as if your motel room had its own little portable setting sun. You became extremely curious about this person you were kissing so strongly but also felt you knew everything about her at the same time. You wanted to tell her that it was all fated—you'd come from Madrid and happened to take the flight to L.A. If you'd arrived at the airport ten minutes earlier or later you would have gone to New York. You hit the streets, her street, because you couldn't sleep. If you'd taken your pill ten or twenty minutes earlier you might have fallen asleep and never met. But you did meet because it was all fated, just like your mother's kidneys were fated to fail and you were fated to be alone and do something important in the world—once you got your woman addiction under control—nothing else made sense, why even spend the money you had now if you didn't do something important, something great that would make you live forever.

You were inside her now and you looked directly at her face. "My name's Barry," you blurted. She looked puzzled for a second and then smiled.

"Barry Auer," you added, as you continued to penetrate her. You kept on doing her but stopped yourself before you were going to come. You didn't want it to end so soon and more importantly you wanted her to come too.

You began sucking her, half remembering that this was something you never did with prostitutes but no longer sure why, or (again) what exactly a prostitute was. She had been sucking you for a while at the same time but you stopped her, sliding down on the bed and just devoting yourself to her. You put your heart and soul into it, until you were in a world where nothing else existed but your mouth and her. You sensitized yourself to her moment-by-moment responses and made the appropriate adjustments. You were consumed by the desire to bring her pleasure.

When she got really excited she started producing a pattern of exotic sounds. It was as if each person carried around their own hidden music, which only the right musician could reveal, and that music was as individual as their fingerprints or speaking voice. It was the music of their sexual soul and you wanted to hear hers before she heard yours.

You kept building her music—it was really a lot like building a fire which you learned to do at the camp your mother sent you to years ago after she got her inheritance. It was the one thing you learned to do at camp and now you were doing it again because it was all fated.

Just as her fire was at its peak you went inside her again and felt her writhe and come on your dick and then and only then— watching her face the whole time—did you try to come too.

"I'm not Gordon," you said just before you came and made your own music—more uncontrolled than you'd imagined it could be. And then you two fire musicians collapsed into each other's arms, and for a short while just held each other.

…You were an unlikely couple but it didn't matter. You could figure that out later, the point was you had traveled across the ocean to meet her. You had fled from one dangerous world to another—you with your urn and your ten thousand memories of your mother and now you weren't alone anymore.

You gave her hand an exploratory squeeze. She didn't squeeze back but she let you hold her hand. She didn't say anything either. She was very still, as still as a corpse. You wondered vaguely if you had killed her but that made you think of Madrid—that perhaps the hooker there had really died, had run for a while after she escaped from you and then had a heart attack or just died from what you did to her. .

"Jordan," you said, "are you all right?" You looked at her and saw that she was sleeping. Should you feel insulted? You felt a mix of anger and tenderness. Her sleeping could be a sign of how powerful the experience had been or else simply indifference. You needed to find out though you were reluctant to wake her, there was something fascinating about the transition from writhing woman in heat to corpse-like body in repose, something that mesmerized you.

You propped yourself up on your elbow and examined each part of her. It was a young woman's body—the breasts were so firm—she was probably in her early twenties, maybe younger.

She had shaved a lot of the hair around her genitals but left a little in a kind of heart shape. It looked nice. She looked kind of sad while she slept, serene but sad—which, you had to admit, was a little disconcerting.

    …"Stop sleeping on the job, bitch," you muttered to yourself. You were aware that your transcendant feelings had left you and you looked at the ashtray hoping to find part of a joint. There was about a half inch of one of them left, next to the still flickering candle—like a low flame in the bowl of death, you thought. Your mother was in her bowl and soon enough you'd be in yours. You'd read an interview with a writer once who compared the bombing of Hiroshima to human life in general. He said he couldn't see much difference between the two. "Life is Hiroshima, only stretched out a little." If that's all life was, why did people, including yourself (when you thought about Madrid), get so hysterical about death? Was it just biological programming? When you tried to remember your life there wasn't really that much to it—sometimes it seemed like two instants—your mother washing your face in Santa Barbara (but you weren't in Santa Barbara, why weren't you?) and the last time she looked at you in the hospital in New York.

    You smoked the remainder of the joint as quickly as you could and got another buzz again, almost instantly. Suddenly you couldn't bear to be alone and you shook her shoulders until she woke up.

    "What's up?" she said.

    "You passed out. I didn't want to be alone so I got you up."

    "Oh, OK. That's cool. Good high, huh?"

    "I'm still high, I smoked again."

    "That's cool, it's all good. Hey, Gordon, can I use your bathroom?" she said, already half out of bed.

    "Go ahead," you said, pointing to it. You watched her nice pop-up ass as she walked to the bathroom but you were mad that she called you Gordon. She must have been really stoned when you told her your real name, but still, you'd said it twice. Didn't she listen to anything you said? That was extremely insulting, soul killing, really.

You were angry but you still missed her while she was in the bathroom. She seemed to be in there an extraordinarily long time. When she came out she looked half dressed which was another shock since you hadn't noticed her carrying any clothes.

"Hey, what're you doing?" you said, putting on your underpants as you got up from bed. "Why are you getting dressed?"

"It's getting late. I've got to get on my pony."

She was already half in her short little purple skirt when you reached her, grabbed both wrists and threw her down on the bed.

"You're not going anywhere. What do you think you're doing leaving me now, when I'm so stoned? What about all the things we said to each other?"

Finally she looked a little nonplussed, finally a crack in her confidence. "You only pay me for an hour man, I know I've been here almost two."

You dug your nails as hard as you could into the palms of your hands and your arms shook like you were having a seizure.

"How can you do this to me?" you screamed at her.

"OK, calm down, man."

"My name's not 'man,' bitch."

"OK Gordon. Calm down and don't be calling me 'bitch.' No need to."

"My name's Barry. You weren't listening to me, were you? You were just lying and manipulating my emotions and now that you've got your money you're leaving me in the state I'm in."

"How long you want me to stay?" she said, looking at you seriously.

But it was too late to talk. You had already jumped like a praying mantis, screaming and covering her. You had already snuffed out the flame and covered her in her bowl. She would scream but you had covered her and what did a scream mean in a Motel 6?

…You don't remember when you left her and got out of bed, but you do remember watching her in the half dark. As breathless and inert as you were, it was hard to say which one of you was more dead. "It was an accident," you muttered to yourself. "It was an accident." Then you wanted to scream again but of course you couldn't risk drawing attention. So far you didn't think anyone had seen you or probably heard anything either—not this late. Besides, Motel 6 residents were not exactly known to be community watchdogs.

You knew already what you had to do—it came to you like a vision. The first thing was to leave her in the room and get a cab on the street. The next thing would be to find an all-night car rental. Then you'd have to get rid of your fingerprints and give the body a shower. Probably you would have to do all this in the dark but there was still time for that and to put the body in the car before it was light.

Thinking about all this you noticed that you were pacing and had to make yourself stop. It seemed that you were born to pace.

...You were on the street again, walking towards Sunset. You had made a decision but it wasn't really a decision because it was all fated. You got a cab on Sunset and told the driver to take you to the nearest car rental that would still be open. You thought you'd have to go to the airport but he took you to a place only ten minutes or so away. You remember that you gave him a five-dollar tip.

At the car rental you were nervous for a moment but you reminded yourself that no one suspected anything, that they only cared about money. Then your lines came to you easily as if you were reading a script. They accepted your Gordon I.D. without a thought and gave you very good directions back to Sunset.

Once in the car you thought only about getting to the motel as fast as possible. Your mind cooperated the whole time, you were not even aware of yourself.

...It was much more difficult in the motel, however. It was awful to face the body and even worse to wash it and the sheets in the shower. You felt yourself about to buckle then, you were actually sobbing for a while but you stuck to the task, you did it.

It was almost four when you finished washing it and wrapping it in the wet sheets with a sock on each hand. Then you opened your suitcase, took out a scarf you'd bought (but not opened yet) in Madrid and wiped every inch of the room at least twice. At twenty past four you opened your door and carried the body into the trunk. Your mind was still leaving you alone. Your mind was still cooperating—you'd remembered everything—it was a miracle.

The last thing left to do was the most important—where to put the body. A river would be the best place but were there any in L.A.? You drove away from Hollywood. Once you got rid of her you would take the first plane to New York. How could they trace you? Gordon Green didn't exist, your fingerprints didn't exist either. You drove down side streets looking for alleys or some kind of deserted area. You seemed to be looking for a long time but still your mind didn't panic. Then you thought you saw something and you pulled to a stop. You realized that you didn't even know where you were but it was probably better that way. It was another miracle—there was no one around the alley wedged between two buildings. There was even a trashcan too. You backed into the alley, opened your trunk, put the socks on your hands again. Then you folded the body up and the cover even fit over it. You remember staring in disbelief—it was like a perfect marriage of geometry and fate.

You were functioning impeccably. You were stronger and more competent than you realized. Now you would take the first plane to New York you could get at L.A.X. You still had a few thousand dollars in cash in your pockets. It was starting to get light out, you wanted to cry because you were so relieved, almost happy in a strange way, and for a second you wished Jordan were with you. But you couldn't let yourself think of that, not with the way your mind had been functioning. You couldn't begin to open the door to regret when you'd worked so hard at keeping it closed.

...More time passed and you continued to do what you were supposed to. You were playing life like Bobby Fischer played chess—daring but with no mistakes. It was only after you dropped off the car and you were already in line at the airport (when it was too late to do anything about it) that you realized you'd left the urn in the motel—your last direct link to your mother lost under the bed in that room. It was heart breaking, you literally felt a break in your heart.

Then you realized (as you were now realizing again in New York, a month later) that her name was engraved where anyone could see it on the urn. If a detective were ambitious enough to follow up on it, it would inevitably lead to you. It was a permanent clue, a piece of evidence that would last forever. You felt your knees buckle then while you held your place in line. Then you dug your nails into your hands as hard as you could (just as you were doing now in your living room in New York) and shivered at the power of fate.

The Victims

I t was twenty-two years ago that my eighth-grade baseball coach decided I should be his starting shortstop instead of Andrew Auer. As he announced the starting line-up a half hour before game time, I looked at Andy four seats away from me on the bench and saw an expression I've only seen since in children who have suffered a disappointment so great it doesn't seem comprehensible. I think it was that expression more than anything else that encouraged me to become his friend. Maybe I felt he was someone who would never hurt me. Besides, at that time I could appreciate his sensitivity while luxuriating in a secret sense of superiority. In school we were about even, but besides beating him out for shortstop, I lived in a large house with professionally successful parents, while Andy was the only child of a young divorcee who lived in one of the less fashionable parts of Newton.

For the next four years our friendship flourished. We seemed to discover the same things at the same time. By our junior year in high school I would listen to Thelonious Monk or to Mahler symphonies with him, and we'd share our first attempts at writing poetry or fiction. Outside of my family, Andy was the most important person in my life. He was almost unfailingly compassionate. Even when I lost my virginity before he did, he forgave me. He became especially important to me then, because I could never confide anything like that to my sister or parents.

But a year later when he lost his, I was considerably less charitable. Andy didn't simply lose his virginity with another teenager, after all, he had an affair with a thirty-one-year-old German woman named Lizette who seemed shockingly attractive. How had this happened? It was such an outrageous coup I couldn't comprehend it. She was a former model from Munich and a divorcee, while Andy was a Jewish virgin and a second-string shortstop. They kept their trysts secret from everyone except me, meeting once or twice a week in her apartment for an entire summer. I was so shaken I even told my father about it, who assured me that I, too, would have many triumphs in my life and that I should "let him have his."

Finally Lizette went back to Germany, but no sooner had she gone than I discovered that Andy scored eighty points higher than I did on his college boards, and that despite my parents paying for two years of private school for me, he got accepted by a more prestigious college. Still, Andy was far from insufferable about it. He was in his anarchistic phase then, very much under the influence of Henry Miller, and assured me all he wanted to do was to become a great writer. I somehow wasn't surprised to see him knocking on my front door four months after Antioch started, having hitchhiked all the way from Ohio and vowing never to return. I was surprised, however, that Roberta, his mother, didn't force him to go back. I never knew precisely what her reaction was, only that that year he stayed at home with her.

The next year, Andy decided he had to live in New York. Newton, in fact all of Massachusetts, was "too small and provincial" for a writer with his "concern for the world." As a concession to his mother he agreed to enroll at Columbia. This time he stayed for about a year and a half before quitting in a rage. I never learned exactly what went wrong. He was doing well academically (his mother said he was offered a university scholarship) but he began fighting with his professors or intermittently losing his concentration in class. At night he'd suffer from insomnia. His mother called me and pleaded with me to talk him into going back to school. "Marty, you're his best friend, he'll listen to you. His uncle is going to wash his hands of the whole thing and then he'll never be able to get a degree."

I called Andy and gave him all the standard arguments (which I only half believed) for finishing college, but he wasn't convinced. He stayed in New York reading and writing and "exploring life," supported by his mother and her brother. "If he doesn't straighten out, he'll never get a job. His mother can't support him his whole life," my mother said. But getting a job, despite occasional threats from his mother and uncle, was literally the last thing on Andy's mind. Not only did he still worship Henry Miller, he'd discovered Gertrude Stein's entire "lost generation." It was both the most natural and imperative thing in the world, as he saw it, to escape "the absurd contradictions and crass materialism of America," and to move to Paris. Now his uncle did stop contributing money but in a strange turnaround Roberta defended her son's ambitions, fought with her brother, and told him not to bother calling her again. Then she left her secretarial job at a Boston hospital and began selling life insurance. She didn't enjoy her new work with its increased responsibilities, for Roberta was not a person who reacted well to pressure, but she felt she had to do it for Andy. Eventually she grew quite adept. For the next three years she was able to support him in his studio apartment in Paris. "I believe in him, Marty," she would say to me whenever I questioned her. "You know how brilliant he is. Isn't he brilliant? Isn't he as talented as anyone his age?"

"He's very bright."

"All right then. He's going to make it. He'll support himself from writing. Look at Norman Mailer, look at Gore Vidal. It can happen. He'll do it. He just needs some peace of mind to develop. He says Europe's the place, he must know. Look at Hemingway and Fitzgerald. It will happen."

At that time I had finally left Newton, and was going to graduate school at New York University. School wasn't easy for me but I was a steady, if unspectacular, student. When my parents sometimes complained about how expensive my tuition was I'd feel the same envy for Andy's life that I used to feel when he was sleeping with Lizette. But it wasn't envy alone I felt. I also admired him and felt he deserved his life in a way I never could. Secretly, I'd conceded a number of things to him. He had a greater intellectual curiosity than I did. I struggled to pass my foreign language requirement at N.Y.U., but he could speak fluent French and German and was teaching himself Italian. For every book I'd read, he'd read two; not only literary books but philosophy, psychology, even books about painting or sculpture. Why *did* he need school? He also had an intensity, a generosity of spirit that I didn't. By comparison I felt petty and spiteful, even ordinary. It's true that by conventional standards I might have been considered better looking but Andy had raven-black hair, in fact the blackest hair and greenest eyes I'd ever seen. Even his personality made a bigger impact on people. He had a better sense of humor and was more trusting. People gravitated toward him and seemed ambivalent about me. No wonder he was able to get his way with his mother, even at the expense of her breaking off relations with her brother.

Of course, there were my undeniable advantages over Andy— my family's financial success and status, the sad fact that he hadn't had any contact with his father since he was eight. But more often than not the absence of a father seemed to me one more romantic detail about Andy. It gave his life, like Gatsby's, a certain self-created quality.

While I always thought Andy remarkable, I only rarely thought I was. Maybe that's why I left graduate school after I got my master's to teach in a prep school in western Massachusetts. I was twenty-three then and felt uncomfortable taking any more money from my parents. Meanwhile, Andy and I continued to exchange letters from Northfield, Mass. to Paris. In his letters he always seemed on the verge of a major breakthrough in his work. He said he was friendly with Michel Foucault, that he was contemplating going to the Sorbonne, that he was writing a novel, a screenplay, and a book on aesthetics, that he'd slept with Ingmar Bergman's daughter and a certain prominent American critic whose name I can't mention. I began to suspect he might be exaggerating but I couldn't be sure. With Andy anything seemed possible, there was never a way to prove him wrong.

That summer I visited him in Paris for two weeks. I must have been very excited since it was the first time I'd been to Europe, but what I chiefly remember is the awe, the infinite hopefulness in his face as he told me about his new life. I think we were walking in the Tuileries, though we could just as easily have been in his studio. It is his face, the excitement in his green eyes that I am sure of, as he told me he'd increased his "overall grasp of literature exponentially. The people that I've met here are incredible, the entire ambiance—it's become my spiritual home. I only wish you could stay longer."

After a passionate description of his French female conquests he told me that his mother was now seriously involved with a very wealthy Boston businessman. Roberta was only eighteen when Andy was born, twenty-six when she was divorced. Since then she'd only dated a handful of colorless men. Although she was extremely youthful and attractive, I'd somehow never imagined her with anyone but Andy. I pressed him for more details but he held up his hands to stop me. "I can only talk about it so much," he said, forming a short space between his thumb and index finger. "It could mean so much to her but I just don't want to say more until something definite happens."

Andy's revelation dwarfed whatever else I did in Paris, and I returned to Boston wondering how much of what he'd told me was true. Within a week, Roberta took me into her confidence and told me about "the special man" in her life, Benjamin Walters, who had invested prophetically in communication systems, and was indeed a wealthy man. Not only was he rich, but he was investing in Broadway shows and other theatrical endeavors which put him in touch with people that Roberta, who'd never been out of Newton, had previously only read about. Suddenly she was eating dinner with these stars and accompanying Benjamin for quick trips to Las Vegas or Hollywood. It was clearly the adventure of her life.

Eventually I had dinner with them in the more expensive apartment she'd moved into in Beacon Hill. Benjamin Walters was overweight, shy, preoccupied with his work, but he did exude a certain gruff charm. At times he looked and acted a bit like a New England Broderick Crawford. The morning after her dinner she called me to ask me my impressions, not so much of Benjamin but of how serious I thought he was about her. It was a question she would ask me in many different ways over the next three years. Of course, I never gave her an absolute answer. I was always embarrassed, although also a little flattered when she asked my opinion. Generally, I tried to encourage her because when she felt encouraged she'd be happy and she was wonderful to talk to when her basic optimism resurfaced.

Andy, meanwhile, had made some important career decisions. He'd abandoned his attempts to write novels or screenplays and concentrated instead on what he was best at, literary and social criticism. He began publishing book reviews in literary quarterlies, then longer and more theoretical essays. Within three years he was occasionally reviewing for *The New Republic* and *The Nation*.

I felt competitive and a trifle envious, though, of course, I was happy for him too. Besides, I had distractions of my own, principally a series of short, intense love affairs. As for my career, I had managed to publish a few stories in little magazines. (I thought of them, at the time, as proof of the important creative distinction between me and Andy. So what if they appeared in magazines with circulations under a thousand. They proved I was "an artist," didn't they?) I'd also left the private school in the country and become an English instructor in a junior college in Boston. What I was concentrating on chiefly was getting tenure. I saw that as the necessary first step to anything else I wanted from life, so I methodically plugged away at it. That's how it was in those days: I was plugging away after tenure, Roberta was plugging away after Benjamin Walters, while Andy was pursuing the legacy of Edmund Wilson and making impressive progress.

Finally, after three years Roberta got discouraged, then angry that Benjamin wouldn't marry her.

"He says he's got a hang-up about marriage, but I think he's just a cheapskate. He doesn't want to part with any of his big bucks. I don't care for myself; it's Andy I'm worried about."

"Andy seems to be doing fine, he's flourishing."

"Marty, I still have to support him. I may always have to help him."

"At the rate he's going he'll probably be making his own 'big bucks' from writing," I said, surprised that I was assuming the argument she usually used to defend Andy's life. "Maybe you should give Benjamin, you know, an ultimatum of some kind," I said softly. Roberta ran her fingers through her own raven-black hair, only slightly flecked with a few silver streaks. Her eyes were also sharp and green; she looked like a feminine version of Andy.

"I probably should, but the truth is, Marty, I'm afraid he'd say no….Anyway, he's promised to always take care of me."

A few months later Andy moved back to New York to capitalize on his initial successes. I think we were both so busy with our careers that in some ways we had less contact than when he was in Europe. Also, I had become seriously involved with Lianne, an assistant art professor at my college, and within a few months we were virtually living together. During his last visit to Boston I only found time to have one lunch with Andy. Every time I spoke I ended up mentioning Lianne, as if my mouth took a compulsive delight in pronouncing her name. When I asked Andy if he was seeing anyone he alluded to his usual list of glamorous one-night stands and then changed the subject.

I felt guilty for not spending more time with him during his visit and a month later, after a new review of his on Samuel Beckett had been published, I wrote him a long congratulatory letter.

Andy wrote me back eight pages. Typically, his references ranged from Proust to Heidegger to Miles Davis to the Abstract Expressionists. But it was the confessional part near the end that I still remember:

> You praise me for having so much to say about Beckett, but there is so much more I want to say, so much more inside me that I need to utter and I feel thwarted and ashamed that I still can't fashion it into decent prose. If only I could write poetry! Besides the desire to write something I am not disgusted with, I want only three things in life: happiness for my mother who has sacrificed everything for me; happiness for my friends—most of all for you since you are my most treasured friend; and a little taste of the love you have found with Lianne. I realize now that I have not yet been able to fall in love.

I decided to never let too much time pass without seeing Andy. That summer he was in Boston a lot and I would see him two or three times a week. He and I and Lianne would sometimes go to the movies together or walk around Harvard Square, but I was careful not to let him spend too much time with her. It wasn't that I didn't trust them—it was just easier for me to deal with them separately, perhaps because each required such an intense and different kind of attention. I also realized that I didn't understand Andy's sexuality—it was so ferocious yet detached, like a caged lion that was only temporarily calm. He was constantly evoking this or that starlet (usually European ones) as the apotheosis of beauty or sex appeal but the only woman I'd ever seen him express any strong emotion for was his mother. It was Roberta who could provoke his temper as no one else could, Roberta who could still induce his screaming fits the same as when he was an eighth grader, and it was Roberta whom he would still unabashedly smother with kisses, even in my presence.

One weekend in July, Lianne went home to visit her parents and I went to Roberta's apartment to meet Andy. We were planning to go to a literary party of some kind. When I arrived Andy was still dressing, and I saw Benjamin Walters sitting on Roberta's sofa. Corpulent, slow moving, he was wrapped in his dark blue suit like a mummy. We exchanged five minutes of awkward small talk while Roberta, dressed in a tight-fitting pink gown that showed off her slim figure, fluttered around him like a cocktail waitress. That evening she was obviously going to cook him another dinner.

"You know, I can't stand him," Andy said to me in his car as we searched for the party in Cambridge. "If it weren't for my mother I probably would have punched him out a couple of times by now."

"But he seems to make your mother happy. I've never seen her so animated."

"Of course, and that's everything to me," he said, as his voice softened. "But it's ironic that the love of my mother's life should be such a bloated, petty, ignorant, self-involved, penurious nouveau riche…." He searched for more adjectives and then started to laugh. "I wish for two minutes I could be Marcel Proust just to once and for all do verbal justice to Benjamin. The point is, I could forgive him for being so culturally bankrupt, but he has the chutzpah to lecture me and my mother about how I should get a job and work for him in his business. The man is actually trying to parent me. Meanwhile, if he'd only marry my mother she could finally stop working for once in her life, but he's too goddamn cheap to marry her and he's been sleeping with her for four years now."

"Still, you know, he might marry her and you should try to be nice to him. It can only benefit you."

"Believe me he *will* marry her. And within one year after their marriage I'll launch the most important literary magazine in America since *The Dial*. Who knows, since he has millions, I may even start a small publishing company that will only publish books of real quality."

As if sensing the pang of envy I was feeling, he quickly added, "Of course, Marty, you'll leave that little college where they're mistreating you and be my partner."

At the party there were a number of attractive women. I told Andy that I was being faithful to Lianne and that he should go after whomever he wanted. But Andy found something wrong with every one of them. One of them was a little too plump, another looked too Jewish, a third, who was obviously pretty, he claimed had "no hips or breasts, she might turn out to be a boy."

We ended up drinking a lot at the party and then walking along the Charles River afterwards to sober up. "If Benjamin ever double-crossed my mother I think I'd be justified in killing him, don't you?" he said as we walked past a series of couples making out on the benches or on the grass by the river.

"What are you saying, are you serious?"

"You don't agree, you think that's sick?"

"I think you're too close to your mother. Can't you find a girlfriend, instead of all those one-night things?"

"You're right. It's because I know she needs me; she's given everything to me."

"But she has someone. She has Benjamin and you're still alone...."

"You're right, Marty. As soon as I get back to New York I'm going to work on it. I'll have a girlfriend within two weeks."

A few hours later, at two or three in the morning, I was asleep in my apartment when the phone rang. Andy's voice was saying words to me I could scarcely absorb.

"Something unbelievable happened. Benjamin had a heart attack. I'm calling you from the hospital. My mother's in shock."

I went to Benjamin's funeral with Roberta and Andy. Roberta cried throughout the service and then intermittently during the reception at Benjamin's brother's home. Andy was by her side every moment, his face rigid with a kind of heightened alertness.

A few days later it was determined that Benjamin hadn't left a will. As the next of kin, Benjamin's brother put in a claim for the whole estate and offered Roberta $10,000. He had grossly underestimated her. Of course, at this time palimony suits were still unheard of, and in all those years Roberta had never technically lived with Benjamin. But Roberta's claim was that Benjamin had verbally promised her his estate in lieu of marrying her, and that she had faithfully rendered to him the services of a wife.

A month later, Benjamin's brother claimed to have located a homemade will leaving him everything. The controversy wound up in court and dragged on for a year, with handwriting experts contradicting each other, with appeals and counterappeals. I was one of the witnesses who testified for Roberta. It was peculiar; I thought she was probably telling the truth most of the time, but the mere participation in an attempt to get someone's money made me feel a little like I was committing a crime.

Since Benjamin's death Andy had moved back with his mother. Like Roberta, he became obsessed with the details of the trial. He stopped writing, and even read very little. He was too nervous to attend the various hearings. Of course it was impossible to get much pleasure from his company in those days, but in some ways our friendship was stronger than ever. Not only did he and Roberta need me as a confidant about the twists and turns of their case, I needed them as well. I was having my own crisis. Lianne and I had broken up (I'd found out that she'd slept with someone in her department) and the pain of adjusting to living alone was worse than I'd anticipated. Also I found out I was coming up for tenure a year earlier than I'd expected and was very anxious about it. My own rate of publishing had fallen well behind my expectations. In short, listening to Roberta's and Andy's monologues about their case (as well as their occasional epiphanies about all the things they could do when they finally got their money) seemed a small price to pay for some genuine empathy for my loss of Lianne, and my troubles with tenure.

Another year passed before Roberta was finally awarded her settlement. It was far less than Andy and she had dreamed of, but it was more than a half-million dollars. I had meanwhile managed to postpone the decision on my tenure for another year. What better time was there to finally discuss with Andy our long-planned magazine which we both needed to revitalize our careers?

A month after the Auers won their case, when they'd returned from a short vacation in Europe, I invited Andy to dinner at a small French restaurant in Harvard Square. Perhaps because we hadn't talked about the magazine in a long time, or because I wanted it so much, I led up to it gradually. I waited until we had our main course and were on our second bottle of wine before I mentioned how much I needed to publish to get tenure. Andy stared past me and gave me a rather perfunctorily sympathetic nod. I switched to another approach and began railing against those young critics in Andy's field who were publishing everywhere and whom we both knew to be mediocrities. Again he didn't take the hint.

"So when are we going to start working on our magazine?" I suddenly blurted.

Andy focused his eyes on me darkly.

"About the magazine you have to understand something, Marty. It's not my money, it's my mother's. She deserves so many things and now she has a chance to get some of them. She's going to decide how every penny is spent."

"Of course, I understand. But you could ask her. I mean, it's only $5,000 or $10,000 we're talking about, initially."

"Maybe if we'd gotten the whole estate, but now? No, I won't even ask her."

"I don't understand. What have we been talking about the past four or five years?"

"I don't care about the past. My mother and I are starting a new life."

"But..."

"No more buts," he screamed, slamming his fist on the table. The veins stood out in his thin forehead the way they did when he'd have a temper tantrum playing baseball as a kid, or else fighting with Roberta. "Is that why you testified at the trial? Is that why you've been my 'friend' all these years, because you want your cut? You want to rob me too, like Benjamin and his brother, and the courts, and my father. I'm nauseated. I never want to see you again!"

He got up from the table and left the restaurant. A few minutes later I went home, shaken. During that sleepless first night, I was sure he would call and apologize. I'd seen him have these temporary rages before and then become profoundly apologetic an hour or two later. But the call didn't come. Then I thought he'd write me or that Roberta would contact me, but neither happened and soon a week had passed.

I began to wonder if I were all the things he accused me of. Who had betrayed whom? Who was the victim, Andy or me? Yes, I had wanted to do a magazine, but I'd never made a secret of it, and it was Andy who'd suggested it first. Would I have testified for Roberta if there were no magazine involved? Of course. Would I also have listened so religiously to all his anxieties if there were no hope of my benefiting from it? I was still sure I would have. After all, we'd been friends since childhood.

Another week went by. I almost called him many times but my own pride and sense of justice stopped me. I finally told my parents what had happened and my father shook his head and walked out of the room. My mother had a few things to say, however.

"They're the schemers, they're the opportunists. They're what they accuse you of being. I say good riddance. Andy's gotten a free ride through life. He's just jealous of you because you work like a normal person and don't live off your parents. If you ask me, they're both *meshuga*, and you're lucky to be rid of them."

But I didn't feel so lucky and I finally wrote Andy a long conciliatory letter. He didn't answer me and when I phoned him a week later I learned that they'd already moved.

Four years went by, maybe five. I had new love affairs, new disappointments. I didn't get tenure, but I managed to get a series of one-year teaching jobs near Boston. I published a few more stories. Through the grapevine I heard Andy and his mother had moved to Lexington, then to New Hampshire, then to Cape Cod. I was hurt by Andy, but I felt so clearly wronged that it grew easier to forget him. Eventually, I only thought about him once a week or so, as if he were a relative who had died years ago. I never saw his name in print again (although I instinctively avoided those magazines most likely to publish him), which made forgetting him still easier.

Shortly after Christmas each year, the Modern Language Association holds its national convention. Although a number of academics present various papers, the main purpose of the convention is for college English chairs to interview various candidates for their departments. Last year's convention was in New York, and I considered myself fortunate to have secured two interviews, although one was for a junior college, and the other (which was a "tenure track" job) was for a college in an obscure town in Arkansas.

After my last interview I walked out of the Hilton and began replaying the sequence of questions and answers that had just occurred five minutes before. It was bitter cold outside. The sky looked drained, as if it were too depleted of energy to send out any color that day. For no particular reason I headed east. When the wind blew it seemed to cut into my face. Around Second Avenue and 55th Street I stopped at a red light. Someone had called out my name loudly and shrilly two or three times. I turned and saw Roberta.

She was still strikingly pretty, in a white fur coat with her carefully coiffured black hair, and her green eyes under a stylish pair of sunglasses. Physically she had aged, if at all, in very subtle ways.

"Don't turn away, Marty. Come on, give me a hug. Let's forget the past, we can forgive each other, can't we?"

We embraced and at Roberta's suggestion walked into a nearby coffee shop. Once at our table we continued our small talk for another minute or two. I noticed that she looked a little sad when I told her I'd just come from a job interview.

"So how's Andy?" I finally said.

"You'll see him tonight. I'm cooking him dinner in his loft in Soho."

"Are you…where are you living now?"

Roberta told me matter-of-factly about her apartment in Sutton Place but a moment later she clutched my arm just above my wrist and said, "Promise me you'll come tonight, it will mean so much to him."

"Of course, I'll try."

"No, you have to promise. Marty, you've got to forgive him." She took off her sunglasses and wiped away a few tears. "These last five years have been a nightmare."

"I'd just heard that you moved a lot."

"You've heard of the 'wandering Jews,' right? We're setting a record."

She listed the places they'd lived in that I already knew about, and two other places that I didn't.

"What's the trouble, why do you keep moving?"

"He makes me move. One place is too isolated, the other is too noisy. He has problems now, Marty, he's not the way you remember."

"He's not working?"

"He says he's writing but I can't be sure. We wasted four years on a lousy psychiatrist—he should rot in hell. He put Andy on all the wrong medication. But now he's found a new doctor who he thinks is God. Andy can still turn it around. You know how talented he is."

"He never got a job," I said, immediately regretting my words.

"He can do it with his writing. Look at Truman Capote, look at John Updike. They never taught, they didn't need degrees. If he were healthy and writing he'd be making a million dollars. Marty, just promise me you'll come tonight. Here, I'll write down the address."

I went back to my hotel, dazed by my meeting with Roberta and the prospect of seeing Andy in just a few hours. On my bed I closed my eyes and saw a series of pictures of my past with Andy, one at a time like paintings in a gallery: Andy in his Paris studio, Andy walking out of the movies with Lianne and me, Andy like a sentinel at Benjamin's funeral, Andy on the bench at the baseball game twenty-two years ago.

I forced myself to get up—I had to buy them a bottle of wine, after all, and I'd fallen asleep in my suit. Roberta was probably exaggerating about Andy's condition. Like my own mother, she was hopelessly melodramatic.

Andy lived on Spring Street in one of the more elegant parts of Soho. He shook my hand with a quizzical but benign smile on his face.

"I'm sorry about what happened between us."

"Forget it," I said quickly.

"I guess we're both nervous," he said, as he led me into the living room. Waving at me from a distance, Roberta immediately walked into a bedroom and left us alone. Andy was wearing jeans and a sport shirt and I made a joke about showing up in a suit. He laughed and handed me a glass of champagne. I noticed that his hair had receded even more than mine, and that he now had as many crow's feet around his eyes as Roberta.

"Let me show you the loft," he said, walking ahead of me. The walls were covered with paintings, prints, and photographs. Some of them, like a print by Pollock or Chagall, were of real value. He gave me a brief history of each picture but I forgot most of what he said. Where there weren't paintings, there were high white shelves completely filled with books.

"How many books do you have?" I said.

"Guess."

"I don't know. It looks like a library."

"Five thousand, all alphabetically arranged," he said, beaming with pride. He continued his walking tour, stopping periodically to give me the history of a lamp or quilt. "I always wanted to live here, some incredible people live around me, you know," and he rattled off a list of art-world luminaries. "They're here now and in the summer they go to the Hamptons. By the way, this summer my mother's going to buy a place there. She's already trying to sell the Sutton Place apartment."

We continued walking slowly in circles around the loft. I realized he was no longer nervous, but the angry wit, the edge to his personality, was missing.

We finally stopped walking and sat down on a couch by a window.

"I'm sorry I didn't answer your letter," he said softly. "I don't know how much my mother told you but I've been having some troubles…the past few years."

"She mentioned you were seeing a doctor."

"Marty, I'm on a lot of medication. Thirteen different pills a day."

"What's the matter?"

He smiled ironically and shrugged his shoulders.

"Maybe you shouldn't spend so much time with your mother?"

"Oh, no, I'd be dead without her. I owe her everything. The only thing is she's never been able to enjoy her money. I mean, how can she be happy as long as I'm sick? My sickness is keeping her from everything she wants," he said sadly, with a strange smile on his lips.

"So you've been living with her?"

"This is the first time we've been apart in five years. It's an experiment. My doctor ordered it."

Roberta came out of the bedroom in a bright blue skirt with a matching sweater and began making her final preparations for dinner. Andy signaled to me and we changed the subject. But it had been so long since the three of us had talked, and even longer since we'd talked about anything but the trial, that it was awkward. When Roberta sent Andy to the store to get some last-minute things for dinner, I knew she was going to take advantage of her time alone with me to talk about Andy.

As soon as he shut the elevator door she led me by the arm to the sofa by the window.

"So what do you think about Andy?"

"I don't know what to say."

"How bad does he seem to you?"

"He seems pretty down on himself."

"Marty, his ego's on the floor. He's a thirty-five-year-old man who's never accomplished anything in his life. Think how he feels."

"So the main thing is that he's stopped writing, that's the main symptom?"

"Marty, he hasn't been with a woman in years. He sleeps twelve hours a day and he lists."

"Lists?"

"He has hundreds of rituals that he goes through every day. His doctor calls it 'listing.'"

"You mean writing things down compulsively?"

"Sometimes it's that, other times it's just in his mind. His doctor calls it a 'rage for order.'"

"So what do his doctors say has caused all this?"

"They contradict each other. One says it's congenital, another says something else. Between all the doctors and the moving I'm starting to go through my capital. I'm still trying to sell our house in New Hampshire. The real estate market's collapsed. I'm losing so much money with all this buying and selling I'd be ashamed to tell you."

"So stop moving."

"I shouldn't listen to him, I know. I tell him the problem's inside him, it's not where he's living."

"You gave up your job too?"

"I couldn't work. He'd call me four or five times a day at my office, every time he had a problem. It was impossible…Marty, you've got to be his friend again. Stay the night. He needs to know that you're his friend again."

"Of course…"

Roberta was an exquisite cook. Her chicken crepes were so delicious that we all became engrossed in our dinner, without worrying about safe topics of conversation. By the time we got to her chocolate mousse and the champagne, we began reminiscing about our high school years and even our grammar school baseball team. Andy grew especially animated and told a couple of jokes. For a few minutes he was just like his old self. But when Roberta warned him not to drink too much because of his medication he glared at her for a moment and turned somber.

A few minutes later he got up from the table and sat down in a chair in the middle of the loft and turned on the television. I continued talking with Roberta, quietly but ineffectually. Every half-minute she'd turn her head and look at Andy. A little later we heard him snoring.

"This happens every night. He sits in the chair, turns on the TV, and in half an hour he falls asleep."

I noticed that it was only 9:30.

"Well, I may as well go to sleep too," she said, yawning. "In a couple of hours he'll wake up and go to his room. I'll fix up the couch for you by the window."

"You're sure you don't want the couch? It's much bigger."

"No, no," she said, handing me my sheets and pillow. "I always sleep on that little bed in the living room when I visit him."

A half-hour later Roberta and Andy were snoring in unison. I lay on the couch unable to read or sleep, feeling trapped and abandoned. I couldn't remember the last time I'd tried to sleep so early. When I turned off the bed lamp I started to think about Lianne. When that got too painful I began reviewing my job interviews and I thought of all the vain and foolish things I'd done to try to get hired at schools I already had contempt for.

I got up and fixed myself a drink. Mother and son were still snoring loudly. In the vastness of the loft it echoed like a bizarre kind of church music. My mother was right, they are *meshuga*, I thought. But when I lay down again I began to feel sorry for them. They're the victims, I said to myself, answering my question of five years ago.

I finally fell asleep, but a few hours later I woke up from a nightmare that involved both my parents and Lianne. My heart was pounding and I could hear someone pacing in the loft. When I shifted the venetian blinds there was just enough light for me to see Andy walking. I saw him making some vague and frenzied gestures in the air, like a conductor frantically cuing his wayward orchestra. I realized he was doing one of his rituals, and I watched him continue his pattern of gestures in a slow, methodical circle around his loft. When his walk brought him a few feet in front of the couch I felt an impulse to get up and stop him. I almost said, "Stop pacing, or listing, or worrying. Whatever it is, just stop. Lie down in bed, next to me if you have to, but just stop."

Christ, I'm starting to lose it, I thought, as Andy began walking away from me toward the TV. Then I remembered that in my nightmare Lianne, whom I'd been kissing, had turned into Andy. I forced myself to analyze the dream for a minute, because I always analyzed the dreams I could remember.

"So what if Andy and I have always been a little in love with each other, and with our mothers too, and with all the wrong people. Just a lot of bad career moves."

I said this in the jokingly cynical tone of voice I usually used in talking to myself, but tears came to my eyes anyway.

"We're all victims," I said, but softly enough so that Andy couldn't hear me.

The Liar

S he's lying! he thought. Paul was standing about five feet
behind her, though he didn't intend to make a call, and had
been listening to everything she'd said the last few minutes. At
first he thought she was some kind of prostitute, but when he
heard her say she didn't like football he thought she might simply
be answering a singles ad. Then came the lie about her height,
although it wasn't so outrageous a lie that he could be positive
about it (for instance, she could have been quoting her height in
the high heels she was wearing instead of her bare feet). But after
her seeming to make herself taller remark, he was sure he heard
her say she had long black hair. He looked at her again—her hair
barely reached her shoulders and was red. Was she wearing a
wig? It certainly didn't look like it. Then why the lie? Wouldn't it
be immediately discovered as soon as she and her phone friend
met? Or did she plan to wear a long black wig when she met him?
He felt disgusted by her lying—wasn't that just the essence of
everything—but also oddly fascinated.

"I'm in Barnes and Noble at a pay phone," she was saying
more softly now, "I can't really get into it now, people are waiting
to use the phone. Can I call you sometime later tonight, say 9:00
or 9:30 after you're back from your dinner?"

Paul felt a pang of anxiety that she'd be getting off the phone
and probably leaving the bookstore soon. She definitely didn't

look like the bookish type who'd be doing much browsing. Fortunately, having visited the bank a half-hour ago, his pockets were bulging with money and he quickly got an idea. While he went over it, he moved a little to the right to observe her profile again, which he admired, though she looked to have collagen-enhanced lips that were made even bigger by a generous amount of garish red lipstick.

She was making more protestations. Again she used the words "I can't get into it now." It had to be something about sex, what else would someone like her be afraid to discuss on a pay phone? The phone was situated between the men's and women's bathrooms and a fairly steady stream of people were passing by them—entering or exiting with the sound of the flushing toilets audible more often than not each time one of the doors opened—sometimes annoyingly drowning out a crucial word of hers.

Then, suddenly, she was off the phone and moving towards the other side of the floor without once turning around to look at him. There was no reason or time to bother faking a phone call. He followed behind her as she entered the bookstore cafe and ordered a coffee. To save time he bought a biscotti, managing to sit at the table next to hers. He didn't like or trust this kind of food but figured he had to make concessions. He was feeling a strong desire to talk to "the liar," as he'd nicknamed her in his mind, and without fully realizing it was openly staring at her. When there were only a few sips left in her cup she finally looked at him and said with a perfectly cryptic smile, "Was there something you wanted to say to me? I mean you are sort of following me, aren't you? It's not my imagination."

Paul hesitated at first. "Yes I have been. I seem to have a very strong desire to talk with you."

"Well," she said, looking at her watch, "I have a couple of minutes. What do you want to say?"

He knew what he wanted to say, or part of it, but also knew he had to be tactful. "I wish there were more time to talk. It's hard to do this in two minutes....Do you come to this store much?"

"Sometimes."

He nodded. He'd already pictured her using the pay phone as her "office" for her dealings with men. That way nothing could ever be traced.

"My name is Paul," he said, stopping just short of extending his hand.

She said hello but didn't offer her hand or her name either, and he felt tricked and angry and thought then of leaving his table and this liar and making a clean exit, perhaps walking through the park outside to feel still cleaner. Instead, he stayed in his chair and said, "Of course, I think you're very pretty."

"Thank you."

"And mysterious."

"What would make you think that? You just now started talking to me."

"It's in the atmosphere that surrounds you, I guess."

She smiled slightly. "I find it mysterious that you've been following me."

"I told you, it's because I have a strong desire to talk with you. I would love to invite you to dinner at Eden," he said, naming perhaps the most expensive restaurant in the city, "or any other place you'd like to go."

"Would you? Well, I'm quite impressed."

Then for a few minutes they talked about the bookstore and the weather. He wished she could see all the fifties and hundreds in his pockets and, in fact, without fully realizing it, had removed a few of the bills and was caressing them with his fingers in a way that she would notice, perhaps, if she were the observant type. When he reiterated his invitation she said, "But that's a lot of time to spend with someone you've just met."

"How about a drink then to help you decide. Is the Forum OK?"

"You're quite persuasive in your own way," she said, moving to get up from the table after looking, he thought, at his hand holding the money. They said nothing while they rode the escalator down to the first floor but as soon as they were on the sidewalk Paul asked her name.

"Andra," she said.

What did it matter what she said, he immediately thought, it could just as easily be Lydia or Carmen. "Andra" sounded almost

overly poetic, although possibly too strange a name to spontaneously make up. At any rate, it was nothing he could press her
about. She, in turn, asked him how he made his living and he told
her he was an entrepreneur considering various investments.

"How did you manage that?" she said as they walked into the
dark, high-ceilinged restaurant. The place was filled with white
marble columns that alluded to the Roman Forum. Everyone in it,
especially the waiters, seemed to have very white theatrical skin
that contrasted with their dark suits or dresses.

"I used to have a software business supplying programs which
I sold. I guess I lost interest in computers just as the world was
developing its…well, interest is too small a word, passion or
sickness really, because I've come to see it as a sickness."

"Why is it sick?" she asked after they ordered their drinks from
the waiter.

"Because it pretends to tell the truth but lies. In some
fundamental way the entire Internet is a lie, but there's way too
much money at stake for anyone involved to admit it."

She fell silent. He couldn't tell if she was bored or else waiting
for him to elaborate. "Well you're admitting it, so kudos to you,"
she said raising her glass as if toasting him. "And did you make
a nice bit from selling your business?"

"Yes, yes I did."

"And now you're looking for a new business?"

"I'm looking for something with meaning…for me. I'm
looking for truth, you could say."

She smiled and he felt himself getting somewhat aroused. But
he had certain things to find out about her before making any
kind of move.

The drinks came more quickly than he imagined. He drank
his slowly to stretch out the time before she'd have to go. He
said there were illusions everywhere and she asked him what
he meant.

He said there were the well-publicized ones like religion
and money and sex and then the less publicized ones like art
and immortality.

"Wait," she said, "why is sex an illusion?"

"Is there anything about it that isn't?"

She laughed. "OK. That was a good answer...so I guess you're a pretty skeptical guy who's soured on just about everything."

"It's not a question of that."

"It's not like I can't understand," she said, taking a generous swallow of her rum and coke. "I've soured on a lot of things too."

For the first time her smile left her face.

"To make truth a real value in your life doesn't make you a negative person," Paul said. "It just means you're sick of lies and illusions. You don't want to chase after them anymore."

"Who does?"

"Right. No one. I think the only reason we do is our minds are built to cling to them. We're programmed that way."

"Now you've lost me again," she said, putting down her empty glass. He looked at it as if she'd suddenly revealed an amputated finger and he quickly asked her if he could buy her another.

"I really shouldn't."

"But why? We've hardly spent any time here at all. Don't you like it here? We could go somewhere else if you don't."

"No. This place is fine, very classy. I just really shouldn't."

"Please, just one more."

"Well, OK, one more and that's it. I guess I should give you more time to explain all this complicated stuff to me about mind programming, huh?" she said, laughing.

"What I mean is our brains aren't built to face the reality of our situation in the world. For instance, we can't really conceive of our death, grasp that there's where we're headed—not until we've lived most of our lives, anyway."

"Well why should we? You think little kids should think about it? How could anyone enjoy anything if they did?"

"All right. I'm just saying, just observing that this is the way it is. And even when we acknowledge death we don't really acknowledge it. We invent an afterlife. Or we pretend our accomplishments will last forever. Like our books and paintings and..."

"So what are you saying?"

"It's a paradox, isn't it? If time isn't infinite then the world ends. If time is infinite then everything we do will be forgotten...eventually."

She was already attacking her new drink, much to Paul's chagrin. She would be walking off soon into the early evening, free of him and thinking more of the drinks in her stomach than of anything he'd said.

"I don't know Paul, it sounds kind of weird to me."

"What does?"

"All this stuff about our brains not being built to think about death and…"

"Not only death. How about time itself—ever think about that? We know through science that time can't really be separated from space yet we don't think of it that way."

"I don't know about that. Whenever I think of the past there's always a place involved, usually with a creepy guy in it…no offense Paul. I don't mean you. You've been pretty nice so far."

He nodded in acknowledgment and forced a smile, but he felt stung. How absurd of him to prattle on in these grandiose abstractions. She was right to make fun of him and pull him up short.

"So this is what you think about?" she finally said.

"It's really just the backdrop of what I think about."

"I mean, why do you let it get to you so much?"

He shrugged and forced another smile. "Why, what do you think about?"

"I'm much more practical. I find myself thinking a lot about money, for example."

"Why don't you let me free you from that distraction, then, at least for tonight?"

"Really? How would you do that?"

"I'd like to buy you dinner for one thing. Here or at anyplace you want, and since I've already taken you from part of your afternoon, I'd like to make you a small gift for the gift of your time that you've given me."

Then he slid her one of the hundred-dollar bills he'd been holding and placed it next to her hand.

"This is very strange, Paul. You assume that I'll take it."

"I assume nothing. But I really would like you to accept this small gift from me, that's all."

"And what do you think this is buying?"

"Nothing. It's a gift. Think of it as a philosophical gesture. I put money on the table for you in order to take money *off* the table—of our discussion. You said you think about money and I want your mind to be money-free for one night. So please just do me the favor and complete my gesture by taking it and then we don't have to think about it anymore."

"Well, in the name of philosophy, I guess I can take it," she said, picking up the bill. "And if you like, here is fine for dinner. It's very atmospheric, don't you think?"

"Yes, certainly," he said, pretending to look around himself for a moment in appreciation. So that was that. He felt pleased. He had her attention now and the knowledge that she would stay through dinner. The restaurant itself suddenly seemed less like a haunted house and more like a romantic one. The waiters, too, now seemed less like vampires and had become unintimidating like peripheral figures in a dream.

They ordered dinner from one of them and he faded away, blinking and then disappearing like a firefly. Then he and Andra made small talk for a while which suited him fine. She even told him she liked the sport jacket he was wearing and the haircut he'd gotten earlier in the day. She seemed to like saying nice things to him—a trait that was always welcome.

At first, when dinner came, they concentrated on eating, speaking only to compliment the food. But this wasn't what he ultimately wanted. He still hadn't found out about the things she'd said on the phone. He ordered more drinks. Perhaps he should just ask her directly, not worrying about the right kind of transition, and she would say something, she would have to say something, wouldn't she, unless, of course, she got offended and took her last swallow of roast lamb, leaving the restaurant, his hundred in her hand, never to lay eyes on him again.

Life was like that—didn't he know it. Like a minefield, where at any moment you could lose everything. He was 41 years old—his hair thinning and receding already, his eyes dimming, though he still didn't wear glasses, and he was alone—he who had once loved so much—so he did know about that. He was an expert on loss, he figured, and so he postponed his question. But now, ironically enough, she was asking him one. Was he married, she wanted to know? Yes, but not now. Was he involved, then, with anyone? Yes, always until the last time, but not now. He didn't think he'd really loved these people like he'd thought he did, he heard himself saying. "I have come to see that there are no thoughts—only addictions."

"There you go, talking weird again. What's that supposed to mean?"

"I used to think about the psychologies of the individual women I was involved with. I used to try to understand why I was attached to them, why we were in a relationship and then inevitably why the relationship got in a downward spiral and ultimately ended. I believed I was having my own free thoughts about very different people and situations but then one day after enough time went by I started to see through myself. Some writer said, 'Love is a dance of your own ego.' You think it's your partner who's creating a new dance with you with so many new steps but it turns out to be…"

"Don't tell me—an illusion," she said, laughing.

"Yes," he said. He noticed a little dab of gravy just above her thick red lips but dared not say anything. "It turns out to be, in the end, the same dance with yourself that covers roughly the same area. Just another addiction, in other words.

"But then something did change in my life. Not with the woman—Claire—who I'd married and then gotten divorced from, but with our child, our son Daniel."

"Oh."

"Who was an accident and only two or two and a half when we divorced."

"A cute kid, I bet."

"Sweetness itself. The irony is I began to get much closer to him after I was separated from him and could only see him a few hours a day while his mother was working. This is in Foxgrove, by the way, do you know it?"

She shook her head no.

"It's a mix of mostly suburban sprawl with a few pretty patches of country. Maybe it happened because with the pressures of my divorce over, I was freed up to concentrate on him more. Or maybe it was because he was starting to talk which, of course, changes so many things. Or else that he was taken away from me, because I'd meekly agreed to give her custody.

"Whatever it was, we grew closer and closer. Seeing him soon became a dramatic event and I'd find myself counting the minutes until I could be with him. Soon I began driving up from the city three days a week instead of two. Then four and five days a week as my interest in the business world and all its silly hustle continued to decline. On the weekends, without Danny, I would suffer acutely.

"I rented a second apartment in Foxgrove as close to where he and his mother lived as I could find and started staying there on weekends in the hopes that his mother might use me as a babysitter for an hour or two. But often I was completely alone on the weekends, waiting for a phone call that never came. I knew something new and very powerful was happening to me. I would cry just thinking about him almost every day and no longer thought for a second about all the thousands of extra dollars I was spending on my two homes, nor about the career I was almost totally neglecting, not to mention the company of women, or any adults for that matter, that I'd completely given up.

"All of that ceased to exist when Danny and I went on our walks in the land around his mother's condo complex. Words that I'd never thought of or almost never said began to dominate my conversation, and thoughts took on the power of mantras."

"What words?"

"Words for the things he loved that ruled his world. Pine needles and ice cream cones, only by ice cream cones he meant the narrow green pine cones that we'd find that sort of looked like pistachio ice cream cones. Then there were holly trees and the green and red berries he loved to pick from them. Stones that he loved to throw into the pond and that he later called boulders because there was a boulder that chased after some trains in one of the videos he watched so religiously.

"The names for his trains were also magical. Henry and Thomas and Thumper and Boco and Rheneas, that he pronounced 'Frheneas.' And then the names of the characters from his animal videos: Little Bear and Maisy and Franklin and Duck and Pip, which was his name for Duck's baby. One day he said to me, 'Pip loves you,' and I almost swooned in ecstasy.

"But best of all were the names of the characters he and I invented. Anything could become a character just by our talking about it that way. Just by eliminating an article Danny didn't ride in a wagon but 'Wagon' gave him a ride and 'Wagon' missed him and waited for him. He didn't sleep on a mattress; 'Mattress' let him sleep on it.

"We called a large bush thick with foliage 'Bong Tree' and when he threw his pink beachball into it we said 'Bong Tree ate the ball.' I earned my hero's stripes and his peals of laughter by rescuing the ball, though Bong Tree would always bite my hand in the process. Then I'd hand Danny the ball and he'd throw it back to Bong Tree again. Similarly, I bought what looked like a toy raccoon or squirrel, tucked it between the back of my shirt and pants and announced to him that I was wearing my tail. Danny would then sneak up behind me, take my tail, and run away laughing hysterically as I bellowed, 'oh no, Tail is gone!' I'd find it in the same hiding place he always used—on top of the kitchen table. Then 'Tail' would chase after and tickle him and return to his home with me only to be taken again twenty seconds later by Danny.

"When we'd go to the condo association's swimming pool—with life preservers up to his skinny neck—'Fish' would alternately chase and bite me, and then chase and bite him. It's odd, or maybe not odd, how scared he used to be to go in the pool with me. Of course he spent much more time with his mother and he was sometimes nervous about doing things with me. The first time he stayed overnight with me in my apartment when he was already three, he was so excited he had insomnia.

"'I can't sleep,' he said, 'Mattress keeps biting me.' Later he said, 'Is mommy here?'

"'No.'

"'Is that her at the door?'

"'No, mommy's in her house sleeping.'

"'Let's go wake her up.'

"'No, that would make her mad. You can fall asleep right here. Just close your eyes!'

"I tried him on my bed, on my mattress on the floor, in my La-Z-Boy, before he finally fell asleep on my living room carpet, clutching his silky, his little head propped up on a pillow at 1:30 in the morning with the same Little Bear video he'd demanded playing for perhaps the fifth time.

"Now I, myself, was way too excited to sleep. Instead I watched him sleep, listened to his breathing, watching and listening for signals to know when to add or subtract a blanket or sheet."

"He sounds like an adorable kid," Andra said. She'd finished her roast lamb, Paul noted, and had pushed her plate to the side. Soon the waiters would come with the dessert menus.

"Yes, of course, adorable by any measure and beautiful. Beautiful blue smiling eyes and golden brown hair. Like a child Renoir would paint. I tried not to focus on Daniel's physical beauty because he was such an intelligent and sensitive child, always giving me drawings or running out into the yard to pick leaves off the maple tree so he could give me 'lettuce' for my lunch. But I was in awe of his beauty too.

"I began making a big effort to be nice to his mother and not only always paid my support check on time but bought Danny a new bed, a piano, a train table, and her a new coat. Twice I paid for them to fly to Florida to visit my mother with me. Also I constantly bought him presents, invariably trains from Thomas's stable, and was paying for the two apartments, of course. All these efforts, especially with his mother, began to pay off. As a result, the three of us occasionally went to dinner or to the park where he loved the swings and slides and most of all being with the two of us. He would look at us and exclaim in ecstasy, 'Mommy and Daddy!' I would even fantasize about how we could possibly reunite for his sake but Claire was more controlling than ever and more manipulative too. Danny's manipulations were nakedly honest; hers were steeped in deceit.

"I admit I would also have moments when I'd be jealous of her relationship with Danny—whenever he'd spontaneously kiss her or tell her he loved her directly instead of the way he'd tell me through one of his characters. What was inhibiting him with me was that I was constantly leaving him after spending two or three hours of time.

"'Can you stay with me?' he would say when I'd start to leave at the time I'd agreed on with his mother. 'Will you stay with me a while?' Then, the next time, 'You always leave. Why do you go?' Then, 'I don't want to say good-bye, Daddy.'"

Andra made a sympathetic sound and Paul quickly said "that's why I would cry about him, do you understand? Finally Danny just stopped asking. But it was still, of course, all worth it. I essentially transcended my jealousy of his mother, I essentially transcended my loneliness in Foxgrove too because in some fundamental way I was at peace inside and often happy. The only thing I couldn't transcend was fate...of course."

"Did something happen?" she said. She had a serious look on her face that almost frightened him.

"Yes."

He was watching her, wondering what would happen if he simply stopped speaking.

"To your son?"

"Yes."

"Something sad then?"

He nodded.

"I'm sorry."

"Yes. It all ended. My son had an accident, you see. He drowned in the swimming pool at his grandparents', his mother's parents, who lived maybe three miles away."

Andra put her hand over her mouth.

"He was in his mother's care, but she fell asleep. He loved the pool, and he got in it, we're not sure how. Maybe he climbed up on the rocks and unlocked the door that way, though I don't think he had the reach. Maybe he crawled under the one part of the fence that didn't go straight into the ground—but, small as he was, he wasn't small enough to do that, I don't think....These were the theories, hypotheses that were offered to me after the fact. Or they were lies. Maybe they just forgot to lock the door on the fence and it swung open and Danny saw it out on his run and couldn't resist the water. His mother fell asleep—she said she didn't. She said that she'd just gone to the bathroom a minute and that happened to be the time when Danny ran out, but I think she was lying about that and about the fence too. I think she was afraid I might sue her parents or perhaps go after her in some way, financially.

"It didn't matter. At least not then. Danny had died. That was the only thing in the world to me for a long time. I was sympathetic to Claire for a few weeks, she suffered horribly, of course, but then, after all her lying, my feelings changed. And when we finished our legal and financial stuff I stopped talking to her, completely. The odd thing is, though, a month or so after I stopped talking with her, her lying about the fence and her not falling asleep began to bother me profoundly. I found myself thinking about it, those moments when I wasn't directly thinking about Danny. The whole idea of lying, in general, began to pre-occupy me. How difficult it is to not do it, yet how painful and wicked a thing it is to do. How the whole economy and all of human relations is based on it. That was when I started thinking about the Internet and so forth and ultimately sold my company."

Which brings me to you, he wanted to say, but didn't. She had a look on her face that made him nervous. "I've come to see that the only thing we can control is our thoughts, and—I'm all right now," he added, hoping that would make Andra's nervous look go away, but it didn't. He thought then that perhaps he would not confront her about the lies she had told on the phone. It would only make her leave sooner.

"You see, I'm all right because I've told this story before to people like you who were kind enough to listen."

"You've suffered a lot," she said. There was a kind expression on her face, he thought, but was it real?

"You were very kind to listen so long…I don't want you to worry about money…" he mumbled, sliding two bills towards her. He thought he had meant to give her one but had placed two in front of her plate. Maybe, since they were new, one was stuck to the other. He hoped one was a fifty but they were probably both hundreds.

She picked them up, unable to hide a brief but clear look of pleasure that replaced her expression of concern.

"Thank you," she said softly, and smiled at him. They talked a little bit about the restaurant and how good the desserts were. Then she said, "I'm going to use the little girls' room now, if you'll be OK?"

"Yes," he said. He would be all right. He watched her walk down an aisle and disappear around a corner. He would sit still and wait. When he closed his eyes to rest them a second he saw an image of Danny's smile as the two of them walked to the holly tree holding hands, his other hand holding Danny's train bucket, which they'd put the berries in.

He opened his eyes, shaking his head to dispel the image, and swallowed more of his new drink. Andra seemed like the right type for him. So what if she was some kind of prostitute, he still felt he could break through with her. She would be the first one since he'd lost Danny.

He stared out at the high ceiling and at the Byzantine columns of light. At that moment he realized the restaurant was laid out in such a manner that she could leave the ladies' room and then the restaurant without his noticing. A high wall would block his vision.

The vampire waiter approached him. "May I take this?" he said, meaning the plates, but Paul instinctively placed his hand over his heart before saying yes.

He waited some more, saw Danny's face as clear as a flower, his voice ringing in his head like a song he would hear forever. Then he finished his drink thinking no matter what, his life had had great beauty and truth in it and she couldn't take that away even if she didn't come back, any more than Claire had taken that away from him either. He kept consoling himself that way twenty minutes later, when he knew she'd left, and then even later than that, when it was finally clear to him that he must also leave the darkness of this restaurant to begin his long walk home.

My Sister's House

There were rows of stairs, a waterfall of stairs, and I was high up on one of them, yet there were many more above me. I was a spectator in the house, which was also my house, but when you're a child it's like being a small mushroom in a forest. It's your forest but you're compelled to think of it as *the* forest that belongs to others, perhaps to the trees.

Later I thought of the house as a castle that somehow included me. It was white with twenty steep cement steps in two rows that led to the black front door. The castle had four floors and twenty-one rooms including an outdoor patio surrounded by a gray cement wall, colored stained-glass windows in the sunroom, and large eye-like oval-shaped windows on the top floor through which it seemed one could survey the entire activities of the town. From there I could see my friends on the playground, friends whom I loved so dearly then though none of them really lasted and by my mid-twenties were virtually all gone. The castle-house had an ample front and back yard that were protected from the street by two hills, one on each side of the stairs. Similarly, there were fences and two rows of trees that shielded the entire length of the yard from each neighbor.

It's the oddest thing. You are born into a kingdom and you spend the rest of your life remembering it. That's what happened to my sister and me. Only much later did we become detectives and try to understand how the kingdom worked. All your archetypes are in the kingdom. Thus, flowers will always mean the trellis roses and lilac trees that bloomed in our backyard and snow will always mean sledding down the hills of our front yard or down the alley in back.

Over this castle-house presided the King. Like all kings he had a paradoxical nature that mystified his subjects. He had a deep authoritative voice, yet he was short, perhaps 5 feet, 6 inches. But so authoritative was his voice or demeanor that for many years I thought him to be much taller than he was, and years later my sister told me she thought the same thing. The King was from Norway and spoke with an accent, yet far from being an impediment this only contributed to his mystical aura. One couldn't really expect him to speak ordinary, uninflected English. The accent suited him, just as it suited him perfectly to speak six languages fluently and to ostensibly know everything about politics and philosophy.

The King was so many things—a renowned director and character actor, a distinguished cofounder of a theater who was honored nationally, and, of course, a towering figure in the Philadelphia theater world. He'd been a child prodigy who helped support his large family in Norway for years. He was also a man who endured unspeakable pain and isolation for twenty-seven years, between his first marriage and his final one to my mother. Surely that was endurance worthy of a god.

His contradictions were also deity-sized. He was a fervent Marxist who played the stock market and lived in a palace. He was an imposing man who inspired if not exactly terror then an ongoing low-level anxiety in me. Yet he was often surprisingly gentle and forgiving, as when he forgave me so easily for breaking one of the sunroom's stained-glass windows with a baseball, or years later when he opened my door and saw me kissing my first girlfriend, whom I'd snuck into my room. He was able to joke about it with me that very night.

It was so different with my sister, Daneen. She never experienced the King's forgiveness simply because in his eyes she never did anything deviant enough to require it. Their communication was so close and harmonious that she soon learned to speak Norwegian from him. How she loved speaking in a foreign language which neither the Queen nor I understood! Like the King, my sister had a real gift for foreign languages and would have pursued that field I'm sure were there not one thing that pleased the old Commander even more, namely that she become a drama professor (which she did) where she could teach and eventually write about his work. So it was I alone who heard the King's disapproving words that shook my little mushroom soul, which perhaps was more like a wind-ripped leaf while he said them than a mushroom. I could only metamorphose from leaf to mushroom and resume my former place in the forest hours after his words had ceased. But later he might do something magnificently restorative where I would once more temporarily feel intact. Such was the case when he accompanied me to the playground to demand the basketball the big kids had taken from me. How frightened I was for him as we walked there. He was short (I suddenly realized for the first time) with gray hair—already over sixty years old—yet he walked right up to them, the delicate director/professor, with the accent which he lost only while performing and said, "I'll take the ball now," and they gave it to him without saying a word. That was my favorite memory of him except for a much earlier one where he stood over me, removing and then placing back a blanket over my shoulders, because I was too hot with it and too cold without it, until I was finally able to sleep.

Yes, my King could be brave and tender but he was always old. I remember lying in my bathtub calculating what age I'd be when he'd die. I'd read that the average life span of a man was seventy and concluded I'd be fourteen when it would happen. Whenever the telephone rang late at night or even in the afternoon when he was late arriving from the theater, I worried that it was the doctor in a hospital or else the police calling to inform us of his death.

But I'm making it seem as if the King dominated my life. The truth is he was often away traveling or absorbed in his work and did very few things alone with me. My sister, too, would tell me later that she often felt she was inventing him more than she was remembering him. That's one of the problems when you become a family detective, you think you want knowledge but your wishes interfere, so when the knowledge finally comes it's clouded. I want to see things in a balanced way now above all else, and kings can make you lose your balance. Actually queens can too. One of the first things I realized in my early years was that despite the vast power of the King, it was she who decided when we would entertain and who we would invite. It was she who decided when we needed to hire or fire a maid, where we would go on our vacations, even which restaurants we would eat at or which movies we'd attend. (Alas, despite her talents as an actress, she was an inveterate fan of Hollywood kitsch.) Worst of all were her monumentally indiscreet stories, often sexually outrageous in content, sometimes teeming with not-so-subtle references to her own sexual frustration. (For years she and the King had lived in separate rooms.) But why did the King permit this? Why did he so rarely challenge her? It seemed a self-defeating way to show one's love, even if one were a king.

With the King away so much, I was left alone in the castle with the two women. To be with the Queen often meant lying in her bed while she rehearsed her lines but then getting to kiss her hundreds of times when she was through. She was soft and pretty and so funny, especially the way she could become other people. In her comic scenes she could make people laugh whenever she wanted and I laughed harder than anyone. But more often than not it also meant listening to the same stories about her dysfunctional and traitorous relatives or the dysfunctional and traitorous directors, actors, and critics who stabbed her in the back. As I got older it meant seeing how upset it made her to meet my girlfriends or any friends of mine at all. And when I got still older, long after the King had died, it meant learning that she'd betrayed the King once with an affair. She told me, after a few drinks, less than a year ago while I was visiting her in the Castle during Thanksgiving. (I was shocked at first but not really surprised since they'd lived in separate rooms all those years, and though I felt some sense of anger and hurt for the King I ultimately decided not to comment.)

My sister, on the other hand, liked to hear about my friends. She was four years older and competed against me in every sport, especially baseball and badminton and also in games like Chinese checkers and Parcheesi. Her name was Daneen, but she wanted to be called Victor, appropriately enough. It was fun to beat her in the sports and games, as I often did, but I also felt bad when she'd pound her fist on the board and cry sometimes after losing. As I got older we began playing our own games together, inventing a group of characters and a kind of ongoing soap opera between them. Once my character kissed her character and a thrill unlike anything I'd ever felt surged through me.

My sister had a beautiful face and a full bosom that I admired but she didn't seem proud of her large breasts. She was always overweight, sometimes fat, consequently she didn't have many boyfriends or go to the dances in grammar school or high school, and the Queen worried out loud about her though the King never said a word against her. The King simply adored my sister, and one had to accept that.

One day I went into her room to sharpen my pencil and saw her naked in bed with one of her girlfriends from school.

"I just wanted to sharpen my pencil," I said, eyes straight ahead and aimed at the wall away from them, as soldier-like I sharpened the pencil, about-faced, and exited in a daze. I roamed the hallways, then up and down the waterfall stairs for countless hours. Finally I wandered into the Queen's room and she tearfully guessed what happened and tried to reassure me. The Queen's softness could be exquisite.

Years passed. My sister and I moved away from the King and Queen, who continued to live in the Castle with the help of a series of live-in maids. (After the King died, a series of nurses were added, who continue to care for the Queen to this day.) I moved first to New York and then other states, wherever I could get a teaching job but my sister moved just a few miles from the Castle in Rosemont to an apartment in Philadelphia. I was no longer close to Daneen, though I wasn't sure why: during a visit to the Berkshires I bumped into her during the intermission of a play in Williamstown (at the theater the King and Queen had both been associated with), and when I went to hug her she turned away from me.

Meanwhile the King and Queen continued to prosper in their careers. Even after the King retired from the theater he cofounded he continued directing, sometimes plays that featured the Queen (she'd always been quasi-dependent on him professionally), well into his eighties. He was admired and beloved everywhere, it seemed. He'd been a fine chess player in his youth and people still loved to play with him. He inspired reverence among the chess players as he did with his former students who wrote or telephoned and often visited him from all over the country. He was a man who knew how to get along with people. Not so the Queen who lost best friend after friend because she thought they didn't sympathize with her or appreciate her enough. These breakups were horrible, like broken love affairs. Only her family didn't leave her. We were, all of us, including the paradoxically meek King, ultimately under her control. And ultimately in many ways I suppose I myself loved her more than I loved the King or anyone else.

When he was eighty-eight, the King had a stroke while playing chess and died three months later in a hospital. At the memorial in the Walnut Street Theatre in Philadelphia a number of celebrated theater people spoke. The King's accomplishments as a director, actor, and theater-owner were all reviewed. One of his colleagues referred to him as a noble man. He'd helped so many young actors and directors, he was honest, selfless—all of which, I suppose, added up to noble.

At the memorial I read a poem about him, which along with a variation of it remain the only poems I have ever written. After the ceremony my sister told me she was touched by it and we experienced a moment of closeness again before returning to our separate lives. In many ways her fate mirrored mine. We both wrote, or tried to; my sister eventually wrote a whole book about the King's life in the theater but neither of us, of course, could support ourselves by writing the way the King and Queen supported themselves by their art. We were both teachers (an apt profession for the truly dominated) who lived alone. She was simply more successful at it, getting tenure in her drama department long before I got it as a musicologist. There was no particular shortage of women that we could sleep with but neither of us had children. When we talked on the phone we talked almost exclusively about the Queen. It was that way for years. Meanwhile, the Queen's ailments were increasing exponentially. Despite inheriting virtually all of the King's money, she was reluctant to spend any of it, even on her health. Her fears of her childhood poverty recurring were worse than ever, as was her ability to listen to others—now that she was half deaf, the one physical problem she had that she wouldn't acknowledge. Yes, there was a lot to talk about as my annual visit to my sister's house approached in the summer of my forty-fifth year.

Something else. I'd developed an interest, that began a number of months ago, in Margo, a homeless black woman who lived on my block in Boston not too far from the school where I finally got tenure. She looked to be somewhere in her middle thirties and was pretty and quite fastidious. She spent a great deal of her time on her makeup and wore bright red lipstick. She was also neat with her belongings and the cardboard box she slept in. Occasionally she ranted a bit, but most often she was warm and extroverted in a friendly way. I talked to Margo at least every other day and gave her about fifteen dollars a week.

The last few weeks I'd wanted her to visit my apartment and had invited her several times. She laughed each time and said with a quasi-Caribbean accent, "You want to add some dark meat to your plate, sir, is that it? Oh no, I don't think so sir," or other words like that. I assured her that wasn't the case but when I was with myself I wondered what I did want. I'd been lonely lately and enjoyed Margo's company, and I did have a desire to give her a good dinner and have her sit on my relatively comfortable furniture and take a long bath if she wanted. Certainly, I wouldn't have minded eventually having some kind of physical contact with her, if she initiated it. I knew I'd never force myself on her, my sexual ego being far too fragile for anything like that. But, yes, I did wonder about her sexually and even fantasized about having a child with her from time to time. At any rate, I reassured her that sex was not my goal, that I simply enjoyed her company.

"You stay in front of my building; don't you want to be inside it once? Watch some TV, listen to music, hang out for a while?"

She laughed again. "Your money is fine sir, I don't need your house."

That line made me laugh, too, it was delivered so well. She had a gift for banter and I enjoyed the fact that our relations were light and pleasant, so I didn't press her too much. At last there was a woman in my life with whom things could be friendly and humorous. It was the very opposite of what awaited me in the Berkshires, where I'd undoubtedly be engaged in a long, intensely painful dialogue with my sister about the Queen's failing health and what exactly we should or could do about it. It was the certain knowledge that that was what was in store for me that made me ask Margo if she wouldn't like to accompany me there. After all, I knew that Jean, my sister's girlfriend, would be in the house and that she always stayed with my sister whenever I visited. If my sister could use Jean as a buffer, why must I visit my sister alone?

"Wouldn't you like to go to the country?" I asked Margo. "My sister has a pool that overlooks the mountains."

"Oh my God, no," she said smiling. "It's fine here where I can overlook the alley and other people in their boxes and know that I have the cleanest, best-looking box in Boston. That's good enough for me, sir," she said quasi-sarcastically.

There was no point pursuing my idea further, I decided, so a week later I got on the bus for the interminable ride that took me to Stockbridge where my sister was waiting for me in her new red sports car. We exchanged a rather awkward hug and then sped away on the road to her house in Interlaken.

One big difference between my sister and me is that because she got tenure well before I did she was able to stay in Philadelphia essentially her whole life. She's moved only once that I recall, from one apartment in Philadelphia to another, and then four years ago managed to buy her country house not far from the Stockbridge Theater, where the King and Queen once performed. Her house is large and roomy and filled with pictures and memorabilia about the King. (There he is with his arm around John Gielgud. There he is at a party with Edward Albee and Tennessee Williams.) Tiger lilies and other wildflowers grow around her house and in the backyard, which slopes uphill steeply to the pool. Behind the pool is a badminton court, a gazebo, and a fine view of the hills.

I, on the other hand, have been the proverbial gypsy scholar, moving from one part of the country to another—wherever there was work. As a result, there was never a real chance for me to buy a house, and I've lived exclusively in a series of one-room apartments. These apartments were never spectacularly bad to live in, incidentally, yet each had an Achilles heel of a kind that really was quite horrific. Even in my current post-tenure apartment, which has two bedrooms and to which I've often invited Margo, there's a bad problem in the bathroom where, due to a running faucet, a small window, poor ventilation, and decaying plaster, a tropical rain forest level of humidity has developed and a mushroom-like fungus has actually begun blooming near my bathroom mirror.

In the car I asked my sister two questions. "How about this new car?" was question one.

She smiled. "You like it?"

"It's very chic. How do you afford it so soon after buying the house?"

"You know me, I'm a spender. I have nothing in the bank." That's true. She's like the King that way, whereas as I've gotten older I've become more of a hoarder like the Queen.

I laughed, "Where's Jean?" was my other question. My sister answered that Jean was reading by the pool. So Jean has granted us this private moment, I thought. I didn't expect there to be many more. Jean has blondish, slightly graying hair and intense eyes like my sister and is also an academic, but there the similarity ends. While Jean is more outgoing and has a more charming social presentation of self, I suppose (which has helped her a lot professionally as an administrator), she's also much more controlling and possessive than my sister. Jean generally makes sure she and my sister stay close to each other in most social situations, and I was surprised my sister had ventured forth to meet me alone. Looking out the window at the trees and hills, I wondered if that meant anything special, but there was no sign of it during the rest of the ride home.

Jean was by the pool, as advertised. She exchanged a minute's worth of pleasantries with me before returning to the newspaper she was reading on a chaise lounge. I sat in a chair neither too near nor far away from her. It was strange. Having thought so intensely about my family on the bus trip, I suddenly couldn't stop thinking about Jean. It was as if my mind seized upon the chance to think about someone else and wouldn't let go. I thought about how I never knew whether to hug Jean when I saw her or not and ended up never even touching her. Then I thought about how Jean and my sister never touch in public and how I've never seen them touch in private either. When Jean and Daneen fell in love, Jean was married with two young children. For the next seven years she stayed married, living a double life with Daneen, who had to accept that Jean was regularly sleeping with her husband and that she had to pose as a mere friend of their mother's when she was with Jean's children, to whom she got quite attached. It took Jean twenty-three years to finally, partially, come out of the closet. She divorced her husband much earlier, of course, but still kept up a kind of heterosexual pretense. Even now it still isn't clear to me what she's told her children about my sister.

I'd have to say, though, that in spite of all the unusual circumstances, both of Jean's children turned out well. I don't know Louise as well, though I hear about her various successes in business, but Phil is a charming, funny man with a good starting-out job in a law firm. He's married to a quite attractive woman who just got pregnant, and both he and Louise appear to have excellent relationships with their mother. They joke, they respect each other, there's nothing overtly possessive or neurotic between them. Not that Jean is without her faults, but as a parent she appears to be Supermom. I give her all the credit in the world for that, though lately I've felt a pang of envy when I see her with her kids and also some resentment when I watch my sister cater to her every whim. Meanwhile, my sister was like a second mother to Jean's children, without her having any of her own. Of course, Daneen could have had children despite her sexual preference. She even has lesbian friends who did it with a sperm donation from a gay friend and a turkey baster with quite happy results. I think my sister wanted to have a child, or at least part of her did, but something in her feared it too and so she ultimately didn't. To be around Jean, then, is a constant reminder for both my sister and me of our childlessness and all that that means. Rationalize it as you will, but for most people if you don't have children by a certain age it's like having a permanent wound that the world manages to irritate every day.

At this gloomy and dramatic moment in my thought progression my sister suddenly emerged from the house in her bathing suit. She didn't see me at first since her slightly worried look was directed wholly at Jean. I was a mere mushroom again for the next few moments, lost among the tiger lilies. "Hi Daniel," she said, without waving when she did see me, and I tried with my usual lack of success not to stare at her large, still youthful-looking breasts.

Although my sister has always been overweight, she's always been very athletic. She is not a person, even at forty-nine, to spend much time sitting by a pool. She sat next to Jean for a couple of minutes, then got up and made a graceful dive into the pool, which made me remember that she was on her college swimming team. A minute later, I got up from my chair and went into the water myself. My sister had been doing a vigorous backstroke and for a minute or so we were in the water together. Then Jean began reading a review of last night's concert from *The Berkshire Eagle* and Daneen stopped swimming to listen. Soon both women were laughing and hooting with glee as they discovered that the review agreed exactly with their low assessment of the piano soloist and the guest conductor.

I got on one of the floats, as my sister left the pool to sit next to Jean, and paddled off into a far corner. I was thinking about how many chances to have children I've had in my life. It's strange that I've been reviewing this intermittently in my mind the last few years, since it's not as if the number's changed and it's not as if it's a great and complicated number to remember. I define a real chance to have a child as the conscious attempt by each partner to do it even if (as in my case) that conscious attempt happened only once or twice before a change of heart or a breakup or abortion occurred. My total number of chances has been seven for some time. If a TV drama were made of my life I think they should call me, and the show, "Daniel Seven," a name both catchy and symbolic like the old "Peter Gunn" show. Floating around in the pool, looking up at the tops of the tiger lilies and the hills in the distance, and at an unusually bright blue Berkshire sky almost the same color as my sister's bathing suit, I actually wondered if Henry Mancini, the "Peter Gunn" theme composer, were still alive so he could write the theme for "Daniel Seven," and then when I realized what I'd been thinking about I started to laugh. Jean said, "What's so funny Danny? I could use a laugh." But, of course, I said nothing about it, which made Daneen say, "He's always been secretive."

At dinner the usual conversational pattern prevailed. It began with Jean and me praising my sister's roast beef, then got into fairly light-hearted shop talk, though not without some edge to it, because like most academics they were angry about their lot. I was angry too, but no longer bothered to talk about it. Inevitably, there was a political argument, as if the anger having been aroused by shop-talk foreplay had to climax in a more important forum. These discussions made me uneasy because my sister was so excitable, and I feared her temper when she got excited. She would pound the table, sometimes, like she did as a child, or yell, and her face would contort in a fearsome way. When she drank, as she did that night, it made such outbursts all the more likely. To top if off, Jean made a joke about lesbians. My sister is very sensitive about women jokes in general and lesbian ones in particular, and not wanting to witness her reaction I got up from the table, saying I had to go to the bathroom. I did, in fact, go to the bathroom, not to use it but to hide from the conversation. On the way there I was struck by how few photographs of the King were left in the house. What had happened? My sister's house looked almost naked with so few images of the old Commander and I felt as if she'd somehow betrayed him.

I never did discover what the argument was about, something to do with Newt and Candice Gingrich. It was like listening for an explosion of thunder after first hearing some vague rumblings. But the thunder didn't come. Daneen surprised me by not erupting. I returned to the table and it was like the calm after a storm, except that the storm never happened. It was true there was still more tension in the air than usual, but fortunately there was a concert at Tanglewood to go to which we all had to get dressed for. The concert soon became the focus of all our discussion and energy and, as it turned out, it rewarded us well. When we got back home we all agreed it had been a fine performance and that we were all tired now, and so the first day at my sister's house ended without any real catastrophe.

I was extraordinarily tired the next morning. Despite sleeping a long time, I stayed in my room longer than usual. I'd had a disturbing dream the night before in which I saw the King talking very intensely and privately with Margo. It was as if even in my dreams (and from beyond the grave) the old Commander was still controlling my life with women. When I finally left my room I heard some strange sounds—a combination of half-muffled crying and talking coming from my sister's room. They're probably making love or having a quarrel, I thought, or possibly combining them, so let it be. But the little sneak in me couldn't ignore it. Dedicated family detective that I was I tiptoed down the hallway to get closer to the door, fully aware of how absurdly comical I would have looked if anyone had seen me. I didn't listen long and I didn't hear much. There was an exchange that sounded like, "It happened again."

"What?"

"I remembered again."

Then I didn't hear anything intelligible except for the crying sound until two minutes later when Jean said, "Does Daniel know?" at which point I instantly began to feel more guilty than curious and started backpedaling on my tiptoes as if I were executing an awkward ballet step.

That morning incident was on the edge of my mind all day, though Daneen seemed cheerful enough. Yet I had the feeling that she was acting. This was especially disturbing since I thought of her as belonging to the emotionally nontheatrical part of my family, along with the King.

That night they invited me to go to the movies with them. They'd had enough of high culture and wanted to see a "fun" movie that was playing in Pittsfield. Having my father's aversion to movies, however, I said I wanted to go to the concert instead, so they dropped me off at Tanglewood.

There was a short Haydn symphony, and then the romantic part of the program began. Prokofiev's Third Piano Concerto followed by Tchaikovsky's Sixth—two pieces that capture the very essence of bittersweet love. But I didn't think of any of my past loves as I thought I might and I didn't think much about having a baby either. Instead my mind fastened on my sister's remark about me that she'd made in the pool the day before. "He's so secretive." It was said jokingly, but it was also meant as a true observation, one she'd said intermittently over the years. It hurt me to hear it, though I could hardly deny it was true. But how, I kept wondering during both concerto and symphony, could I have become any other way, living as I did in such a house full of secrets, a house that made me a perpetual detective of my own family?

Then I remembered that last summer I'd seen some odd notes on the writing table by my sister's bed describing something erotic while using the pronoun "he." Perhaps that's how she thought of Jean—I didn't want to know at the time, having wandered in merely to talk to my sister. So I left the room and more or less blocked out the notes, which were definitely in Daneen's writing. Yes, it was a house full of secrets. There was my sister hiding her attraction to girls as she grew up, and there were the King and Queen living in different rooms. There was also the King's otherworldly harmony with my sister compared to which his kindness toward *me* had an almost guilty or forced quality, and then after years of closeness my sister literally turning away from me. There was also the sudden disappearance of the King's photographs from her house and, finally, her strange notes and Jean's asking, "Does Daniel know?" Know what, of course, was the question.

By the end of the concert I felt an urgent need to talk alone with her but it was impossible. When she and Jean picked me up they were telling dirty jokes and making fun of the movie and were very much in their inseparable mode. During the ride I suddenly wanted to say, "Why don't you two kiss or at least put your arms around each other? You're obviously in the mood and you know that I've known about you two for twenty-five years." But, of course, it didn't happen. Reticence and secrecy were still their way.

"Do you want to play badminton?" I suddenly said to Daneen late the next afternoon while Jean was napping in a chaise lounge by the pool. My sister hesitated for a moment, perhaps wondering if it would disturb Jean, or perhaps she was simply surprised that I casually suggested doing something we'd last done so long ago. But she agreed and when she returned with the rackets there was a smile on her face. Almost immediately we began slamming the birdie back and forth just like we did thirty-five years ago, still pretty evenly matched. We didn't play a game, though I was keeping a kind of unofficial score in my mind and felt she was, too. What a woman, I thought, while she was playing. To be a college professor of drama and to appreciate music and to be so good at sports! No wonder the King loved her so much; no wonder she couldn't find her niche with other men who were so vulgar and limited by comparison. She was too good for them, she was too good, generally speaking, for the male sex and had to be with women, I thought, just as I broke my racket while hitting a vicious overhead. For a moment we both stood stunned at the sight of the birdie wedged in the space where the strings spread slightly too far apart and then we started to laugh. They were cheap rackets, so we could afford to laugh about it. We sat down on two chairs by the pool, breathing heavily, as was Jean, who was still asleep. Then a minute later the laughter seemed a part of the distant past as we began talking about the Queen.

"I've noticed a real difference in her the last month or so. She's not the same person anymore," my sister said, pushing two locks of blondish, light brown hair away from her eyes. It occurred to me that she had approximately the same color hair and eyes as I did and that we also shared the same general facial shape.

"What do you mean?" I said, although I did know what she meant.

"It's like she's crossed over into another world."

"You're exaggerating, tremendously exaggerating."

"No, Daniel, I don't think so. Her depression, her denial of what's happening to her. Her complete unwillingness to face reality."

"What reality?"

"The reality that she'll never walk again, that she'll have to spend the rest of her life in a wheelchair. No matter how often the doctors tell her, she doesn't believe them or accept it."

"She's probably not even hearing them. The one thing that *has* gotten worse is her hearing, but, of course, she's far too vain to ever acknowledge that and get a hearing aid. She'd rather not hear a single word you or I say the rest of her life than admit she needs a hearing aid."

"It isn't that. She does know what the doctors say. But when they tell her what the situation is she simply sees another doctor and continues believing what she wants to believe. The woman survives, has always survived, by believing what she needs to."

"What do you mean?" I asked, but she didn't answer me.

"The thing that really worries me," she continued, "is that she's in real danger living at home with these nurses coming in different shifts. The reality is she's alone too long every day and her vertigo is worse now and when she tries to walk, even with the walker, there's always the chance that she'll have another serious fall. What she needs is constant, supervised care in some kind of place where that care exists."

"You mean a nursing home? She'll never do that. Her whole life is in her home. Her career, her memories. Katharine Hepburn was in that house. She'll never let that happen."

"The point is the time may come, may already have come, when that has to happen."

"In the name of what?" I said excitedly, suddenly feeling tremendously protective of the Queen.

"In the name of saving her life. I'd like to feel you'll be my ally if and when that happens."

I didn't say anything to that. I stayed silent while my sister talked some more about it. I was chastened, diminished. I was a mushroom again among the giant trees that shaded my sister's pool. I might have left it at that—I was never as good or as relentless an arguer as Daneen—but apparently there was still some adrenaline residue in me from the badminton match. I let her finish about how we would have to be allies in all things concerning our mother. I conceded the point, knowing that my blunt sister was correct again, and then I changed the subject. I asked her why there were so few photographs of the King in her home now? In fact, as I asked the question I couldn't remember seeing one. A strange look swept over my sister's face and I knew I'd not only caught her off guard but hit a nerve, as well.

"I find it especially odd when I remember what your house was like last summer. I mean it used to be like a shrine for him."

"I went overboard with that," she said. "I got a little carried away and so I stopped. Don't you think we've both been too overwhelmed by our parents for too long?"

"What do you mean?" I said, knowing, of course, what she meant.

"That we've been so caught up in their lives it's kept us from doing some things we wanted to."

"What things?"

"Having children, for instance. You told me once you wanted to."

"True enough."

"So? It's too late for me but maybe you should do something about it. I know you'd be a good father. I'm sure you'd honor that."

Again I changed the subject, not wanting to be sidetracked from my investigation.

"I heard some crying this morning, you know, by accident. Was that you?"

I sensed Daneen would be looking away from me, and not wanting to see that I looked past her at the still sleeping Jean.

"Yes, that was me," my sister said, half-looking at the ground. "I didn't know it was that loud."

"I just heard it for a few seconds in the hall, but, of course, I was concerned. I heard my name mentioned, too."

"What did you hear?"

"Something like, 'Does Daniel know?' So naturally I wondered if I'd done something to upset you."

"No, nothing like that."

"I mean you must admit we've had a kind of strange history."

"How so?"

"We were so close growing up and then I always felt you turned away from me somewhere in your twenties and I didn't have that much contact with you after that until a few years ago, so I don't want anything to go wrong now. I'm touchy about that."

"Nothing's gone wrong with us," she said, but she looked slightly nervous.

"I guess I always wondered what went wrong all those years ago, why we…"

"We were too close then, almost incestuously close, and I just couldn't handle it. It was hard enough deciding to be a full-fledged lesbian. And it was a lot harder to be one then than it is now, believe me. Not that it's so easy now. Look, do you really want to talk about this?"

"Yes."

"Then let's go inside. I need a drink, and…" She gestured toward Jean and I nodded and began to follow Daneen down the stone steps that were cut into her lawn.

It was like descending a waterfall. As soon as I went down two steps I felt a curious shortening of space. There was nothing but my sister and me, the trees around us having blurred like watercolors. We sat across the table in her kitchen. A dragonfly was hitting its head against the window. It had to do with the King, did I want to hear? She'd been wondering for some time if she should tell me but she guessed she should because it had to do with a lot of my questions she supposed—why she turned away from me and men in general, though, yes, she'd always liked women more, but she'd liked men, too, for a while, should she go on? I nodded. It was chaos, her words, but I expected that in the beginning. I was on a cataract of water and sat still at the table to hold on.

At first, when she thought of it, it was like dreams, or rather she turned the memories into dreams, though it still affected her and made her repulsed by men for a while. That was in her middle twenties. Then it went away.

"What? What went away?" I said.

Then she told me. It was like a roaring in my ear. Like human yelling in a mushroom ear. It was so loud that I didn't hear even as she said it again. She told me next that her mind found a way to keep it away such a large percentage of the time that when it did happen she could dismiss it as a fantasy or a new way of punishing herself. But last summer it came back during my visit. She guessed she identified me with him, she said, and in spite of everything, for a moment I couldn't help feeling proud to remind someone of the King.

But the roar came back, stuck with me this time, and I focused more clearly. "How bad was it?" I blurted.

Maybe not what you think, she said. There was no intercourse. She didn't even know if any orgasms were involved. Not hers, anyway, though she used to think about him during sex with men. She used to think about him all the time. She was afraid to think about anyone else. But with him, no intercourse, no penetration. Just a lot of fondling and touching in "bad places."

I felt myself shake inside. I felt curiously light and hollow. "When was this?" I said.

"He waited until I was a teenager," my sister said. She said it was shortly after he and the Queen started living in different rooms. That's when the Queen had her affair, I thought to myself, though I didn't say it, still didn't know if my sister knew that or not.

"You say that with a lot of sympathy," I finally said to her.

"His first wife hurt him and then his second wife did, too," she said quickly. He could master a lot of things but not that. Love, sex, it was like water in his hands, he couldn't control it, he nearly drowned in it, like a waterfall over his head.

"You don't even hate him, do you?"

"No. It was the worst of him, not all of him. Remember he was incredibly kind to me, to all of us most of the time."

"You still sympathize with him, don't you? Even now."

"Don't you? I can't help it. It was only for a year or part of a year, and it wasn't that many times. I mean, of course it was awful and I hated it. I'm not trying to minimize it. But it wasn't all of him, it wasn't the whole story, and I know he suffered a lot and felt enormously guilty."

"Christ," I said, interrupting. "Why did he do it?"

He was alone, she said. After the Queen's affair he changed. So you knew, I said. Yes, she knew. That's what changed him, she thought. He lost himself. It was no excuse, of course.

"Jesus Christ," I said.

"He'd get tears in his eyes every time," she said, with tears in her own eyes.

"It's probably why he never criticized you. He treated you like a goddamn princess, the hypocrite."

Then I noticed that she was crying softly, but I couldn't let up and I asked her if the Queen knew.

"I don't know. I can't be sure, she's such an actress."

"Did he tell you not to tell her, did he threaten you?" As if I could do anything about it, as if the King hadn't been dead for thirteen years.

"Yes, no. He didn't threaten anything, but he said it was part of our secret world and he'd ask me not to tell."

Christ. The thought of the King talking that way. "Christ," I said.

"Yes, Christ...Danny? Are you all right? Danny are you all right? It was very hard to tell you this."

"Yes, I'm all right. I'm sorry for you, that's all."

She thanked me. She said she loved me and told me she meant what she said about my being a good father. I told her about Margo, then, maybe to try to lighten things up a little. I said it quickly in a half-joking way, although my hand was still trembling. But my sister listened seriously, before encouraging me to try to meet women I'd have more in common with background-wise. Suddenly there were tears in my eyes too. I was still shocked in one way but not shocked in another. The oddest thing. Like all my detective work was a sham, a game I played with myself because I always half-knew.

Then I hugged my sister. She was shaking. I said, "Maybe you should be with Jean now," meaning maybe you want to be with Jean. She nodded and fell out of my embrace. I sat at the table. The dragonfly was gone. I watched Daneen climb the steps one by one. The trees came back into view. But before she got a quarter of the way to the pool Jean met her on the stone stairs. I watched my sister talk to her. I watched the two longtime lovers talking. My sister put her arm around Jean and I watched them hug each other. I saw the tiger lilies, the other flowers, the high trees. Then I looked around myself at the table and chairs and at the paintings on the walls. Everything had an order to it; everything seemed to sparkle that second in my sister's house.